The CITY under SIEGE

Also by Michael Russell

The City of Shadows
The City of Strangers
The City in Darkness
The City of Lies
The City in Flames

The CITY under SIEGE

MICHAEL RUSSELL

CONSTABLE

CONSTABLE

First published in Great Britain in 2020 by Constable

Copyright © Michael Russell, 2020

1 3 5 7 9 10 8 6 4 2

The moral right of the author has been asserted.

*All characters and events in this publication, other than
those clearly in the public domain, are fictitious
and any resemblance to real persons,
living or dead, is purely coincidental.*

A CIP catalogue record for this book
is available from the British Library.

ISBN: 978-1-4721-3037-2 (hardback)
ISBN: 978-1-4721-3038-9 (trade paperback)

Typeset in Dante by SX Composing DTP, Rayleigh, Essex
Printed and bound in Great Britain by Clays Ltd, Elcograf S.p.A.

Papers used by Constable are from well-managed forests and
other responsible sources.

Constable
An imprint of
Little, Brown Book Group
Carmelite House
50 Victoria Embankment
London EC4Y 0DZ

An Hachette UK Company
www.hachette.co.uk

www.littlebrown.co.uk

For my mother and father

Dark Angel, with thine aching lust
To rid the world of penitence,
Malicious Angel, who still dost
My soul such subtle violence!

'The Dark Angel'
Lionel Johnson

PART ONE

A MAN OF NO IMPORTANCE

We are sorry for the Irish people if the storm breaks on their shores and over their land. We know what others in a similar situation have suffered, but Mr de Valera and his friends have sheltered behind neutrality, and they may have cause to wish that they had drawn the sword with the remainder of the great representatives of freedom and democracy. We in Malta have no regrets. In Malta we have suffered, and we are prepared to suffer more until final victory . . . We must not forget that there are many Irishmen fighting in this war against Nazism – with units of the Imperial forces in Britain and over-seas. It is the fact that the Free State is still neutral that is regretted by all who love Eire. The poet sings that a nation born where the shells fall fast has its lease of life renewed.

Times of Malta, 1941

1

The County Hospital

Naas, Co Kildare, 1939

In the white, tiled room the two porters carried the body from the mortuary drawer and laid it down on the porcelain slab in the middle of the room. Detective Inspector Stefan Gillespie turned the pages of a manila file of statements, reports and photographs. The photographs showed the body as it had been when it was discovered, in a grove of trees by a river, surrounded by the debris of a picnic: a tartan blanket, a wicker basket, a piece of cheese, a half-eaten loaf of bread, apples and apple cores, two empty beer bottles, a bloody kitchen knife, a bicycle on its side. Then the body up close, partly clothed; the stomach and the tops of the legs drenched in blood. In black and white, the pictures of the picnic site and the river, in wide shot, looked almost elegant. The sun had been shining. In some photographs its light reflected off the water. The detective looked from the photographs of the body to the body itself.

Beside him Sergeant Dessie MacMahon smoked a cigarette, looking at the young, dead man with disinterested curiosity. He had read the State Pathologist's report. There would be no more to learn. They were in the mortuary at Naas Hospital for reasons he didn't much like, checking up on the work of other police officers, looking for mistakes, failings, shoddy work. It was the kind of thing that went with the job he now, suddenly, found himself doing. He didn't much like that either. It was a job he hadn't asked for.

Stefan Gillespie continued turning the pages of the file. The only other sound was the slow tick of a bank clock that hung above the mortuary door.

The body of James Corcoran was a fortnight old. Cold storage in the hospital at Naas was cold enough to slow decay, but not to stop it. The smell of rotten flesh had risen up as the porters pulled open the drawer. It wasn't strong, but as the Sweet Afton Dessie MacMahon was smoking went out, he lit another. Stefan Gillespie closed the file and moved closer to the slab.

It was a boyish face. He looked younger than his twenty-four years. A mop of dark hair covered his forehead, the only part of him that was unchanged by death. The opening that reached from the throat to the chest and stomach, where the flesh had been pulled back for the examination of the internal organs, had been closed up and loosely stitched. As always, with the State Pathologist, it was neat, tidy work. He was a man who gave the dead care and attention; it was something the dead were always owed, whoever they were, whatever reason had brought them to the slab. For Stefan, his work was unmistakable. The body was immaculately clean, washed and tidied, ready for the undertaker when that time came, as it would do soon. The flesh was pale, almost luminous. The colour was deceptive. In reality it spoke not of the cleanliness outside, but of the rot spreading beneath the skin, which would eventually break through and consume it.

There was nothing to surprise Inspector Gillespie, having seen the photographs taken at the scene of death and afterwards, as the body had been stripped and opened up and explored. The wounds around the groin were obvious. They

4

were what made this so striking. There were seven: in the lower stomach, in the thighs, in the penis and the testicles. Now they were only uneven tears in the white flesh, thin, broken lips lined with black, long-dried blood. What was visible did not record how deep the kitchen knife had gone, how hard and how furious the strokes had been. The gushing blood that had covered James Corcoran's body and his clothes, his trousers and his clean, white shirt, had long been washed and sponged away. The bruising around the throat was still clear, though, grey and yellow, red in places. The fingers that had throttled him had pressed so hard that the hyoid bone had broken. But the savagery of his death had been left behind now. His face was oddly calm.

The doors into the mortuary opened with some force and the tall, bearded figure of the State Pathologist, Edward Wayland-Smith, entered, with the air of impatience that was familiar to Stefan and every other detective.

'What's all this to do with you, Sergeant Gillespie?'

'Your office told me you were here today. A good time to catch you.'

'That's not an answer, is it? I'm in the middle of an important meeting. Administration, that's the thing. Never mind the dead.' Wayland-Smith grinned. 'Still, you gave me an excuse to leave the buggers to it. This one's done, isn't he?' Wayland-Smith glanced at the body. 'Inspector Charles's, Maynooth?'

'You might call it an administrative matter, sir. The case seems to have ground to a halt. I've been asked to look it over . . . see if there's more to do.'

'To see if Inspector Charles has made a bollocks of it, you mean? It wouldn't surprise me. I don't think it's an investigation that fills anyone with . . . I don't know if enthusiasm is the right word, but if it is, there's probably a considerable lack of it. There's an element of the proverbial bargepole with which some things are not to be touched, however. I'm sure you know all that.'

'Do I?' Stefan smiled.

'You'll have read he was training to be a priest.'

Stefan nodded.

Wayland-Smith shrugged, as if that explained everything.

'But I'd forgotten, they've moved you into Special Branch. And it's Inspector Gillespie now. Good for promotion, but not for making yourself popular.' He looked at Dessie. 'He's dragged you along too, MacMahon.'

'That would be the word. Dragged. Special Branch wasn't my choice.'

A look passed between Stefan and Dessie. There was a smile in it, or at least the hint of a smile, but something else from Dessie that wasn't a smile.

The State Pathologist registered the exchange.

'You've lost weight, MacMahon. That's no bad thing.'

'That'll be something to thank Special Branch for, sir.'

Wayland-Smith laughed.

'Well, I'm sure we can't have too many policemen keeping an eye on what we're all saying, now that there's a war on that we intend to play no part in. I'm sure Ireland will have a lot to thank you for. I don't think the state has a great deal to fear from Mr Corcoran, however. You've seen him. Is that all?'

Stefan Gillespie said nothing.

All three men were silent, looking down at the body.

'It was a very vicious attack,' said Stefan quietly.

'Very. Unusually so, I'd have to say.'

'An attack by someone he knew?'

'I can't say that, but it seems a reasonable conclusion.'

Stefan opened the file and turned several pages.

'In the investigation, there seems to be some resistance to talking about the details you've given. They beg certain questions that I don't see asked.'

'I can imagine that's so, Inspector. Are you surprised?'

'Can you tell me what happened – what you think happened?'
Stefan asked.

'You've read my report.'

'I'm a great believer in the horse's mouth.'

'He was strangled. Asphyxiation was the actual cause of death.' Wayland-Smith moved closer to the slab, looking at the young body with a kind of tenderness, unlike his brusque, impatient manner with the living. He walked around the body slowly as he spoke. 'The wounds around his groin were inflicted immediately after death. I mean immediately, almost simultaneously. The quantity of blood left that in no doubt. He could barely have been dead.' He stopped and looked up at Stefan and Dessie. 'Perhaps he wasn't, not quite.'

'He was partially dressed. Did that happen before or after death?'

'He was as you will have seen him in the photographs, Inspector. His shirt was open, as were his trousers. That's how he was when he was attacked.'

'The trousers pulled down.'

'Some way down.'

'And he was lying on the ground, before the attack.'

'Yes. That would be my interpretation.'

'Was he killed where he was found?'

'Not for me to say. Given the circumstances I can't see it could have been otherwise. And I gather that was the con-clusion Inspector Charles came to.'

Stefan Gillespie turned over another page in the file.

'There was semen present.'

'There was.'

'Not only from the victim.'

'No. I would have made that observation, simply on the basis of common sense, from the two areas semen was found on the body, but I was able to establish the two specimens of semen do represent two different blood groups.'

'We know the killer's blood group?'

'In all probability.'

'So, we assume some sort of sexual act took place, possibly – even probably – consensual, followed immediately by a brutal, murderous attack.'

'I can only give you simple facts. That's what it feels like. And you can see, already, why there are a lot of questions no one would be eager to ask.'

'There's no evidence there was anyone else involved?'

'Nothing that I've seen. My evidence stops with the body.'

'There's nothing that gives us any more information about the other man?'

'Nothing I could find, Gillespie. I understand there are some fragments of a fingerprint that don't belong to the dead man. On a beer bottle, I think it is.'

'Would the killer have had a lot of blood on his clothes?'

'Some, certainly. Whether it was a lot would depend on how he was positioned when he delivered the blows. There was no resistance, obviously. The wounds were inflicted with ... I suppose frenzy was what came to mind when I first saw the body. That still doesn't mean the murderer was covered in blood. I gather the investigation has produced nothing on who he was, where he came from, where he went. An isolated spot ... did anyone see anything at all?'

'No. There's barely a thing,' said Stefan. 'He's almost invisible.'

'Is that so surprising, Inspector?'

'I'd have hoped for something, sir, more than we have, working out from the scene of the crime. It is isolated, but there's not even a sighting of two men cycling together. And there's nothing in terms of the victim's associations, his friends, things he might have said. He set out on a picnic, after all. This wasn't something that happened by chance. Time, place ... must have been arranged.'

For a moment, again, they looked at the body. It offered no answers.

'However this encounter came about, Inspector Gillespie, it was, by its nature, secret, utterly secret. Whether the second man was someone James Corcoran had just met or knew well, what they were doing had to be hidden. That's the point, isn't it? It's what we're fighting. Every effort, presumably on the part of both men, went into trying to make sure they were invisible.'

The black Ford pulled away from Naas Hospital. Dessie MacMahon drove.

'Maynooth?' he said in a flat, unengaged tone.

'Yes. St Patrick's College.'

'Not Donadea?'

Stefan Gillespie reopened the file on the death of James Corcoran.

'I wouldn't mind, if there's time. But the scene of the crime can't mean much after a fortnight. If we were actually investigating this, maybe. We're here to tick Inspector Charles's boxes and see if he needs to go back and do it again.'

Stefan didn't notice the sour look from his sergeant.

'But I think we should speak to this man Dunne. He seems like the only one in the seminary who was close to Corcoran at all. He wasn't exactly blessed with friends. Or if he was, Maynooth CID didn't get very far unearthing them.'

'There's a good reason for that,' said Dessie. 'They'll all know enough about what happened, however tight Andy Charles tried to keep it. If any of them are queer they'll be more worried about that coming out than a dead body, friend or not, and for the rest, they'll all want to keep well away from it.'

'We'll take what we've got, Dessie. And I'd like a look at his room. I'm assuming that's still locked up as part of the investigation. There's a list of things that were taken to the barracks in Maynooth. Nothing that matters; at least, nothing that produced any evidence. But that doesn't mean they didn't miss something.'

'This is a fucking waste of time, Stevie, you know that?'

'You could be right.'

'Andy Charles is a good detective. What are we chasing him for?'

'We're not chasing him.'

'We're looking for what he's done wrong, what he missed, what he didn't do. What else is this for? Does he even know we're on it? Have they told him?'

'I'm sure he'll find out.' Stefan smiled.

'Yes, he fucking will, Stevie.'

'A friend of yours?'

'If he is, he won't be for long.'

Stefan took out a cigarette. He lit it, glancing sideways at Dessie.

'You're not that pissed off about Inspector Charles, Dessie, or a couple of fellers in Maynooth CID. You're just pissed off. Well, I am too. I didn't ask to go into Special Branch. And I didn't ask for you to be pulled along to work with me either. I don't want to spy on anyone, let alone other Guards. It's shite and we both know it. But it's Superintendent Gregory's shite. It's his decision.'

'His shite is our shite now,' muttered Sergeant MacMahon.

'All right, Dessie. I don't know what the hell it's about, and I'm no happier than you are being in Dublin Castle with the Commissioner's collection of old IRA men and narks and all-round arseholes. But if you don't like it, get used to it, because Terry Gregory will cheerfully tell you it'll only get worse. I don't trust any of those gobshites in the Castle, Gregory least of all. And I'm not even welcome there. Anyone they don't know is an informer . . . and since they're all fucking informers themselves, why not? But the last thing you and I need to do is stop trusting each other. We're here, Dessie. We may get on with it, so.'

Dessie MacMahon did not reply. Eventually he produced a shrug.

2

St Patrick's College

Inspector Stefan Gillespie walked across the grass of St Joseph's Square, the great quadrangle of St Patrick's College, Maynooth. With him was a young man in the black priestly uniform of a seminarian. The small square of white at his throat was the only break in the black. He wore wire spectacles and a look of seriousness that reflected the conversation he was about to have, as well as his nature. He looked to Stefan unsettlingly like the young man he had seen earlier in the mortuary. He was about the same age. He had the same pale features, even the earnestness that was still, somehow, in James Corcoran's dead face. There was no real sense that the trainee priest was nervous being asked to talk about his dead friend, but because Stefan could see he was wary, he had said nothing yet. He had asked no questions. He had left Dessie MacMahon to search out a cup of tea and talk to the porter, who had extracted Aidan Dunne from the library. He wanted the conversation to be as informal as he could make it.

St Joseph's Square was empty save for a few young men hurrying along the straight central drive, late for a lecture. The square was laid out as a garden and Stefan and the young seminarian were walking among trees. The buildings of the college made up the quadrangle, surrounding them on four sides, but the buildings felt a long way off. The space was huge. Long, high, grey walls full of windows, hundreds of them, with the spire of the chapel at one corner. It was a place that had been built to declare its seriousness and its immutability. The rows of windows carried the barest echo of the grace and light of the Georgian terraces being built in Dublin at the same time. In the dark stone and the insistent formality, in the relentless repetition of mullioned windows, there was something fortress-like. The college had been established at the end of the eighteenth century, when the Penal Laws, which tried to make Catholicism invisible in Ireland, were being abandoned. The Penal Laws failed. St Patrick's was a grand statement of Catholic visibility. This was the biggest seminary in the world. Training priests was one of the few things that Ireland did on a bigger scale than anyone else, anywhere. If there was one place that proclaimed the permanence and the power of Catholic Ireland, it was calmly, peacefully here.

'I don't know what I can tell you that I haven't said already, Inspector.' Aidan Dunne spoke quietly, breaking the silence Stefan Gillespie had let sit uneasily between them as they walked slowly through the college gardens.

'You can tell me about your friend being happy.'

'What do you mean?'

'That's what you said, when you were talking to Inspector Charles. He had been happy, noticeably so, in the days . . . the week before all this happened.'

The young man nodded. He looked slightly puzzled.

'I don't know how much you know about what happened . . . the details.'

'I only know he was attacked and killed.'

'Maybe that's all you want to know,' said Stefan.

'Maybe it is. I know it was . . . it was all very unpleasant.'

'Unpleasant is certainly one word for it, Mr Dunne.' The words were spoken quietly, but there was an edge that was

13

almost an accusation. 'I think you know enough to know . . . you don't want to know more. You're not alone.'

The seminarian looked away; it was true enough.

'But back to what you told Inspector Charles, Mr Dunne.'

'If I knew anything, do you think I wouldn't have said?'

'You say he was noticeably happy, does that mean he wasn't usually?'

Aidan Dunne frowned. He wasn't sure how to answer. Questions he had been asked before were about times, dates, facts, when he last saw his friend.

'It's a simple question.'

'He had his ups and downs; we all do. A vocation isn't an easy thing. We all face questions, all the time. You can be very sure about your faith and still be unsure whether the priesthood is the right way, if you're doing the right thing.'

Stefan Gillespie said nothing for some seconds. Then he continued. 'That's not what you meant, is it? Is that what you think about when you're asked about a friend who's dead, who's been murdered? His vocation? You were talking about something else you were conscious of. It was in your head. So, there was something unusual about it. It stood out. When I read it, in your statement, it stands out for me. It was . . . exceptional in some way, is that fair?'

'Yes, I suppose that's right, Inspector.'

'What made him so happy, then?'

Aidan Dunne shook his head and walked on in silence.

'Let's look at it from the other end. If being happy was so obvious, his unhappiness was more than the ordinary ups and downs of life at St Patrick's. If he did have doubts about his vocation, they must have gone deep, is that true?'

'I don't know what you want me to tell you, Inspector.'

'Were those doubts there only because he was homosexual?'

Aidan Dunne stopped, staring at the detective. There was a startled look on his face, but not only shock; there was a sense of fear, as if something that should not be said had been spoken, casually, idly; others might be listening.

'It's just the two of us, Mr Dunne,' said Stefan. 'I won't be writing down your answers. I simply want to understand your friend, and to see if there is anything at all, anywhere, that can help us find the man who killed him.'

Aidan Dunne walked on, looking at the ground.

'You knew he was homosexual?'

The young man nodded.

Stefan took out a packet of cigarettes and offered him one. Dunne took the cigarette. Stefan took one himself and lit both. They walked on again, smoking.

'You did know?'

'Yes.'

'Did he talk to you about it?'

'Never.' There was a hint of uncertainty in the word, but only a hint.

'Until those last few days?'

'He still didn't say anything, as such. But I knew. I guess he knew that.'

'There are other men in the seminary who have the same problem.'

Dunne frowned and said nothing. He looked straight ahead.

'I'm not asking about you.'

'I'm not! Jesus! I'm not that way at all.'

'I'm only interested in your friend. Did he associate with other men, other men here who were that way? I'm sure you have a sense of it. It may be that no one says anything, or looks too hard, but sometimes it's not so easy to hide, is it? James was your friend. He didn't say a word about it. You knew anyway.'

'I can't talk about this,' said Dunne.

'It's another simple question. I'm assuming he was happy because he'd met someone. Isn't that what it was? Isn't that what he said . . . in some way?'

'James was very shut in on himself, that's the only way I can put it. He didn't make friends easily. I'm not sure he wanted to. I knew because he had the room next door. We got on. I sensed things about him, yes, but I know he had little to do with anyone here. He worked all the time, that's almost all he did. I think he wanted to work himself into believing he really did have a vocation.'

'But he didn't?'

'I thought . . . he was using the priesthood to run away from something.'

'Suddenly he was happy. Someone had made him happy, is that it?'

'Not someone here. I know that, Inspector.'

'So, what did he tell you?'

'He'd been in Dublin for a few days, working at the National Library. He'd met someone. I suppose . . . he was in love. He didn't use those words, but it's what he was saying. And it had made everything clear. He knew what he had to do. He couldn't stay at St Patrick's. He knew he didn't have a vocation.'

'And that didn't trouble him?'

'No, quite the opposite. He said he was going to go home the following week and tell his mother and father. He was going to leave the college. He said he might even leave Ireland. He talked about going to England . . . I don't know what that meant, and he didn't either. Most of what he said didn't make sense. When I asked what he thought he was going to do . . . in the middle of a war, he laughed and said it would all be fine, it would all be grand. All he had to do was find a way to live his life the way he wanted. And he believed he could.'

'And what about the day out, the picnic? You've said he talked about it.'

'He said he was going to meet his friend. That's all he called him . . . I think somehow he managed to avoid even the word "he". It was a day out, they were going to cycle down to the country . . . there was a place he knew, a place he loved . . . They were going to make plans about a holiday in England, that's what he told me. These weren't long conversations, Mr Gillespie. He was in and out of my room . . . talking, then going away. He came back to borrow a picnic rug I had . . . and then he needed a knife for the bread or something . . . and I had one . . . that was the last evening he was here. And the next day he was gone . . .'

'James told you nothing about how he met this man, where he met him, what the man did? There was no name, no description? There was nothing?'

Aidan Dunne shook his head.

Stefan nodded. He had more than Inspector Charles had got. He had a clearer picture of James Corcoran's last days, but that's all. The killer had an existence in his head that he hadn't had before, but it was only a shadow. Stefan knew Corcoran better, but he knew nothing that helped. He did not tell the dead man's friend what had happened to the borrowed bread-knife. Stefan looked round to see Dessie MacMahon walking towards him, a mischievous smile on his face.

'The Dean wants a word with you, Stevie. Canon Mulcahy.'

'Does he now?'

'He's profoundly unimpressed by your lack of courtesy.'

'Is that what he said?'

'His exact words: "profoundly unimpressed".'

'Thank you, Mr Dunne. And I'm sorry for your loss.'

Stefan Gillespie and Dessie MacMahon walked back towards the college. The young seminarian stayed where he was, as if unaware they had gone. He wasn't looking at them. He was looking at nothing. He was crying, noiselessly.

Detective Inspector Stefan Gillespie stood in the Dean's study. Behind him stood Sergeant MacMahon, and behind him the college's head porter. The room was lined with books on every wall, except where the large windows looked out to the drive and the gardens where Stefan had just been walking with Aidan Dunne. Canon Mulcahy sat at his desk, a slight, tight-faced man, wearing a look of almost puzzled benevolence on his face, as if he had been done some small but inexplicable wrong. Stefan imagined he had been standing at the window, not long before, watching the conversation with Dunne, and not liking it. Mulcahy's face softened into something like a smile. He was comfortable giving instructions.

'I think your sergeant can wait outside, Inspector.'

'As you wish, sir,' replied Stefan. He looked at Dessie MacMahon. The sergeant grinned and walked out of the room. The porter left too, pulling the door shut. Mulcahy did not offer Stefan one of the chairs in front of the desk; instead, he stood up himself and walked round to stand very close to him.

'I am surprised, Mr Gillespie, that you should come into the college to speak to one of our seminarians without asking to do so, without approaching a senior faculty member. In matters of discipline, I am the first port of call here.'

'There is no issue of discipline that concerns the college, Canon Mulcahy, just a conversation I needed to have with Mr Dunne that continued conversations he had had with Inspector Charles and detectives from Maynooth.'

Canon Mulcahy drew himself up, regarding Stefan with less benevolence.

'There is an issue of courtesy, Inspector. It may not be your strong point, but no one walks into this college to question its students without permission.'

'It's about the investigation into the death of one of your seminarians.'

'I'm glad for that information. But you might want to enlighten me about what precisely you have to do with the investigation into that tragedy. I have only just put the telephone down from speaking to Superintendent Mangan at the barracks in Maynooth. His men have been conducting the inquiry ever since poor Corcoran was found, in particular Detective Inspector Charles. Superintendent Mangan has no idea who you are, Inspector, even less idea why you're here. He was flummoxed altogether, though he put it more colourfully.'

If the last words were some sort of joke, the Dean did not smile.

Stefan did. 'Ah, I'm sure he'd know me if he saw me.'

'Then perhaps you'd like to do something about that. He's in his office in the town, and he asked me to tell you to call in there, as soon as you leave here.'

'I see,' said Stefan.

'Thank you. Before you do leave, perhaps you'll tell me exactly what you wanted to know from Mr Dunne, given that he has already made a statement.'

Stefan was surprised at the ease and assurance with which Mulcahy asked that question. He obviously had every expectation that he would get his answer.

'I don't know how Superintendent Mangan and Inspector Charles do things in Maynooth, but that's not how police inquiries work, Canon. Not quite the confessional, but still, as these things go, it's near enough, at least until it comes to court.' He shrugged. 'Judgement . . . well, not so different even there.'

'Do you think you help your case by insulting the Church?'

'The case is not mine. The case is about finding who killed your student.'

'And it is a very sensitive matter. I shouldn't have to say that, Inspector.'

'Perhaps a little too sensitive.'

'What do you mean by that?'

'I mean that so many questions have not been asked from the start, particularly about homosexual associations or relationships in the dead man's life, that more work has gone into what isn't being said than trying to find the killer.'

'Do you think being blunt and offensive is clever, Mr Gillespie?'

'I think being honest might have brought us closer to a brutal murderer.'

'If you want me to be honest, there are things we now know about Mr Corcoran that mean he should never have been here at all. He was not a suitable candidate for a vocation. He must have known himself that he was . . . in sin, perhaps very deeply in sin. He needed to be closer to God, certainly, but not as a priest. We can only hope that he is now closer to God. The problems he had, which are still only conjecture, are not the business of St Patrick's, except in so far as he was a seminarian. He was, however wrongly, one of us. We pray for him. The whole community prays for him. As for the questions you seem so interested in, I'm not frightened by the word homosexuality. I'm not frightened by any sin. But we all owe something to James's memory and to his family, his mother and father especially. They have been hurt enough by his death, without having to suffer the exposure of things in his life that, if true, should be decently forgotten. Any judgement on that belongs . . . in a more compassionate place.'

'Surely his parents know what happened?' Stefan pushed aside most of the Dean's words, except for what told him again that questions had not been asked.

'I don't doubt the Guards left many details alone, out of charity.'

'You mean they probably said nothing and asked nothing.'

'You seem to have an unpleasant appetite for all this, Mr Gillespie.'

'You should look at what the killer did to your seminarian,

Canon. Charity's grand. Maybe begin with making sure he doesn't do it to anyone else.'

The Dean looked at Stefan with cold contempt, as if he was something very grubby. He didn't expect anyone to speak to him like this. He didn't expect anyone to disagree with him. It certainly wasn't the place of a policeman. He turned away towards the big window, his back to Stefan. He looked out over the quiet lawns and the elegant drive to the college. He would not show anger.

'There is nothing more to say, Inspector. I think you're finished here.'

Canon Mulcahy walked back to his desk and sat down, smiling.

'I'm sorry, Canon. I suppose I wish the investigation had been more urgent when it started. Time was lost. I still . . . I wanted to look at his room.'

The Dean opened a cigarette box and took out a small, dark cheroot.

'Did you? I'll repeat myself. Whatever it is you're doing you're finished with it now. Anything else, you can discuss with the superintendent. He can discuss it with me. If there is a reason for you to come back here, we can discuss that as well. It may be that if you're with him, I will agree to it. My impression, however, is that the investigation is in good hands, and that won't be necessary. In fact, when I did speak to Superintendent Mangan, he suggested that the best approach to you would be to tell you to fuck off. I think he has you summed up well, Mr Gillespie, but I'll let him elaborate himself, as I'm sure he will.'

The Special Branch offices took up one side of the Police Yard at Dublin Castle, away from the buildings of state that had, not long ago, been the heart of British rule in Ireland, away from the chapel and the gardens and grand spaces. The entrance to the yard, through the stone archway of the Carriage Office, owed something to the look of the rest of the Castle, but the yard beyond, circling the Special Branch building, consisted of scruffy rows of garages and old stables and stores. Inside the building, Stefan Gillespie sat in a chair facing Detective Superintendent Terry Gregory. Gregory stood behind his desk, turning the pages of the file on the murder of James Corcoran, smoking a cigarette. The superintendent sniffed and shut the file. Stefan was aware his boss had looked at nothing at all in the file. He had certainly taken nothing in.

'You spoke to Superintendent Mangan?'

'I phoned him from St Patrick's. It was a one-sided conversation. He wasn't happy the case file had ended up in Special Branch. There didn't seem any point going into the station to see him. I did . . . well, what he told me to do. Fuck off.'

'I had a similar conversation with Andy Charles.' The superintendent grinned. 'Let's just say I was shocked by his lack of due deference to my rank.'

Stefan smiled. It wasn't much of a smile, but he had worked out, in his short time in Special Branch, that when the boss made a joke, you smiled. He wasn't yet sure what he made of Terry Gregory, except that he didn't like him.

'And the Commissioner has had a phone call from the President of St Patrick's. Obviously, the Dean thought your attitude required some comment from the top man. Insolent, rude, offensive, all those things that I wouldn't particularly have you down for, but then I'm not a fucking priest, am I? It would have all been very polite, but it hardly puts you in Ned Broy's good books.'

'You told me it was the Commissioner who wanted the case looked at.'

Gregory sat down and leant back in his chair.

'I wasn't expecting quite as much of the Protestant work ethic, Stevie . . . I can cope with a bit, but you're going to have to learn to keep it under control. Ned Broy gets a letter that expresses concern about the fact that the investigation into this murder has ground to a halt. The daddy of the dead feller is an up-and-coming member of parliament. So, since the letter's from a TD, on Dáil Éireann notepaper, Ned asks for the file from Maynooth and then he asks me to make sure it's all been done by the book. I ask you to have a look and tell me what you think. What you think, Inspector, that's all. I didn't tell you to go out and start the fucking investigation up again, all on your fucking ownsome.'

'You might say it was done by the book, sir. It's a shite book.'

'And so you thought you'd show Maynooth CID how to do it?'

'Why ask me the question if you don't want an answer, sir?'

'The answer the Commissioner wants is along the lines of: there may be a few minor criticisms, a few things to chase up, but apart from that it's a thorough, workmanlike job. Is that so hard? You didn't have to leave the office, let alone start a row with CID in Kildare and the bloody Catholic Church. Three years ago, Ned Broy put you back in uniform for punching a priest. You're in CID a couple of weeks and you've got the hierarchy foaming at the mouth about you.'

'I didn't ask to come into Special Branch, Superintendent.'

'Don't try to be clever with me, Inspector. If I want you, you're here.'

Stefan didn't reply. Now there was an edge to Gregory's voice.

'So, what should Inspector Charles have done, Stevie? You tell me.'

'It starts with a lack of urgency, sir. You can't list the consequences of that. You can't buy back the time. But the main thing is the relationship between Corcoran and the man who killed him. They must have met shortly before the murder. A week, not much more. I'd say they didn't know each other before. They probably met in Dublin. They arranged to meet again at Donadea. This was a big thing for Corcoran. Not some quick pick-up. So, where they met, how they met, these are questions that should have been asked. There's not so many places in Dublin two queer men can hook up, or many places to go if they did. I'm not saying that's the way it was, and I'm not saying it was that obvious, but it should have been tried. Were there places Corcoran regularly went to in Dublin – pubs, bars, pick-up spots? Was he known? Had he ever been noticed by the Guards? We should have been in Dublin with photos of him. Who saw him? Was he with anyone? It's a shocking murder. The investigation was too small.'

'And what do you think the Church would have made of all that? Not to mention his family. Photographs of a seminarian in every queer pub and public convenience in Dublin? And for what? You think every faery in town would queue up to tell us who was at it on a dark night in the Phoenix Park bushes?'

'It's not just any killing, Superintendent. It was fucking grim.'

'You know the complaint came from the lad's father?'

'He's a TD. Yes, you said.'

'A Fianna Fáil man – with a career ahead of him right now. Word is he's about to become a junior minister. A Cabinet seat soon . . . if he doesn't mess up.'

Stefan looked harder at the superintendent's smile. It seemed as if those words were meant to offer an obvious conclusion; they were self-explanatory.

'Your man has a feeling the investigation wasn't what it should have been. He passes that on to the Commissioner, because he's an important feller, and he can. But he doesn't know very much, except that his son was killed, brutally killed, in an attack that must seem almost random. He knows about the brutality. But it all came out of nowhere. Maybe a madman, what else? And does he know his son had sex with the man who killed him? I don't think so. And I doubt anyone's

24

stuck a piece of paper in front of him and his wife with a description of what was happening by the lake minutes before their son was killed, with details of two different specimens of semen. Discretion, Inspector, doesn't make for good investigation. But do they want pictures of their boy up in every Dublin toilet now? I doubt it very much. And one thing's for sure, if that was happening, Rory Corcoran TD could say goodbye to his ministerial career.'

Stefan Gillespie nodded. That was the simple truth.

'He'd be finished. Unfair, unreasonable bollocks, but who can doubt it? So, I'll send this file back, with a few critical observations. Ned Broy will write a letter expressing his full confidence in his officers in Maynooth. And life goes on.' Terry Gregory got up abruptly. 'That's it, Inspector. If you want to fit in, don't show too much initiative. If you can't be arsed to fit in . . . same advice.'

Gregory looked at Stefan, as if waiting for a response. There wasn't one.

'Why did you join the Guards?'

'I'm not sure I had a reason.' Stefan shrugged. 'If I had, I've forgotten it. I left Trinity because . . . I didn't like it. There was no point staying. I needed something to do. Maybe it was because my father was a policeman. Or maybe because they were looking for recruits and I couldn't think of anything better.'

'That'll do. As long as you didn't bring any principles with you.'

'Perhaps that's what I've forgotten, sir.'

Superintendent Gregory laughed. He walked across the room and stood looking out through the glass at the detectives in the room beyond. He had his hands in his pockets. He watched his men as if he didn't much like what he was looking at. It was clear, without more words, that the conversation was over.

Stefan walked to the door. As he opened it, Terry Gregory turned.

'You're right. The investigation was shite. If there was a chance of identifying the killer, it's long gone. Too much time spent keeping too much quiet. And if you read between the lines, a bit of . . . well, your man was fucking queer, and he got what happens to queers. So, you're right about all that too.'

The man who killed James Corcoran left Ireland long before Stefan Gillespie saw the body in the mortuary at Naas Hospital. He left even before Inspector Charles arrived at the picnic site by the lake at Donadea, the morning after the murder. He took the mail boat from Dún Laoghaire on the night of the killing. By the time a poacher found the seminarian's body, walking out of the Donadea woods towards the lake early the next day, the murderer was getting off a train at Euston Station in London. A great calmness had come over him after the frenzy of the assault. He knew the danger he was in and he knew he had to get away unobserved. He had gone to Donadea almost unseen from Dublin, taking two days to cycle by a roundabout route, sleeping the first night in an empty lock-keeper's cottage by the Royal Canal and the second in the ruins of the castle at Donadea, among the all-enveloping trees. That morning he swam at the lake where they had arranged to meet. The water was cold and clean. The September sun was still warm on his body as he lay on the grass to let himself dry. They met at midday. James had cycled from Maynooth, taking backroads and boreens as well. All the secretiveness of getting there, unknown, unnoticed, was part of the excitement. This would be their place, this deserted estate, overgrown and unworked, thick with trees, with a sparkling, hidden lake at its centre. It was James's place first, at least somewhere he had discovered, a secret space. But the man he came to meet was good at finding his way. And afterwards the man had to find his way back to Dublin, even more unnoticed, more unremarked than when he'd come. That was the sole thought in his head. He had an Ordnance Survey map and a compass. He had a change of clothes. There was blood, of course. That was easy to dispose of. He stripped naked and swam in the lake again. He put on new clothes and wrapped the old ones in a tight bundle. He wheeled his bicycle out of the trees to the road and set off, heading north towards the Royal Canal. He saw no one for several miles and when he did hear a car, then later a tractor, he had time to slip through a gate into a field. When he rode through a village, his head was down and whatever attention he attracted was the work of seconds. And it wouldn't matter. Someone would have to stumble on the body, in a place few people went. He would be gone. He made good, fast progress. He disposed of his clothes, weighted down with stones, and then of his bicycle, in a deserted stretch of the Royal Canal. He followed the towpath into Maynooth, where he got the train into Dublin, making sure he arrived at the station with only seconds to spare, so he wasn't standing on the platform, waiting, noticeable. By then he was very confident. And Dublin asked no questions. He ate a meal in a restaurant on Stephen's Green, with more to drink than he was used to, then travelled out to Dún Laoghaire for the night boat to Holyhead. He had never killed before. The thought had been there sometimes, the anger had been there, perhaps a need, building in him. It had still happened without him wanting it, or knowing he wanted it. He was sorry for what he had done. He wished it hadn't been James. He shed tears for what had happened, looking back from the boat as it steamed away from Dún Laoghaire's lights; tears for himself rather than the dead man. Yet there was a sense of relief, too. And for a time, a very short time, it made him feel that he had torn something out of himself, that he had rid himself of the darkness, of all the passions filling him with disgust about who he was. It was done, and done in such a terrible way that surely none of those feelings could ever come back again, those feelings he could not control. Hadn't he put a stop to it? Hadn't he done that at least? It was a kind of sacrifice. He didn't often pray, but he did as Ireland disappeared into black night; not for James Corcoran, the man he had butchered, but in the bright hope that what he had done had truly cleansed him.

3

Kensal Green

London, 1941

Row upon row, across London's great suburban cemetery at Kensal Green, the avenues of the Victorian dead stretched in every direction. A derelict community of black slate and mildewed stone, modest headstones and crumbling mausoleums, miniature Greek temples and skewed Egyptian obelisks, and the red Gothic arches of a dozen tiny Albert Memorials. Watched over by angels with broken wings and chipped and blackened faces, the straight paths echoed the streets that spread out around the cemetery for mile after mile, with a kind of cacophonous decay that brought a hint of chaos to the solid certainty of the houses the dead had inhabited when they were alive.

A middle-aged man was walking along one of the tomb-lined avenues on a clear, chill January afternoon. He knew the place well. It had been a part of his childhood. He had lived in one of those solid streets. Walking through the cemetery had been the ritual of so many endless, empty Sunday afternoons. Now the cemetery had an easy, casual familiarity that he felt more comfortable with than the roads he had just taken from the Underground station at Kensal Green. Perhaps it was that hint of chaos in the tumbled stones. They reflected a truth of sorts. You had to wait for death to discover all had not really been well, in the best of all possible worlds; nothing had been certain or solid. It was part of an unwanted past as far as the man was concerned. But it was there even if he had made himself a stranger to it.

He was just over forty. A fastidious, almost obsessive concern with his appearance meant that he did worry about being forty. It felt older than it should. There were plenty of people to reassure him it was really no age. He was, after all, Ireland's greatest actor and theatre director. He liked to say he wasn't, but he was not unhappy to be contradicted. If growing older concerned him, mostly he pushed it aside, amused that it mattered to him at all. But here, in this forgotten place from a largely forgotten past, the awareness of age was less easily shrugged off. He already felt coming had been a mistake. The streets beyond the cemetery walls were dead to him. That hadn't changed. They always were. They were before he knew they were. He had grown up here, but he'd left it behind in a strangely absolute and final way. He had invented a past for himself in which Kensal Green played almost no part. The child who had lived there was a ghost. It was fitting that on this rare visit his companions were ghosts too.

Along the avenue, between bare trees, in front of a crop of tombstones that leant in every direction, several dozen people stood by a heap of newly dug earth, watching as the undertakers lowered a coffin into the ground. The smell of fresh soil was in the air. The drum of a rusty gasometer rose up behind them.

Micheál Mac Liammóir was late, though there were others still behind him. No one was in a hurry. The actor's presence was a gesture, one he was unsure he should have made. There wasn't even an audience to appreciate it. It was unnecessary; it was inconvenient. It had involved the mail boat from Ireland, and a train through an England full of delays and wartime darkness. But as the Irishman he had become since leaving

Kensal Green, funerals mattered. He had decided this one did. He owed the man a lot, though he hadn't seen him in many years. It was the kind of sentimentality he was usually too scrupulous to allow himself. But there was a debt. There had been kindness, generosity, friendship, when he'd been unsure how to find that. The man had helped him become who he was.

Most of the mourners were men, older rather than younger. Mac Liammóir recognised some: actors, directors, artists; people he would have expected to see. He nodded and smiled the quiet, uncommunicative smiles that go with a funeral where the deceased doesn't matter so much to the mourners' lives. But for a moment he mattered enough. The words of the burial service surrounded these people briefly – friends, acquaintances, strangers – and bound them together. They were words that somehow you were born knowing.

'Thou knowest, Lord, the secrets of our hearts; shut not thy merciful ears to our prayers; but spare us, Lord most holy, O God most mighty, O holy and merciful Saviour, thou most worthy Judge eternal, suffer us not, at our last hour, for any pains of death, to fall from thee.' The minister looked round at the faces for some seconds, blankly, then continued. 'We commend unto thy hands of mercy, most merciful Father, the soul of this our brother departed, and we commit his body to the ground, earth to earth, ashes to ashes, dust to dust.'

The look was an invitation to come and cast earth on the coffin. No one moved. Then one man stepped forward. An undertaker handed him a brass trowel of soil. He tipped it on to the coffin. Micheál Mac Liammóir moved to the grave more dramatically. He bowed his head and scattered the earth, with purpose and flamboyance. As he turned there was a queue. He smiled. This was a performance at least. The dead man had every right to expect it to be properly done.

As the actor turned away from the graveside, he passed a young man, dark – Indian, he thought – looking at him with a fixed, frowning gaze. Their eyes met for only seconds, but Mac Liammóir felt a surprising intensity in the other man's stare. There was a sort of smile, too, boyish, awkward, but it was the intensity that unsettled him. The young man wore a grey overcoat, well cut, elegant. He clutched a brown, square canvas box to his side. It hung from his shoulder. The gas mask case that not long ago everyone carried, but now seemed less essential than a tin hat. The actor nodded uncertainly and carried on. The man was still watching him. He could feel it. It was someone who knew him, perhaps someone he should have known. He didn't recognise him. The man saw that and didn't like it. He expected a response. There had been anger in those eyes. Mac Liammóir shrugged it away. The Indian was attractive, unquestionably. A forgotten encounter? It must have been a long time ago. Those days had gone. Well, gone for the most part.

The last scatterings of earth fell on the coffin.

'O Father of all, we pray to thee for those whom we love, but see no longer. Grant them thy peace; let light perpetual shine upon them; and in thy loving wisdom and almighty power work in them the good purpose of thy perfect will; through Jesus Christ our Lord. The grace of our Lord Jesus Christ, and the love of God, and the fellowship of the Holy Ghost, be with us evermore. Amen.'

Micheál Mac Liammóir crossed himself.

Then everyone was leaving, turning back into the avenues of the dead, exchanging quiet words about plays and friends and the war and last week's bombing in London, unfinished sentences. The great actor was conscious of the dark young man again, gazing from some way off. He walked on, following the other mourners. He was puzzled, but more than that, he was annoyed. It was as if the man wanted something. There was an etiquette. Not remembering was a part of that. You never imposed. You never reminded. Except by invitation. It wasn't about politeness. For some men it was about survival.

A brief encounter, if that's what it had been, should be exactly that. He had almost decided to speak to the young man, but something stopped him. It was that intensity again. Mac Liammóir's instincts were to go. There was something troubled in the young face, a mix of desperation and anger.

A familiar voice pushed all that away.

'Alfred!'

There was no mistaking the voice, lazy but razor-sharp, or that the name he had once been called was from the past. No one used it now. In Ireland hardly anybody knew he once carried this most English name.

'It's a while, Noël.'

'Well, I suppose we've nodded across a crowded room from time to time. Not so long as all that. Let's not make ourselves any older than we are, Alfred.'

Noël Coward took out a cigarette case. He offered one to Mac Liammóir. They stood for a moment, saying nothing, as one actor lit the other's cigarette and then lit his own. The two men had known one another in childhood. They had acted together as children. For both of them it was a world that had been left behind, though only one of them had entirely erased it from his present.

'I'm sure you're rather a stranger to London now,' said Coward.

'I thought I should come. Eric did a lot for me.'

'I saw him last year. Very ill. I can't say I kept in touch with him, but at least I did something. He spoke a lot about old times. I have to be honest and say I couldn't remember most of what he was talking about. I think he invented some of it, and even that wasn't particularly entertaining. Well, nothing wrong with that. If I am ever so ancient that I find myself spending most of my time talking about the past, I shall make everything up. Anyway, there he lies. He mentioned you. I think he'd rather you'd come to see him . . . when he was still alive.'

'I should have done.' Mac Liammóir smiled. 'Thank you, Noël.'

'Not often I can be self-righteous, Alfred. Don't begrudge it me. And I still can't call you Michael, let alone say it the way one is supposed to in Irish. I don't do it to irritate you. It's how I see you. I still resent the fact that you're a serious actor.' Coward laughed. 'And rather too serious, I sometimes think.'

'If my father had given me a more interesting name, I might have kept it.'

'There's something in that. As a child I took some pleasure in you having an uninspiring name. I might have come to nothing without my diaeresis.'

The two men joined the drift away from the graveside, heading along the avenue towards other avenues and the entrance to the cemetery, walking slowly.

'I have a car waiting, if you want a lift into Town?'

'I think I'll get a breath more air and take the Tube.' Mac Liammóir wasn't sure why he suddenly said that, except that he wanted some time on his own. 'I gather a few people are going for a drink, at Billie's. I might do that. I don't know. I have a night in Town before I go back to Dublin. Are you going?'

'I have work to do. Well, dinner with tedious people is always work.'

'I'm sure you'll amuse them.'

'You see what I mean, Alfred. You're the serious one, I'm the clown.'

'Ah, but what a clown!'

Noël Coward laughed. 'There is that.'

They walked on for a moment, silently. Mac Liammóir smiled.

'I remember you at ten, Noël, auditioning for a goldfish in one of Miss Lila Field's thankfully forgotten productions. We met at the audition. You asked me if I'd done much work. I'd no idea you meant acting. You also asked me if I knew what I wanted to be when I grew up. I didn't. You were unimpressed. You said people should always be clear about what they want. You were. I don't think you ever doubted or lost your way. I opted for uncertainty.'

'You finally discovered what you wanted to be, Alfred. An Irishman.'

Micheál Mac Liammóir laughed.

'I hope I make a better Irishman than I did a goldfish.'

'I'm sure you do, but I have never forgotten that Miss Field cast you as King Goldfish. I was stuck with Prince Mussel, not on until the third act.' Coward grinned and shook his head. 'The *Morning Post* review singled you out as the pretty little boy with the curls. It left a scar on my heart that never went.'

'I don't remember that at all,' said Mac Liammóir.

'Terrifying that I do,' replied Noël Coward. 'Ten or not, a low point in my career. You were earning two pounds a week and I was only on thirty bob!'

'You've made up for that since, Noël.'

'Money is a small compensation.'

'But you're busy enough, from what I read.'

'I suppose so. I've tried to find an obviously heroic role in the business of war, swanning around the world on some vague Intelligence mission, all grand hotels and secret assignations. They did give me a diplomatic passport, but it seems Winston didn't think I was achieving much by travelling the empire. They decided I'd be better singing while the guns fire, or words to that effect. Jolly songs for the troops. Positive propaganda. Which sounds like an exercise in boring the Germans into submission. I hope it doesn't do the same to Britain.'

'I doubt it will, Noël.' Mac Liammóir said what he knew his old friend expected him to say, but perhaps without the conviction that was required.

'It is a work in progress, dear boy. Some argument about whether a dressing gown and cigarette holder is good for morale or not. However, Herr Hitler has been helpful in making me a normal Londoner. The Luftwaffe dropped a bomb on my flat. I'm at the Savoy now. Beggars can't be choosers.'

The last joke, as if scripted for it, coincided with Noël Coward's arrival at his Rover. It was perfectly timed. The chauffeur was holding open the door.

'You're sure about the lift, Alfred?'

'I'm sure. Take care.'

The Englishman took out another cigarette, fixing it into a black cigarette holder with a shrug that was a rare moment of self-deprecation. He was on stage, even in the back of a car driving through suburban London. But the conversation with Mac Liammóir had been a performance too. It was something the Irishman understood. They were very different men, with very different ideas about what they did, but they shared something in that need to keep performing, whether on stage or not, in public or in private. Performance was a way to survive. It always had been. They knew it as children, even before knowing why survival was necessary.

Leaving the cemetery for Kensal Green Underground Station, Micheál Mac Liammóir slowed down. There were several people ahead of him from the funeral. He chose not to catch up with them. He might talk to them later, over a drink. For now, he turned away from the station, towards College Road. Burrows Road, Ashburnham Road; the turnings were still familiar. They were in his head, though he had forgotten they were. And the houses were as drab and as heavy as they had been in his teenage years. On Purves Road he stood outside number 150. He looked at it for only seconds before retracing his steps. He had a dread of this place that bore no real relation to what it was, or what it had been. If he felt any guilt about the battered scenery stored in the back of his mind, perhaps it was because his mother and father had never been as interesting as his story needed them to be. They were as solid and as ordinary and as English as these houses. They belonged in a place where he had been unable to breathe. But it was the reason he couldn't breathe that separated him from this place. That was the truth. The real desires that were his real identity.

The platform at Kensal Green Underground Station was empty now. The funeral contingent was gone. Only a few people stepped forward on to the red Bakerloo Line train as the doors opened. Micheál Mac Liammóir got in and sat down, conscious that a drink would be no bad thing now. He had not noticed the young Indian man who had been waiting by the platform entrance and ran to get into the next carriage at the last moment. He had already forgotten the uncomfortable encounter at the graveside. He had not registered that the man had been following him, keeping far off in the quiet streets of Kensal Green. He would not notice, as the journey into London continued, that the man had him in sight through the windows at the end of the adjacent carriages and was ready at every station for him to disembark. He was less likely to notice anything as the train went into the tunnels and filled up with passengers, and as it passed through stations closer to the West End, where the platforms were filling with people settling down to spend the night underground, in anticipation of the bombing. He was absorbed in what he was looking at, interrupted by the stretches of darkness in the tunnel. It was a rhythm he still knew, the rhythm of the stations that had been like a heartbeat when he was young. Queen's Park, Kilburn Park, Maida Vale, Warwick Avenue, Paddington, Edgware Road, Marylebone, Baker Street, Regents Park, Oxford Circus.

He counted them, as he used to count them once. He did not notice, at Piccadilly Circus, getting off the train, threading his way through the crowds to the escalators and emerging into late-afternoon London, that the young Indian man was still following him.

4

Billie's

In the bar at Billie's, in cellars beneath Little Denmark Street, a quartet of black musicians played 'Somebody Loves Me' with lazy familiarity. A woman with a peroxide-blonde perm, who might have sounded better without the American accent she was failing to imitate, sang in a breathy, slightly off-key whisper.

> Somebody loves me, I wish I knew
> Who can he be worries me,
> For every boy who passes me
> I shout, 'Hey maybe
> You were meant to be my loving baby.'
> Somebody loves me, I wonder who,
> Maybe it's you.

There was a buzz of conversation and laughter from the bar and the tables that were barely visible along the dark walls. There was little light anywhere except around the bar. No one was listening to the music, not even the dancers who shuffled round the small dance floor in front of the band. The couples dancing, most of them draped around each other, would have been unusual elsewhere. There were men and women dancing together, but among them white women danced with black men and black women with white men. Men danced with men and pressed their bodies close, slowly and sinuously, keeping time to what their bodies were saying more than to the music. Women dancing with women, in the face of men too busy at the bar, was familiar in any dance hall, but here two women's lips touched in the darkness. The club was full, though it was still early. It had been barely dark when Micheál Mac Liammóir had walked down the steps from the street. But things happened earlier in London now. What the night had in store in terms of bombing, no one knew. At any moment the silence and the darkness outside could be pierced by the moan of engines overhead and the sounds of the first explosions. There were nights when nothing happened. There were nights when the bombing was elsewhere. Some ran to shelters or hurried home to the suburbs at the first sign of German planes. Others made fine judgements, forcing another half-hour of pleasure from an evening before seeking safety. Some diehards stayed in Billie's basement, drinking their way through a raid.

Mac Liammóir had walked from Piccadilly Circus in the dusk. He had spent only two nights in London since the Blitz began. On neither occasion had bombs fallen close to where he was. He registered bombsites and shattered buildings, the broken windows of shops he knew, the sandbags at every entrance, the criss-crossed tape over every window. He had not seen the dead; he was conscious of that. But tonight, he was conscious of more. The walk from Piccadilly, along Coventry Street, to Leicester Square and Charing Cross Road, was another return. Coming out of the Underground he saw the Café Royal, still the safest place in London for a man like him; if you were welcome there you were important enough to be safe. Passing the Criterion, he smiled. The site where Eros stood was boarded over, but some things didn't change. Two young men, barely boys, were eyeing passers-by, wearing too much rouge and too much lipstick. The Dilly boys, bombs or no bombs. Outside the Lyons Corner House in Coventry Street a noisy gaggle waited for tables. The queue was full of men in uniform, like everywhere, but this was a Corner House where the codes and signals of queer London were learnt and practised. He had learnt them as a young man, with a kind of bewilderment and then with joy, finally knowing he was not alone. No one said anything; all was discretion. No one suggested the first-floor restaurant was different from any other floor. But the waitresses never sat women there. It was a public space but a private club.

Mac Liammóir didn't like the centre of London any more than its suburbs. It had always felt as if it was crumbling behind its imperial façades. The theatres mattered, but nothing else. Yet he felt an unfamiliar warmth for the city that night, with darkness closing in; such complete darkness, like a curtain coming down in the blackness of an auditorium, but with no lights to come up. Now the London he had turned his back on was being destroyed, he had time for it.

In Billie's, a handful of men who were at the funeral occupied one end of the bar. Micheál Mac Liammóir joined them. The conversation was bright enough. They were theatre men, in one guise or another, acquaintances rather than friends. The talk was of before the war, of old friends, and as ever on such occasions, who had died. But the war was quickly there, even in the cheerful relief that the theatres had reopened. Someone had decided entertainment mattered; that meant there were still jobs. The bombing was always present, too, though mostly in black jokes and unlikely stories. Mac Liammóir listened and laughed, but he offered no jokes of his own. He had some, but it felt as if the right to joke came with being under the bombs. And if these old acquaintances were amiable enough, he knew that not every comment about him being safely tucked away in Dublin was well intentioned.

There was no sign of an air raid, though the maître d'
appeared at intervals to say that there were bombs along the
Thames, beyond Greenwich. No one took much notice, but
people were beginning to drift away. Whether the West End
was to be spared for another night or not, evenings finished
early now, just as they started early. Micheál Mac Liammóir
ordered one more drink before setting off to his hotel. Suddenly
the drummer at the side of the dance floor delivered a crashing
drum roll that had nothing to do with the slow version of
'Caravan' being played. The trumpeter blew a discordant wail
before, abruptly, resuming a muted solo. The actor noticed
several customers moving across the dance floor at speed to
disappear through a back door, among them a couple of men in
uniform. Everyone else continued as before, talking, drinking,
dancing. Two men in raincoats, hats still on, approached the
bar. The maître d' stood in front of them, smiling his broadest,
apparently most welcoming smile. He knew who they were, as
did most. The warning had already been sounded.

'Are you friends of Dorothy, gentlemen?' asked the maître d'.

There was chuckling from the onlookers.

One of the newcomers produced an identity card.

'Military Police.'

'Lovely, dear,' continued the maître d'. 'I wish you'd come in
uniform.'

'We're looking for service personnel. This club is
off-limits.'

'Really? That makes us sound very exciting. Would you like
a drink?'

'Don't come the faery with me.'

The second MP walked away from the bar, through the
club. He was watched with distaste by some and laughed at by
others. He looked ill at ease, uncertain what exactly he was
supposed to do, unless he actually saw someone in uniform.
The music continued. The first MP glared at the maître d'.

'I have information that men in uniform were seen entering this club.'

'Well, I don't see any. Are you going to ask us all for our identity cards?'

The military policeman looked more doubtful.

'I'm only interested in service personnel.'

'I don't blame you. Aren't we all, dear?' There was more laughter. Then the maître d's tone changed. 'I'll give you a bit of advice, soldier boy. A lot of people who come in here are VIPs. That means Very Important Poofs. The police know that. And we're surprisingly friendly with the police. They leave us alone. That's how it works. You need to do the same. Or you could find your cushy job patrolling the West End cut short. If you bump into a senior officer, who knows where they'll post you? Could be somewhere you might get shot at.'

The second MP returned from a fruitless circuit of the club.

'Now piss off,' said the maître d', grinning cheerfully again.

As Micheál Mac Liammóir watched the two military policemen head for the exit, he saw a figure at the bar, watching him. The man was familiar, the young Indian from Kensal Green. The actor was unaware that the man had been sitting in Billie's for some time, at a dark corner table, waiting until Mac Liammóir was finally on his own. He was smiling. He walked forward with his hand outstretched. The actor responded as he had to and shook, but he knew now that he had been followed.

'Mr Mac Liammóir, you don't remember me, do you?'

'I'm sorry. You'll have to remind me. I did see you at the funeral, and I had a feeling I really should know you. You'll just have to put it down to age!'

'Vikram Narayan. It was Cairo, the Royal Opera House, 'thirty-six. I was a stage manager. You gave me a part in *Romeo and Juliet*. One of your chaps was off with the usual Delhi belly, or whatever the Egyptian equivalent is.'

43

The young man grinned. Mac Liammóir nodded.

'Yes, of course. I remember now.'

He did remember. The Indian had played Sampson in the opening scene of *Romeo and Juliet*. He remembered that it had been a mistake, all the more glaring because it was the beginning of the play. It was a mistake born of another mistake and a row he'd had with his partner, Hilton Edwards. There had been a night, a very drunken night, when he had fallen into bed with the, admittedly very beautiful, young stage manager. He had barely recalled anything the next day. He wasn't convinced anything had happened except that he had passed out, though Hilton was never going to believe that. But he felt some kind of awkward obligation to Vikram Narayan; the result was the second mistake. That was the one Hilton Edwards had not let him forget. Narayan was appalling.

'I can handle you fucking the boy, Micheál, but not fucking the Bard!'

Hilton's words came back to him and he smiled.

Vikram Narayan was smiling too, an oddly fixed smile.

'You're living in London now, Vikram?'

'I spent some time back in India, after Cairo, but I've been here a while.'

'Are you still . . . working?'

Mac Liammóir was not finding it easy to say anything. It was not a problem he had normally, but the man unsettled him. As the words left his lips, he regretted them. For someone in the profession, the word working meant one thing. He knew, before he finished, that it was unlikely Narayan was acting.

'I'm not in theatre at the moment, no.'

The great director thought that was probably an understatement. The season in Cairo was in focus now. The man hadn't been much better as a stage manager.

'I want to get back to it, though. That's where my heart is.'

The young man stepped closer, smiling more broadly. Mac Liammóir wanted to step back, but he was wedged against the bar. He thought Narayan was going to make a pass, there and then. He couldn't get away. He glanced at his watch. He was usually better with words, much better, but he felt he was going to be reduced to something like, *Good God, is that the time already?*

Narayan said nothing. The Irishman began to waffle.

'You knew Eric Lake, anyway? He was a very old friend. I hadn't seen him in years. He was a very kind man, kind to me . . . but you knew him too.'

'Not well. He helped once . . . with a job. Front of house. It meant a lot.'

The words were pointed, as if they connected to Mac Liammóir.

'I think we were meant to meet again, Mr Mac Liammóir. I had no idea I would see you today. But I have thought about you. The idea of coming to Ireland, you see, that's the thing. The idea of working with you again. So, when I saw you, I was more than surprised. I was delighted. If I hadn't gone, it wouldn't have happened . . . Things are destined sometimes, don't you think?'

Mac Liammóir didn't think so at all. He was more uncomfortable than ever. And something in Vikram Narayan's voice reminded him of what he had seen in his face before. A kind of desperation. His eyes were fixed, unwavering.

'I think I can be honest with you. I need help. To get out of London. That's what's in my head.' He reached forward and touched the actor's arm. 'I'm sure all sorts of things are in my head, seeing you again . . . all sorts.'

Jesus Christ! Mac Liammóir barely stopped himself saying the words.

'I have some money,' continued the young man, changing his tone suddenly. 'Enough to get to Ireland, maybe enough to keep me a while. But I need the papers to travel. I need a job to go to if I'm to stay. And we're old friends, aren't we? We've worked together. You see why I was thinking of you. And of course, the opportunity of working at the Gate with you . . . wonderful.'

The Irishman could hear an emptiness in those last words. Narayan's face was blank. The words meant nothing. All that was there, behind the smile, was the desperation. He didn't appear to be drunk. For a moment Mac Liammóir wondered if he'd been taking drugs. He was sweating profusely.

'You will help me, won't you?' he spoke quietly, but it was a plea, deep and troubling. He whispered, 'I have a room we can go to . . . if you want to go.'

'I don't, Mr Narayan,' said Mac Liammóir. He tried to sound kind.

The young Indian reached into his pocket. He took out a business card.

'Take this, please.'

The actor took the card.

'My address. I'm sorry if I said the wrong thing. We should approach this professionally, of course we should. Please . . . if I am too eager . . . forgive me.'

'Vikram, I can't take you into the company just like that. I hardly know you. We met for a few days, five years ago. We're a small company . . .' The actor trailed off. He could hardly tell the man there were no circumstances on earth in which he could offer him a job, even if there was a job. 'Impossible.'

The young man shook his head. He spoke more softly.

'It's not safe for me here. Something happened . . . Ireland would be safe.'

Mac Liammóir said nothing, because the words meant nothing.

'It's the same for all of us who are working for Indian independence. I have, I always have. I told you, in Egypt. We

46

talked about Irish freedom, Indian freedom. Do you remember? Ireland showed the way. We all look to Ireland.'

'I see.' The actor said something because he felt he must. He remembered no such conversation, but it could have happened. It was the kind of conversation he might have had. It was a conversation he had had with others.

Vikram Narayan moved closer, almost whispering now.

'If you could offer me a job, then I could get into Ireland. I need the papers, that's all. You shouldn't believe what you hear about India. There are those of us who don't want Britain to win this war. We feel like you. We know the words. We hold the thought.' He smiled, as if he knew he was saying what Mac Liammóir would want him to say. 'England's difficulty is our opportunity too. Aren't we all fighting in the same cause, in Ireland and India?'

Micheál Mac Liammóir had no ready answer to this unexpected appeal to his Republican instincts. It wasn't long ago that he might have echoed the Indian's words with enthusiasm. There was a cause that India and Ireland shared. There was a fight for freedom in the face of the British Empire that Ireland had not fully won, and India had still to win at all. But the war that was happening now made for less easy conclusions. His antipathy towards Britain had to be put beside his hatred of the darkness that was sweeping Europe. He could have that conversation, as people across Ireland did, and find himself in conflict with himself, but he didn't want it now, here. And he didn't believe Vikram Narayan wanted it either. These were words meant to impress him or put pressure on him. He could feel it. They were spoken with the intensity that was driving the young man's voice. But they carried no conviction. Mac Liammóir wanted to get away. Narayan could see it.

'You should help me. You have to help me.'

'Mr Narayan, please . . .'

The young Indian's tone changed.

'I don't care what I do. I need to get away. Do you understand?' There was a quiet aggression in the voice. 'I think you owe me that.'

'Owe you?' The actor frowned. 'Dear boy, what do you mean?'

'You know what I mean.'

'I don't think I do. But I do think I've had enough. A brief encounter in Cairo that memory tells me probably didn't even happen . . . is hardly a debt.'

Narayan's face came closer.

'How does being queer go down in Ireland, Mr Mac Liammóir? It doesn't go down well here, but with all that Irish holiness, what would they make of you, if they knew what you got up to? How about a story like that? I could say a lot that would make the newspapers sit up. I wouldn't stop at Cairo. Papers don't care if it's true. What would Ireland think of the squalid old man you are?'

Micheál Mac Liammóir stared in disbelief. This had come from nowhere.

And then he laughed.

'You think I'm a candidate for blackmail?'

'Every queer's a candidate for blackmail. I could do it.'

'My dear boy, you're right to say this isn't a topic much talked about after Mass of a Sunday in Ireland. And you might think that Ireland, of all the places on God's Holy Earth, would be the last to give a man like me protection. But you'd be wrong. Ireland is a land of glorious hypocrisy, and if I made a paragraph in the *News of the World*, the whole island would pretend it was never there. There may be a couple of deaf old ladies in Cahirciveen and Malin Head who are unaware of my sexual predilections, but that's about the extent of it. Perhaps you missed the conversation with the military policeman just now, but on Eireann's sacred shores, I really am a Very Important Poof.'

It seemed that abruptly all the energy had drained out of Vikram Narayan. But Mac Liammóir could see there were, surprisingly, tears in his eyes. At that moment the maître d', who had watched for the last few minutes, approached.

'Is there a problem, Mr Mac Liammóir?'

'No, not at all. I think Mr Narayan is leaving.'

The young Indian looked deflated, beaten. He glanced nervously at the maître d', as if he was a new kind of threat. He turned quickly and went, pushing past people as he did.

'Do you know him?' The actor looked at the maître d'.

'He doesn't come in often. I don't think he has the money. Rather down on his luck. I'm sorry if he upset you, sir, but I'm sure he meant no harm.'

The maître d' walked away. Mac Liammóir was less sure Vikram Narayan meant no harm. He finished his drink, collected his coat, and left.

Walking back towards his hotel in the blackout, Micheál Mac Liammóir was still troubled by the face of the young Indian. It pushed aside his awareness of the dull thud of explosions. They were a long way off. Along the river, the maître d' had said. Only a few days in London had made that seem ordinary. The sense of desperation he had seen in Vikram Narayan's face, even at a first glance, across the coffin at Kensal Green, would not go away. Whatever was wrong went deep. It was not idle, and whatever anger the actor felt himself about the attempt to blackmail him into helping the young man, he felt something else too. There was no reason why he should feel sorry for Narayan after what had happened, yet he did. Something made him think he should have tried to help. It was an uneasy feeling. It was the kind of thing you might feel for a stray dog that snapped at you in the street. What could he do? Why should he bother? But the tense, hopeless face remained in his head when those last angry, mad words were already fading.

He put his hand in his pocket and found the business card. It was bent and dog-eared. It read: *Vikram Narayan, Actor, Flat 6, 24A Greek Street.* Mac Liammóir shook his head. There was something almost pitiful about the printed declaration. The man was afraid of something. And there was a connection, however slight. It meant almost nothing, but perhaps it was wrong to turn aside on the road. He had five pounds in his wallet. If he could help in no other way, he could give him that. He was very near Greek Street. It would take only minutes.

Micheál Mac Liammóir reached the door at 24A Greek Street, sandwiched between an Italian restaurant and a delicatessen. There was a list of names and some bell pushes. Narayan's name was there, but when he pressed the bell, he knew nothing was happening at the other end. Probably none of them worked. A man cycled past, an air raid warden in a tin hat.

'The front door'll be open. You won't get nowhere pressing those!'

The man disappeared into the darkness.

Mac Liammóir opened the door. It swung back to reveal a corridor and some stairs. There was a faint light from the landing above. It didn't seem the best idea to be here, but he had made his decision. For whatever motive, a conscience he had no reason to salve needed salving. He walked up the stairs, looking at the door numbers. A second flight of stairs took him to the top of the house. There was only one door: Flat 6. It was ajar, and the room exuded a warm, orange glow. Narayan was home. Mac Liammóir wished he wasn't. He could have stuffed the money under the door. But he would do what he had come to do. He knocked on the open door. There was no answer. He pushed the door and looked into a small, cluttered room, lit by a bedside lamp. There was an armchair, a table, a chest of drawers, a bed in one corner. The blackout blinds were closed. There was another door across the room.

If Narayan was in the other room, maybe that would do as well as being out. He would leave the money on the table and scoot. He took the five-pound note from his wallet. He laid it down. It was as he looked up that he saw the bed in the corner. And the body of Vikram Narayan stretched across it. He saw the blood everywhere on Vikram's clothes and on the sheets. The young Indian was dead. There was so much blood Mac Liammóir could taste the iron in the air.

5

West End Central

Inspector Stefan Gillespie sat at a table in the window of the Lyons Corner House at Piccadilly Circus, looking down at London going to work. The night had been quiet in the West End and he had slept well enough in the small attic room at the top of the offices of the Irish High Commission, across the road in Regent Street. No one lived at the High Commission, but for two months now, either side of Christmas, Stefan had shuttled back and forth between there and the Department of External Affairs in Dublin, carrying the briefcases that were the diplomatic bag. A train of Irish and British diplomats, politicians, businessmen and Army Intelligence officers followed the same route. He knew many of them now, British as well as Irish. Sometimes they spoke on the mail boat or the train, sometimes there was merely a nod, often there was nothing. He knew those whose journeys were public property and those whose travel arrangements led them into the offices of the British Army and British Intelligence – the men who weren't meant to be noticed at all. Irish neutrality was a business that showed itself, clear and transparent, above the waterline, in all its necessary dealings with the British, but what mattered was the invisible iceberg beneath the surface.

In many ways Stefan's work as a courier was about what could be seen and defended, even if some of what he carried might not have been viewed positively in Berlin. There the conviction that Ireland was a constant thorn in the side of the British war effort was an article of faith.

Stefan found the job tedious and repetitive. It meant a lot of time doing nothing except sit on boats and trains, but if it was undemanding, it kept him out of Special Branch. He didn't mind that his time wasn't spent spying on other Irishmen and cataloguing dissent. He was used to London now. He knew the routines of the shelters and the Underground. He knew its atmosphere, intense and resigned, slow, yet full of a strange energy. He didn't dislike being there. He found the anonymity of the city an easy thing.

It was still early, just after eight o'clock. There was a newspaper in front of him, but he wasn't reading it. There was a break ahead, when he got back to Ireland: two days at home in Wicklow, with his young son, Tom, and his parents. He would take the mail boat that night. He looked at his watch. Shortly he would walk up to Charing Cross Road to find a book to take back for Tom.

He smiled. He knew he had to do better with the book than his effort at Christmas. It was the price of being at home so little. The *Beano Book* had not been unwelcome. It lasted for Christmas Day and it provided a series of bad jokes to repeat for several days more. But he had lost his sense of what Tom read, even what he thought. He had seen the book next to Tom's bed was a translation of *The Iliad*, from the library in Baltinglass. It was something he had never read. Tom would be twelve before long, and in the last year, without Stefan seeing it, he had changed. He had grown quickly into someone Stefan didn't know as well as he had. Being away so much it felt as if it had happened abruptly, when it really hadn't at all.

'Gillespie!'

Stefan looked up to see the High Commissioner, John Dulanty.

'Miss Foye said you were here.'

Dulanty pulled back a chair and sat down. He had just arrived from his commute into London from a quiet house in the suburbs. He travelled into Waterloo every weekday, like any Londoner, and he was as unnoticeable as anyone else on the Southern Railway trains through Wimbledon and Clapham Junction. Stefan was barely ten years younger than the High Commissioner, but Dulanty's balding head made him look older. His voice gave little indication of his Irishness. He had been born in Liverpool; he grew up in Manchester. He was one of a cohort of British civil servants and diplomats with Irish parents, who had left the service of Britain to work for the Irish state when it came into existence. His loyalty to his country now did not disguise the fact that the skin he inhabited seemed, at times, as English as Irish. In the midst of London's war especially, he was as much a participant as an observer. He took out a cigarette. The Nippy, the waitress, in crisp black and white, hovered.

'Just a cup of tea.'

The waitress disappeared.

'I had a message from Scotland Yard when I got in. One of the assistant commissioners. I don't know quite what to make of it. He didn't know much himself. It was something he picked up, that he heard, that could become . . . I don't know if embarrassing is the word . . . but awkward. As I say, I don't know exactly what's happened. I imagine you know who Micheál Mac Liammóir is?'

'Yes, of course. I know him . . . well, I've met him.'

'That might be helpful. I suppose, if you know him . . . you'll know that he is a man with . . . with some less than normal social . . . when I say—'

Stefan smiled. 'He's queer. I'd say we can take that for

granted, sir.'

Dulanty frowned. It was what he meant but he didn't like it said. The waitress brought the tea. The High Commissioner waited as she walked away.

'So, Mac Liammóir has been arrested. I don't know if arrested is the right word, but he's in custody or he's being questioned. He was in some club in Soho.' The High Commissioner said 'club' with an expression of distaste. He glanced round and lowered his voice. 'That's the gist of it. That's all the Assistant Commissioner knew. Something happened between Mac Liammóir and . . . some chap . . . and the long and the short is that someone – I assume this man – is dead.'

Stefan Gillespie found it hard not to smile, listening to Dulanty's delivery of a narrative he did not relish talking about, but those last words were serious.

'Dead?'

'Yes. It seems Mac Liammóir is . . . a witness . . . perhaps a suspect.'

'Well, I find suspect very hard to believe, sir.'

The High Commissioner shrugged. He stubbed out his cigarette.

'It appears Mr Mac Liammóir was over here for a funeral. I have had no request for consular help, but he may need it. I hope this is a mistake of some kind, but I'd like to know what's happening. He is . . . a prominent figure at home – and to some extent here. It is a private visit, but he does . . . Well, with the Gate Theatre, as a director, an actor, he has represented Ireland all over the world. He is much admired. If he is involved in something . . . squalid . . . it's not what we want splashed all over the newspapers. And if it's more serious than that, it is something that Dev won't . . .' Dulanty shook his head. 'He will go berserk.'

Stefan said nothing. He was a policeman. If there was a dead man somewhere, whatever the circumstances, his first thought was not what the Prime Minister of Ireland might object to in the newspapers.

'We need to find out what is happening, Inspector. Do you see?'

'Do you know where he is, Mr Dulanty?'

'A police station . . . West End Central.'

'I can't just walk in there and ask what's going on, sir.'

'The Assistant Commissioner recognises . . . a diplomatic element to this. That's why he called. No one wants waves, wherever they come from. You can't tell where anything leads just now. Mac Liammóir has influential friends here. And if we want to avoid embarrassment this end, the British don't want to see him turned into a cause célèbre in Ireland. Mac Liammóir is strident about his nationalism. If it looks like he's being persecuted, nobody needs him dressed in the Green and turning himself into a martyr. The man is not beyond that.'

Stefan laughed. 'No, he probably isn't.'

The High Commissioner ignored the laughter. He wasn't amused.

'I don't want to involve a solicitor. That's not our business. Mac Liammóir may have done that himself. That's up to him. I'd rather the High Commission isn't directly involved at this point. The Assistant Commissioner is happy for you to go into West End Central. He will provide any bona fides.'

'Go in to do what exactly?'

'Help with inquiries, with anything they may want to know.'

'Why would they want to know anything from me, sir?'

'All they have to do is tell you what's happened, why the man is there, whether he is actually being charged with anything. They will be instructed to let you talk to him. I want to know what I tell Dublin. I want to know if this will stop where it is, or whether there is worse to come. As far as Scotland Yard is concerned, it's a request from me, and the request is being accommodated as a courtesy to the Irish government. You won't need to explain yourself at all.'

'I should think there's every chance they'll tell me to fuck off.'

The High Commissioner drained his tea and stood up.

'I think they'll do what Scotland Yard tells them. And if there's nothing to this, except keeping insalubrious company, I'd say the police will do us a favour and forget about it. If so, I want Mr Mac Liammóir out of London and on a boat to Dublin as soon as possible.' He smiled for the first time. 'You might offer up a couple of prayers to St Anthony for that happy outcome. I certainly will. He was my mother's favourite saint. I'm sure she's still got some credit with him.'

The sergeant on the front desk at West End Central gave Stefan Gillespie a smile that was almost a sneer. It was clear he was expected, but not welcome.

'Garda Síochána, eh, Inspector? We don't get many of those.'

'I think someone should have phoned, Sergeant.'

'From Scotland Yard, that's right. To the superintendent. If we'd known Mr Mac Liammóir was putting on a show, we would have sold tickets.'

The sarcasm was wasted on Stefan. He didn't reply.

'You'd better come through then, Inspector.'

The sergeant lifted the desk flap.

'Who do I need to talk to? Is it CID?'

'The super can't be arsed to see you. He said get on with whatever you're here for. As for CID, I think they'll leave you with the feller from the Yard. They've already sent a chief inspector. He beat you to it. In with them now, for what it's worth. My bet is they'll let you two at it . . . and go for a fucking drink.'

Stefan followed the sergeant along the bright corridors.

West End Central was a new police station. One day it would have the stale smell of sweat and smoke that all police stations had. Now it smelt of polish and new paint. The sergeant knocked on a door and went in. Inside were three detectives, standing at a desk, looking at photographs, statements and diagrams.

'It's the Irishman,' said the sergeant. He turned and walked away.

Stefan Gillespie stepped into the room. The three men looked at him. Only one of them smiled and walked forward, hand outstretched. He was tall, slightly gaunt, with pale hair and skin that was darker than it should have been, as if he had been a long time in the sun. He was older than Stefan; not by much.

'Frank Nugent.' He shook Stefan's hand and turned towards the other two, a man in his fifties, heavy and sour-faced, and a man in his twenties. 'Inspector Hardy and DS Dillon. They've been working on the scene of crime. And they've tied the murder into several other similar killings. The body was only discovered last night, but that's what's come out already. It's good work.'

Stefan registered the word murder. The English detective was talking to him as if he knew something. He had known about a death, but not a murder.

The older man walked across the room and shook Stefan's hand now. He did not do it with any good grace. The atmosphere in the room was uncomfortable.

'It's Inspector Gillespie, is that right?'

'It is. It's Stefan.'

'I don't know exactly what you're here for.'

'I'm not sure I do myself,' said Stefan, trying to keep the conversation as light as he could. He sensed that whatever the atmosphere was, it had been there before he walked into the room. 'You have an Irish citizen . . . I don't know if he's in custody or whether he's a witness to something . . . I think it's just that I was here, and the High Commission wanted to offer . . . some assistance.'

Inspector Hardy laughed. 'To us or to him?'

'Maybe both,' said Stefan more quietly.

'The man you want to talk to is Chief Inspector Nugent here,' continued the DI. 'He seems to be taking over. Who knows why he's here either?' He looked at the man who had introduced himself to Stefan a moment before. 'Murder. Why would they hand that to Special Branch, but what the fuck, eh?'

'No one's handing anything to anyone, Dick,' said Nugent.

'You're not here for your health, sir.' Inspector Hardy made a point of the formality of Nugent's higher rank. 'I don't suppose you are either, Mr Gillespie.' He made the same point, in a different way, ignoring Stefan's rank. 'When you sort out what you're doing, give us a shout. The office is yours.'

Detective Inspector Hardy nodded at his DS. He walked out and the younger man followed him. For a time Stefan stood looking at Nugent, who had a faint smile on his lips. The Irish detective had no idea what was going on. But he knew that if the chief inspector was from Special Branch, the West End Central CID man was probably right. He was there to take over, whatever the reasons for that.

'Not much of a welcome, Inspector.'

'I wasn't expecting much of a welcome. It's Stefan.'

'I think you're slightly more welcome than I am.'

'I'm here to find out what's happened to Mr Mac Liammóir.'

'I know.'

'Has he been arrested?'

'No. Helping with inquiries. I think Inspector Hardy had him down as a killer in the early hours of this morning, but it's clear enough that his own description of events is probably true. He discovered the body. And that's all. I say that's all, but if you look at what he found . . . he won't forget it in a hurry.'

Nugent turned to the table. He pointed at a row of photographs.

The wide shots showed a room, cluttered and small, lit by the harsh light from a flash. The close shots showed a bed and the body of a young, dark man; the full body, stretched out on the bed, then closer views of the head, the swollen neck, the legs, the stomach, the groin. The photographs were black and white, but the blood-stained clothing showed sharply all round the stomach and thighs. There was a great deal of blood. The man had been stabbed repeatedly.

'This is the crime. This is what Mr Mac Liammóir saw when he walked into the flat where it happened. The dead man is a young Indian, Vikram Narayan. Mr Mac Liammóir found a policeman and reported it. However, inquiries by CID established that he and Mr Narayan had met earlier that evening, at a club in Little Denmark Street – Billie's – where they had some kind of argument. The long and the short, as Mr Mac Liammóir happily told Inspector Hardy, was that the dead man tried to blackmail him in some way, threatening to reveal his homosexuality, which Mr Mac Liammóir has no problem revealing himself. The idea was that he followed Narayan back to his flat . . . and killed him.'

As the English detective spoke, Stefan stared at the photographs.

'That's extremely unlikely, however, Stefan. Even a cursory forensic examination shows that Mr Mac Liammóir did exactly what he said. He walked into the room, saw the body and walked straight out again. Still, you can't altogether blame Dick Hardy. This is a very distinctive murder. The knife wounds round the groin and the genitals, I mean, all adminis-tered, with great violence, immediately after death. There have been three similar murders over the last year. Two in London and one in Berkshire, in Reading. All the men were young, and they were almost certainly queer. Dick Hardy had seen reports of the other deaths. He thought he'd not only stumbled on a fourth murder, he'd caught the killer red-handed. He was right about the murder.'

Chief Inspector Nugent picked up a large manila envelope. He took out several photographs. He was too busy with his story to register the intensity with which Stefan Gillespie was gazing down at the pictures on the table.

'These are a couple of photographs from two of the other murders. I think one on Hampstead Heath, another along the Thames, near Richmond. I've only seen these today. The basics are the same. A man is killed, a blow to the head, strangled or suffocated. Then he's attacked with a knife, same way each time.'

Stefan looked up, frowning. He took the photographs Frank Nugent was holding out. He was not at all surprised by what he saw.

'This needn't concern you, Stefan. Mr Mac Liammóir has given a detailed statement. It seems to clear him of any involvement. The forensics tend the same way. So does the fact that there is a pattern of murders. Assuming he was not in England when the others took place. He says he wasn't, but you can verify that in Dublin. Hopefully, these are just loose ends. I think even Inspector Hardy recognises Mr Mac Liammóir's a lost cause. He's no use as a witness – he saw no one. So, I guess that's you finished.'

Stefan laid the new photographs on the table, next to the others.

'I don't know that I am, Frank.'

'What do you mean?'

For the first time Frank Nugent realised something else was going on.

'I've seen this before,' said Stefan.

'Seen what?'

61

Stefan glanced back at the photographs. He was familiar with what he was looking at. He had known straight away. He had not forgotten that image.

'The same thing. In Ireland, nineteen thirty-nine. A young man, strangled, then stabbed, over and over again, in exactly the same way . . . in exactly the same places.'

Stefan Gillespie stood in a small, square room. There was no natural light, simply a bright bulb overhead. Even in a new police station this room had been made as bare and uncomfortable as possible. The only furniture was a table with a chair on either side. Micheál Mac Liammóir sat at the table. He wore a grey overall. He looked tired. There was a cup of tea in front of him, but it was untouched. There were cigarette ends in an ashtray. The actor stared at Stefan without recognition. It was a while since the two men had seen each other, but hardly more than a year. They were only acquaintances, yet Mac Liammóir knew him well enough to recognise him. Now there was only bewilderment in his eyes; behind that something more fragile, a dull and uncertain fear.

'Mr Mac Liammóir.'

The actor kept staring, looking through him.

'You'll remember me, so.' Stefan smiled.

'I'm sorry, whoever you are. I can't think of anything else I can say.'

Stefan pulled out the free chair and sat down.

'I'm not here to ask you anything. My name's Stefan Gillespie, you've seen me in Dublin. At the Gate. And in New York, when you were on tour. I'm an Irish policeman. I'm a Guard. The High Commissioner sent me here. Mr Dulanty.'

'Dulanty?' Mac Liammóir still looked confused.

'You can leave soon. They're pretty well finished with you.'

Micheál Mac Liammóir shook his head.

'They think I killed a man . . . a man I knew . . . Jesus, the way he . . .'

A wave of shock seemed to roll over Mac Liammóir. He was shaking, but slowly. There were tears in his eyes. Then he was still again.

'How long have I been here?'

'Since last night.'

'I found him, that's all. I wanted to help him. Then he was there . . . just there. I can't believe how . . . like a piece of meat . . . blood . . . I ran . . . I ran and there was a policeman . . . Then I was here . . . they kept saying I did it . . . and they were talking about other men . . . other dead . . . I told them what happened. They wouldn't let me sleep. They—' Mac Liammóir stopped, staring harder at Stefan. He was looking at him now, not through him. And there was a smile, almost a smile. 'Stefan. Jesus Christ! What in God's name are you doing here?'

'Among other things, getting you out of this place. And hopefully home. The High Commissioner wants you on the mail boat, sir, out of harm's way.'

The life that had drained out of the actor was returning.

'I only came for a fucking funeral. A fucking funeral!'

Mac Liammóir stood up. He stumbled and leant against the table.

Stefan moved round to help him.

'I'm grand. I'm just exhausted. They did put me in a cell, but I couldn't get any sleep. The beds are terrible here. I shall say something before I go. There certainly won't be a tip.' He breathed deeply; the joke faded. 'There was someone crying. The next cell. It seemed like hours. Just crying. It didn't stop.'

'They have your possessions at the front desk. I think they want you to reread your statement and sign it. But that's all of it. Where are you staying?'

'A hotel, in the Strand, the Regent Palace.'

'I can arrange for a taxi.'

Mac Liammóir looked at the overall he was wearing.

'What about my clothes?'

'They were being examined by forensics . . . I don't know . . . it's just . . .'

The actor shook his head. He understood what the examination was about; the blood that the police were looking for on his clothes. He stepped forward and stumbled again slightly, his limbs stiff from sitting for so long. Stefan put his arm round him. The tears that had been there briefly before returned. Mac Liammóir's head was buried in Stefan's shoulder. He was sobbing. But it was only for a moment. He moved back, smiling, for the first time, the wry, almost insolent smile that Stefan recognised so well.

'I think I'd rather not have them back. But I can't walk through a hotel lobby like this, can I? I have a suit in my room, a shirt, a tie, and whatever else. I don't suppose you could be a real saviour and go and fetch them for me? And bring them back? I'm sure your consular services could stretch to it, Stefan. If they can provide me with some washing facilities here, that would be helpful. I'd like to exit this den of the whoreson English with rather more dignity than I entered!'

They walked to the door. As Stefan opened it, Mac Liammóir stopped.

'He was frightened. It feels like that, looking back. Desperate, anyway. But I couldn't do anything. When he threatened me . . . I've no idea what it was about. Afterwards, I felt guilty. I thought some money might help . . . but I don't think it was about money. How . . . why did someone do that to him?'

6

Charing Cross Hospital

Little more than an hour later, Stefan Gillespie left Micheál Mac Liammóir at the entrance to the Regent Palace Hotel in Piccadilly, now in a grey suit that had been brought from his hotel room. There had been not much conversation. Stefan had been surprised to find Chief Inspector Nugent waiting for him outside West End Central Police Station in a car, first to take him to the Regent Palace to collect Mac Liammóir's clothes, then to make a second journey to the hotel to drop the actor off. The first leg had been surprisingly silent. Nugent made only a few remarks about traffic and the blackout and fuel shortages. At the Regent Palace he went upstairs with Stefan to Mac Liammóir's room. He walked around the room as Stefan took clothes from a suitcase. He looked at a book by the bed and glanced into the suitcase. He bent down and picked up a pair of tan brogues that were on the floor, inside the door to the corridor, with a printed note on them to say they had been cleaned. Stefan recognised that despite everything, the English detective had the Irishman at the edge of his mind. He was getting a better sense of who the man was.

'He'll need shoes. The ones he had on are evidence. The soles are the only place they found blood. I don't know if he'll get them back. He'll miss them. From Lobb's, handmade. I don't suppose even great actors have many of those.'

'I don't suppose they do.' Stefan noted attention to detail.

They walked to the lift and down to the street. As the car pulled away, Stefan took out a cigarette. He was surprised the English detective had said hardly anything about the similarity between Vikram Narayan's death and the death of the young man by a lake in Ireland. It had been less than two years ago.

'Any observations about Mr Mac Liammóir? You were looking.'

'I didn't expect to see much in a hotel room, Stefan.'

'No.'

'Though it's not every Irish nationalist who gets his shoes in St James's.'

Stefan Gillespie laughed. 'Is that useful?'

'You never know, do you, in our line?'

Stefan heard the edge in Nugent's voice.

'Our line?'

'I checked on you with the Yard.'

'They have a list of Gardaí, do they? That doesn't sound very likely.'

'They have a list of Garda Special Branch.'

Stefan Gillespie lit the cigarette. It wasn't his business how they did things at Scotland Yard, but if Nugent had observations to make, so did he.

'I don't think it's odd the Irish High Commissioner asked the only Guard in London to see what the Metropolitan Police were doing to Ireland's favourite actor. I'd say CID at West End Central were more puzzled why the Yard sent a senior Special Branch officer to take over an investigation into a dead queer. Even if there's been a few of them. You get to be jack of all trades in Dublin Castle, but that's not how it works here. Not that it's any of my business.'

'Not that it is.' Frank Nugent laughed. 'Give me a fag, will you?'

Stefan passed him a cigarette and held up his lighter.

The Scotland Yard man went on. 'There's a list of dates. The killings I told you about. While there's no evidence I can see that says your actor killed Mr Narayan – in fact, I'd say the opposite – there is all the circumstantial stuff. An argument, threats, he was at the scene of crime and, of course, the whole queer business, which makes for suspicion in itself. You know what I mean by that. If a man's a pervert, then why not a murderer?'

'That's not much of a case, Frank.'

'Men hang on less,' said the chief inspector. 'Anyway, dates.'

'Dates,' said Stefan.

'Where was your actor on the dates of the murders, all of them? I'm assuming he's not going to turn up in the environs of London and Reading on the dates specified, but it's belt-and-braces from his point of view. And there's no point wasting time on a dead end from our point of view. With a murder in Ireland, those loose ends do need some tying up. But he's an actor. I'd expect to find fairly clear evidence of where he was on a particular day or night. Of course, that includes the date of the murder in Ireland now. If that really looks like the same killer. It doesn't help Mr Mac Liammóir. Quite the opposite.'

Stefan Gillespie nodded. He had already had the same thought.

On the second journey to the Regent Palace, Micheál Mac Liammóir had sat in the back of Nugent's unmarked car saying nothing until they reached the hotel.

'I'm booked on the mail boat tonight. If I'm able to get the train ...?'

Mac Liammóir didn't finish the sentence. Despite the reassurances, he could not feel free of what had happened. Stefan looked round. The words were a question, addressed to him. But he couldn't answer it. He looked at Nugent.

'I'm sorry, sir,' said the chief inspector. 'There may be more questions. I know there's probably nothing you can add. But we would appreciate you staying in London a few more days. It's nothing to be concerned about. Something may come up. It's early days. You may even remember something.'

'I'm more inclined to forget than remember,' said the actor quietly.

'And you know you're quite at liberty, sir.' Nugent smiled.

Micheál Mac Liammóir smiled too. 'Except that I just can't leave.'

'I wouldn't put it like that at all, Mr Mac Liammóir. And if you need any reassurance, you have Inspector Gillespie here. Helping us out. Right, Stefan?'

Stefan nodded as he seemed required to do.

Mac Liammóir looked at him for a moment. He didn't look reassured. Stefan got out of the front passenger seat and opened the door for the actor.

'I'll keep in touch, Mr Mac Liammóir.'

'It's early, but I'll probably be in the bar. Until they carry me upstairs.'

He walked towards the entrance. The porter tipped his hat and opened the door for him. Stefan heard a bright, jokey voice he knew was a performance.

'Thank you, Stanley. Quiet night again last night!'

Stefan got back into the car. Nugent pulled out into Piccadilly.

'I'm helping you out then, Chief Inspector, am I? I didn't know that.'

'You know now. You're here, aren't you? I don't suppose you've got much else to do. I haven't seen the body yet. And it could be you've seen one of these before. You're one up on me. I need to know if you're right. You do too.'

In little more than six months, the mortuary that made up only a small part of the basement of Charing Cross Hospital had spread: from an office and two theatres and the refrigerated chamber where a handful of bodies could be kept in storage, to now filling the corridors all round. As other storerooms, off the same corridors, had been turned into emergency theatres and overflow wards, the living and the dead were in closer proximity than had been the case in peacetime, and for many the shift from one state to the other involved a short journey in every sense. For the living, only the seriously injured came to the hospital from where the bombs dropped night after night, so the numbers that died were high. But the dead came too, when they were pulled from the buildings and the wreckage, disfigured, crushed, torn, often burned beyond recognition. And if they were unidentified, they stayed until they could stay no longer. The refrigeration plant could only cope with so many corpses. Many waited in the corridors, in cardboard coffins and bags, men, women, children, for a vacancy that might keep their flesh from rotting long enough for someone to claim them.

It was along one of these corridors, stacked with the dead who had been brought in over the last two nights, from bombing in the East End and the Docks, where other hospitals and mortuaries were overflowing, that Inspector Stefan Gillespie and Chief Inspector Nugent pushed their way into a theatre. Mortuary assistants and pathologists gathered what information they could from the unidentified dead, most of them laid out on trestle tables and the floor.

No one could grasp what Inspector Nugent was looking for. The idea of a murder victim puzzled the men and women who were examining the dead. It seemed out of place as the waiting bodies came in and out, with the details that could be noted – noted as quickly as possible. The night shift had gone. There must be a note somewhere. There had been a pathologist on through the night. There would be one somewhere now, at some point.

'Would he be here? Was it a fire? There was a lot from the fire at—'

'The Police Surgeon sent him. It was the only ambulance he could get.'

'He'll be here somewhere then, won't he, Chief Inspector?'

'Narayan, Vikram Narayan.'

'If they know who he is he won't be in here. All these are unidentified.'

A nurse called out:

'Was there a man brought in who was killed?'

There was some laughter.

'They've all been fucking killed, haven't they?'

'I mean someone killed him.'

No one responded.

Trolleys with dead bodies wheeled in and out round Stefan and Frank.

An elderly man walked into the room.

'Police?'

'Yes, Chief Inspector Nugent. This is Inspector Gillespie.'

'Next door.' The man walked out into the corridor. The two policemen followed. 'Hawkins, I was on last night. I've looked at your man. I'm sorry, I haven't had time to write a report. I can tell you what happened, but I've only made a cursory examination. Cursory is what we do at the moment.' He pushed open two swing doors. They entered a low, dark room, with a bank of drawers at one end. The room was cold. There were bodies on trolleys and on the floor.

'The Indian chap. Narayan, is it?' Hawkins addressed a round, short man, sitting on a stool, reading the *Daily Mail* and smoking a hand-rolled cigarette.

'The poof?' said the man, with a sniff of disdain.

'The police want a look at him.'

The man on the stool got up and walked to the bank of drawers. He took hold of a handle. The coffin-sized drawer slid out of the wall. Hawkins walked forward. Stefan and Nugent stood beside him. The man went back to his paper.

The naked body of Vikram Narayan lay in the drawer. Stefan glanced at the dark face. It looked peaceful, like Corcoran's. Then he looked at the stomach and the groin and the knife wounds that formed a kind of wreath round his genitals.

'There's a blow to the head. Severe, but probably didn't kill him. He was then suffocated. That's an assumption at the moment, but the signs are right. Your inspector from West End Central mentioned a pillow. That would be about it. The wounds have nothing to do with his death. Inflicted around the same time, probably afterwards. The knife thrusts were through clothes. A sort of circle. Quite neatly applied, but not much of a knife. A kitchen knife of some sort. In fact, the end of the blade broke off in the wound, in what must have been the last thrust. I don't know if you have the knife, but you will want this.'

The pathologist picked up an envelope that lay in the drawer by the body. He handed it to Nugent, who opened it and looked at a blackened sliver of steel.

'Less to do with the violence of the blows than a poor quality weapon.'

Frank Nugent nodded.

'Is that it, gentlemen?' Hawkins asked.

'Will you be doing a full autopsy?' said the chief inspector.

'I can't think there'll be much else to say. Knocked on the head, suffocated, then, for whatever reason, decorated. If you need more, you'll have your own people. I've too much to do. I'll send a report. But we can't keep him for ever. If you want the body preserved, you should make other arrangements.'

'He was fully dressed?' asked Stefan.

'Yes.'

'Was there any indication of sexual activity?'

'I'm not sure what you mean.'

'Semen, for instance?'

'That's a very specific for instance, Inspector Gillespie, but no, nothing of that kind. I wouldn't think he had much time for dalliance between the crack on the head and the asphyxiation. All there was in that area was blood. A lot of it.'

Stefan Gillespie sat in a small office, high in the red-and-white brick building that was Scotland Yard. It was a building he had seen many times, standing at the end of London's great street of government, across the road from the Houses of Parliament. It was an oddly unassuming block set beside the classical stone façades of the government buildings that surrounded it. It could have been a block of flats in a Kensington side street, or a department store that hadn't lived up to the grandeur of Harrods or Selfridges. It was hard, even with the instinctive distrust of the British police that Stefan's Protestant heritage couldn't ignore, not to feel something about this place. Good, bad or indifferent, and inevitably a mix of all three, this was still where policing began. It may have been a monument as much to what policing should have been as to what it was, but it was still a monument. And it was reassuring to see that it was as dirty, as cramped and as full of people who looked like they didn't want to be there, as any police station he'd ever been in, big or small. And in the corridors the smell of dust and old sweat and tobacco was the same too, with the slight scent of ancient urine that always found its way, somehow, up from the cells.

Chief Inspector Nugent's office was close to the attics, to the side of one of the brick turrets that marked each of Scotland Yard's corners. It seemed a kind of outlier. They passed through no big office to get to it. Other doors along the corridor from the stairs were firmly shut. Stefan saw no one, though the floors below had been busy. He wondered who, as a chief inspector, Nugent was in charge of. It didn't feel like he was surrounded by men from a Special Branch department that must have been many times bigger than Terry Gregory's. The office itself was tiny, with a sloped ceiling and a small window that just about gave a view of a patch of the Thames. Nugent had disappeared for several minutes to make some tea. Stefan found himself looking past the box files that were piled up around the desk, a dozen deep, at a large-scale map of India. It looked out of place, taking up most of the wall next to the window.

Now the two detectives were looking at a row of photographs, all of them of the bodies of dead men, marked with some variation of the savage circle of knife wounds round the stomach, thighs and genitals. There were photographs of the bodies as they had been found, naked, partially clothed. The pattern was clear. Photographs of Vikram Narayan, on the bed in his flat and on the slab at the mortuary, were in position beside the others, the last.

'I spoke to my boss in Dublin,' said Stefan. 'He's sending photos from the Donadea murder. There are some statements. They don't amount to much.'

'But you have fingerprints . . . a fragment?'

'Yes, from a beer bottle. What have you got in the way of prints?'

'From the flat in Greek Street, quite a lot. That doesn't mean the killer left anything. Until we find something to compare them with . . . we can't know.'

Stefan Gillespie nodded; nothing led anywhere without a suspect.

'You think your man in Ireland, Corcoran . . . you really believe it's the same?'

'I can't see how it isn't. It has to be. But once you've said that, it just turns four into five. We had fragments of a print, but there was nowhere to look and no one to look for. It was a dead end. But what about the investigations here? What about these other murders? It doesn't seem you're much further.'

'Except in quantity. There's nothing, Stefan. I say nothing . . .' The Englishman turned the pages of a file, opened another and turned more pages. 'I've only just got these from the Murder Squad. Still getting on top of it. No prints at all. That's remarkable in itself. The man may be a maniac, but a meticulous maniac. If we can compare the prints at Narayan's flat with what's coming from Dublin, maybe we will get a break. A break . . . but no suspect . . .'

'So, this is your case now?' asked Stefan.

'It's too big for West End Central.'

'And too big for the Murder Squad?'

'There's the Irish angle now.' Nugent grinned. 'A delicate relationship.'

It was an answer of sorts, but Stefan Gillespie felt it was an answer after the fact. Frank Nugent had arrived at West End Central when the only Irish angle was the Irish actor who found the body and was, perhaps, a suspect. It might have been awkward. It wasn't about a relationship with the Irish police. That relationship was only there now because of new information from Stefan.

'Except for Vikram, all these murders have taken place outdoors somewhere,' continued the chief inspector, 'like yours in Ireland, James Corcoran. So, every time, no real surfaces to get prints from. A few footprints, but nothing substantial. Never the same shoe, but always a size ten or eleven. That's it. The killer leaves almost nothing behind. There are some hairs, a few pieces of wool or fibre. But looking at the file, so far, the fibres don't match each other. One detective wondered if the killer was even destroying his clothes after every attack. With the blood, maybe he'd need to. But he never appears to have worn the same thing twice.'

'You can't destroy your hair.'

'It's brown. That's about it. No hair so far at Vikram Narayan's. Well, two on the pillow, bleached, maybe permed, a woman's. Presumably another visitor, another time. So, we have short brown hair and he may have used Brylcreem once. Hardly enough to identify anyone. No one to identify anybody anyway. Four bodies and we're no better off than you were in nineteen thirty-nine. No witnesses, no sightings of the dead men with anyone near the time of their deaths. Not necessarily surprising. You take the one on Hampstead Heath. It's a place men meet for sex. Men who don't know each other. Men who have never seen each other before and won't see each other again. I'm not saying it's all like that, we can't know, but we're dealing with a level of secretiveness . . . a hidden world. That's what these dead men have in common. They're all some part of that world.'

Stefan stood up, looking out at the patch of light that was the river.

'That's true of James Corcoran, too,' he said. 'But it's not the same. I'm sure he met the man who killed him, in Dublin, sometime before. A few days, maybe a week. Maybe more, but certainly that. They arranged to meet again. Nothing random in it. It was secret, yes, but it was no chance meeting.'

'That's what interests me, Stefan. You've got more there than a dozen detectives have put together over our four murders. We're still hoping for more from Vikram. There's at least a chance he knew the killer or that the killer followed him from Billie's. I know the man could have picked him up in the street, but everything that went before – the argument with Mac Liammóir, the mood Mac Liammóir says Vikram was in – makes that feel unlikely. And this wasn't long afterwards. It wasn't the middle of nowhere, either. It was the blackout, but not a dark night. It was the West End. There were people about. No bombing even close. Inside a building. All that makes for a much higher chance the killer left a trace somewhere, that someone saw him in the area.'

'They've never found a witness before?'

'Maybe one, maybe two. Not close enough to the scene of any murder to be sure, but the only descriptions we have. Two descriptions, both of a soldier.'

'Is that it . . . a soldier?'

'A tall soldier.' Nugent laughed. 'No, that was never going to be red-hot evidence, was it? A bloody soldier! Some place to start in the middle of a war. It could have been anything, anyone. It could have been a fucking Home Guard uniform.'

'So, where do you start?'

'I'm a fresh pair of eyes, Stefan. That's why they've put me on it.'

'Just you?'

'The Murder Squad will do the leg work where necessary.'

'They'll enjoy taking orders from Special Branch, Frank.'

'Maybe we're not as unpopular here as you are in Ireland. It might help that we're not a retirement home for ex-IRA men who still cherish our old comrades, the ones beavering away to overthrow the government, the ones who aren't beyond shooting the occasional policeman, for old times' sake. But I'm sure they're grand fellers, eh? Or don't I understand Ireland at all, Stefan?'

Stefan Gillespie heard the easy mockery in Nugent's last few words, but he wondered if he heard more. He had struggled to place the chief inspector's accent. It was English enough, southern, middle class, but there was something else in it he couldn't place. He wondered if there was something Irish in there. He looked at Frank Nugent and smiled. He didn't know what to make of the man. There was something about him that didn't sit right. He didn't belong in this murder inquiry. However dark, there was no political dimension.

'You don't have to be English not to understand Ireland, Frank.'

Chief Inspector Nugent laughed.

Stefan said no more. What went on in Scotland Yard wasn't

his business. Only James Corcoran was his concern. He had forgotten the dead seminarian, but now he remembered; he also remembered how little anyone had wanted to know about that murder. Something of that atmosphere was still there. Superintendent Gregory didn't relish the prospect of working with the Metropolitan Police on a killing that had been filed away and forgotten. From a phone call only an hour earlier, Stefan got the impression that his boss didn't want the failings of An Garda Síochána under the microscope at Scotland Yard. The Garda Commissioner wouldn't like that either. However, Terry Gregory was no slouch when it came to examining the clouds that came his way for brighter linings. With four bodies piled up, the failings of the police in Britain were on an even bigger scale. The pros and cons could wait till Stefan got home. They would have to look again at what had happened by the lake at Donadea. There had to be a chance of finding who James Corcoran's murderer was. And one thing that did raise Superintendent Gregory's spirits was the sudden realisation that the killer would probably turn out to be an English poof now, rather than an Irish one. There was the silver lining, however small. English homosexuality was safer ground.

7

Veeraswamy

Stefan Gillespie left Scotland Yard, heading back to Regent Street and the High Commission. Assuming the information from Ireland raised no more questions about Micheál Mac Liammóir, Stefan would return to Ireland the following night, carrying the diplomatic bag and bringing an unexpected operation with the British police that no one would be very enthusiastic about on either side of the Irish Sea. In Britain, with the dead all round, and the flow of telegrams arriving in homes to express regrets for the dead men overseas, it felt like there were bigger priorities. He had seen that in the faces of the Murder Squad detectives that Chief Inspector Nugent had sent out to talk to men in the queer pubs and bars and cottages of the West End. Those men wouldn't want to speak to the police and the police wouldn't want to speak to them. The only hope was that someone had seen something; if anyone knew anything, fear might break through the wall of secrecy, but the fear of exposure was still there to prop it up. In Ireland there were a lot of reasons why working with the police in England was viewed with suspicion, and the baggage from the past was complicated by present neutrality. It made every area of contact between the two countries something to be explained away or denied. Five dead men didn't alter the fact that every misstep the Irish government made brought criticism and diplomatic fury from London and Berlin down on Dublin.

It was odd that carrying a briefcase to and fro from Dublin to London had kept Stefan outside that for several months. He was simply part of the show. What he carried was the most official and least significant material passing between the High Commission in Regent Street and the Department of External Affairs on Stephen's Green. What was contentious found other routes. Men from Irish Military Intelligence, G2, who sat in meetings with MI5 along the road from the High Commission in St James's, but were never officially in England at all. Politicians and army officers who marketed a far more cooperative Irish neutrality than the fierce impartiality Éamon de Valera advertised in the Dáil and declaimed on radio for the Irish public. Most of what those men carried, they carried in their heads. It was never to be written down.

The messages Stefan brought related to the most innocuous tasks of John Dulanty, the Irish ambassador, who went by the title of High Commissioner because Ireland was still part of the British Commonwealth of Nations. The difference between Dulanty and the other High Commissioners, however – Canadian, Australian, New Zealander, South African – was that Ireland stood outside the war. It supported neither Britain nor Germany. And it was the only part of the Commonwealth that the British War Cabinet had plans to invade.

In London, as in Dublin, Stefan Gillespie's spare time was something he filled up rather than used. If he could not be at home in Wicklow with his young son, filling up time with not much was how he lived. In some ways it was easier to do that in London, where he knew hardly anyone, than in Dublin. The business of war, still a neutral's business too, was what occupied him in one way or another. And it was an occupation. The weary sea crossing from Ireland to North Wales; the slow, constantly delayed, constantly re-routed trains between Holyhead and London; broken nights shuttling from a hotel room or a camp bed in the High Commission to the Underground or a basement shelter.

There were days in London with nothing to do, waiting for instructions, for the bag; moving around the West End from pub to pub, on a now familiar route, staying long enough to drink but never long enough to do more than exchange a few formulaic bomb-and-war-and-weather observations. A drink in one pub, a drink in another. It passed the time. And anonymity suited him, not because of the job he did, but because he had no inclination for anything else. He drank too much, he knew that. Never enough to be drunk, but enough to know it was too much. He drank because it was something to do, the same way others smoked. He smoked too, but without the same conviction.

London was all motion and anonymity. Because he didn't belong, it didn't mark him out the way Dublin did. There was no need to be anything other than alone. He had worked on one mission in London already that year. He knew it. He was used to the bombs. And, of course, he could take a rest from it. But the darkness of the city at night was undemanding. Most of the time, that would do. It had been this way since the death of his wife, Maeve, eight years before. There had been times, there had been women who made him step away from it, but something always pulled him back. Sometimes that seemed more about laziness than anything else, but it was still where he was. It suited him, to be in transit. Even when he was at home in Wicklow, with his son Tom and his parents, on the farm that was the real fixed point in his life, it sometimes felt as if it was only a pause. It was a pause he needed, but if it lasted too long, he was restless. Movement was a purpose, however empty that was. The war that was not meant to be Ireland's war kept Stefan in motion.

He returned to the High Commissioner, having killed what remained of the afternoon in three pubs on his route from Whitehall to Regent Street. It was dark, and he expected the High Commission to be closed, but as he came out of the lift, heading for the stairs up to the room he was sleeping in, the stairs towards Dulanty's office, he could hear the sound of Miss Foye's Remington. Miss Foye was now somewhere around fifty years old. She was a spinster, as she had to be to work in the Irish civil service, and she used that word as a kind of claim to authority over the men who worked there, whatever their age. She had worked at the High Commission since it was established, with the foundation of the state in 1922. If the High Commissioner was head of mission, it was Miss Foye who ran it, whatever anyone else might think. She was from Cork but there was nothing soft about her voice. It was sharp and crisp, and it did not suffer fools. Stefan liked her, most of the time, but he had not worked out whether she disliked him or simply thought he wasn't serious enough for the job he did. But everyone had felt that at some time, even the High Commissioner. Stefan walked on towards Miss Foye. There was no other route. Three drinks were scarcely a misdemeanour, but he knew she was watching him, though she appeared to be gazing down at the typewriter. Her look would be one of familiar disapproval. She always knew when he'd been drinking. It was the fact rather than the quantity she disapproved of. She looked up, finally, as Stefan Gillespie reached the desk, and pulled a sheet of paper from the roller.

'This is for you, Mr Gillespie, from Superintendent Gregory. The details of Mr Mac Liammóir's engagements on the dates in question. I will send a copy to Mr Nugent at Scotland Yard, but I have telephoned him already with the information. I thought you would want him to have it . . . as soon as possible.'

'Thank you, Miss Foye.'

He smiled. There it was. The tone of voice to go with the look. He should have been there to do it himself and not, as she knew he had been, in some pub.

'The chief inspector says there is no problem with Mr Mac Liammóir returning to Ireland. If there are other questions, he assumes that you will ask them and provide the answers. I told him I was certain that was your intention.'

Stefan nodded. She would be pleased she got two bites of that cherry.

'And Mr Mac Liammóir has been on the telephone too.'

'Is he at his hotel?'

'No, but he wants to talk to you.'

'I'm sure. Anyway, it's good news. Where is he?'

'He's in a restaurant, over the road. The Indian one, Veeraswamy.' She spoke the name as if she didn't entirely trust the idea of an Indian restaurant. 'He said he'd appreciate you joining him. And he did say it was important.'

Stefan walked across the road, following Miss Foye's directions, and found his way up a flight of stairs to the first floor, where a large dining room looked out over Regent Street, though the thick blinds and curtains necessarily blocked the view. It was an unexpected sight. The furniture was full of ornate, intricate carving. The walls were hung with bright tapestries. It was something he knew, but only from pictures. Above the darkness of London's blackout, it was a small world on its own, full of subtle and unknown scents as well as the colours of India. There were only a few customers: several men in uniform, very senior uniforms; others in the dark jackets and pinstriped trousers that were another uniform of seniority, this time the civil service's. He was shown to a table in a corner, tucked behind a carved screen, away from the main part of the dining room. And he saw Micheál Mac Liammóir waiting for him there.

'Dear boy, sit down. Have a drink.'

A waiter in a turban and a kaftan smiled.

'A beer, that'll be fine.'

'I've ordered food,' said Mac Liammóir. 'Just soup and a pilau. Is that all right? I haven't eaten all day. I haven't wanted to. But I need something now.'

'I'm happy to leave it to you, sir. I wouldn't know what to order.'

'It's very good, the real thing – don't be tempted to play safe and have something English or French. This won't be too hot. I'm sure you'll enjoy it.'

Stefan smiled and nodded. The conversation wasn't really about food; it was about Mac Liammóir trying to recover a kind of normality out of the chaos.

'So, Stefan, what news?' asked the actor.

'You can leave tomorrow. The mail boat awaits.'

'Thank God. I gathered from the Gate that you wanted a résumé of where I've been and what I've done since nineteen thirty-nine. I had no idea Scotland Yard took such an interest in the theatre. If they want reviews, I'm happy to oblige. Well, in most cases.' He laughed and raised a glass of wine, as Stefan's beer arrived at the table. He was trying hard to lighten the past twenty-four hours of his life. 'I don't understand what all those dates were. Mr Nugent is satisfied. But why?'

Stefan had decided he would tell Mac Liammóir the truth. The actor had been pulled into this, however inadvertently, but there should be no secret about what was happening now, or about what had happened before. It was hard not to feel that too much secrecy, too much sweeping away what nobody wanted to look at, was one reason why the killer of five men was still killing. Mac Liammóir was surely owed the truth after being a suspect himself.

If it was a truth that Micheál Mac Liammóir was owed, it was not one he was easy hearing. The darkness he had started to push away came back, and it was darker. If he wanted somehow to leave it in London, it touched Ireland, too.

'I don't know what to say, Stefan. It's terrible . . . and it's terrifying. I suppose I wanted . . . I wanted to feel with poor Vikram it was some sort of awful accident. That sounds stupid; even as things stood it was stupid. We're all stupid when we want to hide, I suppose. Five men . . . dead. No one can hide from that.'

'No.'

'It's very strange.' Mac Liammóir drank slowly. He was puzzled now.

'I hope it won't stay that way,' said Stefan. 'We will find him.'

'You have to say that, of course you do. What I mean by strange . . . is that Vikram's sister came to see me this afternoon. She doesn't know any of that, what you've just told me. She went to Scotland Yard. She saw Mr Nugent. She wasn't expecting to see him . . . or that he was in charge of the investigation into her brother's death. She knows him, you see, from India, that's what she said.'

Stefan took this in. It was very odd information.

'He told her nothing, really,' said Mac Liammóir.

'To be honest, there isn't a lot to tell,' said Stefan.

'This will all seem very . . . I don't know what it's about, Stefan, but she doesn't like Chief Inspector Nugent at all. She is disturbed by his involvement. I don't know whether this new development . . . this poor Irishman . . . will help her in any way or if it's even relevant to that . . . ah, but here she is now.'

Mac Liammóir stood up and Stefan did the same as a slim, dark woman, with long black hair, stopped at the table. She was very striking. She wore a dark suit, with an orange and yellow scarf that said something of India. As the waiter moved a chair for her to sit on, it was obvious she worked at the restaurant.

'Mr Gillespie.' The woman reached out her hand.

'This is Miss Narayan, Hindu. Vikram's sister. She is the manageress here, so it seemed a good idea. Nearby for us both. And sort of out of the way.'

'Thank you for coming, Mr Gillespie.'

'I'm very sorry, Miss Narayan.'

'Thank you.' She shook her head. 'I tried to find out what had happened to Vikram. I got very little at Scotland Yard. I was taken in to see Chief Inspector Nugent, but he told me almost nothing. I was surprised to see him . . . There is a connection, an Indian connection . . . It is not a welcome one at all.'

Hindu Narayan was thoughtful. But she did not elaborate.

'I asked at Billie's, the club. Mr Nugent mentioned it. He said Vikram had been there. I got more there. They told me about Mr Mac Liammóir. I found him. I did know he had been a friend of Vikram's. I knew they worked together in Egypt. Mr Mac Liammóir told me what he knew. He said you'd know more.'

Stefan glanced at Mac Liammóir, who looked down into his wine glass. He wasn't as easy with this as he was trying to look. Stefan did not imagine he had told Vikram Narayan's sister everything in his statement. He doubted anything had been said about the young Indian threatening him with blackmail.

'I can tell you what I've just told Mr Mac Liammóir. It's not an easy thing to say. It doesn't find the man who killed your brother. But I hope it will.'

'You can't tell me anything worse than what's happened. But before anything else, I want to know what Mr Nugent has told you. When I asked to see the detective in charge, I didn't expect him. What did he say about Vikram?'

There was a look of anger on Hindu's face.

'I don't know what you mean,' said Stefan.

'He must have said something. It's not as if he doesn't know him.'

Stefan frowned. This was now a conversation about Frank Nugent.

'You've got no idea what I'm talking about, have you, Mr Gillespie?'

'No, I'm not sure I have.'

'Nobody asked me to identify my brother's body. I still haven't seen it.'

Stefan wasn't sure she would really want to see it.

'But he was identified, wasn't he?'

'There was never any doubt. Mr Mac Liammóir found him.'

The actor nodded. 'I knew him, Hindu. You know I did.'

'The sergeant at Scotland Yard said there was no requirement for further identification. I told him I wanted to see Vikram. "No need, miss," he said. "Don't upset yourself, miss," he said. "Chief Inspector Nugent has identified the body."'

Stefan registered the words. It was clear Nugent knew the dead man.

'You don't know Chief Inspector Nugent is IPI, do you, Mr Gillespie?'

'IPI? I'm sorry, I have no idea what IPI is.'

'Indian Political Intelligence.'

'He's Metropolitan Police Special Branch,' said Stefan.

'Yes, but he's come here from India. He's in London to spy on Indian nationalists, people working for Indian independence. He's a spy, that's all. India is not full of people who want to fight a war for Britain. We have our own struggle and it goes on whatever happens here. You're Irish, like Mr Mac Liammóir. You know what it means. Frank Nugent is a spy and a thug. In India, when people are arrested by IPI, they don't come out the way they go in. Sometimes they don't come out at all. In Delhi they took Vikram when he was only a teenager. He did come out, yes, but he was in hospital for weeks afterwards. That was Mr Nugent and his officers. My family has been in the Congress Party since the beginning. They beat my brother because they dare not attack my father. I don't suppose Mr Nugent did it himself. They use Indian officers to do that. Vikram took it all. He never answered their questions.'

She said the words proudly, with a look of defiance, fighting tears. Micheál Mac Liammóir reached across the table and touched her hand. Stefan turned away. He knew what such a beating looked like, sounded like. They didn't happen often in the cells in Dublin Castle, but they happened.

'Mr Nugent has known Vikram for years, in India and in London. The details I won't . . . it is not relevant. They have been watching Vikram here, as he was watched at home, because he is fighting for India. The Congress is in his heart, his head. He has been followed. He told me. His flat has been searched. He has been threatened, questioned. The chief inspector's people report who he sees, who he knows, meetings he goes to. He has—' She stopped, dropping her head. There was anger, but there were still the tears she was not going to show. 'I must say "had", he had . . . it's all *had* now, isn't it?' She looked up again, calmer. 'Why is this man investigating a murder? Why do I go to ask about my brother's death and find *him*? He hasn't told you he knew Vikram, has he?'

'No,' said Stefan quietly, 'I can't say he got round to telling me that.'

It was an hour later that Stefan Gillespie and Micheál Mac Liammóir emerged from Veeraswamy on to Regent Street. The conversation had not moved much further. Who Frank Nugent was and what he was doing was no clearer. Stefan had explained something of the background to the murders that culminated in the death of Vikram Narayan, but he had not said everything. He wondered how the killings came across to Miss Narayan. He had skirted round the issue of homosexuality. And when he did, he felt it was what she wanted. Although she must know the truth about her brother, it was shut away somewhere out of sight, even now. She believed there was something political behind Vikram Narayan's death. She almost insisted on it. Yet none of that related to the violence dealt out to the five men who now included her brother.

However, if there was nothing political, why had Special Branch's top India hand pushed his way into the investigation? And why was he behaving as though Vikram Narayan was a stranger when he had known him for years and had officers following him around London, recording every contact he made.

A good place to start looking for evidence about who the young Indian had been associating with, and where he had been in the days before his death, was the information Chief Inspector Nugent and his officers must already have. And it hadn't even been mentioned. There was no doubt Nugent was hiding a great deal. But Stefan didn't have to look hard to find that less surprising than it ought to have been. In Dublin, Terry Gregory had made a career out of telling nobody anything. It didn't have to mean anything. It didn't necessarily mean what Hindu Narayan was convinced it meant. She had decided Frank Nugent was responsible for her brother's death in some way, whether personally or not didn't matter. Despite the evidence tying her brother's death to a killer who had murdered other men in the same way, she was unwilling to let go of the conviction that seemed driven by her personal dislike, even hatred, of Nugent.

There was something else, too. Stefan could hear it in her voice and see it in the fierce determination in her eyes. She didn't want to believe Vikram's death meant nothing, that he was simply in the wrong place at the wrong time. To find a way to accept his death, she needed him to die for India. She seemed to expect that Stefan, because he was Irish, would think the same way. She was frustrated that he didn't, that he felt, whatever Frank Nugent was, that the evidence that made her brother's murder part of a chain was real. Hindu didn't want it to be real. She had finally turned her distress on Stefan, almost accusing him of being in the pay of the English.

'I'm sorry,' said Mac Liammóir. 'I wasn't quite ready for that.'

'Me neither,' said Stefan.

'The deaths of the other men make it more complicated, Stefan. But I still thought what she said was odd. An English policeman, who turns out to be an Indian policeman, investigating the murder of a man he pretends he doesn't know, after following him round London, a man he beat up years ago in India. I thought you should know. It's still . . . I don't know what it is.'

'I'm glad I know. I am being lied to. That's always worth knowing.'

'Well, we're in England, Stefan. Would you expect anything less?'

Stefan Gillespie smiled. As they walked on, he was more thoughtful.

'I understand Miss Narayan feels . . . that she wants . . .'

'Yes,' said Mac Liammóir, 'if he had to die, she wanted a hero.'

The two men separated. Stefan Gillespie crossed Regent Street, Micheál Mac Liammóir walked on through Piccadilly Circus to the Regent Palace Hotel. Stefan stood, taking out a cigarette and lighting it. He thought he would walk up Regent Street and back before returning to the High Commission. He would probably stop at a pub. He needed another drink. Most of all he needed to clear his head and think how he would handle Chief Inspector Nugent the next day, whether to play the game and see where it led or call him out. What Nugent was doing was only Stefan's business in so far as it concerned James Corcoran and a man who had now murdered five times. It was easy to forget that with Hindu Narayan's face still in his head. And

Frank Nugent's callousness was in his head too. It seemed he had hardly spoken to Vikram's sister. He had been uncommunicative. He owed her more of an explanation, certainly more of his time, surely. He owed her the assurance that her brother's death did matter and that everything was being done to find the man who had killed him. Yet Stefan also wondered, did Hindu Narayan want to listen?

Drawing on the cigarette, Stefan moved back up Regent Street. He noticed a car pull out ahead of him. It moved to the left and drove away towards Oxford Circus. He recognised it even in the darkness. It might have been simply another black car, but it was the car he had been in and out of several times that day. Chief Inspector Nugent would not need telling where Stefan had been that night or who he had been talking to. Wherever Nugent got his information, he was good at his job. He had been watching the restaurant. Stefan smiled, then he groaned. The sound of sirens filled the street as they cranked up and wailed. He could hear bombs – one, two, a third – not close, south of the river. But coming his way. He turned round, heading for the Underground, joining the growing stream of Londoners.

8

Greek Street

The next morning Stefan Gillespie walked through Soho to Greek Street. He had called Scotland Yard and he knew Chief Inspector Nugent was at Vikram Narayan's flat. The morning was cold. In the air there was the smell of smoke; behind it the sour scent of the incendiaries. There had been bombs in Marylebone and the Euston Road, but nothing closer. The city went about its business and the streets were busy with people going to work. The street market Stefan passed was stacked with vegetables. A uniformed constable stood outside 24A Greek Street. Parked in front was the black Austin Stefan had last seen heading north along Regent Street the previous evening, carrying Frank Nugent away from his surveillance.

'Chief Inspector Nugent here?'

'He's upstairs, sir.'

'Inspector Gillespie.'

The constable nodded. His expression said, *Oh, you're the Irish one, are you?* A mixture of suspicion and wry amusement. But he spoke officiously.

'The room at the top, sir, right up. You'll find a couple of footprints marked on the stairs; if you could manage to avoid stepping on those, please.'

'I'm sure I can manage that, Constable,' said Stefan, smiling.

The door to Vikram Narayan's flat was open. It was no more than a room with a tiny bathroom, almost in the attic of the building. The small window let in little light; the bedside lamp and the overhead bulb were on, even though it was a bright day outside. Stefan stood in the doorway, unobserved, taking in the cluttered room. He could see the bed. He recognised the corner of the room from the photographs he had already seen. Elsewhere, books were stacked in piles against the walls. Several suits hung on the kind of rail you'd find in a shop. The room would have been drab and cold – that was its normal condition – but the walls and the chairs were draped with variegated Indian cloths and hangings. It was a kind of brightness that faintly echoed the Veeraswamy, and it made him think again of Vikram's sister. Frank Nugent was looking through a chest of drawers. There was a flash of light; a photographer in the bathroom, taking pictures. After a moment another flash. Across the room, a man in plain clothes placed items in a series of cardboard boxes on top of a small table. Another detective. The chief inspector stood up, catching sight of Stefan.

'Come in, Stefan. The place has been dusted to death, no worry.'

Stefan crossed the room towards Frank Nugent.

The photographer emerged from the bathroom.

'Is there anything else, sir?' he asked.

'I don't think so. You're happy?'

The photographer nodded, putting his camera into a bag.

'Give him a lift back to the Yard, Sergeant.'

The other detective nodded.

Stefan was standing by Nugent, as the two men left.

'Anything new?'

The chief inspector pushed the bottom drawer of the chest back in. It was full of books; it slid shut with difficulty. He struggled to push in two top drawers, overflowing with the unremarkable stuff of a seemingly cluttered life.

The wall behind the chest was covered with pictures of actors and film stars, cut from magazines. They were pinned and pasted over one another. Stefan scanned them, picking up some faces he knew. Humphrey Bogart, Marlene Dietrich, Katharine Hepburn, Cary Grant, Laurence Olivier, Spencer Tracy, Noël Coward. There were some he didn't recognise. He thought they must be theatre actors. He recognised a young Micheál Mac Liammóir.

On top of the chest of drawers were several photographs. Three were in frames, one glass crystal, the other two silver. One picture was of Vikram Narayan. He was in a suit, smoking a cigarette, wearing a monocle. It was a posed photograph, taken on a stage. He was dressed for a part. Stefan recognised Narayan's sister, Hindu, in the second photograph. The third was of an older man and woman, posing stiffly in a studio. Stefan could see they were the parents, from the images of the two faces he had in his head, the dead brother and the sister he had spoken to last night. There were other, smaller photos. They included pictures that must have been taken in India; groups of young men and women; a family gathering where he recognised, again, both Vikram and Hindu; a picture of what looked like a class of schoolboys. Then Vikram on a camel, with a pyramid behind him; a picture of him on the steps of the British Museum. Frank Nugent shoved the last drawer in with a grunt. He took the photographs of family and friends and put them in one of the boxes.

'There's a footprint by the bed, with traces of blood, paper over it now. The same inside the door. Replicated on the stairs. Someone going out and going down. Not Mr Mac Liammóir's print. In fact, his shoe is partly covering the one by the door.

Which confirms he was here afterwards. The killer had already gone.'

As Nugent packed several more items in the boxes, Stefan walked to the bed. It had been stripped of sheets and blankets. The pillows had gone too. It was only a bare, grubby mattress on a brass and iron frame, rusty in places. There was a book on a table by the bed. Stefan recognised the brown cover and the gold lettering of a book he knew, an anthology of poetry: Palgrave's *Golden Treasury*. He sat on the mattress and opened it. Inside the cover was a bookplate: *Vikram Narayan, For Excellence in English, La Martinière College, Lucknow*. He had the same book at home. His mother and father had given it to him as a present. There was a bookmark. Stefan turned to the page; a poem he knew well. He hadn't looked at it in many years, but he knew it. The poem began on one page, but it was book-marked where it ended.

> Ah, love, let us be true
> To one another! For the world, which seems
> To lie before us like a land of dreams,
> So various, so beautiful, so new,
> Hath really neither joy, nor love, nor light,
> Nor certitude, nor peace, nor help for pain;
> And we are here as on a darkling plain
> Swept with confused alarms of struggle and flight,
> Where ignorant armies clash by night.

Stefan closed the book and got up. He was here because of a dead man in Ireland, but he already knew more about the dead man in England. But not as much as the man now writing a list of contents of the cardboard boxes knew, though he pretended he didn't. Stefan watched Nugent. The chief inspector, wearing white cotton gloves, put a black camera and a long steel lens into one of the boxes. It was a striking item of equipment in this room full of books and clothes and bright oriental colours and ordinary clutter. It didn't belong.

'What's that?'

'The photographer tells me it's a Leica camera with a 50 millimetre lens and an Elmar 135 millimetre telephoto lens. He wouldn't mind the telephoto lens himself.'

'And it's Narayan's camera?'

'It's here, so yes.'

'What would all that cost?'

'Enough.'

'A lot.'

'Yes.'

'The conversation in the club . . . the idea that he was on his uppers. Bollocks. But that's why Mac Liammóir was here. Couldn't help him any other way, but he could give him a bit of cash. That camera equipment is real money.'

'He wasn't short of money,' said Nugent. He picked up an envelope from another box. 'Under the mattress. There's over a hundred pounds there.'

'So, what does that tell us?'

'I don't know.'

Stefan Gillespie looked at Nugent for a long moment, then smiled.

'I'd have thought Indian Political Intelligence could do better than that.'

Nugent grinned.

'I did assume Miss Narayan would have filled you in on that.'

'I suppose now you've stopped watching her brother, you've got time to watch her. Or were you just watching me, for the crack, one Special Branch man to another? You need to do better than the car you drove me around in.'

'I can do better when I need to. Come on, I'll buy you a tea, Stefan.'

*

Inspector Stefan Gillespie and Chief Inspector Nugent walked away from the wooden cabman's shelter in Soho Square with mugs of tea. Two taxies were parked outside the green, shed-like building that served hot food and drink to cabmen. There were similar buildings all across London. They kept strange hours and they were open in the early mornings when nothing else was. The steam from their metal chimneys was a welcome sight on a cold night, and all the more so in the blackout. They were meant to be the preserve of taxi drivers, but the men who ran them recognised a detective when they saw one. When there were no detectives around, they said it was simple: simply by the smell.

'I wasn't expecting you to meet Miss Narayan, I have to say.'

'She got fuck all from you. She wanted more.'

'She's a very determined woman.'

'She wasn't very happy to find you in charge of the investigation into her brother's death. And why should she be, given the background?'

'What background is that, Stefan?'

'They didn't send you from India because they're short-staffed on the Murder Squad. You're here to watch Indians, nationalists, politicians, whatever they are, and you've had people on her brother . . . I assume since he got here. It's only a pity someone wasn't watching him the night he died. You knew who he was, that's the thing. What sort of fucking conversation were you having with me about a dead queer in a mortuary, knowing who your man was?'

'I had to decide what was your business and what wasn't.'

'And have you, Frank?'

'I don't know yet. It depends what I'm investigating.'

'I would have thought that was the one thing that was straightforward.'

'Is it? What would you do with an IRA man in Dublin who'd been hacked about like that? Would your first thought be: *He must have been chopped up by a maniac*? Or would you want to know where the feller'd been, who he'd been talking to, what he'd been up to, before you settled on your madman?'

'It's hardly the same thing.'

'Isn't it? There are some very nice chaps who want an independent India, I can assure you, and I've lived in India long enough to think they've got some fucking right to want it. But it's like all these things, Stefan, some of these chaps are nicer than others. Some of them want to march through the streets and join Mr Gandhi in fasting for freedom, and some of them wouldn't mind a holiday in the Emerald Isle to take an IRA course in making bombs. And there are those, given the time that's in it, as you might say yourself, Stefan, who'd like to see if Mr Hitler couldn't help them do things faster than Mr Gandhi. You've got IRA men in Berlin. Well, we've got Indian nationalists there. A Mr Subhas Bose, in particular, there right now. You may remember him coming to Dublin a few years ago. Despite the meetings with Dev, and the reception at the Shelbourne, Terry Gregory was keeping an eye on all the IRA men Bose was talking to as well. Mr Bose has friends in Ireland that are not friends of Dev's.'

'You know more than I do, Frank. It's before my time.'

'I think I do, Stefan. It wouldn't have mattered whether your friend Mac Liammóir wanted to give Narayan a job or not. He's on a list of Indians who won't be allowed into Ireland whatever happens. I know, because I drew up the list. And I don't doubt your Superintendent Gregory has a copy of it, along with G2, Customs and Excise, the Department of External Affairs and Uncle Tom Cobley and all. But then I don't imagine Mr Gregory tells everyone everything.'

Stefan laughed. 'That would be putting it mildly.'

The two men turned back to the cab shelter and put the mugs down at the hatch. They walked towards Soho Square and into the gardens. For a time they said no more. Stefan was aware that he was out of his depth.

'Miss Narayan,' said Nugent quietly.

'Yes,' replied Stefan.

'A remarkable woman.'

'She wouldn't have a great deal of time for you, Frank.'

'No, she wouldn't, I am aware of that.'

'And you wouldn't blame her.'

'I could tell you that I didn't break her brother's ribs myself in Delhi, but I'd be lying if I said I told the men who did to stop. I left them to it. But that's how it works sometimes. You won't like the kind of man who'd go in for that sort of thing yourself, but I doubt you haven't stood by and watched it, or at least heard it. I doubt you haven't shaken your head and ignored it. We're in the same job. I don't do it because I like it. I've long forgotten why I do it at all.'

Stefan had nothing to say. It was a simple truth.

'I should have been prepared for Hindu Narayan. She arrived at the Yard. I didn't know what to say. She's not a woman with any predisposition to believe me anyway. Starting with what happened, the simple facts. Did she want to hear me say her brother was possibly killed by a man he'd picked up in the street? Probably a stranger. A man he'd gone back to his room to have sex with. And the details of the death . . . It's still something I can't put out publicly, for reasons that have to do with the investigation. You understand that. I have men out asking questions, trying to look for sightings, people who knew Vikram. I don't want too much knowledge on the street. I want to ask questions without creating panic. There aren't many homosexual men who will talk to the police. It's softly, softly. It has to be.'

'You'd think Hindu would understand that,' said Stefan.

'Up to a point. She knows . . . and then she doesn't. She's protected him for years, even from his family. I think she's kidded herself into the bargain.'

'But you've had men watching him, Frank. You know all about him.'

'I haven't had anyone watching him.'

'That's not what Miss Narayan thinks. Why wouldn't she be right? You tell me Narayan was a nationalist. He was too dangerous to let into Ireland because he had what . . . contacts with the IRA? If you weren't watching him, what were you doing? She knows it backwards. She knows who you are. She knows why you're here. That's why she thinks you've got something to do with his death. Why not, when she finds you in charge of the fucking investigation? I don't know you and it looks like a cover-up to me!'

'I didn't say there aren't things to cover up.'

'I see. Well, I suppose that's honest enough.'

'It doesn't mean there's not a real investigation. It doesn't mean I don't want to find the man who killed Vikram, as well as the others. I owe him that.'

Stefan heard something different in Nugent's tone, something more real.

'You owe him?'

'Yes. It's not something I can explain to his sister.'

'Because she wouldn't believe you.'

'I don't suppose she would. I'm not sure I'd want her to.'

'I think you've lost me, Frank,' said Stefan.

'The reason I wasn't watching Vikram Narayan was because I didn't need to. He was doing the watching, from inside the nationalist movement. I know what his sister thought. That's the lie. She didn't know. But Vikram had worked for me since he was in India. He was my agent. The first thing I had to do was decide if he'd been murdered because someone found out the truth.'

Stefan nodded. It wasn't pleasant, but it made sense.

'I can't see how that's likely,' continued the chief inspector, 'given what we know about the other murders. But what I have to ensure is that this investigation reveals nothing about Vikram being an informant. He has to remain the man his sister thinks he was. There's a whole chain of connections, other informants – going all the way back to India and the Congress Party – that could just disappear. You know how these things tie together. He wasn't that important, but he knew people. He was trusted. Because of his family. You know that, too. Isn't it the same with Republican families in Ireland? The Narayans are people who matter in the independence movement, in the Congress. It's in their blood. The daughter's not called Hindu for nothing.'

'I'm not here to cover up your shite, Frank. It's about murder.'

'I know. I am here to pursue that. As for what I've just told you . . .'

'I don't care. Just cut the lies. It's not my business to tell anyone else.'

'Not even Superintendent Gregory?'

'If you cared about that, you wouldn't have said it.'

'You'll be heading to Ireland now, but you might want to steer clear of Hindu Narayan. If she thinks you're useful, she's persistent. I don't mind her telling her friends her brother's death has something to do with Indian Political Intelligence. It even suits the story. But I don't want to make my lies your lies.'

Stefan had decided not to talk to Hindu Narayan again. He didn't want to lie to her and now he knew too much to avoid lying, even if what he knew was only part of the truth. He had just one thing to carry back to Ireland and it was nothing to do with India, Indian Political Intelligence or Chief Inspector Nugent's Special Branch operation in England. He would pass what he had been told on to Terry Gregory, though. There were issues between the Irish and British governments, even about what was going on halfway round the world, in India, that mattered to them both. It didn't have to matter to him. It was only another stone he had looked under by chance. But there was a murder no one appeared to care much about in Ireland that would now not be forgotten. In the middle of the mess that was Special Branch and Intelligence and the misinformation of war, there was a real crime and there was real police work to do. He wanted to hold on to that. Not for any principle, but because it was, out of nowhere, something solid. It seemed, despite his doubts, that it was solid for Chief Inspector Nugent too. There was little about Nugent to trust, but what there was related to the murder of Vikram Narayan. Stefan did not think that Nugent had told him the whole truth, but that didn't matter. He believed that when the shite was shunted aside, the IPI man wanted to find Vikram's killer. That would do.

He took the afternoon train from Euston to Holyhead. There had been a message at the High Commission from Hindu Narayan, asking to see him. She left a note with Miss Foye, saying there was something she needed to tell him. He ignored the message. As the train pulled out of London, he regretted it. He did not want to face her, with what he now knew about the brother she so loved and so believed in, but he felt shabby about sneaking away. She was, as even Frank Nugent acknowledged, a remarkable woman. If he did not want to confront her, with a head full of evasions, he was sorry he hadn't seen her again.

9

Thomastown

Thomastown, Co Kilkenny

It was three days later that Stefan Gillespie got off the train from Carlow at Thomastown, the next stop after Kilkenny. It was a small country town on the banks of the River Nore. Once it had been bigger; the street of scruffy buildings still clung to a kind of elegance. It was a Norman town, like so many in Leinster. It lay claim to a ruined castle and a ruined abbey that reflected a long-forgotten importance. Thomastown sat in a softer countryside than the town Stefan had left that morning before dawn, Baltinglass. Apart from the bright colours of the houses in the main street, the Kilkenny town could almost have been English. With the high, bare hill that rose up behind it, and the Wicklow Mountains beyond that, Baltinglass could never have been anything other than Irish.

Stefan had spent the night at home in Wicklow, with his eleven-year-old son, Tom, and his parents, David and Helena. He had been there only a few hours and was surprised to find an atmosphere that was colder than usual. Tom had little to say and spent most of the evening out in the fields or in his room. The book Stefan had bought in London, *The Hobbit*, was, at least, a success, and if Tom was in his room it was partly because he was absorbed in it already. But the atmosphere was not right. David Gillespie had a lot to say about nothing in particular, which was always a sign that he had something else to say that was being avoided. Helena produced more food than anyone wanted and worked at pretending nothing was wrong. There were things wrong that Stefan knew about. There were problems at the farm; there had been for some time now. The year before, the fact that David Gillespie was getting older came as a surprise to no one but Stefan. He could do less work and some of the land was let to a neighbour. There wasn't as much income. Stefan's Garda salary mattered more than it had done. His father didn't want to accept that it did, but he had little choice. There were tensions where there had been none before, but this time Stefan felt it was something else besides. If there was ill-temper, it was between Tom and David. He had not seen temper in his son before, not in a way that somehow felt quiet and resentful. It was more adult than Stefan was used to. Tom was changing. Things that had been simple, childlike, were more complicated. It had been there at Christmas, but barely. Now it filled the farmhouse. Stefan had no idea whether the atmosphere was a spat or something more serious. With only a few hours at home, he took the easiest way and ignored it. He left his questions unasked, hoping that next time he came home they would have evaporated.

James Corcoran's mother and father lived in a house on the outskirts of Thomastown, in the constituency Rory Corcoran represented in the Dáil. The TD was at home for the weekend; Stefan wanted to speak to him. It was there that the contents of James Corcoran's room at St Patrick's College were stored, in the trunk they had arrived in. It was well over a year now, fifteen months, because the months were still counted. There was still a room that belonged to the dead man. Stefan had established that it was virtually untouched. It wasn't unusual. When a death was so far-reaching in its impact, it could be a long time before the dead were allowed to leave. Things that mattered could not just be thrown away. Stefan was grateful for that. There might yet be something to find.

He left the railway station with directions to the house. He walked through the town and out the other side, along the River Nore. He did not call at the Garda barracks, as protocol required, though he walked past them. He knew Superintendent Carberry from his time in uniform at Baltinglass, but he had nothing to ask. He would give the Corcorans what privacy he could. One minute's conversation at the Garda station and all Kilkenny would know.

Stefan had arrived back from England to find that Dessie MacMahon had already established a murder room in a small storeroom, away from the main Special Branch offices. He had brought all the information that related to the death of James Corcoran from Maynooth. The files and statements, the photographs of the scene and of the body, the boxes of evidence from Donadea. The boxes contained the blood-stained picnic rug, the beer bottles, the bread knife that had inflicted the savage wounds, and even a bag that held the remains of the bread the knife had been used to cut beforehand. A note explained that a piece of cheese and some sliced ham had been disposed of. It was an example of attention to detail that Stefan Gillespie wished could be seen elsewhere in the investigation. Another box held the clothes that James Corcoran had been wearing, along with an envelope containing woollen fibres that had probably come from the killer's clothing. Against a wall leant the bicycle James Corcoran had ridden from Maynooth to Donadea. Both tyres were flat. Stefan would look at all this material. He would look again at the reports, the statements, the photographs, the maps. He already knew that he would be lucky to find anything. If there had been more to find at the time, something would have come of it. One thing mattered. One thing that, put together with the investigation in England, might lead somewhere, eventually: the fingerprint.

Superintendent Terry Gregory was less interested in the murder Stefan Gillespie was now investigating than he was in the Metropolitan Police Special Branch, Indian Political Intelligence and Chief Inspector Frank Nugent. That was what he wanted to talk about when Stefan finally sat in his office again. The presence of a small Indian community in Ireland, mainly in Dublin, was not something Stefan was unaware of, but he didn't know it had any significance, let alone that it was under surveillance by G2, Military Intelligence, and had been before the war. Terry Gregory's magpie-like passion for collecting information, including the least shiny and obviously useful information, was in full view. Stefan had information about the Indian community in London; there were links to Ireland. It didn't matter how slight. This was information G2 might want. That made it a precious commodity. Special Branch and Military Intelligence were as much competitors as colleagues. They watched each other as closely as they watched the various players who were in their sights. They had different roles and different targets, but they never let that stop them straying into each other's territory. Terry Gregory, in particular, had a loose sense of where his own remit began and ended. If there were things G2 kept to themselves, they were, by definition, things he wanted to know about.

'You remember your man Bose, Subhas Chandra Bose?'

'Nugent mentioned him. Isn't he in Germany now?'

'Yes. He was here in 'thirty-six.'

'I read something about it. I wasn't in Dublin then.'

'Bose was a big man in the Congress Party. In India he's not as big as Gandhi, but he's there with Nehru, at least he was. Now he broadcasts on Berlin Radio. He was the hard man, so. The others want constitutional change. He wanted a boatload of guns and explosives. The only thing different from Ireland is that the gunmen don't run the show there. I guess he got fed up. If they won't fight, maybe the Germans can instead. Does that sound familiar?'

Stefan nodded. He didn't reply. Gregory mostly was talking to himself.

'So, your man Nugent was in England when Bose was here. At the Special Branch office in Holyhead. One man and a dog to keep an eye on who's on the mail boat.' Gregory took out a cigarette, though he didn't light it. 'Busier now, I'd say. He didn't come here at the time, but they had people watching Bose. He wrote to me, though, Nugent. He said he was only being helpful. He suggested Mr Bose was trying to establish links between the IRA and the Indian Congress Party. He said Bose had met and conversed with people of all political classes of opinion.' The superintendent laughed and then lit his cigarette. 'It's a phrase I've always remembered. But he was right. Bose met de Valera and then proceeded to meet most of the people in Ireland who'd decided, by that time, that the Republican cause would be best served by a bullet in Dev's head. There was a distinct cooling towards Mr Bose on Dev's part. Your man was welcomed with open arms, because we support Indian independence, but the people he ended up with were either gunmen or communists. And his best friends in Europe were Herr Hitler and Signor Mussolini. Mr Nugent said we might want to know the Italians had been caught trying to get money and arms to anti-British elements in India. Elements being Mr Bose's part of the Congress Party. Anyway, Nugent wanted our cooperation. We declined at the time, though I suspect Dev made his feelings about Mr Subhas Bose known to Messrs Nehru and Gandhi. He wasn't asked back.'

'If the IRA can't get Germany to invade Ireland, it's a long march from Berlin to Bombay,' said Stefan. 'Haven't the English got bigger problems?'

'They had bigger problems than Ireland in nineteen sixteen. Look at us now! If the Congress Party isn't exactly supporting Britain in the war, it's standing back. If that changed, if India blew up like Ireland did . . . that would be some problem.'

'I'm sure it keeps Mr Nugent busy, sir.'

'But he's got time for a dead homosexual. Why's that?'

'Well, we have too. What's the alternative? There are people dying by the thousands, tens of thousands, everywhere. So, do we just forget about murder?'

'Is that a bit of principle I see surfacing? Be careful, Stevie.'

Stefan laughed.

Superintendent Gregory pushed a typed list of names across the desk.

'This is from the Department of External Affairs. A list of Indians not allowed into the country from Britain. You'll see your man's name: Vikram Narayan. It's a list the English supplied. We haven't even bothered to have it retyped. They don't give much detail but contact with Bose is one reason Narayan is on the list. In nineteen thirty-six, when Mr Bose was on his way back to India, his ship docked in Alexandria. He wasn't allowed off, in case he stirred up trouble in Egypt. Mr Narayan was one of the people who went on board to meet him. That's the year the Gate Theatre toured Egypt and Narayan had his brief encounter with our great actor. Narayan was one of Bose's people in Egypt.'

'Except he wasn't. He was working for Nugent and the IPI.'

'Who knows?' said Gregory. 'But he was up to his neck in it, one way or another. So? Well, Dev's got a lot to say in support of Indian independence, as ever, but when the political posturing's done, our interests coincide with our friends' across the Irish Sea, for now. Or at least as far as we can throw them.'

'And Chief Superintendent Nugent?'

'The short version is that G2 is now doing the IPI's job for them in Ireland. I doubt there's much that goes on in the Friends of India Society here that won't end up on Nugent's desk. Most of what the less respectable Indian nationalists are doing with the IRA in London lands on mine. Apart from what we chose to keep to ourselves and vice versa, as ever, ad infinitum, Amen! And it's always cosier than you think. Chief Inspector Nugent's boss in India is a Superintendent Philip Vickery, a Fermanagh man, and educated at Trinity, like you. Who knows? If he'd stayed in Ireland . . . he'd probably have my job now.'

'Is that some kind of warning, sir?'

'You can never know too much. These deaths are another contact with English Special Branch. If you get anything interesting from Nugent, tell me.'

'What about the murders, sir? Are they of any interest?'

'Is that a sour note of indignation, Stevie? Tut! The murders are yours. If I've got other priorities, that's what I'm paid for. It might look like my in-tray is populated by clowns playing at spies, and IRA men on the piss, but the line between the clowns and the tanks rolling down O'Connell Street, whether they're German or British, could be no more than a fucking clown with a stick of gelignite. You just do what you're told and leave the moral debate till there's no war to get in the way. There'll be time then and I'll be happy to listen. Assuming we come out the other end as we went in, with God's grace . . . and the fellers who follow the tanks don't arrive with a bullet . . . for every man here.'

Terry Gregory stubbed out his cigarette and grinned.

He crossed himself.

'This is the word of the Lord. Thanks be to God.'

He stood up. Stefan did the same.

'I'll want to talk to Mr Corcoran, sir, James's father. Since I am reopening the investigation, someone should tell him, before I pitch up on his doorstep. I will have to explain what's happened in England. That's what's brought us back to the case. It's hard to tiptoe round. I think we're beyond not mentioning his son's homosexuality out of politeness. Did he ever get his Cabinet post?'

'Not yet. He's still a junior minister. Agriculture.'

'You'll tell him?'

'He complained we weren't doing enough at the time,' said the superintendent. 'I don't know if he'll like it any better now we're back. But that's not a sin, is it? It's not easy looking into the darkness, Stevie. We forget that sometimes. Or we get too used to it.' There was something close to compassion in Gregory's voice. 'You'd hope the wound was healing now.'

He shook his head. He was brusque and businesslike again.

'He's an important man. The Commissioner can tell him.'

'Yes, sir.'

The superintendent frowned; the other story was still in his head.

'Your man Nugent will have a reason for this. Vikram Narayan.'

Stefan wanted to get on with the job; the rest didn't concern him.

'Does it matter?'

Terry Gregory gave him a wry, equivocal smile. It always mattered.

The Corcorans' house was some way out of Thomastown. It was a solid, square, Georgian farmhouse, but it had been built out from an older structure. Once it had belonged to planters; the equally solid English middlemen who bit by bit had become more Irish than English, though they barely knew it. They did the work that kept the Ascendancy, the rootless upper class that England had planted in Ireland, in the avaricious idleness that was its only reason for being there. Now the house was home to the family of a Deputy in the Irish parliament. It was kept with the neatness it always knew. The lawns were tidy. There were dark rhododendrons the size of trees, which an earlier occupant had brought from the Himalayas. The windows were big and bright; the frames had recently been repainted. Old, warped glass and new white paint shone in the winter light.

A young woman answered the door. Sorcha was a maid or a housekeeper; she worked there at least. Stefan recognised the accent of Kerry. He walked into a hall full of dark, heavy furniture. It looked as if it had come with the house. A man in his fifties came out from a room off the hall, thin, grey-haired, balding.

'Cé hé, a Shorcha?' He asked who it was.

'An tUasal Gillespie, an póilín.'

He was introduced, in Irish, as the policeman Rory Corcoran was expecting. The question was only asked so that the Irish-speaking habits of the household were established. Stefan recognised a particular kind of house, where Irish was spoken in a sea of surrounding English. It was a statement of what should be rather than what was. It was likely Corcoran and his family were not native speakers. Sorcha, the woman who let him in, would be. It was one reason she was there. Rory Corcoran stepped forward and stretched out his hand.

'You found us then, Inspector.'

'I did, sir.'

'Come through, will you? Have you come down from Dublin?'

'From Baltinglass, my family are there.'

'Another ruined Cistercian abbey by a river!' Corcoran smiled, but Stefan could feel the tension, as he followed the TD into a big room that was the politician's study. It was lined with books, meticulously tidy. Two sofas stretched out in front of a walnut desk. A turf fire smouldered, as turf fires do.

'Please, sit down.'

Stefan sat on one of the sofas.

'Will you have some tea?' The deputy stood by the fire.

'I won't, sir, but thank you.'

'Ned Broy spoke to me yesterday. I understand the investigation into my son's death is being reopened. There's new information. He didn't go into many details . . . I gather it's because of a murder in England that is in some way . . .' He left the sentence unfinished.

'There have been several deaths in England, in fact: four now. All in London except one.' Stefan spoke carefully. 'All very similar to your son's.'

The door from the hall had opened. A woman had come in. She was pale, slightly fragile. Her face was lined in a way that made her look older than she was, maybe in her late forties. Her hair was black, somehow younger than her face. Her lined features were accentuated by a frown of dark seriousness.

'Cén fáth nach raibh tú a glaoch orm?'

She asked why Corcoran hadn't called her. She was slightly irritated. The Irish didn't hide that. But her face softened. She understood why he hadn't wanted to. Her voice was gentler as she looked from her husband to Stefan and back.

'Ná déan iaracht mé a chosaint.'

She didn't need to be protected, she said. Stefan understood. He imagined that Mrs Corcoran must have been beyond the kind of protection that meant not talking about her dead son for a long time. She was looking at him again now.

'I'm sorry, Inspector . . . I'm Mary Corcoran,' she said.

'Inspector Gillespie.'

'You must think we're very rude.'

'Not at all, Mrs Corcoran. Más mian libh Gaeilge a labhairt . . .'

He had asked them if they wanted to continue in Irish. Corcoran looked surprised. He may have already made enquiries about the policeman who was coming from Dublin

III

Castle. He may have picked up, even in a few words, on the almost invisible signs that told any Irishman who was a Catholic and who was a Protestant. Mrs Corcoran smiled and shook her head. It was a gesture of politeness on Stefan's part, but he also knew the fact that here a knowledge of Irish made him a little more trustworthy than he had been a moment earlier.

'We'll stick to English, Mr Gillespie,' said Corcoran.

He sat down. His wife remained standing.

'You were talking about other men being killed,' said Mrs Corcoran. 'And you think the same . . . the same person was responsible. It's hard to take in. This was in England . . . how can you be sure? You are very sure, I take it?'

'We are very sure. I don't think it would help you for me to say . . .'

'No,' said the deputy. 'I don't think it would.'

'It's terrible,' continued his wife. 'How many . . .?'

'With your son, there are five murders. So, this investigation is now being led by the police in England.' He paused. The point needed making, even if it felt unwelcome. 'I don't know what more we can find out here, but I want to look at a number of things, in particular what came back from St Patrick's. Do you still have your son's possessions – the things that were in his room there?'

'Yes, Inspector,' said Mary Corcoran softly. 'It all sits where it's sat . . .'

'I don't know that there is anything we can really tell you, Mr Gillespie,' interrupted Corcoran. 'Every question that we could answer, we answered. But this awful thing . . . came from nowhere. We knew nothing. It simply happened.'

Stefan Gillespie was silent for several seconds.

'I am interested in how James was, in the days before.',

'He was in Maynooth,' said the deputy.

'Did you hear from him?'

Mrs Corcoran went to the mantelpiece. She took a cigarette from a silver box. She picked up a heavy, onyx lighter and lit the cigarette. She turned back.

'He did telephone to say he would be coming home, the next weekend.'

'And how did he sound? What sort of mood was he in?'

'He was quite cheerful. He didn't say a lot.'

'Did he say anything more?'

'That he'd sent a letter. And we would talk about what was in it . . .'

Stefan watched Rory Corcoran shift uncomfortably.

'And what was in it?'

'In what way, Inspector?' asked Corcoran. 'I don't know what anything my son could have written in Maynooth has to do with dead men in London.'

'I'm trying to understand your son. It may help, it may not. But the days that led up to his death are important. I think they are. I don't want to intrude . . .'

'But you have to.' Mrs Corcoran smiled.

'I do.'

'We have the letter. It arrived . . . after he died.'

'I'm very sorry. Did it tell you what he wanted to talk about?'

'He wanted to leave the seminary.'

Rory Corcoran stood up.

'I don't understand the point of this, Gillespie. Every priest will have doubts about what he's taking on. It's a vocation, not a job. A lifetime's commitment to God. He was dealing with it like any young man. He wanted to talk. He needed reassurance. How on earth does that relate to being killed?'

Mary Corcoran stepped closer to her husband and touched his hand.

'I'll take Mr Gillespie to James's room, Rory. I'm sure I can answer any questions. I know you have a lot to do before you go back to Dublin, darling.'

Deputy Corcoran nodded. He seemed to diminish in stature; the fragile figure beside him seemed to grow. She was the stronger. Coming into the room she'd looked timid, nervous. Stefan could see it was the other way round. The man who was a public figure, a TD, a government minister, a strong pair of hands for his party in Kilkenny, was the one who wanted to run from what Stefan was there to talk about. There was, after all, the Emergency, the word the Irish government used to describe the war that wasn't quite a war, yet. It was all-consuming. The business of running the country was no bad place to hide.

'I'll be here if you need me, Inspector.'

Corcoran walked to his desk and sat down. He opened a briefcase.

'If you'll follow me, Mr Gillespie,' said Mrs Corcoran.

Stefan Gillespie left the study with her. The junior minister looked down into the briefcase on his desk for a long time before he finally took anything out.

Mary Corcoran led Stefan Gillespie through the house and out into the back garden. They walked along a shaded path, where the rhododendrons were bigger and older. They came to a wooden shed-like building, painted in grey with two curtained windows on either side of a door. It was a peaceful, welcoming place.

Stefan followed Mrs Corcoran inside. She walked from one window to the other and opened the curtains. It was a single, large room. A bed, a table; a small kitchen at one end, with a basin and cooker. There were bookshelves against one wall. In front of one window was a desk; in front of the other was a chest with candles, a crucifix and a statue of the Virgin Mary.

'We call it the annexe, and Rory used to work here when we first came to Thomastown. But James always wanted some-where of his own – really his own – from when he was a teenager. And when he said he was going to be a priest, it seemed even more important that he had his own . . . a special kind of space.'

Stefan looked round, taking in the room. It was simple and calm.

'I do understand, Mr Gillespie, that these terrible murders . . . I don't want details. I know enough . . . I know too much . . . too much that will never go away . . . I understand that they have to do with what James was . . . in some inexplicable way these other men died because of that. I don't know what to say about James's homosexuality, except that Rory and I pretended it didn't exist . . . or that being a priest would end it. But if you have something to say, please say it. If there are things my husband can't talk about . . . I am far beyond that.'

'I'd like to look at the things that came from Maynooth. I'm not sure anyone looked at his room in the college. If they did it's not mentioned.'

'There's a trunk, over there, at the end of the bed. I've never opened it.' Mary Corcoran pointed across the room. 'I can leave you, if that's all right.'

She turned back towards the door.

'Thank you. I would like . . .'

'Yes?'

'The letter he wrote. It must have been one of the last—'

She cut him off, almost with anger in her voice. This was very hard.

'I'll get it, Mr Gillespie. You don't need to explain.'

Stefan walked slowly round the room. There was little to see. The bookshelves carried a mixture of books. It was what you would expect in the room of a young man who had not long stopped being a boy. Among the missals and the catechisms and the books on theology and philosophy, there were still books James Corcoran had read as a child. Stefan went to the trunk at the foot of the bed. He pulled up a chair and sat down, opening the lid. One by one he took out the items that were inside. There were clothes, neatly folded and pressed. A black overcoat, sweaters and corduroys and the black uniform of the seminarian. There were more books: bibles in Latin and Greek, a Hebrew Old Testament, prayer books, dictionaries, the works of the great theologians of the Church: St Augustine, St Anselm, Thomas Aquinas. There was a heavy missal, full of underlinings and abbreviated notes. Half a dozen novels, some maps, a guide to Rome. There were folders and notebooks full of essays and notes, in a small, tightly written hand, neat but hard to read. Then a bundle of letters. Most were from his mother; some from people Stefan worked out were brothers and sisters. There were letters written on Dáil notepaper, from his father, short, uninformative, but often funny. There were postcards with pictures of cities: London, Paris, Vienna, Jerusalem, Rome; some had been pinned on to a wall.

That was it. A torch, batteries, some glasses and cups. They were things that should be looked at for prints. There was no reason to believe that the man who killed James Corcoran had ever been at St Patrick's College, let alone in James's room, but it should have been done in any thorough investigation.

At the bottom of the trunk there was a small tortoiseshell box with an elastic band to keep the lid on it. Inside were several pieces of paper and a champagne cork. The pieces of paper included a bill from a restaurant in Dublin, a receipt for the purchase of a book from Hodges Figgis in Dawson Street, and two tickets for the Metropole cinema in O'Connell Street. The restaurant bill and the receipt were dated: five days before James's murder.

There was a knock at the door. Stefan got up and went to open it.

Mrs Corcoran held out an envelope. She looked less strong than she had.

'This is the letter.'

She turned and hurried away.

Stefan walked back to the trunk and the pile of the contents he had laid out around him. He sat down and opened the letter. It was the same neat, slightly cramped hand he had already seen, just made bigger and more legible. The letter was written in Irish. Not a long letter. There was only one paragraph.

I will try to get home next weekend, to talk to you both. I will plant the thought now, without explanation, so the thing isn't a complete shock! I have come to realise that much as I love it, the priesthood is not for me. I think I have to face that and do what's right, what's right for me. Surely God would want that? I think I have to look at my life in new ways. Don't worry about this. I am actually very happy, in a way I have never been, in a way I have never let myself be. I don't know what that means, and I'm not sure where it will take me. It may take me out of Ireland. My life has been all 'odi et amo' till now, even if I haven't let myself face it, hating what I love, hating myself most. There is another way. I have seen that in the last few days. So, don't worry. Trust me. I will make sense of it all. I can now. I know myself better. I'm happy, remember that. That's what I have to tell you above all else. I love you both. See you next weekend.

Stefan Gillespie looked at the date on the letter: four days after the restaurant bill and bookshop receipt; the day before his death. Stefan would not immediately have made sense of 'odi et amo' in the letter, except that the Hodges Figgis receipt told him where to look. The book Corcoran had bought was a Loeb edition of Catullus's poems, Latin with an English translation. Stefan had just seen another copy of those poems on James's bookshelves as he had run his finger along a line of titles. The phrase 'odi et amo' was in there, Stefan remembered. He found the book and flicked through it. 'Odi et amo. Quare id faciam requiris. Nescio, sed fieri sentio et excrucior.' *I hate and I love. Why, perhaps you ask. I don't know, but I feel it and I am tortured.* Stefan reread the letter. There had been torture, self-hatred, now joy. He recalled the conversation with James's friend at St Patrick's, over a year ago. Happiness, a different kind of happiness. Why keep a receipt and a restaurant bill in a box with two cinema tickets and a cork? The champagne was on the bill. A wild extravagance for a seminarian at St Patrick's. Love tokens; only love turned bills and cinema tickets into treasures. The date was right. James had met someone in Dublin. Someone who changed his life. The man who killed him the next time they met.

10

Scoil Naomh Iósaf

In the windowless storeroom that contained the flotsam and jetsam of James Corcoran's murder, Superintendent Gregory read Stefan Gillespie's handwritten report, a series of scribbled notes on two days' work. Dessie MacMahon sat on a chair, leaning against the wall, smoking a Sweet Afton, content, for once, that he was doing something that felt like police work. Gregory was in no hurry to finish. Stefan waited for a response. He had one more thing; some real evidence.

'It's nothing new,' said Gregory. 'You thought he'd met someone.'

'We know now. I can't see there's any doubt it's the man he arranged to meet for a picnic in Donadea. We know the date. We don't know how they met . . . if they'd met before, but we know what they did, where they went . . .'

'None of that identifies the man, or does it?'

'Not yet. Not a year on. CID should have been out in Dublin—'

'They weren't,' snapped the superintendent. 'Next?'

Stefan looked at Dessie. Dessie sat forward on his chair.

'Two assistants in Hodges Figgis recognised a photo of Corcoran, even though he hadn't been in there since then. He was a regular customer, over three or four years. He had an account. Mostly books on theology, the classics, some poetry. They don't remember that day, or him being in there with anyone.'

'The restaurant?'

'No,' said Stefan. 'I showed them a photo. They didn't know him.'

'I doubt they did at those prices,' said Gregory. 'Cinema? Not a chance.'

'I have a theory about the Catullus.'

'Does it identify the fucking killer?'

'No, sir.'

'That's helpful then.'

'There was no Loeb Catullus in his room at St Patrick's. He already had a Latin edition at home. It seems likely he bought it as a present for this man. We know there was one poem that meant a lot to him. It's even in his letter home.'

'I don't need a lesson, Stevie. I was no slouch at Latin.' Terry Gregory grinned. 'I was thinking of going into the Church at one time. You see, no one ever believes that. If they still had the Inquisition, I might have gone for it.'

Stefan and Dessie offered the laugh the head of Special Branch expected.

'When you find a maniac with a knife in one hand and the poems of Gaius Valerius Catullus in the other, I'll get straight on to Chief Inspector Nugent.'

'This has gone cold for over a year, sir. I'm putting together what I can.'

'I know, Stevie.'

'Someone is going to be picked up, sooner or later, probably in England. That's what it looks like. When he is, there's a lot to prove . . . it will all count.'

'All right, I know that too. What about this champagne cork?'

Stefan picked up a cellophane envelope. This was something real.

'You see the metal bit on the top, where the wire's attached?'

Gregory nodded.

'There's a thumbprint. Very clear. The print we have on the beer bottle, from the picnic, is also a thumb, the same thumb. It's a fragment. It might not even be enough to identify. But it matches this. And this is more than enough.'

Gregory sniffed. It was better. It moved things forward, a little.

'Good. That's something, Stevie . . . something solid.'

He walked to the door. He looked back; a decision made.

'It's time G2 put up some fellers for the courier run. You're back on Castle duties. You can keep an eye on this.' He shook his head amiably. 'When you pick up the feller with his knife and his Latin poetry, we'll be laughing. But keep your fingers crossed our friend Nugent is doing better in London.'

The weekend brought Stefan Gillespie home to the farm below Kilranelagh, and more days there than he had spent since a Christmas that had been brief. The conversation he had to have with his father, about the coolness between Tom and David, was unavoidable. When Stefan learned what had happened, though he recognised a problem, he also recognised his father's instinctive urge, shared with most of his Protestant neighbours in Catholic Ireland, to keep his head down. He felt that what had happened didn't mean much; it could be resolved without a lot of trouble. Ultimately it was about those things Stefan had seen himself recently. It was about Tom growing up, thinking new things, finding new ways to look at the world. But if he was rebelling, David Gillespie was right to be cautious about where that led. Tom's new ideas, combined with a stubbornness that made him not unlike his father, were touching on things that affected the family from outside, in particular ways. In the past they had caused deeper problems for Stefan, David and Helena, and for Tom himself, when he was too young to know it.

Stefan went to the fields above the house, the first morning he was home. He saw Tom coming out of the trees, where a steep wooded valley that marked one of the boundaries of the farm led down to a stream. The boy was absorbed in his own thoughts. The sheep dog, Jumble, walked patiently at his heels. Tom and the dog were still inseparable. But a year ago, there would have been a game; boy and dog running, chasing. It was a small thing, but it marked real change.

Stefan waited as Tom saw him and approached.

'You were out early,' said Stefan.

'I wanted a walk.'

Father and son moved together across the field of grubby, winter sheep.

'How's *The Hobbit*?'

'It's good. I finished it.'

'That was quick.'

'I read fast enough if I like something.'

'What's it about?'

'I don't know. *The Iliad* with dwarves and dragons . . . and a lot funnier.'

'I never read it. I wouldn't imagine *The Iliad* being big on fun.'

They laughed and moved on. Tom was anticipating what was coming.

'You're still doing Latin with Mr Cashman after school?'

'Yes, I like it.'

'You know he doesn't have to do the work to get you ready for a scholarship exam. Opa's tried to pay him something, but he won't take it.'

'I know. John Byrne's doing it too.' Tom grinned. 'He doesn't like it.'

They were both postponing the reason Stefan was there.

'I wish you and Oma talked German to me when I was young. I only know a few words. That's what I want to do, German and Latin, and Greek too.'

'That's very ambitious.' Stefan smiled. 'I don't know about Greek, but I did Latin because I had to. And I didn't much enjoy it. I did German because I spoke it, so it was an easy subject. But it depends where you go to school.'

Stefan had delayed long enough.

'You know the parish priest's been to see Opa and Oma?'

There was little left of the German heritage that Stefan's mother had brought to the Gillespie family as a young woman. Helena had spoken German with him, as a child; he still spoke it well. He had visited his cousins in Germany when he was a teenager. All that had faded with time and distance, but Tom still used the German words for grandfather and grandmother, Opa, Oma.

'I know.'

'You haven't been going to Mass.'

Tom shrugged.

'And you've been lying about it to Oma and Opa. You started off making excuses for not going and when you ran out of those, you pretended you were going and never got there. What have you been doing on Sunday mornings?'

'Nothing.'

'Nothing?'

Tom shrugged again.

'There's other lads than me who don't want to go to Mass.'

'Tom, you know enough about how difficult things are . . .'

'What's that got to do with me? Nobody asked me what I thought about all that. I don't want to go. I don't see why I have to.' His face hardened. 'I don't believe in it. What's the point? It isn't school. I'm not learning anything.'

Stefan and his son said nothing for a moment.

123

'You know some of this, Tom, but not everything. Let me say it.'

Tom sniffed, irritated, impatient.

'When I married your mother, because I was a Protestant, I had to promise that any children we had would be brought up as Catholics. That didn't change because she died. It was a promise. You might say a sacred promise.'

'And would you have kept it, Daddy, if they hadn't made you?'

It was a sharper question than Stefan expected.

'All right, maybe the answer to that isn't so easy. Maybe you're right. You know a bit . . . there was a time . . . before you started school . . . I don't know if you remember it now, but you went to stay with your uncle and aunt for a while.'

'I sort of remember. I've stayed with them other times. That didn't seem any different, but I know what happened. I know people tried to take me away.'

'Maybe taking you away is putting it more strongly . . .'

Stefan stopped. There was no point trying to retell the truth.

'There was a particular priest who didn't think you should be brought up in a Protestant home, even if we did take you to Mass and send you to a Catholic school . . . and do everything we had to. It got a bit out of hand, and yes, the Church did . . . but it was sorted out. I think they knew they were wrong.'

Tom was silent. He sensed there was pain, and anger too, which his father still felt. It opened up a memory that time had not softened.

'We've kept the promise, Tom. You went to school at Talbotstown, the way they wanted. We took you to Mass or you went with your friends. You took your first communion with your friends at school. We're still keeping the promise. You've got your confirmation coming up. Then suddenly we have the parish priest complaining you're never at Mass, and

Oma and Opa don't even know. They go off on a Sunday to church in Baltinglass. And you just piss off!'

'I wouldn't have to piss off if they let me do what I want.'

'And you've told Mr Cashman you're not doing your confirmation.'

'I don't believe in it. That's what it's about. Saying you believe it.'

'At least Father Brennan doesn't know that.'

Tom stopped. He bent down, scratching Jumble under his muzzle. He was holding back anger of his own. Stefan turned, waiting for him.

Tom stood up, then smiled slightly. 'Do you believe it, Daddy?'

Stefan saw that although they had never had this conversation, his son knew the answer. It was not something he could sidestep, let alone lie about.

'I believe in what I know about the teachings of Jesus . . .'

It was weak; even Tom, at eleven, knew how weak it was.

'I have read bits of the Bible,' said Tom. 'I quite like some.'

Stefan laughed. 'That's a start.'

'You don't believe it, Daddy. You don't believe what the Church says. And it's not just about Mass, is it? Do you go to the Church of Ireland in Dublin?' Tom walked by Stefan, more confident. 'Oma doesn't think you do.'

'Well, Oma doesn't miss much.'

Stefan took out a cigarette. It felt like Tom had the upper hand.

'But you're not old enough to make that decision. You will be. But you need to make it for yourself. To make it when you know what it is you believe and what you don't. I think that takes more time than eleven years, Tom.'

'Nearly twelve.'

'More time than nearly twelve.'

'Don't you mean, shut up and do as you're told? No one

needs trouble. That's what I get from Opa. He won't say it to me, but I hear him tell Oma.'

Stefan drew on the cigarette. He tried to bring conviction to what he said next, but he knew his son would hear its absence. If he believed what had to be done, what had to be said, it was for reasons that wouldn't bear much scrutiny. He wasn't far from telling Tom to shut up and do as he was told.

'Avoiding trouble isn't such a bad thing, Tom. You need to go to Mass. You need to make your confirmation with everyone else. Maybe, as time goes on, we can say . . . you made your confirmation, that's the promise fulfilled. You'll be leaving Talbotstown next year. You'll be somewhere else, if things work out. You'll be boarding. When you're home, it will be different. For now, it is like school. I'm sorry. That's how I have to put it . . . and you have to do it.'

Later that day Stefan Gillespie took the tractor from Kilranelagh towards the long, high hill of Keadeen and the school at Talbotstown that sat in its shadow, at the furthest edge of the mountains. The tractor's link box carried a heap of cut black turf for the fires in the school rooms at Scoil Naomh Iósaf, St Joseph's School. The turf was a contribution parents made to the school through the winter and it was the Gillespies' turn. There was little else at Talbotstown, except for the crossroads and a farmyard and a shop that was only really another farmhouse, with a bar in the front parlour. It was the school and the church that brought people there. Otherwise it was a peaceful, unremarkable place; a junction of quiet roads, a scattering of fields and then Keadeen beyond.

Stefan and the school principal, Michael Cashman, said little as they unloaded the turf in the store behind the low stone building next to the church. The teacher was in his fifties; a quiet, solitary man, now teaching his second generation of children. He had a lot to say to the pupils he taught but kept his own counsel with his neighbours. He was highly thought of, commanding a respect most priests in the area assumed they had, but rarely did. He was as unremarkable as his school and the battered pipe that was never out of his mouth and was mostly unlit. He kept himself to himself. He worked unassumingly, tirelessly for his school. People knew what they owed him.

'You'll want a cup of tea, Stefan.'

'I will, Michael.'

'And the chat you came for.' The teacher smiled.

'And that, too.'

The two men sat in front of the fire in the big classroom. The fire was too small for the room, and however much turf was piled on it the children sometimes sat in their coats in the worst of the winter. Michael Cashman filled his pipe and lit it till it blazed up, but it was soon out, and he would not bother to light it again.

'I appreciate what you're doing with the Latin.'

'Ah, I enjoy it. If I'd been a secondary teacher, that's what I'd have done. So, it's a bit of recreation. I'm hammering it into Tom because I want to.'

It wasn't true, but Cashman was uncomfortable with gratitude.

'I think Tom enjoys it too,' said Stefan.

'I hope so. It's not something he has to do for a scholarship, but he can, and it will help. They like some Latin. And it will help him when he starts.'

'Is he up for a scholarship?'

'Oh, I'd say he's well up for it. It might not cover everything.'

'I reckon if we had to pay, we'd find the money,' said Stefan. This was something he had only been thinking about recently – where Tom went when he left the school at Talbotstown – but his mother and father had thought about it longer. If they needed to pay, the way the farm was now, with Stefan's Garda salary subsidising it, it would be harder than it might once have been. But a way would be found.

Michael Cashman looked into the fire, chewing his pipe.

'There's the question of where he goes.'

'Well, Knockbeg would be first. It's closest, even when he's boarding. Maybe Clongowes with a good scholarship. I doubt we'd run to that otherwise.'

Stefan listed the two Catholic boarding schools that were nearest.

'That's the conversation the parish priest had with me, so I imagine he's had it with David and Helena too.' The principal laughed. 'He'll be having it with you soon enough, if you're not fast on your heels and keep out of his way.'

'I don't mind if he does. I've nothing to argue about with him.'

'No?' said Cashman, with a look that was almost conspiratorial.

Stefan frowned. 'Should I have?'

'We should talk about the other thing, Stefan. God and confirmation!'

Stefan laughed. 'A conversation I'd like to avoid having with Father Brennan.'

'He doesn't know anything about the fact that I now have a declared atheist in sixth class, nor does he know Tom's told me he doesn't want to make his confirmation. Obviously, he does know Tom's been missing Mass. He's on the warpath. I don't need to say he takes it seriously, more seriously than if Tom was living in a Catholic family. There's a point he has to make, do you see?'

'Oh, I see very clearly, Michael.'

The principal got up and bent down by the fire, knocking the contents of his pipe, largely unburned tobacco, into it. He stood up again and put the pipe in his mouth, not caring to refill it. He was serious, thoughtful.

'The trouble is all this goes quite deep with Tom. That's what I think.'

'How do you mean?'

'I only have the gist of what happened, before he started school here, between you and the Church. I'd be bound to know something when it involved you punching the curate in the face in Baltinglass.' He smiled briefly. 'And I'm sure Tom has only a bit of it himself, but he has enough, so. Too much, I'd say.'

Stefan nodded, not sure what this meant, but recognising a truth.

'I think he'd be better off out of it, Stefan.'

'Out of what?'

Michael Cashman sat down again.

'This isn't a conversation anyone else can know about. Tom is strong willed. I don't mean he's difficult, but he's hard to shift from what he thinks. That's true on everything. Sometimes it's good and sometimes not. At his age, not everything he thinks is reasonable. Not that I'm saying it's unreasonable for him to reach a point when he doubts the existence of God. He's got there earlier than most. What he now sees . . . is that in Ireland, you keep your mouth shut.'

'Yes. I don't think he takes to that idea.'

'He doesn't. He's too young to see why he can't say what he thinks.'

'It's a strange time,' said Stefan. 'I don't know him as well as I did.'

The principal smiled. 'You'll know him again . . . in a few years.'

'You still haven't told me what "getting out of it" means.'

'What Tom feels about the Church goes deeper than whether he believes in God, or whether he's asking questions and not getting honest answers. Whatever happened when he was younger, along with all the years he's had to lead a separate life from his family on a Sunday morning . . . they have left a mark. Some children would deal with that more easily. Tom's not easy. He doesn't take things easy. Partly, it's that thing about not knowing where you belong. Being outside. Even if you rebel, you need to fit first, I think.'

'And where does that take us, as far as school goes?'

'I don't mean you give up. He could go to the Tech in the town, and it wouldn't be hard. He'd fit in well and he'd come out in a few years looking for a job. And the only effort it would have cost him would be to sit tight and shut up. You're right to want more than that. My worry is that if you put him in a Catholic boarding school, it's doubling down on everything he doesn't want. He might be getting a great education, but he'll be in and out of the chapel, on his knees, on a daily basis. If he fights, they'll give him a hard time. I don't want to say they'll knock it out of him, but he has it in him to be bloody-minded. There's no room for that. Not believing is . . . he's turning it into a way of saying who he is. I wouldn't want to put money on him staying the course.'

'That all sounds good, Michael! Thanks.' Stefan shook his head.

'I'd say you need to take another course,' said Cashman gently.

'And do what?'

'Take on the Church again. Leave it behind. It's time to change.'

Stefan said nothing, waiting for the teacher to explain.

'Take him out of it all . . . and send him to a Protestant school. Not because it's Protestant, but because it's simply something else. Put him in for a scholarship at Kilkenny or Wesley College . . . Wesley's where you were. He knows that. He won't tell you, but he's talked to me. He wants to know why he can't go there. He won't even say it to David and Helena, because you'll all tell him he can't. You'll tell him he has to do what Father Brennan says. That's it.'

'If Father Brennan's on the warpath about him missing Mass . . .'

'Time has passed, Stefan. You've done enough. You've done what you promised. Tom's had eight years of being taught how to be a Catholic, most of it from me. Until the last few months, he was the best Mass-goer in the school. He made his first communion. He's about to be confirmed by the bishop. You can stand your ground now. He's a Catholic, in every way the Church means. You only have to say that's not going to change. Tom can say it too, whether he wants to or not. Send him to the school you want to send him to. Just do it. We'll keep it quiet as long as we can, so the fuss doesn't last when it comes. There'll be a row with the priests. But he'll be twelve, going on thirteen, when he moves. I'll pretend I'm disappointed . . . while I'm working my arse off to get him a scholarship. That's my advice, Stefan. But I never said a fucking word.'

Stefan laughed.

'You do one thing, though,' said the principal. 'You tell Tom what's happening, and you tell him to keep it to himself. He will do that. I know it. Then you tell him he goes to Mass every bloody Sunday and never misses it. You also tell him he will be confirmed . . . along with everyone else in the class.'

'I see,' said Stefan, taking it in. It was another way to think, after many years of thinking only one way. It seemed to bring clarity, though he was still unsure. 'It's one hell of a lesson in deceit, Michael!'

The principal took out his tobacco and started to refill his pipe.

'Maybe it's a lesson in survival. Sometimes we have to learn those.'

Almost a month and a half had gone by at Dublin Castle. The door of the room which held the evidence from the murder of James Corcoran was locked most of the time. There was

131

nothing more to gather in Ireland, no more information to pass on to Chief Inspector Nugent at Scotland Yard, and no information from him to come to Ireland. The Metropolitan Police had pursued their inquiries, spreading out from the scene of Vikram Narayan's killing, looking for witnesses, for anyone who had seen anything, looking for the Indian's friends and contacts. The results produced nothing that tied anybody to the events of the night of the murder. There was nothing that led anywhere as far as witnesses were concerned. Shadowy figures in the streets of Soho in the blackout; a man on a bicycle, or maybe a woman; a car parked nearby, black or grey or dark green, quite big, not that big. All the other murders, with the exception of James Corcoran's, looked like chance meetings: two men who met for sex, in places where men did meet for sex; two men who almost certainly didn't know each other. But even putting together the last days of Narayan's life wasn't easy. The two areas of his life that the police were looking at were both environments where the police were unwelcome. In London's homosexual world the police were always to be feared. The ability to live any kind of ordinary life depended on secrecy. For some of the people who were working for Indian independence, the war had brought a new need for secrecy. They were being watched as they had never been watched before. For both of these groups, giving information to the police was to be avoided.

Stefan Gillespie had returned to the business of watching and reporting on his countrymen. On those who were at the fringes of the IRA. On the hard-line Republicans waiting for the defeat of Britain and, if it could happily coincide, the replacement of de Valera's government. On those with too many connections to Germany or Italy or, in anticipation of events elsewhere, to Japan. On those who were too loud in their enthusiasm for Britain as well, and on those who kept quiet about their connections with Britain but were working for the British government. As always, too, there were the reports and records kept on the men who left Ireland to fight with the British forces. The lists of these did not tell the whole story, as so many found their way to England to work and then joined up. For the first time, Stefan was sent to report on meetings of the Friends of India Society, who gathered at the Country Shop in Stephen's Green. Superintendent Gregory seemed to have decided that his relationship with Frank Nugent in London qualified him to do this.

He attended several lectures on Indian crafts and one on the life of the Buddha. The society was mostly a way for Indians in Dublin to meet socially, but there were a few IRA men who showed an unusual interest in the crafts of the subcontinent and occasionally disappeared into the back room of the Country Shop for tea and biscuits. The prime movers of the Friends of India Society were an enthusiastic English couple, Mr and Mrs Hurley-Davis, who had moved to Ireland at the beginning of the war. They were more vehement in their support of Indian nationalism than most of Dublin's small Indian community. Terry Gregory, who had little interest in what happened at the Country Shop, thought they were British agents. Stefan's reports on the society were passed to Military Intelligence, from where, once anything useful or revealing had been removed, he assumed they went to British Intelligence, probably to end up on Chief Superintendent Nugent's desk.

Stefan had not heard from Nugent on the murder cases for over a month, when he was called into Gregory's office one evening. Frank Nugent was phoning from London. There was a development, although it had not come through the investigation, and it had arrived from a very long way away.

'Nugent's got something,' said Terry Gregory. 'Another murder.'

Stefan took the telephone.

'What's happened, Frank?'

'Another one.'

'Jesus! In London?'

'No, not in London. In the Mediterranean, in Malta.'

'Malta?'

'That's right. It's come straight to the Yard because a Military Police sergeant in Valletta remembered something similar, when he was a copper. He wasn't on the case, but he couldn't miss it. The same way you didn't . . .'

'No doubt?'

'None, for my money. I've seen the photos.'

'Everything the same?'

'Yes. Happened in a park, near a queer pick-up place. The dead man was a young Maltese. No doubt he was queer. No evidence again, not so far. Don't know what the forensic work's like there. No witnesses to speak of, but maybe a sighting of the dead man with a solider, not long before. No real description of the soldier, but it fits in with what we already know. And there is some hope . . .'

'Which is?'

'Well, Malta's under siege at the moment. It's being bombed round the clock by the Germans and the Italians. No shortage of soldiers. But getting people in and out isn't easy. Everything comes by convoy, and they're being attacked. So, what we know is that since Vikram Narayan was killed in Greek Street, seven weeks have gone by. In that time only a couple of hundred soldiers have arrived in Malta. Some were already in Gibraltar when Narayan died. In terms of soldiers who were here seven weeks ago and are in Malta now . . . we're talking about less than a hundred. That's suddenly a small pool to fish in.'

'Very small.'

'He has to be there, doesn't he?'

'Well, I'd say so.'

'So, I've booked your flight,' said Nugent, laughing.

134

'Booked my what?'

'This is a Metropolitan Police and Garda inquiry. You're the one who's produced the fingerprints that are going to hang this feller. I don't know whether there'll be an argument about where he's hanged. I suppose we have the numbers. But I assume you want to be in Malta, to find him and arrest him.'

'And how do I get there, Frank?'

'Get to London and the RAF will do the rest. Plane to Gibraltar, on to Malta. Always a chance of getting shot down over the Med. Apart from that . . .'

Stefan looked up at Superintendent Gregory.

'Do you know about this, sir? Am I going to Malta?'

'I'll talk to the Commissioner, but we want this off the books.' He grinned. 'And done right. Plenty of room for Scotland Yard to cock it up.'

The words were for Nugent to hear. Stefan returned to the phone.

'Well, seems that's what's happening . . .'

'I'll fill you in when you get to London. You'll need to leave tomorrow.'

'All right.'

'One thing . . . Hindu Narayan, Vikram's sister . . .'

'Yes.'

'She was knocked down by a car. A month or so ago. She was lucky. The car was going some. She was injured but she came away with not much more than a broken ankle. It was her head more than her leg they were worried about.' Stefan almost heard a smile. 'But she was fed up carrying her tin hat, so she'd put it on. These things happen in the blackout, of course. You wouldn't think so with everyone crawling along. The car drove off . . . driver didn't stop.'

The last words were slower, almost hesitant.

'Anyway, she came out the other side,' said Frank Nugent after a pause.

'You make it sound as if you don't think it was an accident.'

'She doesn't think it was.' The chief inspector laughed. 'She reckons Special Branch did it, because she was asking too many questions about her brother. You've met her. You won't be surprised she doesn't trust anybody.'

'Let alone you.'

'Let alone me. I have tried.'

'So, who do you think would want to harm her, Frank?'

'I don't know what I think. It was very odd . . . that's all I can say. She was just coming out of the restaurant. I don't know why I'm telling you this. It's nothing to do with the investigation.' Nugent stopped, as if not convinced of that. 'Anyway, if we find the murderer, she won't need to ask any more questions. She might not want to know what really happened, but I think she ought to understand that I've done everything I can to find Vikram's killer.'

The change of subject had contained a change of tone. Stefan heard concern and uncertainty, different from the breezy assurance of what went before. And there was some-thing personal in it. It seemed to matter that Narayan's sister knew what Nugent had done. But the breeziness returned. A few more words set up another phone call to finalise the arrangements. And then the Englishman was gone. Stefan handed the phone back to Superintendent Gregory, who was scribbling notes in his familiar, virtually illegible scrawl.

'What do they want me for, sir?'

Gregory looked up and shrugged. He considered for a few seconds.

'I can think of a number of reasons. Given where all this started, they still have it in mind this feller might be some mad Irish queer. Once the English get hold of an idea, you have the bollocks of a job getting them to let go. And if he is Irish, whether he's a British soldier or not, a Guard's name in the papers will hammer that home. And to be fair, Chief Inspector

Nugent needs to be sure. They've got a lot of murders, but they don't have much on this man. They're not going to catch him red-handed. Mad or not, he leaves no trace. It's only a bit of circumstantial evidence that will identify him. Now there's a chance. And we have the only solid evidence. You're the officer who found the complete print. So, if you're there when the arrest is made, that looks good in court.'

Stefan nodded.

'Then there's the politics,' continued Gregory. 'If it all goes wrong, and you don't find anyone, it spreads the blame. Scotland Yard won't mind shrugging it off as if we're the ones who pushed the thing when there wasn't enough to go on. Sure, wasn't it all about keeping on the right side of the fucking ungrateful, neutral, bastard Irish? Because you can bet your life there's already a row about this in London. The British Army won't take kindly to a civvy policeman poking his nose into their business in the middle of a war. They won't care about the other crimes. You know how these things go, Stevie. This is Military Police territory. If there's a butchering maniac in the ranks, he's their butchering maniac. Nugent will get a cold reception in Malta, I'd say.'

Superintendent Gregory paused for a moment, then grinned. 'It may do him no harm if an Irish detective gets an even colder one.'

PART TWO

DE PROFUNDIS

*T*he much looked-forward-to Charlie Chaplin film, The Great Dictator, has arrived at long last in Malta, and will be shown at the Manoel Theatre. The Great Dictator was produced, written and directed by Charlie Chaplin, and in it he plays the dual role of Hynkel, Dictator of Tomania, and a Jewish barber . . . This is the first film in which Charlie Chaplin talks. The Great Dictator has been shown all over America and in the non-dictatorship countries of Europe and has been everywhere acclaimed as one of his greatest comedies.

The following qualified in a Colloquial Maltese Test and have been awarded £10 each by the General Officer Commanding: - L/Cpl. Gaunt, J., C.M.P.; L/Sgt. Andrews, W., 24th (F) Coy, R.E.; Capt. Bolton, J.R., R.A.M.C.

Times of Malta, 1941

11

Mare Nostrum

Malta, 1941

The Sunderland flying boat flew east from Gibraltar through the night. It would reach Malta just before dawn. The plane was safe enough leaving the Rock. It would not be at risk from the fighters of the Luftwaffe and the Regia Aeronautica until it came close to the tiny island that sat between Italy and the coast of North Africa. It was at its most vulnerable there, where German and Italian planes from Sicily dominated the skies, but as a solitary plane, emerging from the western darkness, close to dawn and a lull in the bombing of the island, it had every chance of slipping unseen into the RAF's seaplane base at Kalafrana. The Sunderland carried precious spare parts for the handful of decrepit RAF fighters that barely defended Malta against almost daily bombing. It also carried medical supplies, a generator, a dozen searchlights. It was little enough. The RAF kept its fighters flying by cannibalising the ones shot down in ever-increasing numbers. Food and fuel and ammunition, which were all running out on the island, and the desperately needed replacement aircraft could only be brought in by ship, and it was a long time since a convoy had got through from Gibraltar. Too many ships were being sunk to risk more losses. Malta was under siege and the siege was becoming costly in every way. In Berlin and Rome, it was believed that the island that stood in the way of the campaign to sweep the British out of North Africa and take control of Egypt and the route to India could not last much longer. If Britain was slow to put its ships in harm's way to save Malta, it was because some in London believed the same thing.

Stefan Gillespie sat in the front cabin with Frank Nugent. He had taken the usual route across the Irish Sea to London, then travelled with the English policeman to Poole on the south coast to board the Sunderland. The plane flew across the Bay of Biscay and followed the Spanish and Portuguese coast to Gibraltar, where it stopped to refuel and pick up cargo. The other passengers were senior army and navy officers, along with three young pilots, barely out of training, eager for action. The military men would travel on from Malta to Alexandria and Egypt, the Sunderland's final destination. The pilots were for Malta itself. The older men chatted cheerfully with the young to begin with, but after a while they ran out of things to say. They knew what the pilots hadn't yet begun to think about: outnumbered and with equipment the Luftwaffe could outpace and outgun, the young men would probably not be in Malta for very long. Like spare parts in the seaplane's hold, the pilots were there to replace what had already been shot out of the island's skies. The odds against them not being shot down in their turn were not high.

Between England and the Rock, Stefan Gillespie and Frank Nugent said little about the case. For a time, they asked each other more personal questions than they had before. Stefan spoke about his home in Wicklow, his son; he spoke briefly, in the matter-of-fact tone that went with the passing years, about the death of his wife Maeve, Tom's mother, simply as something that had happened that was no longer very different to many things that happen. At least that was how it could be talked about. Nugent spoke a lot about India. There was, as Stefan suspected, something Irish buried in him. His father had been from Waterford, his mother was English; he had been born in Cork. The family moved to India when Frank was a young child. He grew up in India; that was his place in the world, though he didn't say it. He went to school there; he spoke Hindustani and other Indian languages as easily as he spoke English. His father had worked for India's vast railway system and loved the country. His mother hated it. She did what she had to do, but when Frank's father died, she left for England within a week of his funeral. She lived in a bungalow in Worthing that contained not a single memory of over thirty years of her life on the subcontinent. Nugent had tried living in England himself. He lasted two years. He told the story easily, in little more than a few wry sentences. But Stefan was surprised how abruptly it stopped. The English policeman, who saw himself as an Indian policeman, was comfortable with the past and with some well-rehearsed anecdotes. However, he had very little to say about the present that wasn't work. He didn't say he was single, but no family was mentioned. Stefan recognised that silence as a barrier.

It was obvious to both Stefan and Frank that there was at least one Intelligence officer on the plane. He was the only one who showed interest in the two policemen. When they were waiting at Gibraltar for the Sunderland to refuel, he insisted on buying them a drink in the mess at the seaplane base. He introduced himself as Major Courtney, also en route to Malta. He expected some kind of explanation of what they were doing and was irritated by Nugent's cheerful refusal to give him one. He was more irritated to discover that Stefan was not even a British policeman. Frank Nugent offered no explanation for his journey to Malta, or for the fact that an Irish detective was travelling with him. Stefan offered no more than a polite interest in the Rock and went out to look at it. Nugent followed him, still amused. And then they boarded the plane again.

As the seaplane continued east in the darkness, the cabin was much emptier. The young pilots had drunk what they could during two hours in Gibraltar and had brought a bottle of whiskey on board. They started into that shortly after taking off, with the result that they were quickly asleep. Several officers sat further forward in the cabin, including the now sour Major Courtney, who sat as far from them as he could. Stefan Gillespie and Frank Nugent had the seats at the back of the cabin to themselves. Chief Inspector Nugent took a folder from his briefcase. He passed several sheets of paper over to Stefan: they were a closely typed list of names and army ranks.

'These are all – almost all – the soldiers who travelled to Malta between the date of Narayan's murder and the death in Malta. It may not be complete, but they should be able to fill in anything that's missing when we get there. Most of these men arrived on one ship, within a couple of weeks of Vikram's death. A few came in by plane over a longer period. There are only seventy-three. They include regular troops, Royal Engineers, medical corps and some Intelligence officers. I've also got a list of RAF bods. Naval personnel are more difficult to track. They come and go from Gib, North Africa, Egypt. But we start with the idea the man we're looking for is a soldier. If witnesses said they saw anyone in the vicinity of any of the murders, it was a soldier. That's consistent.'

'So, we just pitch up and fingerprint the lot of them?'

'That's the deal.'

'The deal?'

'This hasn't gone down well with the army.'

'Terry Gregory didn't think it would.'

'He was right. There's been a bit of political argy-bargy. In fact, we're only here because the Colonial Office managed to overrule the Ministry of War. I think they pointed out that the empire on which the sun never sets is asking the people of Malta to sit there while the Jerries and the Eyeties drop bombs on them. From what I hear, apart from some Hurricanes, there's only a few clapped-out fighters, including fucking biplanes, for God's sake, to stop them. The last thing they need is a British soldier roaming the island with a carving knife. And that's what they've got. It's a small place. They want him caught and they want him out of there with a noose round his neck. Someone had the sense to realise the Military Police are too busy directing traffic and picking up drunken squaddies. Don't quote me. They do have an investigation branch. Officially, we're to assist the Provost Marshall and his merry men.'

'What about the Maltese police?'

'I don't know. Nobody mentioned them.'

'Isn't the dead man a Maltese civilian?'

'You're not in Eire now, old son,' laughed Nugent. 'In the colonies the military outrank the colonial police. I should know. I'm an Indian policeman. We're only a step up from the damned natives. Hardly to be trusted, let alone in the middle of war.' He looked more serious. 'And I'm not joking, Stefan.'

As the Sunderland droned through the night, more of the passengers drifted into some kind of sleep. Frank Nugent was one of them. Stefan Gillespie stayed awake for a time. He looked through the files the Englishman had laid out on the seat beside them. These were extracts from the investigations into all the murders that stretched from Donadea in Kildare to a park beside the Grand Harbour in Valletta. Stefan had seen the full files only briefly, in Nugent's office at Scotland Yard, fat yet empty of any useful content. He had not read them through in any detail but then there wasn't any detail, at least not detail that did anything other than describe the dead bodies. He was struck again by the barbarity and viciousness of the attacks. He was also struck, for the first time, by how little evidence had been left behind. It seemed unreasonable. So many killings, so little to hold on to. It was no different with the latest. No witnesses, no forensic evidence, no connections that led anywhere as far as the victim was concerned. They had only what came from Dublin, the fingerprints, and the assumption that the man was a soldier, now in the Malta garrison. Stefan Gillespie gathered the files together and pushed them into Nugent's briefcase. He took a cigarette and lit it and stared through a window at the dark.

Stefan had spent one night in London, sleeping in the room above the High Commission's offices in Regent Street. He knew from Frank Nugent that Hindu Narayan was back at the restaurant after the accident in Regent Street. She was only across the road. He felt he ought to see her. He phoned her at the Veeraswamy. She was cautious when she spoke to him. She assumed he was still in contact with Chief Inspector Nugent. He told her he was, but it wasn't the reason he wanted to see her. That wasn't entirely true. Frank Nugent had suggested he make contact with her, since she wouldn't talk to him. It wasn't a suggestion Stefan followed only because of Nugent, however. He was curious about Hindu Narayan.

He met her outside the restaurant in Regent Street, not long after arriving in London. They went to the Lyons Corner House at Piccadilly. She talked about her ankle and the time it took to heal and how inconvenient it all was.

'I did take to sleeping in a shelter or in the Underground. Otherwise it took me so long to get out of bed and get somewhere safe, if the sirens went off . . . normally, I used to wait for a raid and then make a dash.' She laughed. 'But dashing was out of the question for a while . . . So, I tried staying in shelters, but I gave up in the end. I hobble a bit, still . . . but I dash as quickly as I can, when dashing is required. I can't live down there like that . . . not every night.'

Stefan nodded. He had been in London enough to take more risks than he had at first. It wasn't entirely rational, but it went with the way of life in the city. There was a belief, almost in London's air at night, that if your number was up, it was up. Otherwise, you had as much chance as anybody else, inside or outside a shelter. It wasn't that people didn't care about their safety, but the bombing had been going on long enough to be familiar. People took chances.

Hindu Narayan pushed him on his contact with Frank Nugent.

'That's why I'm in London.'

'That's cosy. I'm surprised Indian politics is so interesting in Dublin.'

The remark was a kind of sneer, but Stefan was aware it interested Garda Special Branch and Irish Military Intelligence more than he had known himself until recently. He thought it was unlikely she wouldn't know that too. But if her words were meant to show contempt, they were also probing.

'I'm here because a man was murdered in Ireland. I did tell you about it before. It was over a year ago. He died the way your brother died. He was strangled, then mutilated with a knife, very violently, when he was dead. The reason I'm involved is because we're looking for the killer. That's all it is.'

Hindu said nothing. She stared past Stefan at Piccadilly Circus.

'There has been another murder now,' said Stefan. 'The same, exactly the same. In Malta. I think Chief Inspector Nugent tried to tell you that, didn't he?'

'He's tried to tell me a lot. Even when I was in the hospital.'

'Hindu, whatever's going on in terms of India and the English Special Branch and who Mr Nugent's watching and who he isn't . . . I don't know. You do know. You have friends who know. Your brother knew, I suppose.' Stefan spoke carefully; he knew more than he was saying. But he was used to half-truths. 'This is something else. Nothing to do with any of that. It's about a vicious killer.'

'Perhaps,' she said quietly. 'I wanted to believe something else. It makes it much harder ... much harder, when a man like him ... like Chief Inspector ...'

'There is a good chance we can find Vikram's murderer now. That's why I'm going to Malta with Chief Inspector Nugent.'

'But why him? Why is he the one doing this?'

'It just turned out that way,' said Stefan.

It had turned out that way. He was unsure the word 'just' explained it.

The Indian woman nodded.

'I still can't be sure Mr Nugent had nothing to do with my "accident".'

'Why? What could he gain from that?'

'I kept asking questions about Vikram.'

'And did you find out anything?'

'I don't know. I tell myself it's all paranoia sometimes, I suppose. Or am I trying to make myself believe what I want to believe? Frank wants me to know he's trying to help. I don't want his help. I despise him. That's the truth.'

Stefan was conscious that Hindu had used Nugent's first name.

'The man still has to be caught,' he said.

'I tried to find out what I could,' continued Hindu Narayan. 'Whether I was right about what I thought or not, I didn't trust the police. Even if Vikram wasn't killed by them or IPI or some thug who worked for Chief Inspector Nugent, there were things nobody was asking. That's how it felt. My brother had been ... frightened is the word, in the last few weeks of his life. He was suddenly desperate to get out of England. I still think ... I thought that had something to do with why he died. I couldn't believe something so ... arbitrary, so futile. I tried to talk to his friends, people he knew ...' She waited for a moment. 'I am not talking about Indian friends, or political friends, I mean men he was close to. They avoided me. They got angry. There's a man he was . . . someone Vikram cared about a lot. He has a photography shop in Brixton. I went to see him. When I started asking questions he told me to go. He was shouting at me . . . upset, yes, but angry with me . . . then he cried. He begged me to leave him alone. It was the same . . . the same as Vikram, as if he was afraid of something. Yet the only people Vikram needed to be afraid of were the police.'

'You have to understand that the world your brother—'

'I know all that, Mr Gillespie. This was more. It was more.'

She looked at him for a moment and then shook her head. 'Am I looking for things that aren't there? I don't know any more.'

The conversation was over. Stefan knew Hindu Narayan believed what he had told her. It mattered that she did. He was aware that it mattered too, by proxy, that Frank Nugent wanted her to believe him. And it was the truth. What was happening in Malta, the search for the murderer, was all true. Stefan wanted to believe that the other things he knew, that Hindu's brother had been a double agent, working for Indian Political Intelligence, had nothing to do with it. He believed it, but he carried the deceit like a weight, nevertheless. By Lyons Corner House, at the entrance to the Underground, Hindu reached out and shook his hand.

'I hope you find this man in Malta, Mr Gillespie.'

'I think we will, Miss Narayan.' He smiled. 'You know it's Stefan.'

Hindu Narayan smiled too, for the first time with amusement.

'I do.'

She walked down the Underground steps, hobbling a little. He watched her disappear and turned away. He was glad most of what he said had been true.

*

149

The conversation with Hindu Narayan came back to Stefan Gillespie as he looked out of the window at streaks of pale, orange light spreading in the sky. The flying boat was descending. He could feel the change in pitch and hear a heavier drone from the engines. One of the crew moved through the cabin, telling passengers to fasten their safety belts. Frank Nugent had been asleep. He stretched, yawning. Dawn was barely visible, but as Stefan looked out again, he saw the waters of the Mediterranean, now darker than the sky.

'Almost there,' said Nugent. 'And still in one piece. Not bad.'

'You thought we'd be shot down?'

'Apparently it doesn't happen a lot.'

'I'm a neutral.' Stefan grinned. 'The word is probably out.'

Chief Inspector Nugent gathered up papers and clipped his briefcase shut. Stefan's head was still full of Hindu Narayan and the Lyons Corner House.

'When I saw Hindu Narayan, she was talking about a friend of her brother's. He has a photography shop in Brixton. Did you ever speak to him?'

'I think she was trying to run her own investigation at one point.'

'Because she thought you weren't.'

'Something like that.' Nugent's voice was brisker. 'But yes, I talked to him. Eddie Hopkins. I don't know if he was a boyfriend or they were just acquaintances. Hopkins is certainly one of the fraternity, put it that way. But he doesn't seem to know anything. He wasn't around at the time. He's not part of the Soho crowd. He hadn't seen Narayan for a week or more. What about him?'

'Well, I was wondering about that photographic equipment.'

'Yes, he bought it all there. Still can't see why. It was professional stuff. Expensive. And sod all use to anybody for taking snaps. Hopkins didn't know what he wanted it for. But I'd say he was happy enough to take the money.'

Stefan nodded. Nugent's investigation had been thorough, whatever Hindu thought. But it had been no more than a series of loose ends till Malta.

'You found a used film in his pocket, didn't you?'

'Yes. Didn't get anything out of it. Couple of shots of a man and a woman in a café, probably a railway buffet . . . could have been one of the big stations. Then there were some shots of the funeral at Kensal Green . . . where Mac Liammóir saw Vikram. Mostly out of focus. He could hardly use these lenses. Noël Coward was at the funeral.' Nugent grinned. 'The only surprise. There were some decent shots of Mac Liammóir with him. Who knows why?'

Stefan laughed. 'Perhaps he was a fan.'

Nugent shrugged. 'Whatever he was, he wasn't a photographer.'

The morning was suddenly there, as the heavy Sunderland glided down to the sea, closer and closer. There was enough light to catch the waves. Stefan could see the coast. Low, white cliffs, and beyond that what seemed like white, flat land and white stone in the pale light of dawn. What he glimpsed through the window was the corner of an island of tiny, stone-walled fields and bare, rocky land, scattered with small buildings that were simply another shade of white. The hull of the plane hit the water with a judder that could be heard as well as felt. The shock pushed Stefan into his seat. Engines raced; then they were quieter. The hull rocked as the Sunderland sailed into the RAF's seaplane base.

12

Kalafrana

The tender carried the passengers from the Sunderland flying boat to the quayside at Kalafrana. Even in the early morning, Stefan Gillespie could feel the heat the day would bring. At home winter was barely over, but the scent in the air, here where the sea met the shore, had warmth in it already. There was a brightness about the sky that gave clarity to the broad strokes that painted the dark sea, the grey-white land, the blue sky with its last tinge of orange on the horizon. At the quayside, a row of corrugated-iron sheds and breeze-block huts were draped in pale camouflage nets and painted in shades of brown and white. The soldiers and airmen, waiting by a row of Bedford trucks for the Sunderland to unload, wore the British Army's sand-toned tropical gear in various combinations of shorts and trousers, shirts and jackets. At either end of the quay two camouflage-covered anti-aircraft guns pointed up at the clear morning. Vans and staff cars waited by the steps up from a pontoon, and as Stefan Gillespie and Frank Nugent reached the top of the steps, a tall, lanky soldier walked towards them. He wore the red peaked cap of a Military Policeman. His shirt and his shorts were neatly pressed, in sharp contrast to most of the men in crumpled, sweat-stained outfits that were barely uniforms.

'Chief Inspector Nugent and Inspector Gillespie?'

He held out his hand. In the other he held two tin hats. He was older than either Stefan or Frank Nugent, but not much. His face was lined; dark and tanned from many months of Malta's sun. He exuded a kind of orderly calm, but a broad smile broke up the clipped officiousness of a very military voice.

'Jack Yates, Lieutenant, Provost Marshall's office.'

'Good to be here, Lieutenant, finally,' said Nugent.

'Bit of a trek. You'll need these.'

He handed them each a tin hat. They put down their cases.

'You'll want them soon enough. You've hit a bit of a lull this morning. It's not good at the moment. We get Jerry and Eyetie bombs. Hard to tell which is worse. The Jerries know what they're aiming at, so we can work out what they're doing mostly. The Eyeties drop them anywhere. No idea what they're after. If you're here long . . . you'll be glad to get back to London for a break.'

Yates turned to a younger man behind him, in a less well-presented combination of khaki shorts and tunic that bore an MP's armband on one sleeve and a corporal's stripes on the other. He wore thick-lensed glasses. In contrast to the officer's tanned face, his skin was pale. If Yates fitted, he looked out of place.

'I'll take that, sir.' The corporal took Nugent's case as the chief inspector reached for it. He took Stefan's too. 'And yours, sir . . .' He grinned. 'That's the way. Officers don't carry their bags. Can't have them straining themselves.'

'Jimmy Gaunt,' said Yates. 'If you want anything, ask him. Never mind if he looks a bit of a twit, he knows his way round this island, don't you, Corporal?'

'On a good day, sir.'

The lieutenant got into an open-topped, camouflaged Humber Snipe. Stefan Gillespie and Frank Nugent sat in the

153

back. Corporal Gaunt was at the wheel. They left the Sunderland, Kalafrana and the Mediterranean behind.

The Humber pulled out of the base on to a dirt road. As it joined a metalled road, cracked and pitted, Gaunt stopped, waiting for a low-loader to pass. On it was the fuselage of a Hurricane fighter, along with sections of wing and cockpit. The fuselage was black, buckled. It had been burning not long ago.

'Bastards,' said Lieutenant Yates. 'Most of our fighters belong in a bloody museum. u/s the lot. They only keep them flying by cannibalising what's shot down. Let's hope the poor fucker got out OK. We're running out of pilots too.'

The moment of harsher reflection fell away almost immediately, and as they drove to Valletta and reached the perimeter road that ran between the city's great walls and the Grand Harbour, the lieutenant chatted idly about the city and the island, the bombing and the food shortages, and the weather, in more or less the same easy voice. The walls of rock and stone that rose up around the peninsular on which the tiny city of Valletta was built were enough to drown out Lieutenant Yates' commentary, for Stefan at least. The sand-coloured bastions soared high above them; massive stone blocks built from the hewn rock on which they had their foundations. It was monumental building on a scale Stefan Gillespie had never seen. He heard the Military Police officer describe the building of the city, almost four hundred years ago, by the Grand Master of the Knights of St John, Jean de Valette, after his tiny force of knights had defeated a vastly superior Turkish army of invasion. The city was to be both an impregnable fortress for the future and a celebration of victory. A recognition of sacrifice; a place of beauty that gave thanks to God. As far as the knights were concerned, they, and God, had saved European civilisation. Jack Yates delivered his words on the saving of civilisation with a wry smile.

'So, nothing new under the sun.'

He turned back, offering Stefan and Frank a cigarette.

'But times change. I'm not sure God allowed for German bombers.'

Stefan Gillespie had heard only snatches of what Lieutenant Yates had to say about the ancient siege and the siege that was happening now. Corporal Gaunt broke into the commentary intermittently, to correct his lieutenant. It was clear, when Stefan did catch a few words, that the corporal knew the city's history in detail, while his superior didn't think details mattered. Eventually the two Military Policemen were talking to each other. Neither Stefan nor Frank Nugent was listening anyway. Nugent was absorbed in his own thoughts. He had been here before, on a ship that had stopped over, en route from India. Stefan continued to take in the great walls of Valletta; they needed no explanation. He also took in the rubble and the broken buildings that lined the harbour; that needed no explanation either. Looking across the Grand Harbour to the buildings on the peninsulas opposite Valletta, which Stefan now knew were called the Three Cities, thick smoke rose from recent bombing. In the moorings along the road into Valletta, there were British ships, large and small, in battered disrepair, smashed and holed, many half-sunk in their berths.

The Humber Snipe reached the end of the harbour, with its breakwater on one side of the road and the seaward end of the city walls on the other. Here stood the fortress of St Elmo, guarding the approaches from the Mediterranean. Once the headquarters of the Knights of St John, now of the British Army, St Elmo was built of the same sandstone as everything else; and like everything else it was the target of the Luftwaffe and Regia Aeronautica. The Humber crossed the bridge over the great ditch surrounding the fort, into the outer bastion. Corporal Gaunt slowed to a crawl to negotiate a building and part of a wall that had been bombed the previous night. Dozens of soldiers were clearing rubble from the roadway. There was a heavy cast-iron skeleton in the debris.

'Lost an ack-ack last night,' said Yates. 'Junkers.'

Jimmy Gaunt halted the vehicle as two men walked across the road with a stretcher. The man on the stretcher was dead, only now pulled from the rubble. He was the drab colour of the dust and stone that had crushed the life out of him.

The Military Police vehicle turned up a ramp and drove through a dark archway, into an inner courtyard, bright and elegant, cloister-like. The corporal stopped in front of a pair of high open doors, leading to a cool, stone interior.

'Provost Marshall wants to have a chat first, gentlemen.' Yates smiled. 'That's how he is. Urgent, whether it is or not. Accommodation front . . . afterwards.'

The two policemen followed the lieutenant into the building.

Inside it was almost cold. The roof was high, leading up through two storeys with a wide stone staircase to one side. Ahead were more double doors, heavily carved, and a large, shadowy room. Stefan could see an altar on the far wall, but between the doors and the altar were packing cases and wooden crates. The Military Police officer turned to the left and knocked on a door. He opened it immediately and then followed as Stefan Gillespie and Frank Nugent entered.

It was another big room, with a huge mahogany desk at the centre. There were bookshelves and filing cabinets. The walls were lined with maps of the Mediterranean and the island of Malta. A small, nervy-looking man sat at the desk. He didn't get up, but simply watched Stefan and Frank curiously.

'Chief Inspector Nugent, Inspector Gillespie, Colonel.'

'Thank you, Yates.'

The lieutenant left, closing the door.

'Colonel Macgregor, Provost Marshall. IC Military Police, Malta.'

Only now did the man stand up and walk round to shake hands.

'So, welcome to Malta.' The accent was Scottish, though barely.

'Thank you, sir,' said Nugent.

'Yes, sir.' Stefan echoed the words.

'I'd appreciate your ID.' The colonel smiled amiably. 'Form's sake.'

The chief inspector opened his briefcase and took out his British identity card and his police warrant card. Stefan Gillespie took his passport and his Garda warrant card from his jacket. Macgregor took them and returned to his desk. He sat and peered at the documents. He wrote a long note in a ledger.

'I'll hang on to these for a bit. Jack Yates will get them back to you.'

He picked up Stefan's passport and looked at it more closely.

'A diplomatic passport, Mr Gillespie.' He used the word 'mister' purposefully, as if he was deliberately avoiding the use of the police rank. He laughed. 'Don't see many of those. It won't confer any special privileges here.'

'I wouldn't expect it to, Colonel.'

'Good.'

The Provost Marshall looked at them for a few more seconds. He was being scrupulously polite, but both men knew that they were not welcome.

'I won't say the announcement of your arrival wasn't a surprise, Nugent.'

The colonel made a point of addressing only the English policeman.

Frank Nugent made no reply.

'You do know what's happening here, I presume?'

'I know what I've read in the papers, sir. And I was briefed in London.'

'I take it you've read something in the papers too, Gillespie?'

'I have.'

'Really?' Macgregor sniffed. 'I'd be interested to know what the Irish papers have to say about the situation here. Since you get your news from Berlin as well as London, you may have a different perspective on it all, eh?'

The words were said pleasantly, but there was a sneer behind them.

'I don't know, sir. We're mostly kept in a state of terrible ignorance in Ireland. It's the censors. They do a grand job, altogether. We're so busy making sure what comes from Berlin doesn't offend London, and what comes from London doesn't offend Berlin, that we get hardly any news. A lot of blank spaces but plenty on what's happening round the country's cattle markets.'

Stefan spoke with an expression of almost puzzled seriousness. Frank Nugent's smile struggled to avoid broadening into a grin. The colonel pursed his lips. His words were intended to insult the Irishman, not give amusement.

The Provost Marshall got up and walked to where a map of Malta hung.

'Slap bang between North Africa and Italy, which means we're a pain in the backside for German and Italian convoys trying to get troops and supplies to North Africa. We sink a lot of their ships. It started with the Duce invading Egypt and wanting to make Malta an Italian province, but he made such a cock-up that Herr Hitler had to go into Africa and sort out the mess, and that means they have to see this little island rather differently. They're reluctant to invade for some reason, though God knows why. If they hammered us hard enough and put in enough troops . . . But in lieu of that the aim is to blast Malta into as many pieces as possible and starve us of supplies, especially fuel. They're doing a pretty good job. They assume a tipping point, at which the Malta Garrison surrenders.'

Colonel Macgregor returned to his desk.

'You might as well sit down.' He sniffed again, as if bored now.

The two policemen moved to chairs in front of the desk.

'Most of what we have in the way of aircraft consists of knocked-up Gladiators and obsolete Swordfish. The Messerschmitts fly them out of the sky. The RAF has some Hurricanes now, but too few to even things up. We've yet to see a Spitfire. There's a limit to how many ships the Navy can send to the bottom of the Med to get supplies in. And when you look at the map . . .' Macgregor gestured to the map on the wall. 'You see where Sicily is. Full of bloody airfields. They come when they like. And mostly they do what they like. Sorry if that's a statement of the bleeding obvious, but when we're being visited by one of our neutral friends from the Emerald Isle, it is worth stating.'

The Provost Marshall took out a cigarette.

'You won't find many people with a lot of time for Irish neutrality, Mr Gillespie. When people are dying, one does know where one's friends are.'

Stefan said nothing.

'So, the dead man, this Maltese chap. A very unpleasant murder.'

The colonel had said what he wanted to say. It was time for business.

'Of course, I'm very unhappy that this man was killed in Valletta – even more unhappy that it seems, as things stand, that the perpetrator may have been a British serviceman.' Macgregor opened a file on his desk. 'This is the information I have been sent from Scotland Yard, Nugent. These other murders, which I've only just found out about, do appear to be related. Hard to see it any other way. The thing is appalling . . . bloody appalling.'

'Yes, sir,' said Nugent. 'That is why we're here and why—'

The Provost Marshall cut the chief inspector off.

'Looking at this frankly disgusting evidence ... we're dealing with a pervert. We know that. Let's be honest, with a world of perverts. In a world like that, we can't be surprised at some of the things that ... shocked, but not surprised.' The Provost Marshall stubbed out his cigarette firmly. 'I have kept details about the death, the manner of the death, as quiet as possible. As far as these other murders are concerned ... I have not let that go beyond these four walls ... My Special Investigation Branch officers are handling it.'

Frank Nugent and Stefan Gillespie exchanged a glance. Macgregor had stopped, abruptly, as if he had said all that was necessary.

'Presumably the Maltese Police are involved, sir?' said Nugent.

'In so far as they need to be, I think, Chief Inspector. They were called to the scene when the body was found. They have attempted to find civilian witnesses ... to no avail it has to be said. A couple of people saw a man in uniform somewhere nearby, around the time ... in the blackout. There are thousands of soldiers in Valletta some nights. In reality, there's nothing. Looking through the details from these other investigations, it's much the same story here: no evidence, no forensic material, no fingerprints, and no weapon.'

Chief inspector Nugent nodded.

'It's very consistent, sir. Very brutal ... almost frenzied. Yet the man has enough about him to make sure that nothing gets left behind ... hardly anything. Isn't that a good reason to cast the net quite wide, in terms of the public?'

'I want this pervert caught as much as anybody,' replied Macgregor. 'But I will be frank with you: there are other considerations, as far as the public goes. This is no time to put an announcement on the front page of the *Times of Malta*, about something that could be a major embarrassment to the

British Army. We rely on the loyalty of the Maltese people; they have to have faith in us.'

Nugent looked at Stefan Gillespie again. Stefan shrugged. He already knew his opinion was not something the Provost Marshall would want to hear.

'And what if there's another murder?' asked the English policeman.

Colonel Macgregor didn't answer. He was not used to being contradicted.

'If it did happen again, sir, if it looks as if things have been covered up.'

'It's not a question of covering up, Nugent. It's a question of discretion.'

'As you have no suspect, sir . . .'

'I've told you that, Nugent. You know anyway.'

'But we do have the fingerprints, courtesy of the Garda Síochána.'

Colonel Macgregor looked at Stefan Gillespie, almost reluctantly.

'I can't say I'm happy with the way I'm being asked to approach that.'

'It seems like it's all there is,' said Stefan quietly.

'If it works,' continued Frank Nugent, 'if the man is identified, he can be arrested and returned to Britain. Minimum of fuss. You have your . . . discretion.'

'I am acting on it, Chief Superintendent. I have instructions to do so, after all.' The Provost Marshall did not like being told what to do either. 'Soldiers who arrived in Malta after the date you've given us will be fingerprinted. I have a good man in my Special Investigation Branch. Again, it is not necessary to involve the local police. It is an army matter. But it's wishful thinking to say some connection with the murder won't be made in the garrison. That kind of rumour isn't easy to control. Once loose, Extemplo Libyae magnas it Fama per urbes, etc.'

161

'Rumour than which no other evil is swifter,' said Stefan wryly. 'But in this case, six murders on, there seems to be a greater evil than a few rumours.'

'Thank you, Mr Gillespie.' Macgregor looked surprised that the words of Virgil he had thrown out as if they proved something had been understood. 'I take your point, obvious as it is. I think the interests of the British Army, in a theatre of war, are probably not best served by the opinions of an Irishman.'

Colonel Macgregor stood up.

'I know what I have to do. I'm doing it. If it produces the result we want, the man will be arrested and handed over to you, Nugent. You can take him back to England to be tried and hanged.' The Provost Marshall glared at Stefan. 'Or to bloody Ireland. I can't say I care. Dead bodies are the business of every day here, soldiers, sailors, airmen, civilians. Frankly I don't have the luxury of concentrating all my resources on what the queers are doing to each other. My men will take the finger-prints. You two will simply wait until the job is done.'

'Colonel Macgregor, I think as far as police work—'

'Don't give me a lecture on police work, Mr Nugent. You'll wait, whatever the outcome. My instructions are to cooperate with you. That's what I'm doing. The men on the list are not going to take too kindly to this. I won't be asking them to take orders from a bloody civilian. The top brass doesn't like this. They don't want you poking around on military establish-ments, let alone our friend here. I don't know what clown in the Colonial Office decided this was a good idea, but Malta is a battlefield. There's a fucking war on!'

'Whatever you say, sir.' Chief Inspector Nugent smiled amiably.

The Provost Marshall snapped at him.

'You think you could do this in Civvy Street, Nugent? Gather up a collection of Londoners at random and demand their fingerprints. How many would tell you to fuck off? You might find a lot of soldiers doing the same.'

'This is the army, isn't it, sir? I assume they'll do what they're told.'

'They will. But you have no authority here. My men will take the prints. As for the sodding Garda Síochána!' Macgregor was angry now, and his anger was directed at Stefan. 'I suggest you stick very close to Mr Nugent and keep your head down, Gillespie. For all sorts of reasons. Axis bombs and bullets won't be able to spot your neutrality, even if you wave at them as they fly past.'

A sharp look from Frank Nugent stopped Stefan replying.

'You're responsible for Gillespie, Nugent.'

'I'll do my best to keep him under control, Colonel.'

'Don't waste my time trying to be clever either. I have to tolerate this business, no more. My lieutenant will take you to your hotel. Your reason for being in Malta is simple. If this fingerprint process gets a result, you have a prisoner. That's the point at which you have a job to do: to remove him from Malta. Meanwhile, keep out of the way. There are military facilities you can use in Valletta. If you do have any reason to be on military premises, your ranks entitle you to use the officers' mess. You will be issued with temporary passes.'

There was silence. Macgregor had finished.

'I think that's all.'

'Thank you very much, sir,' said Frank Nugent, with pointed politeness.

He nodded at Stefan. They both stood up.

'Thank you, Colonel Macgregor,' said Stefan, with stiff obligation.

'We rely on your thoroughness, Provost Marshall,' continued Nugent.

'What the fuck is that supposed to mean?'

'I note there are a number of officers on the list for

fingerprinting, including two pretty senior ones. I assume the job will involve everyone, regardless of rank. That's my understanding from London. And it's only fair.'

The Provost Marshall eyed the chief inspector warily.

'We're looking for an ordinary soldier, Chief Inspector. That's what all this evidence about the other murders says . . . all this material you've provided. Whatever sightings there have been, here too . . . it's been an ordinary soldier.'

'It's a supposition, sir. Probably correct, but we can't be sure. And as you say, a lot of men will resent being asked to do this. Not without justification. But it won't be any use unless it includes every name. And if ordinary soldiers feel they have been singled out . . . officers need to set an example to the men.'

The chief inspector ended with a shrug, as if he said this reluctantly. The Provost Marshall didn't like the idea. He knew many officers wouldn't like it. But it was not easy to argue. He also didn't like Nugent having the last word.

The two policemen emerged into the bright sunshine of the courtyard at Fort St Elmo. Corporal Gaunt was sitting in the Humber Snipe, reading a book, too absorbed to see them. Lieutenant Yates was following them from the building.

'Come on, Jimmy. Start her up!'

The corporal put away the book and started the engine.

'All in order, gentlemen?' asked the lieutenant.

'Well, we've got temporary passes for the officers' club in Valletta.'

'Never mind.'

'You wouldn't recommend it?' said Stefan.

'No.' Yates grinned. 'But I'll show you a couple of bars in Strait Street. That's more like it, as they say. We can set you up there. You won't look back.'

Stefan and Frank Nugent got into the open-topped Humber.

'Isn't that right, Jimmy?'

'If you say so, sir.'

'Jimmy's a bit of a prude,' laughed Yates.

The two detectives smiled as if they understood the conversation, but as the Humber turned in the courtyard, Frank Nugent spoke quietly to Stefan.

'You in a hurry, Stefan?'

'Why?'

'Sightseeing,' answered Nugent.

Stefan looked puzzled.

'Hotel then, gentlemen!' announced Lieutenant Yates.

'Where's the body, Jack?' asked the chief inspector.

Stefan understood.

'What body's that, Frank?'

'The murder victim. We've come a bloody long way to see him.'

The lieutenant shook his head. He had no instructions on this.

'Where is he?' asked Nugent again.

'Mtarfa Hospital,' said Yates.

'How about a detour to Mtarfa Hospital, then?'

'Did the colonel say that was all right?'

'He didn't say it wasn't,' said Nugent.

'We forgot to ask him,' added Stefan.

Lieutenant Yates shrugged, then laughed.

'It's not a state secret. You heard the man, Jimmy. Mtarfa.'

13

The British Hotel

The open-topped Humber bumped out of the fort and turned north, away from the Grand Harbour, to follow the city walls in the other direction. Stefan glimpsed the streets of Valletta for a moment, rising up in straight lines inside the walls, and then they were gone. More walls; bastions and sea again; the city shut away, somewhere above. Stefan was aware of the sound of explosions. They had been there some time, he realised, barely heard inside Fort St Elmo. They were not close, but deep, heavy. There were also sharper sounds, harder to hear, faster, almost rhythmic. They were not close either, but they came from every direction. He was familiar enough with bombs and anti-aircraft guns to know how they sounded in tandem. There was a lower hum too, much closer. Looking up he saw a wing of aircraft in formation move across the sky, south of the city, coming from the sea. Lieutenant Yates glanced up. It was the daily routine.

'Heinkels, with some Messerschmitts to hold their hands. South and west. Looks like the airfields today: Hal Far, Luqa. Handy we're going the other way.'

They went west from Valletta. The landscape didn't change. There were few hills. The domes of churches stood out above everything, bigger than the small villages seemed to justify. They drove for half an hour, seeing few vehicles except army trucks. The sound of bombing, ack-ack fire and tracer bullets still rumbled and clattered in the bright, clear air, for now somewhere else. It was hot. At regular intervals the long nose of an anti-aircraft gun pierced the sky. By each one, half a dozen soldiers sat smoking and staring upwards, waiting to see whether the Luftwaffe and the Regia Aeronautica would come their way.

The Humber Snipe passed the hill where the walled city of Mdina rose above the island, on a high point that would be hardly a hill anywhere else. Close to it they came to a grand square building that occupied another hill, behind Mdina. The Naval Hospital had been built where there was light and air, and where breezes blew even on the hottest, stillest days. It had not been designed for war from the air. Around it was the familiar sandstone rubble that showed that the great red crosses painted over it offered little immunity.

The hospital was full of the island's wounded, both military and civilian. The business of war here, as in London, pushed the death of one young man into a place not so much of indifference as irrelevance. The dead, however they died, were the dead. The business of this place was with the living. This was a brighter place than Charing Cross Hospital, though it dealt with the dead and the dying in the same way. As Stefan walked along Mtarfa's chaotic, bustling corridors, to see a third dead body in a third hospital mortuary, there was a noisy, almost cheerful banter. There was a strangely intense sense of life.

The body of Anthony Zammit offered nothing new. He was as clean and well presented as James Corcoran and Vikram Narayan had been by the time Stefan Gillespie saw them. The wounds that ringed the abdomen and thighs were harshly delineated, but the fury of the blows was clear. They were gaping, ragged, as if the knife had twisted as it plunged. Stefan had forgotten that violence. The anger the wounds expressed had not been washed away. It had been there in the same way on Corcoran's corpse. On Narayan's body the stab marks were more tentative, shallower; the knife had to penetrate clothing. Zammit, like Corcoran, had been partly naked.

The inspector and chief inspector took in the details and mentally ticked them off against what they already knew. The sight left no doubt about the reason they were in Malta. The killer had killed again. He was close by.

Returning to Valletta, Corporal Gaunt dropped Lieutenant Yates at Fort St Elmo and drove back round the perimeter road to the great stone gate that was the main entrance to the city from the harbour. Two dark arches gave access to the city above, but the gate was a statement as well as a point of entry. It was named after the Queen and Empress in whose reign it was built. The arms of Malta and Valletta were carved in relief over each of the arches, but above them, at the top of the gate, standing alone, grander than both, dominating, were the arms of Great Britain, supported on each side by a lion and unicorn rampant.

The British Hotel was only yards from the Victoria Gate, a flat, sandstone building, sandwiched between others, that looked down to the gate and the Grand Harbour beyond. It fronted Battery Street and emerged at the back, that was really the front, on St Ursula Street; narrow, steeply cobbled, stepped, like many of the city's streets. Only in Battery Street could a vehicle get close.

Jimmy Gaunt carried the policemen's bags into the small lobby. There was little more than a desk, a brightly tiled floor and a ceiling fan that circled lazily overhead. A staircase wound up through several storeys behind the desk and formed a narrow, open stairwell. A round, dark man in his fifties, emerged from a door that led to a small bar. He smoked a thin, black cheroot.

'They're here then, Jimmy.'

'Il-pulizija Ingliż . . . u l-pulizija . . .'

The corporal faltered in Maltese; the English policeman . . . and the . . .

'Irlandiż, Irish,' laughed the man. 'That's easy enough, isn't it?'

Gaunt flushed and adjusted his glasses. He turned to Stefan and Frank.

'This is Mr Sacco. He runs the hotel.'

'The British Hotel,' said the hotel owner pointedly. He reached into a box for two keys. 'You're welcome. Rooms on the third floor, 301 and 302. Balconies and a view of the Grand Harbour.' He shrugged. 'Bombs allowing.'

Gaunt reached across and took the keys.

'I'll do it . . .' He stopped to say it again in Maltese. 'Se nag ħmel dan.'

'All right.' The hotelier shrugged, turning to the two policemen. 'You'll excuse us. Jimmy's doing his Maltese lesson. He has me confused sometimes.'

'This way, gents,' said the corporal.

He started up the stairs. Stefan and Frank Nugent followed.

'That's impressive, Corporal,' said Stefan.

'I wish it was. I've got a bloody army exam in Colloquial Maltese.'

'Do you have to do that?'

'No, it's just,' Gaunt looked down and mumbled, 'just an interest.'

Stefan stood in the high, square room, looking out through the blue shutters of the boxed-in balcony that pushed out above the street. There was an explosion, much louder than anything he had heard so far. He saw smoke rising, black and grey, a great pillar of it across the harbour. There, he now knew, on three fingers of rock, stretching out into the harbour between sheltered creeks, were the Three Cities: Vittoriosa, Senglea, Cospicua. There too were the dockyards of the British Navy. He saw cranes rising beside the sandstone buildings that mirrored Valletta in miniature. Another explosion sent up a plume of smoke.

'Jerries are dropping what they've got left after the airfields. Most days they drop something over there. Some days that's where they drop everything.'

Jimmy Gaunt stood in the doorway.

'I'm off, sir.'

'Thanks, Corporal. Not much to stop them,' said Stefan.

'Not a lot. They'll be back for Valletta soon enough. Maybe tonight, tomorrow. There are plenty of shelters, well signed. Caves and tunnels under the city are best. Mr Sacco can show you where. You've been in London?'

Stefan nodded.

'Same sort of thing,' the corporal grinned, 'but nowhere to run.'

The bombers had gone. There were no more explosions. No more anti-aircraft fire. Stefan sat in a chair in the balcony, smoking a cigarette, still looking out at the smoke over the Three Cities and a view that, in another time, would have been calm as well as beautiful. He heard laughter on the stairs, the sound of women's voices. The door to his room was open. He looked round suddenly.

'Are you the English policeman or the Irish policeman?'

A woman in her twenties, blonde, looked in from the landing.

Stefan stood up. 'The Irish policeman.'

'It sounds like the beginning of a joke. An English police-man . . . an Irish policeman . . . but there should be a Scottish policeman. There are always three.'

Stefan walked to the door.

'I'm sorry. We should have brought another one.'

'You'll do.'

Another woman appeared, a little older, dark.

'What's he like?'

'Not bad. For a policeman.'

'Has Jimmy gone?'

Stefan realised the second woman was asking him.

'Corporal Gaunt?'

'Of course, Corporal Gaunt.' She turned away, as a third woman appeared, the youngest, very much darker in complexion. 'You just missed Jimmy, Maria!'

'I'll see him later.' The woman called Maria carried on upstairs.

'I'm Jane,' said the woman who first spoke to Stefan. 'That was Maria.'

'I'm Alice.' The second woman looked back into the room.

'Stefan Gillespie. And the English policeman is Frank Nugent.'

'Is he any better looking?'

'You'll have to judge for yourselves.'

'Is he any funnier?'

'Not a lot,' laughed Stefan.

'Oh, well, beggars can't be choosers,' said Jane. 'Catch you later.'

And they were gone, still laughing, now running up the stairs to the next floor. They all wore the light khaki that was the colour of almost everything.

Stefan sat in the bar at the British Hotel, gazing out to the street. Frank Nugent walked in and sat at the table. There was already a glass of beer waiting for him.

'Sorry, I was waylaid.'

'You met the girls.'

'I did. They've just occupied the bathroom.'

'I hope you said something funny.'

'What?'

'It's a test. I think I failed.'

'Well, I did all right on the Intelligence front,' said the chief inspector. 'They work in the War Rooms. Up the road, underground. That's where they plot the bombers, fighters, what's coming in and what's there to stop them. Well, we know that's a bit of a one-way street. Jane and Alice come, respectively, from Bournemouth and Norwich. Maria is the daughter of Mr and Mrs Sacco. And she is the particular interest of Corporal Gaunt, who is, after a fashion, walking out with her, at least trying to. I think Jane and Alice take a more enlightened approach to these things, but this, of course, is a very Catholic country. In fact, I'd say if you were looking for a country more Catholic than your own dear native sod, Stefan, this is it. Jimmy has asked permission to walk out with Maria, which I imagine amounts to exactly that . . . if approval is given.'

'Doesn't sound too promising,' laughed Stefan.

'The problem is not the old man,' continued Nugent, 'but the old woman. We haven't had the pleasure, but it seems she is a woman of Gorgon-like instincts, with a dislike of soldiers, sailors and airmen; in fact, probably of any male under the age of sixty-five who crosses the threshold of the British Hotel.'

'What about policemen?'

'Even policemen, Stefan, I'm sorry to say. But love will find a way, as you know. Mrs Sacco has Corporal Gaunt on probation. He has to demonstrate his bona fides by learning Maltese. Fair play to him, he's calling her bluff.'

'Ah, that makes sense of . . . well, just an interest, he said.'

The two detectives were aware of a man standing by the table. He carried a tray with three glasses of beer. He wore another version of an all-purpose, sandy-cum-khaki uniform.

He had a sergeant's stripes, but the cap and the tunic didn't look like the British Army. He was younger than both detectives; dark-haired, olive-skinned. He put the tray on the table and pulled up a chair.

'Chief Inspector Nugent, Inspector Gillespie. A pleasure to meet you.' The man put out his hand to shake theirs. 'George Spiteri, Malta Police.'

'It's good to see you,' said Nugent. 'Colonel Macgregor didn't appear too keen on us meeting you. That's the impression I got. What about you, Stefan?'

'Well, it might be a Maltese corpse, but it's a British Army murderer.'

'Exactly.' Sergeant Spiteri laughed. 'We should know our place.'

'I take it you don't, though,' said Frank Nugent, 'know your place.'

'My inspector does. He's ex-British Army. I'm not here officially.'

'Good.' The chief inspector grinned. 'Do you know what's happening?'

'Most of it. I know about the fingerprint from Ireland. I know about some similar murders in England. I know there's a list of soldiers to fingerprint.'

'The colonel's right to distrust rumour,' said Stefan.

'Malta's a small place,' said Spiteri. 'We can do better than rumour.'

'What about the colonel's Special Investigation Branch?' asked Nugent. 'We've been told to leave it all to them. Has he got any real detectives there?'

'There are a couple. Ex-UK police. One from the Met, one from Liverpool. Shaw's the Liverpool man – Irish originally, I think. He did work in fingerprints. I don't know if anyone's even been near a murder investigation. They're mainly involved with pilfering stores, theft from the dockyards. But I can't knock them too much. We're not exactly the murder capital of the Med.'

'Well, you're still working on this,' said Stefan. 'And ignoring the fact that the Military Police have decided it's not the business of the Malta Police.'

'That seems to sum it up,' said Spiteri.

'And you're ignoring your own Inspector . . .'

'Inspector Simmons,' said the sergeant. 'Ignoring is overstating it.'

'So, why?' asked Stefan.

'First, because I want to find who killed Anthony Zammit. He has a family. We all know each other here. That's how it is. I don't think the Military Police have any business shutting out the Maltese. And practically, I don't think that's going to help find the killer. Colonel Macgregor is more concerned about how it looks than getting results. I don't mean he doesn't want to find the murderer, but he has priorities. So do I. I don't want this man to do it again.'

'Yes,' said Nugent, 'none of us do. If this fingerprinting is thorough—'

'Secondly,' said Spiteri, interrupting, 'because you have it wrong.'

Stefan and Frank Nugent looked hard at the Maltese sergeant.

'What does that mean?' asked Stefan.

'The fingerprints. I don't mean you haven't got the man's fingerprint. I don't know, but I assume you're fairly sure of what you've got. But if you're only looking at men who came to Malta since the last murder in London, then there's a problem . . . and that problem isn't the seventy or eighty soldiers who are being fingerprinted from your list, it's the twenty-five thousand who aren't.'

'You've had a lot more than hearsay to go on,' said Stefan. 'You've obviously seen some of the material Scotland Yard sent Colonel Macgregor.'

'I couldn't possibly access that, Inspector.' George Spiteri smiled.

'Since you have,' said Nugent, 'you know the man was in England at the beginning of the year. A murder in London, the next here. The dates are clear.'

'They're not,' replied the Maltese policeman.

'Why not?'

'I can't explain away the evidence. What you have is convincing. I'm not arguing with that. I can't argue with it. But in spite of the evidence, the dates do not make sense, not here. This isn't the first murder in Malta . . . it's the second.'

'And when did the other murder happen?' asked Stefan.

'I'm not exactly sure about a date. But at the back end of last year.'

'That's impossible,' said Frank Nugent, 'unless we've got a soldier who was in Malta then, back in Britain after that, then back in Malta again. All right, well, that isn't impossible . . . but there hasn't been that kind of troop movement. Anyone moving around like that . . . you'd be talking about very senior officers.'

'I'm not offering an explanation, Mr Nugent. I'm just telling you.'

'All right, tell us, George.' Nugent glanced at Stefan and shrugged, puzzled. 'And make it Frank and Stefan. We're not the fucking army, are we?'

'A body was found in December. In bombed buildings on the other side of Valletta, Old Theatre Lane. It's an area that was badly hit. It took a while to start clearing. So, the body. Badly decomposed. Under rubble, but not much. Covered up by old doors and beams. But in an area that was very thoroughly checked after the bombing. The man could have been missed, of course. I don't think he was, though. I think he got there later. Either he died there or he was put there. Either way, I think he was killed. Nothing to do with the bombing.'

175

Mr Sacco hovered behind the bar. Stefan signalled for a round of drinks.

'The body was in quite a state. Hard to get much from it. Death probably from a blow to the head. Nothing to stop that happening when a building collapsed. But we still have the question . . . how was he missed? Then there's damage to the lower body. Abdomen, stomach, top of the legs. The flesh was falling away, but you could see the marks. What caused them? There was talk . . . had rats been at him? Did something fall on him . . . with nails or spikes? Where was it? It should have been on top of him. And he was partly undressed. That only makes sense now. Our suspicion was that the body had been put there after the building collapsed. The pathology and the forensics didn't tell us anything then . . . or anything that made sense. Not at the time. But it's become clearer . . .'

Mr Sacco put down three more glasses of beer.

'And when did it make sense?' asked Stefan.

'When I looked at Anthony Zammit's body. It explained what I'd seen on the first body, a man called Kenneth Borg. Wounds we couldn't understand . . . they weren't clear, half rotten . . . but the same circle of stab marks. It's not like anything else, is it? I've looked for parallels between Borg and Zammit. Borg's body was near a place that men meet. A pick-up spot. He was homosexual. I found out later, when I started to look into it. A lot of things do match.'

'Have you got any photographs of the body?'

'No. Once he was identified his family wanted him buried. There wasn't enough to justify us investigating. Some days there are just a lot of bodies. But there's a sketch of the wounds the doctor drew. And it's very striking. It's a lot more striking now I've seen other things that look the same. Once you've seen what we have all seen, when you know what it is, it's like stigmata.'

14

The Upper Barrakka Gardens

The day that followed Stefan Gillespie's arrival in Malta was a day of heavy bombing. It started in the late morning and continued with short breaks until dark. Most of it was directed at the Three Cities and the dockyards, across the Grand Harbour, but later it spread to docks and storehouses in Floriana, on the Valletta side of the harbour, beyond the Victoria Gate. It spread into the streets of the city and down to the end of the peninsula and Fort St Elmo.

Stefan and Frank Nugent spent most of the day in the tunnels under the Upper Barrakka Gardens that looked out over the Grand Harbour, close to the British Hotel. There were tunnels everywhere under Valletta, carved out of the soft stone that built the city. Now they were full of people. Families had claimed their own corners of these cavernous spaces; they had even dug deeper into the tunnel walls to create spaces of their own that could be curtained off and filled with deckchairs and mattresses. It was not unfamiliar to Stefan. It was like the Underground, rough-hewn and without trains. But beneath the Barrakka Gardens, it was as if the street above had been brought into the depths. Spaces were the property of a family or a shop or a business. In one large alcove there was an altar.

A young priest said Mass. There was the smell of incense, the tinkling of the communion bell. In the light of guttering candles, people cooked and read and slept and argued about who several yards of tunnel wall really belonged to. Children had lessons and played hopscotch and fell over their sleeping parents. The British Hotel had its own small recess, where two tunnels branched. There were several chairs, a table and three camp beds. Mrs Sacco provided soup to the hotel patrons and, it seemed, to most of her neighbours as well. Mr Sacco brought down a crate of beer in the afternoon. Corporal Gaunt arrived towards evening, looking for Maria, and quickly found himself pulled into a Maltese lesson that he had not bargained for by her mother. Everyone was bored. Everyone was tired of what was happening. Yet everyone seemed to accept it with an equanimity and good humour that Stefan had never seen in the Underground tunnels under Piccadilly Circus.

There were lulls in the bombing or times where it was further away. Stefan and Frank walked up and down to the Barrakka Gardens above them, all day, to smoke cigarettes and look out over the Grand Harbour at the smoke that was everywhere, and to watch the waves of bombers. Stefan watched his first air battle. He saw two Messerschmitts peel away from the bombers they were guarding, as two British planes suddenly appeared out of the smoke. The British planes were the old, slow Gladiators. The biplanes looked as if they belonged to another age. But they had the benefit of surprise. Black smoke burst from one of the Junker bombers. It flew on for some minutes and then its nose dropped. There were flames from the cockpit and it was falling. Almost straight down into the harbour. The biplane turned away, heading back into the smoke it had emerged from. The two Messerschmitts split away from each other, one to chase the retreating Gladiator, the other to tackle the second plane. The first British plane reached the smoke and dived into it.

The Messerschmitt followed. The second Messerschmitt flew straight towards the other Gladiator. The two fighters were firing as they tore towards each other, head-on. But the Gladiator was heavily outgunned. As the Luftwaffe pilot pulled up above the RAF plane at the last moment, there was smoke from the biplane. The engine coughed and stalled. Within seconds the Gladiator had followed the Junker into the Grand Harbour. The first Messerschmitt reappeared out of the smoke over the Three Cities. He had lost his quarry. The whole thing had taken a few minutes. Not even long enough for Stefan to finish his cigarette.

The next day was quiet. When the bombers came from Sicily that afternoon, they would leave the city and the Grand Harbour for another attack on the RAF airfields at Luqa and Hal Far. That morning Chief Inspector Nugent had gone to St Elmo for an update on what Colonel Macgregor's Investigation Branch was doing with the fingerprint list. Pointedly, Stefan had not been invited. The colonel told Frank Nugent that Military Intelligence had some reservations about an Irish policeman having free access to military bases. He was apologetic, but only slightly. He added that it was nothing personal, more a matter of policy. They were, after all, in a war zone. Frank Nugent thought it was probably a policy the colonel had dreamed up in the officers' club in Valletta over a couple of whiskeys with the Intelligence major they had met at Gibraltar.

Stefan spent part of the morning with Sergeant Spiteri of the Malta Police. Since neither he nor Chief Inspector Nugent could get into the Military Police investigation, it was useful that someone wanted to talk to them.

The day was warm and bright. It would be hot later. Although thin smoke drifted over Valletta and the Three Cities across the harbour, it was peaceful. Stefan Gillespie and George Spiteri stood by the Customs House, on the waterfront below the Victoria Gate. This was where the ferry from the other side of the harbour landed, and where dozens of dgħajjes moored, the small water taxies that shuttled around the harbour. This was where Anthony Zammit's last visit to Valletta had started, shortly before he was killed.

'He lived in Senglea. He worked in the docks there. He came over in a dgħajjsa, early evening, just getting dark. Quiet night here. No bombing. The man who brought him over knew him. He was on his own. Someone else saw him, minutes later. He took the Barrakka Lift. A girl he knew was getting off.'

The two policemen crossed the perimeter road. They walked through a dark archway into a kind of gully, cut out of the rock beside a turn in the city's bastions. A thin, almost fragile tower of criss-crossed scaffolding rose up against the rock to one side, reaching high above, bolted into the cliff face and the city wall. George and Stefan stepped into the lift and the iron-grille doors shut behind them. The cables creaked and groaned. The cabin shook. The lift rose noisily and unevenly upwards, over two hundred feet. Suddenly there was a narrow view of the Grand Harbour that slid upwards as Stefan looked out at it.

The lift opened into the arched colonnade that made up one side of the Upper Barrakka Gardens. Stefan already knew the gardens. This was one of the entrances to the tunnels he had sheltered in the day before. It was where he had stood, smoking a cigarette and watching German and British pilots die. This was the finest view of the Grand Harbour. Behind the colonnades was the dappled light of a shady garden where the people of Valletta came when they had nothing much to do and wanted to do it in a place that felt a long way from the heat of the sandstone streets. There were few green spaces; the walls that had been built to defend the city had become places where trees and flowers grew. Now the view of the Grand

Harbour from the gardens was framed by the guns of the anti-aircraft battery that took up the platform below the colonnades.

'During the day, it's like any park. People walk and talk and sit around. That's what it's for. Visitors come here to look at the harbour, but we go for the trees and the shade.' Spiteri grinned. 'We've seen the harbour now and again.'

They walked through the gardens. They were stacked with sandbags. A group of British soldiers was unloading crates of ack-ack shells from a truck.

'After dark, the atmosphere changes. At least, it does over here.'

The sergeant gestured to a clump of trees and some benches.

'It's away from the harbour. An out-of-the-way corner. And it's always been one of the places men come looking for other men. There are no lights, even without the blackout. No one takes much notice. We might move them on now and again. But there's never that many. If they don't cause trouble . . . if they keep out of other people's way . . . we leave them alone.'

'Did anyone see Zammit here?'

'No. No one I've managed to talk to. It's not easy. You know that.'

Stefan nodded.

'But someone saw him walking out of the gardens. There's a restaurant, by the gate, where you come out into Castille Place. Come on. I'll show you.'

The policemen walked on through the gardens and out into a wide square.

They passed a small café. A few customers were sitting at tables outside.

'I have a statement from the waiter. He saw Anthony Zammit with a soldier, walking towards the bus station. It was night by then. But not such a dark night. The man knew Anthony well. He only saw the back of the soldier. Probably a private. Tall, thin . . . maybe fair-haired.'

They moved on across the square. They turned towards the main street, which the British now called Kingsway, but the Maltese still called the Strada Reale, as the knights who built it had. They passed the great building that was the Royal Opera House, built by an English architect to bring something of Covent Garden to the city of the Knights of St John. Surrounded by classical pillars on every side, it looked like no other building in Valletta, but it had become a much-loved symbol of the city.

They crossed the bridge over the deep moat that cut across the peninsula from side to side. They were outside the city now, in a wide street full of small, colourful buses. George Spiteri turned to the left, following the city walls, past the bus station, to an area of stunted trees, scrub and parched, yellow grass. It was scattered thinly with rubbish. Stefan followed him. The sergeant stopped.

'We found him here. You've seen the photos. When men meet in the Upper Barrakka, they go somewhere else for sex. It's a kind of understanding. People leave them alone. They can find someone there. But they go to some quiet corner to finish the job. And this would be quiet enough, especially with the blackout. Hardly any buses run at night now. It would be empty all around here after dark. And it's out of the way . . . wasteland. It goes nowhere.'

Stefan looked around. There was nothing to see. It was just another place where a young man had died. It joined the list of dark, unimportant corners.

'So, when did Colonel Macgregor get involved?'

'It was our investigation for a couple of days. Then we had the evidence that Anthony was last seen walking in this direction with a soldier. And then the colonel's Special Investigation Branch came in. The investigation was theirs.'

'All theirs.'

'That's how they like it. Interrogating soldiers is not our business.'

'You're still pissed off,' said Stefan Gillespie.

'Pissed off enough to keep at it. I'm still looking. You'll hear a lot of people tell you this is a very small place. It is. It is for everyone. That includes the men who meet each other in the Upper Barrakka. Someone must have seen something. Someone must have noticed something. Someone knows something. I don't even mean about Zammit. Remember, I think I have two murders here.'

Stefan Gillespie walked on along the Strada Reale, Malta's widest street. He already knew his way round the streets that led here from the British Hotel, and continued on, the length of the peninsula, to Fort St Elmo and the sea. Valletta was built on a grid, like a miniature version of New York. Long, narrow streets ran the length of the city and shorter ones crossed it from shore to shore. In a different time, Stefan could have enjoyed the elegant city and the buildings that lined the Strada Reale: townhouses and palaces, churches and public buildings. But his mind was on the dead bodies that had brought him here, and when it wasn't, it was full of the sound of aircraft and bombs and the day he had spent underground. Suddenly a heap of stone stretched almost all the way across the street. It sloped up like a hill. Yesterday it had been a house. Men and women and children were working in the rubble, clearing the road. There were soldiers and sailors with them, filling trucks and trailers with the debris.

A few hundred yards on, Stefan passed the cathedral of St John. He could see ahead that the Strada Reale opened up into a square of palaces and grand buildings. This was where he had arranged to meet Nugent. He saw a sign for the Caffe Cordina. Opposite the café, beneath a stone arch, he saw the English policeman at a table with another man. The man wore the usual khaki fatigues; on the table was a Military Policeman's red cap.

Stefan sat down. He was introduced to Robert Shaw, sergeant in the CMP Special Investigation Branch. He was short, balding, with the accent of Dublin.

'Dead end,' said Chief Inspector Nugent curtly.

'No go,' added Sergeant Shaw with a shrug.

'All the fingerprints have been taken. No matches.'

'Did you get everyone on the list?' asked Stefan.

Frank Nugent sat back, lighting a cigarette. 'Near as dammit.'

The waiter hovered. Stefan asked for tea.

'We got through your list of soldiers,' said the Military Policeman. 'Two officers moved on to Alexandria. One Royal Engineer dead in a raid on St Elmo last week. That's it. No one's going to give you a guarantee someone didn't slip through Malta between your dates. People get transferred, die, go sick, get put in the glasshouse for robbing or fighting or getting pissed. But I think we had all of them. And the idea that the feller you're looking for just happened to be lucky enough to get missed off . . . that would be some fucking luck. Your knifeman isn't on the list. I'd say you're barking up the wrong tree, gentlemen.'

Sergeant Shaw delivered his verdict with a look of satisfaction. He'd done his job. It was the civvies who had fucked up. They had it wrong.

'Those were Colonel Macgregor's words,' said Frank Nugent, 'more or less. He didn't exactly say the fuck-up was entirely ours, but it cost him not to.'

The Military Policeman laughed. He got up.

'Good hunting, lads.' He looked at Stefan. 'How's Dublin?'

'Quieter than here.'

'Ah, you'll miss it when you get back. You get used to it.'

'I'm not sure I would,' replied Stefan. 'Where are you from?'

'The North Strand.'

'Is your family there?'

'They were the last time I was home.'

There was a note of reticence in Shaw's voice. The Irish State didn't take kindly to its citizens fighting in the British Army, even though it only made noises about stopping them. But the sergeant did not want more conversation about Ireland with an Irish policeman. There would be no Ould Irish bonhomie.

'Take care, lads.'

Stefan and Frank Nugent watched him walk away.

'Is he any good?' asked Stefan.

'He knows what he's doing. He was in fingerprints in Liverpool before he joined up. He's a proper copper; I'd say one of Macgregor's better specimens.'

'So, what's the colonel proposing now?'

'He's talking about inspecting a selection of poofs and pansies the army has defending Malta for the empire . . . Well, that's about as much sense as I got.'

'And what does that mean?'

'I think he's going to send his boys in their red caps to knock some heads together in a few queer bars on Strait Street and ask them if they've got any pals who are in the habit of murdering the men they've just buggered. They are, after all, perverts and . . . one thing leads to another in that line of work.'

Frank Nugent laughed. 'I'm paraphrasing his thinking, but unfortunately not a lot.'

'Jesus, that's not going to get him far.'

'No. But I'd bet on it giving him more trouble than he's bargained for.'

The two men sat looking out at the Strada Reale.

'So, that's that,' said Stefan eventually.

Nugent nodded.

'And is that it as far as the dates are concerned?' said Stefan. 'If we're not looking for a soldier who left England after Vikram Narayan was killed?'

'I don't know. That ought to be impossible.'

'It isn't if George Spiteri's right and there was another murder.'

'If . . .' said the IPI man.

'I've been thinking about Narayan,' said Stefan.

'Have you got an explanation then?'

'No,' continued the Irishman, 'but there are questions if you tot up the similarities, in all the killings. That's six, Jesus, seven if there's two here. One can't fit. Either the first one here or Vikram Narayan in London. So, look at them. All outside, in isolated or out-of-the-way places, except one. Most chance meetings in known pick-up spots for homosexual men. Not true in Ireland. Maybe not true for Narayan, but let's come back to that. In every case, except one, there was sexual contact. That's Narayan. The others had sex, whatever that involved. We can't know that for the first man in Malta, Kenneth Borg, but he was undressed, partly or completely, as in every case . . . except one. In every case, wounds to the lower body were so violent that it's still shocking to look at the photographs, let alone the bodies. The amount of violence hits every time. And that's true of all of them, wouldn't you say, all except for one? Vikram Narayan.'

Chief Inspector Nugent nodded, taking in the train of thought.

'He was fully clothed,' said Stefan. 'There was no sex. The knife wounds were shallower . . . almost neat. That's a subjective judgement, but it's one I'd make. It feels different. And where did he meet his killer? Did he know him? We don't know, but I've walked from that club, Billie's, to the flat in Greek Street. We know when he left. We know when Micheál Mac Liammóir found the body. It wasn't that long. Vikram had to meet a man in the street. They had to walk to his flat. Then the killer had to knock him out, smother him, then add the knife wounds . . . instantly. You'd almost say as they walked through the door.'

'You're right,' said Nugent, 'if there is one that doesn't fit, that's it. List it like that, and it misses a lot of the characteristics of the other murders. There could even be fingerprints, just not the fingerprints of the man who killed James Corcoran. We've never found a suspect. Well, we've only looked in one place.'

'Maybe that was a mistake,' said Stefan.

'But how about the stab wounds? They're still so similar. No one could come up with that, Stefan. The chances are . . . you'd have to know something already.'

'And if you did know something,' said Stefan, smiling, 'you'd be hard put to find a better way of making the police look in the wrong direction.'

Frank Nugent said nothing for several minutes. He called the waiter.

'I think we need a couple of beers.'

'What now?' asked Stefan.

'We're still here,' laughed Frank Nugent. 'As people will tell you.'

'What does that mean?'

'Well, since we won't be taking fingerprints from twenty-five thousand soldiers, I reckon we should forget Colonel Macgregor and his Special Investigation Branch. I'd say the feller we need to listen to is Sergeant Spiteri.'

15

The Lascaris War Rooms

The next morning, Inspector Gillespie and Chief Inspector Nugent found themselves with nothing to do. There was no communication from the Provost Marshall's office. Frank Nugent phoned Colonel Macgregor and found that he was either busy or elsewhere. There was nothing from Sergeant Spiteri either; since he was acting without the authority of his superiors in the Malta Police, who had no intention of treading on the toes of the Corp of Military Police, they had to wait for him to contact them. They were in Malta to find a murderer, but the fingerprint trawl had failed, and it seemed the Provost Marshall intended to take their mission literally. Fingerprints had produced no results; that was the end of it for them.

That morning no Axis bombers and fighters had appeared. Stefan and Frank walked the length of the city, down the Strada Reale, to Fort St Elmo. Bombs had fallen on the sea walls the previous day. More men had died; two anti-aircraft batteries had been damaged. The fort was full of soldiers clearing access to the walls and engineers trying to get the guns working before the next raid. The colonel was busy.

As they walked back into Valletta, they heard the drone of planes. German bombers; an escort of fighters; heading inland.

No one took much notice, apart from glancing up with weary resignation. People had good instincts now. There were no sirens, but they knew anyway. Sound, direction, height; you could tell when they were going somewhere else, as you could tell when the rain was coming.

A horn blasted loudly when the two detectives reached the cathedral, heading back towards the hotel. A Military Police Humber Snipe was parked at the corner. Lieutenant Yates was sitting in it, smoking lazily in the sunshine.

'Enjoying the weather, mes enfants?'

'Not a lot,' said Nugent. 'We did try to see your colonel again.'

'Did he have other priorities?'

'That word cropped up, believe it or not,' laughed Stefan.

Yates grinned.

'You're sticklers, I'll give you that. You didn't get the message?'

'I think we did, actually,' said the chief inspector.

'Well, yes, there is that message, Frank. The other one is that there should be a Sunderland in from Alexandria – two, maybe three days' time. Going on to Gib. The colonel thought it would be handy for you, as you've nothing left to do . . .'

'I'm not sure I see it that way,' said Nugent.

'That's between you and the colonel.' Yates shrugged. 'Why bother?'

'Why not? We're here.'

'This is the army. Don't volunteer. Don't do anything you don't have to.'

The lieutenant offered them both a cigarette.

'You've got a couple of days. With a bit of luck, the bastards won't be bombing round the clock. Take it easy. Go down to Strait Street. Next road along. You can drink all day and all night, and the women are so sick of fucking soldiers and sailors they'll eat you alive. And that can be free, gratis and for nothing. It's our job to keep all ship-shape down there, make sure the boys behave. I can sort you out something very nice, very clean. Just say the word.'

'You're too generous, Jack!' said Nugent.

'Up to you.' The lieutenant chuckled amiably. 'Offer's there.'

Stefan laughed. 'I'll pass. But don't let me stop you, Frank.'

'I'll pass too.'

'And there's me trying to do you two a favour! Oh, here's Jimmy.'

They saw Corporal Gaunt, on the steps of the cathedral with Maria Sacco. The two stood as people passed them, coming out of Mass.

'Come on, sunshine!' shouted Lieutenant Yates.

Jimmy Gaunt pecked Maria awkwardly on the cheek. She flushed, seeing the three policemen watching them, and hurried away. Gaunt ran towards them.

'That's the only place she's allowed to be on her own with him, at bloody Mass in the cathedral,' Yates explained. 'He's not even a Catholic! But you got to lend a hand when it's true love. And they say we don't care about our soldiers!'

Laughing again, Yates stubbed out his cigarette and climbed into the Humber. Corporal Gaunt got in and started up the engine. They pulled away.

'Lunchtime, lads!' the lieutenant shouted back at Stefan and Frank Nugent. 'Intelligence reckons bombs over the harbour around then. Stay safe!'

The reports from Intelligence were right. By midday bombs were falling on the docks in Floriana, on the Valletta side of the Grand Harbour, closer to the Victoria Gate and the British Hotel. Stefan Gillespie and Frank Nugent were underground again, in the tunnels beneath the Upper Barrakka Gardens. The routine they were already part of was in operation. The tunnels were filling up. It was cold after the heat of the afternoon, but it would get hotter as the number of bodies increased. They sat against a rock wall. Stefan was writing a postcard that pictured the Grand Harbour without smoke or fire or collapsed buildings or the battered hulls of broken ships. Nugent was trying to read the *Times of Malta*, with some difficulty, in the light from nearby lamps and candles. The sound of the bombs and the guns was there, in the distance. The sound of Mass was closer. In the cavern-like alcove across the tunnel, a young priest was saying the Credo. The people around him, jammed together in semi-darkness, were saying it with him, in Latin and in Maltese and in English.

'Deum de Deo, lumen de lumine, Deum verum de Deo vero . . .'

'Alla minn Alla, dawl mid-dal, Alla veru minn Alla veru . . .'

'God from God, Light from Light, true God from true God . . .'

It was as the Mass was ending, that George Spiteri appeared, standing by them.

'I thought you'd be here. That's perfect.'

'What's perfect?' said Nugent.

'You're where you need to be.'

'For what?' asked Stefan.

'The secrets of the confessional,' said Spiteri, grinning. 'Don't tell!'

The Mass finished and the congregation drifted away into the tunnels and alcoves. The priest saw Sergeant Spiteri and nodded. He moved to the back of the alcove, behind the table that served as the altar. He pulled off the chasuble he wore over his black robes, folded it and put it beside his tin hat.

'Father Zachary, these are the two policemen I told you about.'

They introduced themselves and shook hands.

'That's twice I've seen you in the shelter, Inspector Gillespie.' The priest smiled broadly. 'And never at Mass when it's going on in front of your eyes. And you from Holy Ireland! They say there's nowhere holier than Ireland, but if there is, you have found it. We're in serious competition with you in Malta.'

'I take it you've been in Ireland, Father.'

'I have. But don't worry, I won't report you.'

Stefan laughed and left it at that. It seemed no place to elaborate.

'Father Zachary has been talking to a few people . . .'

'I have. I know what's happened. I know about the deaths. But some of the men you want to speak to have no great trust in anyone, especially the police, and since we're blessed with more than one sort, in any kind of police. I try to give them something to trust . . . it doesn't make me popular with the Church, but that's another story. The story that matters to you is that I've asked a few men I know to talk to Sergeant Spiteri. I trust the sergeant and he says you can be trusted. There are people with things to say. I did hear one confession . . .'

The priest took out some tobacco and started to roll a cigarette.

'I can't tell you what the man said in the confessional, naturally, but I think he would talk to you. And I think what he has to say . . . might help you.'

'He's knows something about the murders?' said Stefan.

'He knows something . . . he saw something . . . please don't think it's very much. I'm hardly a detective, but it is only what he saw . . . and what he felt . . .'

Father Zachary lit the cigarette.

'But that was before . . .' he said with a shrug.

'Before what?' asked George Spiteri.

'It's common knowledge, among the men we're talking about, that the Military Police have carried out a series of, well, raids, I suppose . . . on bars in Strait Street. Bars that cater for a particular interest, let's say that. They can't touch civilians, but soldiers, sailors, airmen, have all been questioned about their associations, their friendships. I put it politely. You know what I mean.'

'We know that's going on,' said Stefan. 'Not a clever idea.'

'Not at all,' said the priest. 'Not if you want people to talk to you. And the result, I'm afraid, is fear. These men fear exposure. We're not only like Ireland in the amount of time we spend on our knees. So, I'm sorry to say that the men who were prepared to meet you and talk to you and tell you . . . perhaps something that might help you find this . . . monster . . .'

'They now think, fuck that for a game of soldiers,' said Nugent flatly.

Father Zachary inhaled, then blew out a cloud of smoke.

'That's about it. You put it very succinctly, Chief Inspector Nugent.'

It was quiet. The bombers had gone. The fighters had gone. Stefan Gillespie and Frank Nugent had spent an hour walking by the harbour. Fires still burned, in the darkness of Valletta and across the water in the Three Cities. The two men climbed the dogleg steps that led from the Victoria Gate to Battery Street and the British Hotel. The steps were closed in, with the street high above and the road from the Victoria Gate below. They were full of cats, as they were every night when people had gone; mangy, moth-eaten, half-starved cats, prowling, roaming, stretching, sleeping. There were dozens. Suddenly, the sound of a shrill screech: in a corner two cats hissing and fighting. A matter of seconds. Then one tore down the steps, past the policemen. The cats barely registered the two men, moving aside only at the last moment. This was their place at night. They held it for themselves and ignored humans unless there was no choice. Some of them glanced up and mewed. People often put food out for them, though there was little to get in a city short of everything, when even scraps were too precious to be thrown out. But the cats knew when someone looked like a provider and when not. These two humans only needed ignoring.

The silence was broken by the weary note of sirens revving up. It stopped almost as soon as it had started. It was a false alarm, quickly turned off. The sound came from across the harbour, from Senglea and Vittoriosa. But it was enough for the cats. They had long known what the sirens meant. They were gone in seconds, scattering up and down the steps, racing into their own shelter holes.

Turning where the steps bent up towards Battery Street, the two detectives saw several men walking down towards them, soldiers in different shades of khaki. The soldiers stopped, forming a line across the steps. For a few seconds Stefan and Frank continued, but then they halted, recognising that there was, suddenly, a threat.

'What's the problem, lads?' said Stefan cheerfully.

One of the men stepped forward; he wore a sergeant's stripes. 'You are.'

Stefan and Frank exchanged glances. For a moment they had no idea why this was happening. These men were looking for trouble and looking for them. This was not happening by chance. Stefan knew it had something to do with why they were in Malta. Things were being stirred up. Here it was. The Englishman shrugged. The same thought was in his head. The Military Police had done the stirring. This was the result.

'I think you've the wrong end of the stick,' said Chief Inspector Nugent. 'I don't know you . . . you don't know me. Whatever you think you're doing . . . whatever it's about . . . this is a mistake. We're just going back to our hotel.'

Stefan looked to one side. As he did so Frank Nugent caught the movement of his head and did the same. Below them, coming up from the Victoria Gate, were another half-dozen soldiers. There would be no escape.

'You don't even know who we are,' said Nugent. 'This is mad.'

Stefan took a deep breath. 'I'd say they know exactly who we are.'

'The Irish fucker's right.'

'OK, you know who we are. What do you want?'

The sergeant who was doing the talking nodded. Soldiers swarmed down the steps from above and up from below. Stefan and Frank were grabbed by the arms. There was no point struggling. They were not going anywhere.

'We want to give you a lesson in manners. You need to keep your nose out of other people's business. I don't know why you're so fucking interested.'

'I'm not interested in your business,' said Nugent. 'I don't give a fuck.'

'I'd hazard a guess,' said Stefan quietly, straining to look across at the chief inspector, 'that it'll be more like Colonel Macgregor's business, Frank.'

'Shut up!'

The speaker moved forward and punched Stefan hard in the stomach. He crumpled up, but the men who were holding him fast didn't let him collapse.

'The sodding Red Caps are pulling us in left, right and centre. You've only got to go for a drink in the wrong bar. They're there. Who do you know? Who do you knock about with? Where do you drink? Have you got pansy pals? Who do you fuck and how often? And do you like to give it or fucking take it, soldier?'

There was laughter from the men.

The sergeant grinned.

'I like to give it. Let's see if you can take it! Because it started with you. That's what we hear. Fucking civvy coppers! We'll give you information!'

'You've got it wrong,' began Nugent. 'It started with—'

195

The sergeant lashed out and punched him in the stomach.

'Shut it! You're not in Blighty now, Mr Inspector Nugent.'

Frank Nugent couldn't speak now.

'Listen! It started with a dead man, Sergeant,' shouted Stefan. 'A lot of dead men. A lot of dead men like all of you. That's why we're here. We didn't tell the MPs to question you. Why would we? We don't have any jurisdiction.'

'Too right, you Paddy bastard. We're here to show you that you don't.'

At that point there was the sound of laughter above them.

Stefan looked up; he knew the voices.

Several of the soldiers turned round, looking up too.

'Ignore your bloody mother, Maria,' Alice was saying.

'I can't. She never takes her eyes off me.'

Stefan saw Alice, Jane and Maria, starting down the steps. They were dressed in their uniforms, on their way to their night shift in the Lascaris War Rooms, he guessed.

'And lie, lie, lie again,' said Jane loudly. 'No decent mother would expect her daughter to do anything else when it comes to men. She lied once!'

Jane and Alice were laughing. Maria, more subdued, smiled.

They saw the crowd of men ahead of them. They saw Frank Nugent and Stefan Gillespie being held. They registered that Frank looked in some pain.

'Hello, Frank; hello, Stefan,' said Alice brightly.

Jane and Maria were frowning, still taking in the tense mood.

'We were looking for you. We said we'd show you the War Rooms?'

This was news to Stefan. He had a vague idea what the War Rooms were. He only knew the women worked there. But now he could think of nothing he would rather do than see them.

Alice looked at the sergeant who had been doing all the

talking. She could see the other men watching him. Whatever was going on, she could tell that he was the focus. She smiled broadly at him. The soldiers would know who they were, from their uniforms, but it had done no harm to remind them. The War Rooms were not far away. They were packed with senior officers. They were guarded by Military Police.

'Still quiet this side, Sergeant,' said Alice. 'Let's hope it stays that way.'

Jane took her lead from Alice's tone now.

'So, are you two coming, then, or have you changed your mind?'

The soldiers holding Stefan and Frank looked at each other, uncertain what to do, and now feeling doubtful. The mood was punctured. They let go.

If it was unclear what was happening, the sense of menace had been palpable in the darkness. There was silence on the steps. In the distance the sirens sounded from the Three Cities. Abruptly the distant thud of ack-acks.

'I hope we're not breaking up a party?' said Alice, yet more brightly.

She stepped forward, down the steps. Jane and Maria followed.

The soldiers moved aside, silent, slightly sheepish now.

'It's probably not the best time,' continued Alice pleasantly. 'Quiet enough here but bombs the other side of the harbour. Who needs that trouble?'

'War Rooms, then,' said Jane. 'You both look like you need a cup of tea.'

She took Stefan's arm, turning him round on the steps. Alice did the same with Frank Nugent. Maria was staring at the sergeant who had been doing all the talking, as Alice and Jane walked down the steps with the two policemen.

'You should go back to base, Sergeant, before a bomb drops on you.'

Jane and Alice walked on with Stefan and Frank; Maria caught them up. Behind them the sour group of soldiers was drifting back up the steps.

Alice grinned at Frank Nugent.

'Well, we've lumbered ourselves with you two now. Talk about "always ask a policeman"! Oh, dear! We'll look after you . . . till your chums have gone.'

Jane clutched Stefan's arm harder, laughing.

'I just think it's smashing you've made friends here so quickly!'

The three women, talking cheerfully about nothing much, took the two policemen along several dark alleys and arches and through two Military Police checkpoints to a dimly lit tunnel that was only minutes from where they had started. It seemed to drive directly under the bastions that rose up above in the darkness. Sirens were sounding in Valletta, but the sound of bombs and flashes of light in the sky came from the other side of the harbour. From the tunnel they turned into a brightly lit chamber where several soldiers and Military Policemen sat smoking and drinking tea. The Military Police sergeant who sat at the entrance grumbled about whether Stefan and Frank Nugent could go in, but he knew who the women were and was happily badgered into it by Jane and Alice. The tunnels that ran into the walls and the rock under Valletta here were the heart of the British defence of Malta, but there was a casualness about this place that mirrored what Stefan had already seen. What happened here, as elsewhere, had become a familiar and ordinary routine.

The corridors and the rooms were full of men and women in uniform, sitting at telephones and standing at great tables painted with the outline of Malta and the Mediterranean coast surrounding it. Stefan and Frank passed these rooms, glancing in at the maps and blackboards that filled the walls, looking like the boards at a railway terminus. They contained all the details of the airfields and the squadrons and the aircraft that could be put up to defend the island from the Luftwaffe and the Regia Aeronautica. The maps on the tables showed attacking and defending aircraft in the form of wooden markers, slotted with cardboard letters and numbers, which were pushed around by women who wore the same uniforms as the three ladies of Lascaris from the British Hotel. There was a constant buzz of instructions, from all directions, and mixed in with that were the crackling voices of men, pilots and observers, coming over Tannoy loudspeakers. In the background, behind the voices, there were explosions and the rattle of bullets. Jane and Maria disappeared into one of the big operations rooms. Alice offered a garbled explanation of what was going on as she hurried Stefan and Frank past the rooms to a canteen at the end of the corridor. It was empty except for four soldiers playing cards.

Alice produced two mugs of stewed, lukewarm tea from an urn.

She lit a cigarette.

'We'd all love to know what you two are doing here.'

'Ah, walls have ears, Alice,' said Nugent.

'He means we're here because we're here,' continued Stefan. 'If we did know when we started . . . who knows now? That's what makes us so popular.'

'We did try to get it out of Jimmy. He wouldn't even tell Maria!'

They were aware of the Military Police sergeant who had let them into the War Rooms, suddenly there. He looked awkward and uneasy and just a little red-faced. Not unreasonably: someone had just given him a bollocking.

'Bit of a cock-up, Alice.'

'You don't say, Sergeant. When wasn't there?'

'My officer said I shouldn't have let the two gentlemen . . .'

'Don't be silly,' replied Alice. 'They're only having a cup of tea.'

'They're not authorised . . .'

'Piffle. They're policemen, for goodness' sake!'

Frank Nugent grinned at Stefan. Stefan nodded. They both stood up.

'It's OK, Alice,' said Nugent, 'you saved our bacon. We're safe enough.'

'No bombing this side, sir,' said the sergeant apologetically. 'Orders from the Provost Marshall's office. That's the thing. Seems your clearance wasn't . . .'

'I'll take them up, Sergeant,' said Alice, irritated.

'Well, finish your tea, anyway . . .' The sergeant grunted and went out.

'Red tape,' sniffed Alice. 'They love it. It's not like what we do here's a secret. And don't you work with the Military Police? That's what Jimmy said.'

'Jimmy maybe says too much.' Nugent smiled. 'We do and we don't.'

'It's all nonsense, most of it.' Alice shrugged. 'Playing at soldiers.'

'It is,' said Stefan, laughing. 'You'd think there was a bloody war on!'

Alice led the two policemen back along the main corridor. They sidestepped the trail of men and women rushing up and down, in and out of every room. But then Alice stopped by the door into the main operations room. Stefan and Frank stood with her, waiting. They had not noticed anything, but she had. It was silence. There were voices along the corridor, but in the biggest room there was nothing, except the crackle of the Tannoy on the wall. No one was speaking. Everyone was very still. The women who stood round the map of the island, the men who sat above them, looking down at the table, the soldiers and airmen carrying messages back and forward from the telephones and the Intelligence and observation desks. They were all gazing at the speaker on the wall. It crackled, hissed again. Somewhere a dim explosion sounded, behind all the interference.

Then a man's voice.

It was the controller, sitting high above, who spoke.

'Striker to Echo 2, come in . . .'

The Tannoy hissed.

'We've lost you, Echo 2 . . . you need to break away . . .'

There was more silence.

Then a voice on the Tannoy, breaking through the interference.

'Striker, am not hearing you . . . not hearing . . . thing's fucked.'

There was a buzz of relief around the room.

The controller's voice again.

'Echo 2, bandits 20,000 feet . . . break away and return . . .'

The Tannoy hissed again. A long, empty moment.

'Hit over Senglea . . . I'll get her home . . .'

'Fast, Echo 2 . . . you need to break away fast . . . bandits above . . .'

'Not hearing . . . not . . . shit . . .'

Over the Tannoy's crackle, something like the rattle of bullets.

Everyone was still staring up at the black box on the wall.

'Shit . . . three of the fuckers . . . they're on . . .'

Another sound. Far away, dim. It could have been an explosion.

'Echo 2 . . . Echo 2 . . . Striker calling Echo 2 . . .'

No one moved. The Tannoy hissed intermittently, but that was all. Stefan saw a woman, standing next to Jane, reach out and put her arm round her. Then the voice of another officer, looking down on the room, broke into the silence.

'Three Hurricanes, Hal Far, now airborne . . .'
The room unfroze. Work continued.
'I'm on now, too,' said Alice softly. 'I'll take you out.'

16

Strait Street

The day was still after the night before. Malta came out of hiding to pick up the pieces, to shovel, clear away, mourn and bury the dead. They went about the life of the island with a quiet determination. Stefan Gillespie and Frank Nugent could only watch. Their part in it all would soon be over. In the morning after a heavy night of bombing, it was hard to believe that what they were doing mattered, especially when they had achieved nothing. If they had a job to do, the Luftwaffe and the Regia Aeronautica were doing everything possible to thwart it. Everywhere the dead piled up. Why should a few more count?

'Are you two busy this afternoon?'

Alice stood in the doorway to the bar of the British Hotel, where the Irish detective and the English detective were drinking coffee. It was a precious commodity in Malta and Mrs Sacco had a supply she kept quiet about. She knew the two policemen would be leaving soon.

'I don't know,' said Frank Nugent, as if he really didn't.

'When he says he doesn't know,' laughed Stefan, 'he means we're not.'

'Ah, but we could be.'

'What, busy packing?'

'I don't like walking away from it. The bastard's here, Stefan.'

'Talk among yourselves,' said Alice. 'Never mind me.'

'The short answer is we're not, Alice. Busy.'

The chief inspector shrugged.

'For an Irishman, you're not very big on optimism,' he added.

'You keep forgetting, I'm the wrong sort of Irishman, Frank.'

Alice was getting impatient.

'You two never say anything to each other we can understand.'

'It takes years of training,' said Stefan. 'Frank specialises in it.'

'Do shut up! Look, Jane's very low. You heard . . . in the War Rooms. He was a pilot she knew. She went out with him a few times. I mean, it's not . . . little things matter quickly here . . . sometimes there's not so long for them to matter.'

'You don't have to explain, Alice,' said Stefan.

'No. Anyway, Charlie Chaplin! That's what we all need.'

'Is it?'

'Yes, you too. Both of you. All you do is sit around doing nothing.'

Frank Nugent tapped his head. 'It all happens up here.'

'Well, the Charlie Chaplin film's on at the Manoel Theatre, *The Great Dictator*,' continued Alice. 'We all want to see it, but I can't get anyone to go with us. So, I've decided you two can come.'

'You have a way with invitations, Alice. How can we refuse?'

'You won't refuse, Frank.'

'It's the opportunity of a lifetime for me,' said Stefan.

'It's Charlie Chaplin. Don't overdo it, old son,' laughed Nugent.

'Forbidden fruit. They've banned it in Ireland.'

'You're joking!' said Alice.

'No, no Charlie. We can't be trusted with that sort of thing!'

'That's just silly!'

'That's neutrality. Hitler and Mussolini are no laughing matter.'

'You're coming, then?'

'Why not?' Stefan said.

Frank Nugent nodded.

As Alice turned to go, George Spiteri walked in.

'Can I smell coffee?'

'Guests only,' said Alice. 'That's what Mrs Sacco says.' She left.

Sergeant Spiteri walked to the table and picked up the coffee pot.

'What she doesn't know won't hurt her.' Stefan pushed a cup towards him.

'This was worth the journey. I haven't had real coffee in a month.'

'Is that all you're here for?' asked Nugent.

'No,' said the sergeant, smiling, 'but it's a good start.'

Stefan and Frank waited. George Spiteri drank the coffee.

'You know what I can't understand,' said the chief inspector, 'if we were in India, and there was a rumour of a British soldier killing Indians, we'd have riots and blood in the streets.' He grinned at the Maltese sergeant. 'Surely any self-respecting colony should have a few nationalists to stir up trouble and throw bricks through the governor's windows. It's not the way it's done!'

'Unfortunately, they're all in Uganda.' Spiteri laughed.

'Uganda?' exclaimed Frank Nugent.

'The British sent them off at the beginning of the war.'

'Well, that's one way of doing it,' said Stefan.

'But as nationalists go, some of them left a lot to be desired.' Sergeant Spiteri topped up his coffee. 'Their vision of independence was Malta becoming part of Italy. There was never a huge amount of enthusiasm for that. And since Mussolini started dropping bombs on us . . . Well, Uganda's probably the best place for them. In the meantime, most of us have made our choice. And it is our choice. We know what side we're on. The future . . . well, that's something else.'

He shrugged and drained the coffee, then he smiled.

'So, first things first. No rumours, no riots, just Strait Street!'

Half an hour later, Stefan Gillespie entered the narrow, canyon-like defile that was Strait Street. The street ran parallel to Kingsway, Valletta's widest thoroughfare. In the city's simple grid, Strada Stretta, too, stretched the length of the peninsula, down towards Fort St Elmo. It was so narrow that two people leaning out of balconies on the upper floors of opposite houses could touch.

Its buildings were high enough that they gave the gullied street a dark and secret atmosphere and kept it cool, even on the hottest days. Once the tall houses had been the homes of the Knights of St John and the wealthier citizens of Valletta. Now it was a row of bars and nightclubs, cheap hotels and brothels, over a hundred and still counting, though the line between any of those establishments was a narrow one. Alcohol, sex and jazz were the blood and the pulse in Strait Street's veins. The British presence in Malta had its pluses and minuses. People differed on where Strait Street stood in that reckoning. It had served the needs of the navy and merchant ships for a long time, and with ever-more soldiers, sailors and airmen arriving in the build-up to war, it had only grown in size.

Strait Street kept strange hours, but they had become more erratic as Malta came under siege from the air. Time had to be grabbed and business had to be done. Whereas the night and the early hours of the morning were when Strait Street had usually seen trade at its busiest, now, whenever there was a respite from the bombing, the bars and their ancillary activities opened up, and any servicemen who could find a free hour, whenever that hour was, made their way into the welcoming darkness of Strada Stretta.

George Spiteri led Stefan and Frank Nugent through the street. It wasn't busy, but there were bars open and soldiers and sailors moved from one to another. The sounds of several jazz bands emerged through open doors from dark interiors, blending and clashing cheerfully as the three men threaded their way along the street that was also known as the Gut. The sergeant stopped at a shabby door bearing none of the garish signs that advertised the delights of the neighbouring bars. There was a name in chipped, gold lettering: The Dorotheum.

The two detectives followed the sergeant inside. There was a bar and three or four tables. Music thumped away through a Tannoy-like speaker. Behind the bar a bearded man nodded at George Spiteri. Clearly, he knew the sergeant.

'Cisk?' was all he said by way of greeting.

'Yes, beer's fine, Karl.'

Only now, their eyes adjusting to the half-light, did Stefan and Frank see two men sitting at one of the tables: a young man, barely out of his teens; an older man, fidgety, suspicious. Spiteri went across to them. There were nods of hesitant uncertainty from the men at the table. The sergeant gestured at the two detectives to join them. More nods; recognition rather than greeting. They sat.

'We'll forget names, for now.'

The older man spoke in Maltese; telling him it was not just 'for now'.

'Mhux "biss għalissa", Surġent.'

The sergeant laughed. 'All right, we'll forget names, full stop.'

Karl put down three glasses of beer. He grinned.

'Friend of Dorothy One and Friend of Dorothy Two.'

'Fuck off,' said the older man.

'This is Mr Nugent and Mr Gillespie,' continued Spiteri. 'They don't know you. Or anybody. But they did come here to find the man who killed Tony Zammit and Kenneth Borg. And other men, too. I want to do the same.'

'You haven't got very far,' said the older man.

The younger man finally spoke. 'And maybe there's a reason for that.'

'And what is that reason?' said the sergeant.

The two men looked at each other, reluctant to say more.

'Father Zachary asked you to speak,' continued Spiteri.

The young man nodded.

'We don't know you from Adam,' said Stefan quietly. 'You can say anything. But we need something. Mr Nugent and I probably won't be in Malta much longer. What we came to do . . . we fucked up on. We came to collect a murderer . . . and we'll go home empty-handed. I know Sergeant Spiteri is doing what he can, but he's at a dead end too. And when the chief inspector and I get on a plane in a couple of days, the man who killed your friends will still be here. This feller's killed six or seven men that we know of. He won't stop. He's here. It's only a question of when he does it again.'

No one said anything for almost a minute.

Finally the younger man spoke.

'There is a soldier we've seen, some of us. I've seen him a couple of times. He watches. That's all you can say. And other men – other friends – have seen him. He watches, where we meet each other. Dark places, at night. He doesn't come close. I could only say he's tall, thin . . . a soldier in a uniform—'

The older man broke in. 'It's not so odd. Some men are very nervous. They want something, but they're frightened. It takes time to have the courage. There's a lot to be afraid of if you're seen, if anyone finds out. And there are other things that stop you. The shame of what you're doing. Some men watch a long time before they . . .'

For a moment again no one spoke.

'But with this man, something is different?' asked Stefan.

'Yes, I suppose,' said the younger man. 'Something doesn't feel right.'

Spiteri looked at the older man again. 'There is more, isn't there?'

The older man nodded.

'Yes. This soldier did come up to me one night. In the Barrakka Gardens. He didn't say much, barely anything, but that's not so unusual. He was English, I know that. I told him we could go somewhere. We could go down in the lift, to somewhere quiet. We walked towards the lift, and when it came up, someone stepped out. And the soldier ran. Fast. Back into the night. I saw his face for a second, just before he ran. He looked . . . I wouldn't say frightened, but angry, very angry.'

'Would you recognise him again?'

'I don't think so. I only saw this soldier briefly. He had a kind of scarf. Just round his neck, but it covered a bit of his face, his mouth. It was months ago.'

'And what about Kenneth Borg?'

The older man was silent again, before he continued.

'Kenneth had met this soldier too, at least once. He told me about it. You notice men. And we'd noticed him. It sounded like the same man to me. Ken tried to talk to him, but the man didn't answer. He just left, as soon as Ken went over to him. Ken had seen the soldier watching, like I had, the way I told you he watched. Ken was intrigued. He liked mystery and strangers. He said he'd have him next time. He'd give that soldier what he wanted. He said it like a joke.'

The man shook his head, looking down.

'And you think this could be the one we're looking for?'

The man looked up again.

'I can't know that. But I know there's something not right. That's all I'm saying. You're looking for a soldier. He's a soldier. You're looking for a man no one knows. That's him. You should look at him. You have to look at him.'

The man stopped, quite abruptly. He looked hesitant, as if there was something more he wanted to say, but he wasn't sure he could safely say it.

'But that isn't the end, is it?' said Spiteri.

'No,' replied the older man. 'There is one more thing. Ken saw more of this soldier's face than anyone else. He'd tried to talk to him. He had a feeling he recognised him. He wasn't a hundred per cent sure, but he said his gut told him he was right. He reckoned he'd seen the soldier somewhere else. He didn't think he was an ordinary soldier at all, even if he was dressed up as one, when he hung about at night in the Gardens. Ken thought he'd seen him in Strait Street, on patrol. He reckoned this soldier was really . . . a Military Policeman.'

That afternoon Inspector Gillespie and Chief Inspector Nugent abandoned the case for a few hours. They had something now, something new, something important, but the next move was going to be very difficult. They had to take what they had, along with George Spiteri, to the Provost Marshall at Fort St Elmo and to the sergeant's superiors in the Malta Police. One thing that wasn't difficult was anticipating Colonel Macgregor's reaction. It would not be pretty.

For now, it would be no bad thing to let it settle for a while. They both needed to marshal their thoughts before they stepped into the furore to come.

They walked to the Manoel Theatre with the three ladies of Lascaris. They sat in its old, golden interior, with its tiers of boxes, more opera house than cinema, and watched Charlie Chaplin mocking Hitler and Mussolini and their strutting dictatorships. Stefan had wondered how easily the laughter would come, with those same dictatorships raining bombs on the island outside the theatre. There had been dead to bury that morning, as there were every day. But it came easily, from an audience of British troops and Maltese men, women and children, laughing with a mixture of relief and some defiance; there was still a world in which simple laughter could triumph. For the British, it was Charlie Chaplin's absurd Hitler-Hynkel who provoked most laughter, but for the Maltese it was often Jack Oakie's Napaloni-Mussolini who produced belly laughs and boos. If Adenoid Hynkel captured some of the real darkness behind Chaplin's comedy, for the Maltese, Benzino Napaloni was their very own pantomime villain.

They came out of the theatre cheerful and refreshed. It was almost dark, but the night was clear and warm and quiet. The bombers might come, but such moments were to be grasped with open arms. Alice, Jane and Maria wanted to go to the Caffe Cordina for some tea and the only cakes in Valletta that still seemed to be made from flour that wasn't adulterated with something unspeakable and inedible. Stefan was happy to go, but Frank Nugent was preoccupied. Sitting in the cinema had not transported him as far from the business in hand as it had Stefan. As they came into the Strada Reale, he hung back a few yards with Stefan. The women walked on, laughing about the film.

'You go with them, Stefan. One of us should.'

'What's the matter?'

'We can't sit on what George has come up with. A Military Policeman. How many are there? Not that many. We have to go back to the Provost Marshall now. You, me, George Spiteri.'

'I know. He is going to love us,' said Stefan, smiling.

'I want to get it all down. Old stuff, new stuff. Point by point. We need to box Macgregor in. He has to realise there's no way round working with the Malta Police . . . and with us. We know more than he does. If he doesn't do it, and there's another murder, he's the one who'll be in the shit, army or no army.'

'I'll leave you to tell him that, Frank.'

Alice called back.

'Come on, you two, no dawdling. Cakes!'

'You go with the girls. When you get back to the hotel, we'll go through it together.'

Jane shouted back now too.

'Don't you two eat?'

Frank Nugent laughed. 'Tell them I've got a bit of Delhi belly!'

It was half an hour later that Stefan was walking down the steep cobbled steps of St John's Street to the junction with St Ursula Street and the British Hotel. He had left Alice, Jane and Maria with tea and cakes at the Cordina. The break that the afternoon had offered was over. Like Frank Nugent, he wanted to get back to work. There was a possibility that the journey to Malta would not be a waste of time. There was a chance that the man who had killed so many could be caught. The answer lay in the British Army. But the Provost Marshall and his men had to be battered into looking for the killer among their own.

The streets were silent, away from Kingsway, but there was a small crowd as Stefan turned into St Ursula Street. The road was blocked. Two Maltese police constables stood talking to an agitated group of men and women. Further up the stepped cobbles more policemen were walking slowly, shining torches in front of them. The conversation Stefan heard was in Maltese and English. He couldn't make out what anyone was saying, but as he moved through the crowd, people stopped talking. They were looking at him, concerned, awkward, nervous. He felt tension. Something was wrong.

A woman spoke to one of the constables in Maltese.

'Dan huwa il-pulizija l-ieħor, il pulizija Irlandiż.'

Stefan could guess the meaning; the other policeman, the Irish policeman.

'Inspector Gillespie . . .' said the Maltese constable.

'What's happened?'

'Mr Nugent, Chief Inspector Nugent. He was attacked.'

'Attacked?'

'The ambulance has come. It's through the hotel.'

The Maltese constable turned towards the St Ursula Street entrance to the British Hotel. Stefan followed. The policeman was almost running, so was Stefan.

'What do you mean attacked?'

'We think he was robbed, at the corner.'

The policeman pushed open the door to the hotel.

'There was a knife.'

'For fuck's sake! Is he all right?'

The two men ran along the corridor to the bar and the lobby and the doors out on to Battery Street, where there was road access.

'They carried him through . . . so the ambulance could . . .'

Stefan came out on to the street on the other side of the hotel. A stretcher was being carried into the back of a British Army ambulance. There was another crowd of people, among them Mr and Mrs Sacco, white-faced, staring. Jimmy Gaunt was by the ambulance door. Stefan stood, frozen, unable to grasp what had happened in only seconds it seemed. Corporal Gaunt turned towards him. Stefan could see blood on Gaunt's shirt and shorts and, as he walked towards him, blood on his hands.

'I found him, Mr Gillespie. I found him . . . just lying . . .'

'Is he . . .?' Stefan couldn't get the words out.

The ambulance's engine started up.

Jimmy Gaunt turned to one of the army medics.

'This is Inspector Gillespie . . . he's the policeman with . . .'

'All right then. Better hop in, mate.'

Stefan, hardly knowing what he was doing, climbed into the back of the ambulance. The medic got in beside him. He pulled the door shut and sat down opposite the stretcher. Stefan sat next to him. The soldier took out a packet of Woodbines. He offered one to Stefan. Stefan shook his head. He gazed across at the stretcher and the face of Frank Nugent, now unconscious. The army medic lit his cigarette. Stefan sank back on the bench.

'What do you think?' said Stefan Gillespie quietly.

The soldier drew heavily on his cigarette. He did not reply.

17

Fort St Elmo

The next morning, Stefan Gillespie waited in the Provost Marshall's office at Fort St Elmo. An ATS corporal brought him a cup of tea. Stefan walked across the room and looked out at the sunlit courtyard. Apart from a truck and a staff car, it was empty. It was a strangely peaceful place. Created by knights who numbered priests in their ranks and had started out building hospitals, the heart of Fort St Elmo, behind its heavy bastions, still contained the faint memory of a monastery. The silence would not last long. Stefan took in the map of the island next to the window. Sicily loomed over it, far bigger; dotted across the Italian island were the locations of dozens of German and Italian airfields. Bombers would leave them again soon enough.

A bookcase reached up to the ceiling next to the map. Stefan let his eyes wander over the rows of books. He saw a shelf of small red and green books; red for Latin and green for Greek. They were sandwiched between bigger volumes; a thick Liddell and Scott *Greek–English Lexicon*, a Lewis and Short *Latin Dictionary*, books of grammar and classical history. This was what the British brought to war. Then he remembered the last time he had looked at one of the small red books, in the garden annexe in Thomastown that was James Corcoran's refuge. There was a Loeb edition of the poems of Catullus and there was a receipt Corcoran had kept for another copy of the same book, probably bought as a present for the man who killed him a few days later.

Colonel Macgregor's books were kept in neat, alphabetical order. Between Gaius Julius Caesar and Marcus Tullius Cicero were the poems of Gaius Valerius Catullus. An old copy, no dust jacket, battered and well read; sandwiched between volumes that looked almost untouched. Stefan took it and opened it. On the fly leaf: *Haydon Macgregor, Edinburgh University, 1919.*

The door opened. The Provost Marshall entered, flustered, irritated.

'Sorry to keep you, Inspector.'

Stefan noted that for some reason his rank was acknowledged today.

'I've been with my SIB chaps . . . and the Malta Police.'

The words were simple, but they contained the suggestion that this was Stefan's fault. Macgregor didn't sit down. He paced as he spoke.

'It's a relief about Nugent. A great relief. You've seen him?'

'Yes, sir. I was at the hospital till this morning. He's grand.'

Grand was stretching it, but Nugent would come through.

'I really don't . . .' Macgregor was shaking his head. 'It's not Malta. Not the Malta I know. People get robbed, yes, but even that is rare enough . . . you know? It's a quiet, peaceful place.' The Provost Marshall smiled. 'Well, you might not think so when you're in a shelter under the Barrakka Gardens, but people are not bombs. They put up with the bombs, though. I've got men who can't stick it the way the Maltese do.'

Macgregor looked at Stefan as if he needed his words justified.

Stefan gave a nod. He had seen the truth of that.

'This business . . .' The Provost Marshall stiffened. 'I have no doubt you and the chief inspector will see something else in what's just happened. I am sure Sergeant Spiteri does too. I don't know. I will admit that. But it still seems . . . if you take one appalling event and shove it next to another one . . . is that evidence or just piling up a series of coincidences?'

'I'm not a great one for coincidences, Colonel, especially when it comes to people getting murdered and then, hey presto, someone trying to murder a policeman who has found out . . . who's stirred things up.'

'You've certainly done that, both of you. You and Spiteri.'

'You can't stir something up if there's nothing to stir.'

The Provost Marshall walked to the window and gazed out.

'I have seen Sergeant Spiteri this morning. It's clear there are issues we need to work on more closely with the local bods. Spiteri's boss will be working with Sergeant Shaw and the SIB, and Lieutenant Yates. I accept that I may have been slow on this. But, who knows, perhaps I might have been more active if you and Chief Inspector Nugent hadn't arrived to lead us up the garden path. It was Scotland Yard, as I recall, that insisted we only had to fingerprint a few dozen soldiers, and it would be done and dusted. Not bloody so, Mr Gillespie.'

'No, sir.' Stefan smiled. The Provost Marshall had enjoyed saying that.

'So, we are on to this. The Corps of Military Police and the Malta Police. I have to say that these allegations about a Military Policeman . . . supposedly from one queer with the habit of picking up men in the Upper Barrakka . . . I simply don't believe it. I won't ignore it, but it's no basis for an investigation.'

Stefan was sure that meant Colonel Macgregor would ignore it.

'It's one place to look, Colonel, if there's a reason to look.'

'Well, "if" is the word, Inspector. I don't go by "if"s. Meanwhile, you and Chief Inspector Nugent are surplus to

217

requirements. You failed to do what you came here to do. You find it impossible not to stir up trouble where there is none. And now, regrettably, Mr Nugent has been seriously hurt. I've spoken to the Officer Commanding and I know he's passed it by the Governor's office. As soon as the chief inspector can travel, there'll be seats on a plane to Gibraltar.'

Stefan nodded. He was in no position to argue. His presence was never really tolerated anyway. Nugent probably would argue, but to no purpose.

'Thank you, sir.'

Stefan realised he was still holding the Loeb Catullus.

'I'm sorry, Colonel. I was just looking at this.'

Macgregor took the book. His face softened, in some surprise.

'You're a classicist, Inspector Gillespie?'

'Not at all. Small Latin . . . and no Greek whatsoever.'

The Provost Marshall leafed idly through the book.

'Looks like you read a lot of Catullus, sir.'

Macgregor's sharp voice was quieter. Somewhere there was regret.

'It's funny, isn't it? I spent a lot of time reading this stuff, two thousand years old – getting on for three, some of the Greek. I carry it around with me, I don't know why. I never look at it. But I remember reading it. That was something . . . worthwhile. It's not a word that comes into my head much now.'

As Stefan Gillespie left the colonel's office, Lieutenant Yates and Sergeant Shaw were walking towards it. Yates smiled and slapped Stefan on the back.

'They make them tough at Scotland Yard!'

'Tough enough,' said Stefan.

'Thanks for leaving us all your work!'

'It'll give you something to do, Jack.'

'Yes, Lieutenant.'

Shaw grinned. 'Bugger all going on in Malta!'

The SIB man knocked on the colonel's door and went in. Yates followed. He looked back at Stefan for a moment.

'You seen Jimmy Gaunt, my corporal, Stefan?'

'No, not since last night.'

'He's disappeared.'

'If he's at the British Hotel, I'll say you're looking for him.'

Yates laughed. 'Whatever's going on with Maria Sacco, if he's not back ASAP, he's on a charge!'

The first thing Stefan saw when he came out of Fort St Elmo was George Spiteri, leaning against the bonnet of a black Austin 10, smoking a cigarette.

'Do you want a lift?'

Stefan nodded. He took a cigarette from the packet held out by Spiteri.

They got into the car. Stefan lit the cigarette.

'I was up at Mtarfa,' said the Maltese sergeant. 'Frank looks good.'

'He's not so bad.'

The car pulled away.

'He knows we've got our marching orders? Back to Blighty.'

'I told him that's what I'd heard at HQ. I've got mine, too.'

How do you mean?'

'I can drive the car and carry the bags, my boss is running the case. He'll do it Colonel Macgregor's way, whatever that is. And that won't impress the people who might be able to give us more information. There's not so many places homosexuals go. The man we're looking for was hanging around them. We know that. Other people must have seen him too. And they all know each other. I think there's more to get. I think we could even start to build up a description. That's the only way to go. But now? It's the kiss of death. You think our friends from the Dorotheum will sit in an interrogation room with a Military Policeman and repeat what they said? It'll be a know-nothing, saw-nothing, heard-nothing job from now on. Not only that. They'll be thinking about what happened to Frank Nugent. They might not want to risk being . . . robbed.'

Stefan Gillespie stepped out of the bathroom at the British Hotel. He had shut himself in there, in the middle of the afternoon. The ladies from Lascaris had come back from their night shift that morning. They were still sleeping. There would be no hot water for them when they finally came to. He knew the consequences. It was the first time he had won the battle of the bathroom. They were sleeping late; he had taken his chance. A bath was not at the top of his list of priorities but being alone was. The skies were still over Valletta; half an hour of silence was worth the wrath of the three women upstairs. Frank Nugent was all right. Stefan had left him recovering in hospital at Mtarfa. That was what mattered most. It had been close, closer than the English policeman chose to say. But he had been lucky, not only in the organs the knife had missed, but in the hospital they had taken him to, where the trauma of bloody wounds was a daily routine.

For the rest, there wasn't much left that Stefan could do. He could only wait to leave the island. If Frank Nugent had little authority, he had none. Colonel Macgregor wanted them both out of Malta. The colonel's predictions had been fulfilled. Sending civilians into a theatre of war, as if ordinary life – even the ordinary investigation of a murder – could somehow continue showed the ignorance of the civilian authorities. There was too much trouble that was beyond the Provost Marshall's control, or anybody else's on an island under siege. The only way to deal with anything troublesome that Colonel Macgregor could realistically control was to remove it. But what Macgregor saw as trouble, Stefan and Frank Nugent and George Spiteri knew was a breakthrough. A Military Policeman. Somewhere behind it all, in Ireland, in

England, in Malta, was a man who was now a Military Policeman. It was something so fragile that it could easily be punctured. And it was likely it would be.

The claims came from people Macgregor would give no credence to; they were only homos, poofs, queers, perverts. And they were making allegations against the Corps of Military Police. Where would Macgregor even start? He'd start by refusing to believe it, thought Stefan. And then another thought, a mad thought. Macgregor was a Military Policeman. It was a wild, unexpected idea, but it was there. Stefan could feel he was grasping at straws, reaching for anything when everything was falling apart again. That's how it was. Anyone could read a Latin poet. A coincidence. And if he was always suspicious of coincidences, wasn't that what they were made of; something here, something there, slammed together only because they were in your head? But how many soldiers in Malta carried a copy of James Corcoran's favourite Latin poet? Stefan Gillespie knew he was leaping at nothing because he had control of nothing. There was only vagary and hearsay.

He was on the landing above his own room, about to go downstairs. He had closed the bathroom door quietly. He had stepped gingerly along the landing. He did not want to wake Alice, Jane and Maria, particularly Alice and Jane. Bath water was a precious commodity. At the British Hotel, the ladies of Lascaris insisted it was their property. He needed a drink before he faced them.

It was the silence of the hotel, in the silent street – where a rare afternoon of peace meant a siesta for most of the residents – that let Stefan hear the noise of a door opening on the floor below. He looked down over the banister. He saw Jimmy Gaunt come out of Frank Nugent's room. The corporal turned to the door and locked it. He waited, listening, looking down the stairs. But he did not look up. He moved quickly, quietly downstairs. Stefan could see the lobby and the desk. No one was there.

Corporal Gaunt disappeared. He was putting the key behind the desk. He stepped across the lobby, visible momentarily, and hurried out through the door to Battery Street.

Stefan waited a few seconds then went down. He passed his own room and Frank Nugent's and continued to the lobby. He walked behind the reception desk and picked up the key Gaunt had put down. He went upstairs and into the English detective's room. He walked to the open shutters of the balcony. He could see Jimmy Gaunt, making his way towards the Victoria Gate. He looked back into the room. It was neat and tidy, as Nugent had left it. On the table next to the bed was a briefcase, files, papers, pages of scribbled notes. There was a map of Valletta marked with hieroglyphs, intelligible only to Frank Nugent. Stefan knew they showed where two bodies had been found, where a witness had seen a victim or an unidentified soldier, where two men may have been picked up by another man at different times. And there were accounts of conversations with George Spiteri and the men at the Dorotheum in Strait Street. Gaunt could have no reason to come into the room secretly, except to look at all this. There was nothing else there. And people had been looking for the Military Policeman too, earlier. Jack Yates had made a joke about it. Gaunt had disappeared. He was AWOL. Why? He must have been at the hotel all along. He had been there to search Frank Nugent's room.

Chief Inspector Nugent was a meticulously tidy man. Stefan, who wasn't, had found himself almost irritated by the way the Englishman squared up piles of documents and numbered and renumbered notes to keep them in chronological order. It was close to obsessive. The state of the papers on the table in Nugent's room was normal for most people, but Stefan had a clear image of what the desk looked like before. The material had been searched. Much of the information it contained was already with the Military Police at Fort St Elmo. Stefan didn't know how difficult it would have been for Jimmy

Gaunt to get access to it. Not that difficult, if he was determined to see it. He wanted more, to risk doing this. But why? What did he want to know so badly?

It was unlikely, even if the corporal had been at Fort St Elmo that morning, that he would have been party to any conversation about a Military Policeman, in the uniform of an ordinary soldier, cruising Valletta. It was something the Provost Marshall was sitting on; something he didn't want talked about publicly. It was also something he didn't believe. It would not be common knowledge. But Jimmy Gaunt must have known something and he had been desperate to find out more. And he must have done in Nugent's room. He must know things now that George Spiteri had told neither his own boss, Inspector Simmons, nor the Provost Marshall. He would know the names of people who were talking. He would know who had pointed to a Military Policeman in disguise, picking men up for sex in the Upper Barrakka Gardens.

The rest of the afternoon was as unsatisfactory as it could have been. Stefan Gillespie thought Jimmy Gaunt might come back to the hotel. He was always hanging around there. But so far, the corporal had not returned. Stefan didn't know what to do next. He wanted to get some perspective on what he had just seen but there was no one to talk to about it. He thought of taking a taxi to Mtarfa, to see Frank, but decided he should stay in Valletta. He needed to know more about Gaunt. Sitting in the bar at the British Hotel, he was interrupted by two Military Policemen who were looking for Gaunt themselves. They were good-humoured enough, but it was clear that Lieutenant Yates was no longer making jokes about the corporal's disappearance. Jimmy was in trouble.

Stefan walked along the Grand Harbour to Malta Police Headquarters. George Spiteri wasn't there. He left a message and was caught, and briefly interrogated, by the sergeant's superior. Inspector Simmons was an English colonial police-man, who was simultaneously curious about what Stefan wanted and half afraid he might tell him. Stefan knew from Sergeant Spiteri that Simmons lived in a state of permanent genuflection to the British Army in general and the Provost Marshall in particular. The inspector was now working with Colonel Macgregor on the investigation of what were two of the most brutal murders the island of Malta had seen, not to mention the ones in England and Ireland that came with it. He would do what the Provost Marshall told him. Stefan knew that anything he said would go straight to Macgregor. The inspector showed all the signs of being a man who worked hard at avoiding trouble. If he ever found it, his first instinct would be to pass the ball on. There was no point telling him anything.

Fort St Elmo was close to Police Headquarters. Stefan had left the fort earlier, with nothing more to say, but something had happened. Corporal Gaunt's behaviour meant something. But what? He couldn't be sure the corporal hadn't been sent there by Lieutenant Yates, or by the colonel himself. Gaunt was handy for a bit of spying. He was never out of the British Hotel, waiting for Maria, being dragged off for lessons in Maltese by Mrs Sacco, to keep him away from Maria. That was a standing joke. But searching Frank Nugent's room wasn't. And something was growing in Stefan's mind: the night before, in Battery Street, the ambulance taking Frank away. Blood on Jimmy Gaunt's shirt and shorts. A lot of blood. The corporal helped carry the chief inspector to the ambulance from St Ursula Street. But hadn't he been the one who found him? The first one on the scene? Wasn't it Gaunt who saw a figure running away in the dark, at the top of the steps? The robber. Wasn't it only Gaunt who had glimpsed this supposed robber?

Frank Nugent had seen nothing himself. He'd sensed some-one behind him in the night, on an empty street. Then the knife, like a sledgehammer in his side. Pain, blackness. He remembered nothing more until the hospital. It was still being called a robbery. And, yes, Frank Nugent's wallet had gone. But he was no more inclined than Stefan or George Spiteri to believe in a chance theft. They had stirred the black pool. Something had come up from the depths.

Stefan returned to the hotel to find Gaunt back again. He was outside, talking to Maria. She was in uniform, on her way to the War Rooms. She was laughing, teasing him about something. It looked like he was hard work. By the time Stefan reached them, Maria's voice showed irritation. She turned as Stefan approached, smiling warmly. Jimmy Gaunt nodded. He looked uncomfortable.

'Mr Nugent's all right,' Jimmy said. 'That's some relief.'

'He'll be fine,' said Stefan. 'I think he was lucky.'

'I can't remember anything like it,' said Maria, with genuine disbelief. 'People do rob. Bags and purses. But no one would do that. I've never heard of it.'

Gaunt shrugged at neither of them in particular.

'Long as he's OK, Maria.'

Alice and Jane came out of the hotel.

'You bastard,' said Jane.

'You Irish bastard,' added Alice.

Stefan was puzzled. He had long forgotten.

'Water, bath,' continued Alice, 'ladies of Lascaris for the use thereof.'

Stefan smiled. 'You'll survive.'

'Don't do it again!' said Jane. 'We'll send in the MPs if you do.'

'Won't we, Jimmy?' laughed Alice.

Jimmy attempted a grin, without much conviction.

'Don't mind him,' said Maria. 'He's been drinking.'

'I have not!'

'I can smell it, Jimmy.'

The three women walked away.

Jane called back. 'If you see Frank, give him a kiss – from us, that is!'

They hurried on.

Stefan headed into the British Hotel.

'Good thing Mr Nugent's OK.' Jimmy Gaunt said it again.

Stefan wondered if he should say something about the MPs who were there earlier, looking for Gaunt, about a now angry Lieutenant Yates. He didn't.

'Yes, it is,' Stefan said, and carried on into the hotel lobby.

An hour later Stefan Gillespie came downstairs. He walked into the bar and stood with a beer. He nodded at Jimmy Gaunt, who sat at a table in the corner, on his own. The corporal nodded in return, but he made no attempt to join Stefan. And Stefan stood at the bar, drinking, because he had no inclination to talk to Gaunt. Not now. When he did, it would be a different conversation from anything that had gone before. But he would do nothing at present. He had to wait for George Spiteri. He had promised the sergeant and he needed his authority.

Mrs Sacco bustled into the bar, looking busy as she always did, but a little put out. Her eyes fixed on Jimmy Gaunt. Clearly, he was what had ruffled her.

'Jimmy, have you got nothing better to do?'

Corporal Gaunt looked up.

'Lieutenant Yates was here earlier. He was looking for you.'

'He can look, can't he?'

'Are you off duty, then?'

'I suppose so.'

She tutted. This wasn't a Jimmy Gaunt she knew. She smiled.

'Come on. If you have nothing to do . . . why don't we do some Maltese?'

She spoke almost tenderly. Stefan saw she was concerned.

'Aħna nitgħallmu l-Malti . . . we'll learn some Maltese, yes?'

Jimmy Gaunt stood up, irritated, almost angry.

'For fuck's sake, give it a break, woman.'

He rushed out of the bar, leaving Maria's mother close to tears.

Stefan put the glass of beer down. He walked out quietly. He went to the door and stepped out into the street. He could see Corporal Gaunt heading towards the junction with St John's Street. If Mrs Sacco was surprised by Jimmy Gaunt's behaviour, so was he. The corporal was obviously anxious, disturbed. He was a worried man. Stefan wanted to know where he was going.

18

Triq Marsamxett

Stefan followed Corporal Gaunt up the steep steps of St John's Street, keeping back as far as he could, always to one side of the street, in the shadow of the shops and houses. There were not many people about, a few Maltese men and women going home, or searching the thinly stocked shops for something that might not be there tomorrow, soldiers and sailors moving from bar to bar, probably working their way from the harbour to Strait Street. Jimmy Gaunt was as preoccupied as he had been in the bar at the British Hotel. He was easy to follow, but full of indecision. He slowed down, stopped, lit a cigarette, walked quickly, threw the cigarette aside half-smoked, slowed and stopped again. As Stefan came up behind him into St John's Square, Valletta grew busier. There were people in the cafés, standing in groups talking in the laziness of an evening that was still calm. There was a line of men and women moving towards the cathedral. The bell was tolling for Mass. Jimmy Gaunt almost passed the Cathedral of St John, but he turned to the cathedral steps and the open doors.

Stefan Gillespie waited, then he walked into the cathedral. It was filling up with people, but he could see the Military

Policeman sitting on one of the chairs that covered the blaze of colour that was the marbled floor. He was close to the doors. He would only have to turn to see Stefan. Stefan went back outside. He walked to a café under a colonnaded archway that partly hid him and ordered a beer. The doors of the cathedral were in front of him, across the square.

It took ten minutes before Corporal Gaunt emerged. He walked on along St John's Street and crossed the central street of the city, the Strada Reale, Kingsway. Stefan followed.

Jimmy Gaunt swung abruptly into Strait Street. The bars were busy here, some behind closed doors, some with doors open on to cave-like interiors that showed no lights. The tight space of Strait Street was crowded with servicemen. Stefan struggled to keep Jimmy in sight, as he brushed off the calls for business from the open doorways and the balconies above. He lost Gaunt for a moment, then almost ran into him when the Military Policeman had to stop to speak to two MPs on patrol. Clearly they didn't know he was AWOL, but Stefan could see Gaunt didn't want to talk.

As Strait Street began to slope steeply down towards the end of the peninsula that was Valletta, the corporal turned into St Christopher Street. There was a red telephone box – a piece of London coming out of nowhere. Jimmy went into it and picked up the phone. He was there several minutes. He came out of the telephone box with irritation, almost anger, adding to the confusion and indecision he already exuded. It was darker now. St Christopher Street was empty, and Stefan needed to stay much further back. He thought he had lost Jimmy Gaunt, but then he saw him, walking across a low hill of brick and stone, to a terrace of houses beyond. Stefan crouched, watching. The corporal passed the row of buildings, looking up at the windows, many of which were broken and unrepaired. Black, empty interiors lay behind them. The houses' fronts were cracked and scarred from shrapnel. Stefan registered a sign in chipped stone at the corner of one of the buildings: *Triq Marsamxett, Marsamxett Street*.

There was a shout from another street and a peal of laughter; it was somewhere behind Stefan. Two voices were arguing. There came the sound of something smashing. The young Englishman stopped at a door now. He pushed and went in.

Stefan walked slowly towards the building. He saw a light in a window at the top of the house. Then it was gone. A lamp had been lit and a shutter had been closed. Stefan reached the door of the house. It was open. Inside was a dark hallway and a set of narrow stairs. There was silence. As he started to climb the stairs, he saw that some doors had pieces of planking nailed across them. There was a smell of warmth that was somehow dry and damp at the same time. There was the smell of rats and mice. Jimmy Gaunt had to be at the top, in the room behind the shutter. Stefan moved carefully, quietly, upwards, listening all the time.

When he reached the top of the staircase, there was a narrow landing. There were three doors. The third was open. The other two had padlocks screwed to them. He could see clearly in the dim light that came from the doorway to the third room. He moved towards it. There was a black alcove and a steep, ladder-like stairway that had to lead to the roof. He could see a padlock on the floor. The door had been broken open. At his feet there was a heavy iron bar. It must have been used to force the lock. Suddenly, he felt his vulnerability. He was unarmed. He had no idea where he was. There was a chance that Jimmy Gaunt had put a knife in Frank Nugent. Could there even be a chance that he had killed six men? It seemed mad, but was it? Gaunt was a soldier, a Military Policeman. The man that had to be found was a soldier, a Military Policeman. That fitted. And Jimmy Gaunt's recent behaviour didn't fit an innocent man.

Stefan picked up the bar. He looked through the open door. He could see a wall and part of a bed in the room. The corporal was bending down at the side of the bed. He pulled out a heavy leather suitcase from underneath it. He undid two straps and lifted the lid. He stood up, looking into the case. He pulled something out, a piece of clothing. He dropped it on the bed and stepped back. Stefan moved out of sight, into the alcove. As he did, he kicked an empty bottle into the stairwell. A few seconds, then the sound of the bottle smashing below. He heard Corporal Gaunt's footsteps on the bare floor. The light from the lamp in the room was casting his shadow along the landing now. He was walking towards Stefan.

'Who is it?'

There was a rustling, a clip unclipped.

Corporal Gaunt had taken out his revolver.

'I said who is it?'

The corporal's voice was trembling.

'Is that …? Who is …?' Jimmy seemed to gulp. 'I am armed, right?'

The outstretched hand and the revolver it clutched moved slowly into the opening to the alcove. Stefan Gillespie lifted the iron bar above his head, and brought it down with all his force. The gun spun away along the landing towards the open door. Jimmy Gaunt collapsed on his knees with a scream of pain. Stefan came out of the alcove and used the bar once more, against the side of the Military Policeman's head, even as he looked up at Stefan in fear and bewilderment. Now Jimmy lay on the floor; out cold.

Stefan Gillespie breathed deeply, leaning against the wall. There came a familiar sound, winding itself up and wailing across the night, over the square streets of Valletta and into the house. The sirens were going, all around. An ordinary night. The bombers were on their way.

★

Stefan dragged Jimmy Gaunt into the room. He was unconscious. He groaned but didn't come round. Stefan pulled him to the iron bed frame that was against a wall, under a shuttered window. He took one of the leather straps from the open suitcase and wrapped it round the corporal's hands, buckling it tight. There was blood on Stefan's hands as well as on Gaunt's. The bar that had smashed into the wrist had a sharp, jagged edge. Stefan could feel the inertia of a broken wrist bone too, drooping as he tied it to the other one. He wound the second strap round the Englishman's ankles and buckled them together. He saw the MP's service revolver in the doorway. He picked it up and put it beside him on the bed.

The room was small and dark. The walls were cracked; there was crumbling plaster. The paraffin lamp lit only the area around the bed. It sat on a box across from the bed, where Gaunt had put it. The bed was quite new; carved, heavy mahogany. There was an armchair next to it, new too, in smart red morocco, with brass studs that gleamed. It was as if someone had started to furnish the room and abandoned the effort. Why? Against one wall there were a dozen boxes and packing cases.

Stefan lifted one of the lids of the boxes. There were bottles of Johnnie Walker whisky stacked inside. The room looked like it was a place where goods pilfered from the army were stored. On a line, stretched across a corner of the room, a suit hung on a hanger; there were trousers, shirts. A pile of unwashed clothes, military and civilian, lay against the wall underneath; shorts, underwear. Yet the room did not feel as if it was lived in.

There was only a dirty sheet over the mattress of the bed. On a packing case, there was a half-empty bottle of Johnnie Walker and several maps of Malta and of Valletta. On the bed was the open suitcase Stefan had seen Jimmy pulling clothes from. Next to it was a khaki army tunic and a pair of khaki trousers. Stefan looked into the case and saw more khaki. He pulled out the clothing. There were two more uniforms in khaki serge. They were the uniforms of an ordinary soldier, with no markings of rank. There were shorts and shirts in the sandy-yellow of tropical kit and two forage caps. Stefan laid the items on the bed. There were no regimental badges, no signs of identity. This was the unidentifiable, barely registered soldier who might have been glimpsed somewhere near so many killings. In blackout, in cities full of plain khaki, these uniforms brought a kind of invisibility. There were two heavy commando knives in oil paper. And there were papers he recognised, copies of reports and statements from the Scotland Yard files Nugent had sent to the Military Police at Fort St Elmo. In the bottom of the case, Stefan found a bag that contained thin, pale kid gloves, almost the colour of flesh. Four pairs. There were never any fingerprints. It was obvious now. All these things were disposable. Uniforms of the night. And whatever bloody state they got into, they could be thrown away. Afterwards.

There was a moan from the floor. Then a cry of pain. Jimmy Gaunt had discovered the pain that was a broken wrist. Stefan sat on the edge of the bed, staring at the young Military Policeman's wide, blinking eyes. Gaunt pushed himself up, his back against the wall.

'Ow, shit!' He held up his bound hands. 'You bastard!'

Stefan said nothing. He couldn't relate this to the pale, boyish face.

'I can't see a thing. Where are my bloody glasses?'

Stefan stood up. Jesus, what was the man talking about?

'You want your fucking glasses? That's it, is it? That's what you say?'

'That would be a start, sir. Why the hell did you do this?'

The note of injured indignation was not what Stefan expected.

The corporal grimaced in pain again, but his mind was somewhere else.

'I knew he had this place, I found where it was. I couldn't fathom what was going on, but I saw him, that's the thing, after Mr Nugent was stabbed, later, near . . . I couldn't make sense of it. He said he wasn't there! I never imagined this, I never . . .'

Stefan stared at Gaunt. What was he talking about? There were tears in his eyes, but it was something that pushed past the pain.

'I didn't know who . . . I was afraid, I tried to phone Sergeant Spiteri . . .'

'What?'

The corporal was staring away from Stefan now.

'Fuck,' he said quietly.

He was looking at the door.

Stefan Gillespie turned the same way.

The uniform was as neat and sharp as ever; the red cap was tightly fixed on his head, at exactly the correct military angle. It was Lieutenant Yates.

'Bit of a party, lads?' He walked forward, smiling. As he did, he unclipped the holster at his side and took out his revolver. He glanced down at Jimmy Gaunt, battered and in pain, his hands tied. 'So, is that an arrest, Inspector?'

Stefan gestured towards the bed and the pile of uniforms.

'You'd better look at what's here, Jack.'

It did not occur to Stefan to wonder how Lieutenant Yates got there, at precisely this moment. He did not register that the revolver was pointing at him.

'Follow my leader,' said Yates. 'There's Jimmy Gaunt, pride of the Corps of Military Police, heading along Strait Street . . . and down here to Marsamxett, with Gillespie of the Garda Síochána in hot pursuit. Not easy to miss. I didn't.'

Stefan saw where the gun was pointing.

He looked at Gaunt. The corporal shook his head.

'Might have been better asking what was going on, sir, instead of . . .' The corporal held up his bound hands.

'Yes.' Stefan nodded. 'It might have been a lot better.'

Yates moved closer, with an expression of weary irritation.

'Don't poke your nose in. That's a lesson in life, Stefan. You and Frank, now Jimmy. What's the point? Nobody cares, not really. It's a fucking slaughterhouse out there. Why fucking bother? But I knew Jimmy was going to pitch up sooner or later. He'd been asking about my little hide-away. I'm sorry to say some idle fucker said something. My fault, maybe. I probably mentioned I had a little place, didn't I, Jimmy, after a drink? Somewhere to bring a woman, eh?'

'You can't walk out of this now, Lieutenant,' said Stefan. 'You have a gun, but where's that going to get you? We're not some fucker in the darkness.'

'You're not clever, are you?' said Yates. 'But then you're a Paddy.'

'Sir,' said Corporal Gaunt, rank still dominant, 'I think it's over, sir.'

Lieutenant Yates turned the revolver from Stefan and pulled the trigger.

Corporal Gaunt slumped back on to the floor.

The revolver was pointing at Stefan again, even as Yates spoke.

'I'm pissed off about Jimmy. I mean that. Your fault, Inspector.'

'How the fuck does shooting him help?' Stefan was almost shouting.

'You're an Irishman, of dubious antecedents. I had Intelligence take a look at you. Irish Special Branch, not your average detective, eh? Trip to Berlin not long ago, right? Family in the heart of the dear old Thousand-Year Reich. You'll be found in the docks. Areas verboten to non-military sorts. When I say you'll be found, I'll find you, taking photos. I'll just do my job! It won't surprise Colonel Macgregor. Neutral, my arse, is his line. He didn't like you poking around. You shot poor Jimmy when he saw you. He'll get a medal. Posthumous. I shot you as you ran. I might get one too. But I won't begrudge Jimmy his if I don't. That'll be that. So, you see, I can walk out of this.'

'Why? To do it again . . . How many men do you need to kill, Jack?'

'You mistake your role here, Inspector. No questions, thanks.'

'Was James Corcoran the first? Or were there others?'

'Shifting you both, that's the bugger,' said the lieutenant to himself.

'He had a name, though. The others didn't have that, did they?'

'Keep me talking? Oh, dear.' Yates shook his head. 'None of us have real names, you see. Queer, that's the name. None of us asked for it. God-given. Can't get shot of it. Whatever you do. You try. Never clean. Never clean again.'

'You can stop this, Jack. Wouldn't that be better?'

'Ah, the old trick-cyclist routine. Don't bother. I'm not going to break down in tears, Stefan. There's a job to do. Marsamxett's empty now. Bombed out, not a lot of people about. That's good. But moving two of you will take some doing . . .'

Yates was talking to himself again, more tense, working things out.

'Even with hardly anyone about . . . getting the two fucking bodies . . .'

Stefan had not moved since he first realised the lieutenant's gun was aimed at him. Now he stepped forward slowly. The slightest shift. Then again.

Still covering Stefan with his revolver, Lieutenant Yates knelt down by Jimmy Gaunt. At that moment there was an explosion. It wasn't close, but it was loud. It shook the building.

Another explosion followed. Yates smiled.

'That's what I want . . . Yes, everyone in the fucking shelters!'

There was the sound of ack-ack guns. More bombs. Yates stood up.

'That's my boys,' said the Military Policeman. 'We need a bit of noise!'

Stefan could see, as Yates stared at him, what he had not seen before. It wasn't something that spoke of madness, but it was a cold detachment. It wasn't confusion, it was more like emptiness. He could also see the MP's attention was no longer on him. Yates was thinking hard, still working out what to do. Stefan used that moment. He inched closer to the bed. That was where he had put the gun down earlier. A khaki tunic covered it. He could see the edge of the grip. He would have to take it and shoot almost instantly. He had one chance. If he missed, Yates would have several. He could not fumble it.

There was a groan from Jimmy Gaunt, half-conscious. Yates spun round.

'You're not dead, you fucker! I need you dead. Damn you, Jimmy!'

Lieutenant Yates levelled the revolver back at Gaunt.

'I didn't want to kill you, you arsehole. But that's how it's got to be.'

Jack Yates' attention was off Stefan for only a second. There was another explosion outside, closer than before. The room shook. Stefan chose that instant to kick out at the box and the lamp. The lamp spun across the room, smashing against the wall. As it did so the light went out. The room plunged into darkness. Simultaneously Stefan had thrown himself hard at the bed.

Yates had turned round and now he fired, but into thin air.

Stefan's hand found the grip of the revolver. He fired two rapid shots towards where Yates had been standing, then pushed himself off the bed. Now he was behind the big armchair. But the MP had moved too. As he did, he fired in Stefan's direction again. But as he pulled the trigger he stumbled over Gaunt.

'Fuck!'

Stefan fired in the direction of the voice.

He heard Yates stumble again.

Something hard, metallic, clattered across the room.

Stefan shot again. He thought Yates had been hit. The noise could have been the gun falling. He fired one more time. There was the sound of feet on stairs. Yates was running. Stefan waited in the darkness, listening. He could hear the steps for a moment more. Another blast outside. The ack-ack guns.

He walked to the door and moved slowly down the stairs.

It seemed lighter outside. He didn't know why. The sound of the anti-aircraft guns was a more distant rhythm, dull, insistent. The raid had passed.

At the bottom of the stairs, the front door was open.

Stefan edged towards it, revolver ready. Yates would be running. Or would he hide? Maybe he'd been hit. Stefan couldn't know. What about the gun? Did Yates still have it? Would he be waiting somewhere, in all the rubble? Stefan knew if he saw the lieutenant, he would have to kill him. If Jack Yates had the gun, he would not hesitate to shoot. Stefan could not wait to find out.

Suddenly, the hall of the house was filled with a bright, almost blinding light. Stefan Gillespie shaded his eyes. He walked through the doorway, out to the rubble-strewn street. Ahead of him was Jack Yates, his hands in the air, yet standing as if to attention in the unexpected brightness. A truck and a car had their headlights on the street and the front of the house, and from the back of the truck a searchlight shone out. Two Maltese policemen had pistols trained on the CMP lieutenant. Walking towards him, over the rubble, was Sergeant George Spiteri. The phone call Jimmy Gaunt had made, in a moment of panic, on his way to Triq Marsamxett, hadn't got through. But his garbled message had. Spiteri stopped. For a moment he looked at the Military Policeman. Lieutenant Yates stared straight ahead, unmoving, with a slight smile on his lips. He lowered his arms slowly. He nodded at Spiteri. He raised his hand and saluted.

The priest had known first, almost before the boy had. All that time ago. It was in confession, after his first communion, that the priest asked him about his thoughts, the bad thoughts, the dirty thoughts. Those were the words. The thoughts were there, of course, thoughts the boy knew he shouldn't have. That they were about sex was bad enough, but it was the wrong sex. The thoughts were still shapeless. Even the guilt was closer to confusion. The boy hadn't grasped how guilty he was meant to feel. The priest told him. He wasn't so old, maybe forty, but he seemed very old to the boy. He was always probing, giving the thoughts in the boy's head a shape they didn't have. They would have found a shape, but in a way that was the boy's own. The priest took hold of those thoughts and gave them a darkness and a bleak, bitter reality the boy could not have imagined. And when the priest pushed the boy's face on to his stiff penis and filled his mouth, calling him names under his breath – filthy, black, hateful, damning names – the boy, barely knowing what was happening, already felt that something inside him had broken beyond mending. The priest knew that too. Breaking was part of it. He knew the shame the boy felt when he found, sometimes, that he was hard too, though he hated the man's every touch and every breath. And the priest made him know how deep that shame had to be, how complete, how everlasting. Only prayer could save him. And silence. But the priest knew, too, that the boy would fight the silence, one time at least. And before the boy could ask for help, the man in the grubby, black, tobacco-flecked cassock whispered a warning, prayerful and kind, heartfelt and compassionate, to his mother and father. He had stopped their son interfering with other, younger boys. He had to tell them that. And when the boy began to protest that it wasn't true, that it was the priest who had— The words were never finished. His father was already beating him, so hard and so long that blood poured from one of his ears. His mother simply walked away. She always knew the truth. But she said nothing. They moved, eventually; that was it. That was all his mother offered. Still she never spoke. And till they moved the priest continued from where he'd left off. Only now, instead of prayers afterwards, there were more threats, darker threats: exposure and shame in this world; damnation in the next. The priest would hit him too. And the priest would weep, calling the boy, between tears and incoherent, pleading prayers, every filthy name he knew.

It was a long time since any of that had been in Jack Yates' head. It was there fleetingly when he stared down at the sea, through the window of the Sunderland flying boat that was carrying him back to England. He had learnt to keep his mind in tight, separate compartments. He was good at it. But the compartments were suddenly not as watertight as they had been. There was seepage now. And there were things to be left behind. Lieutenant Jack Yates, CMP, affable and easy-going, popular and pleasant to talk to, yet a man you never quite got to know. He was gone. There was no room for him. That Jack Yates, along with the Military Police and the war, had been a refuge. He had joined up when he came back from Ireland, after the holiday that had ended in such an unintended but somehow inevitable way. He had returned to England surprisingly calm. The idea of joining up had been in his mind before, but after what had happened in Ireland, he had to change his life. The war was a way to disappear, not from the consequences of his actions, but from himself. He didn't seek out the

Military Police, but they were short of men. Someone looked at his experience as a clerk in the Law Courts and pushed him in that direction. And it suited him. War suited him. He fitted in in a way he never had. He became a sergeant almost immediately. He had a commission before he left for Malta, after his evacuation from Dunkirk. War was all that he had hoped it would be. It was a place in which you could be surrounded by people, and in all the activity no one would ever see your real isolation. No one had to know you. The army and the war were all-enveloping. But that was over. It was all over. And there was nothing to say. They had tried to question him, the Scotland Yard man, Nugent, and the Irish detective, Gillespie. There would be a lot more of that in London. But he had decided to say nothing. Silence. That was all he would give them. He was good at silence. The compartments in his head were full of silences. They did not communicate with one another. He wouldn't let them now. He would stop the seepage. Nothing would come out. No one would know him. He would be no one himself soon enough. He might as well start now. He did not seek death, but he had no real fear of it. In the room inhabited by Lieutenant Yates, CMP, there was a thought of fighting. He knew what they had. He knew most of the evidence was circumstantial. But he couldn't fight without revealing himself in ways that he would not allow. No one could know what was in some of his rooms. And he would make mistakes. He had made some already. The attack on Chief Inspector Nugent had been one. He'd acted out of panic. It was too late to fight. Silence was all he had left. As the hours over the Mediterranean passed, he sat in the seat and closed his eyes. He couldn't sleep but he had a way of shutting down his mind. He was practised at that. The killings did not trouble him. He had come to accept them. They happened. And when they did, they gave him, for a time, a sense of release. He told himself that each one would be the last. He knew better, of course, but he always wanted it to be the last. Yet when the dark came over him, he knew what would happen. The sex and the killing had somehow become indistinguishable for him. He might tell himself that each time was the last time, but he had organised his life so that he could kill again. The men he murdered had no faces. They were never in his head. He encountered them only for minutes. Perhaps they were released from something. He told himself that occasionally, but the words were empty. The first time had been different. He had met James in a bookshop, on a holiday in Ireland. They talked about the books they loved. They walked through Dublin together. They ate and drank and laughed together. They wanted each other in ways that he would not have space for again. There was love; at least he saw it in James. If he felt it too, it was a mistake. The picnic was never meant to end in death. But when they had sex it was as if blood vessels burst in his head. There was darkness and pain and a red, uncontrollable anger. It was over in seconds. He had to destroy what he felt. He had to cleanse himself. Only death was enough. There was too much fury. All he could do was choke and kill, and then strike and strike again, full of despair and shame. The next time, he knew what would happen, what had to happen.

There was a dream that came to him sometimes. He thought he'd dreamt it even before James, but he wasn't sure. Perhaps it had always been there. He had a room for it in his head, shut away with so many shut-away things. In the dream he plunged a knife into himself, over and over, digging out his sex. He stabbed himself, round and round, a circle of blood. He couldn't stop. He had to keep on stabbing, cutting, digging. And as he woke, sweating, trembling, sometimes crying or screaming, the last image the dream left was the smiling face of the old priest, and behind it, framing it, hanging on the sacristy wall from some forgotten Easter pageant, was a black and broken crown of thorns.

PART THREE

AN IDEAL HUSBAND

Sir, – While not questioning the truth, the very outspoken truth, contained in your leading article on Irish neutrality, I feel that the writer has not been quite fair, has stated bare facts in the assessment of the rather peculiar character of the people he is dealing with . . . Please, Mr Editor, be kind to us Irishmen within your charming island, in spite of all our shortcomings (which alas, are known only too well to us). Was it not the ablest of all Irishmen, Daniel O'Connell himself, 'The Liberator', who uttered the immortal words – 'We are a grand people: Glory be to God!'

Times of Malta, *1941*

19

The Salisbury

London

Looking down at Regent Street again, from a window in the Irish High Commission, Stefan Gillespie picked out Hindu Narayan easily enough. The street was not crowded; she stood out anyway, tall, elegant, purposeful. She walked from the Underground at Piccadilly to the small alleyway that led to the entrance of the Veeraswamy restaurant. As she disappeared into the sandbagged passage, he looked across at the windows on the first floor, criss-crossed with tape, like all London's windows, to offer some small resistance to a bomb blast. He watched as if he might see her there.

Stefan had watched Hindu Narayan make the same journey the day before. He wanted to speak to her. But there seemed little point. He had nothing to say, certainly nothing she wanted to hear. He had returned from Malta with a murderer. But however many men Lieutenant John Yates, CMP, had killed, he was not the man who killed Vikram Narayan. Stefan knew that Chief Inspector Nugent would have tried to talk to Vikram's sister. He also knew, without being told, that she would not have seen him. He did not fully understand the gulf between Hindu Narayan and Frank Nugent. At first glance, it was simple. She was an Indian nationalist and he was a member of Indian Political Intelligence, working in London: a spy. It was not difficult to grasp for an Irishman. If Hindu had been an Irish Republican when Britain still ruled Ireland, and Nugent had been a British detective at Dublin Castle, the feelings would have been the same. But there was something deeper in the bitterness Stefan had seen in Hindu's eyes, something far more personal. He had seen how deep it went.

He couldn't guess how much she knew about her brother's relationship with Frank Nugent. She knew something, certainly. She knew that when Vikram was beaten in an Indian jail, if Nugent wasn't there, he wasn't far away. Whether she also understood what Vikram had become – what Frank Nugent and men like him had made her brother: an informer, a traitor – Stefan couldn't know. It was unlikely that Hindu Narayan didn't suspect that, even if she refused to believe it. She wanted to see her brother as a pure, unsullied part of the struggle for independence, as she was, as her family and her friends were, in London as well as India. And she also didn't want to believe he died for nothing, in some squalid, meaningless sexual encounter. She wanted to believe he died for India, in a way she could take home with her, to her parents; in a way she could carry in her heart. That meant Frank Nugent must have played a part in his death, however distantly, however obliquely. It was what Hindu needed to hold on to. It was all she had.

Stefan walked downstairs to the lobby, where the stiff and upright figure of Miss Foye sat pounding at her Remington.

'Is the High Commissioner back yet, Miss Foye?'

'He won't be back today, Mr Gillespie. He has a late meeting and then he's going home. He'll be in first thing. He did leave a message. You're to go to Ireland at the weekend. There will be important papers for the diplomatic bag.'

Stefan nodded, taking out a cigarette. He wanted to get home.

'And there is one more message,' said Miss Foye.

As Stefan lit the cigarette, he sensed a tone of disapproval.

'That man from Scotland Yard, Chief Inspector Nugent . . .'

'Frank,' said Stefan cheerfully.

'Chief Inspector Nugent,' continued Miss Foye, 'said he would be at the Salisbury, in St Martin's Lane. It's a pub, Mr Gillespie. I am sure you know it.'

'I don't, Miss Foye. One of the few! But I'll find it.'

The High Commissioner's secretary resumed typing.

'Nugent's not such a bad feller,' said Stefan, deliberately winding up Miss Foye's Republican prejudices. 'For an English peeler. Harmless enough?'

'I wouldn't have thought harmlessness made for much of a policeman.'

'You may be right, Miss Foye.' Stefan grinned. 'But what about me?'

'How would I know if you're much of a policeman, Mr Gillespie?'

'True.' He gave a shrug. 'I've never been sure about that myself.'

Stefan didn't often get laughter out of Miss Foye; he came close then.

The journey from Malta had been uneventful. A Sunderland flying boat to Gibraltar, an overnight stop, and then on to England. Chief Inspector Nugent had been fit to travel two days after the arrest of Jack Yates. He was walking with a stick, but there was little evidence of the knife wound he'd received from Lieutenant Yates on the way back from the Manoel Theatre. No one had any doubt who did it, though Yates said nothing. He said nothing about anything now. He said nothing in Malta, and he said nothing as he sat in the flying boat.

Frank Nugent had been replaced at Mtarfa Hospital by the last of Yates' victims, Jimmy Gaunt. The gunshot in the house in Triq Marsamxett had done little real damage. Damage elsewhere was less easy to measure. The Provost Marshall's obsession with keeping the investigation of a murder, probably committed by a soldier, relentlessly and secretively in-house, excluding the Malta Police and resisting cooperation with civilian detectives, did not impress his superiors; even though he had been doing exactly what his superiors expected him to do at the time. There was no reason why Colonel Macgregor should not have allowed Lieutenant Yates to figure so prominently in the Military Police investigation, but hindsight didn't make that decision look good. The truth had come despite Macgregor and his Special Investigation Branch officers, not because of them. It came, embarrassingly, from the work of Sergeant Spiteri and his determination to talk to the Maltese men who knew what happened in the Upper Barrakka Gardens after dark. It came from the willingness of Chief Inspector Nugent and an Irishman who shouldn't have been there to listen to Spiteri. There was a net to draw in on Lieutenant Yates, finally, but uncharacteristic panic on his part made him try to dispose of the people who were drawing in that net, in particular Frank Nugent. But he had been careless.

Jimmy Gaunt didn't see his lieutenant try to kill Nugent, but he saw someone in uniform running away. And he saw Jack Yates, in the Military Police Humber Snipe, drive through the Victoria Gate minutes after the ambulance took the chief inspector to Mtarfa. When Lieutenant Yates expressed his shock at what had happened in St Ursula Street, the next day, and told Gaunt he had been in the barracks all evening, the young MP knew something was wrong. He didn't know what. He didn't make a link between his lieutenant and murder, but he was disturbed. He could think no further than what was in front of him, perhaps because he didn't want to. But he had to discover what was happening. He was too loyal, too frightened, to go to the Provost Marshall, but he had to know more. He knew Lieutenant Yates had a room in the town. He had always suspected him of buying and selling contraband, alcohol and cigarettes. It wasn't unusual, even if investigating such crimes was one of the tasks of the Military Police. If that was all it was, he would say nothing to anyone. He'd searched Frank Nugent's room and made his way to Triq Marsamxett to find the truth.

After Jack Yates' arrest, the lieutenant was mute. He would answer no questions. He admitted nothing. He denied nothing. But circumstantial evidence had built up now and there was little doubt it would build further in England. And some evidence was already more than circumstantial. The finger-print that had brought Stefan Gillespie and Frank Nugent to Malta now had a match. Jack Yates' connection to the murder of James Corcoran in Ireland was established beyond doubt. And still he said nothing. He had been handed over to civilian custody with as much speed as possible. The British Army wanted him out of Malta and off their hands. He no longer wore a uniform. But it all washed over him. He seemed to have withdrawn into himself, with a kind of impenetrable finality in everything he did. His face was expressionless. Watching his silence, as Stefan did in Malta and on the hours of the flight to England, he didn't recognise the man he knew as Lieutenant Jack Yates. What he thought he glimpsed, in the strange calmness of the man, was something like relief.

The Salisbury, in St Martin's Lane, was minutes from Piccadilly Circus, and it was still early when Stefan Gillespie arrived there. It was light on customers at that time, but rich in Victorian mahogany and mirrors, in lamps held up by nymphs and long-stemmed flowers. Frank Nugent sat between the nymphs and flowers on the pub's worn leather, closed in by mirrored glass. The barman brought Stefan a bottle of Guinness and a sour, sarcastic expression.

'You here for long, Mr Nugent?'

'A chat with a friend, Kevin, that's all.'

'Any more coppers due? I wasn't expecting a Policeman's Ball.'

'And there's Inspector Gillespie thinking he was incognito.'

'We're born able to spot a copper. If we're not, we soon learn.'

The barman walked away.

'How long are you in London, Stefan?'

'Till the weekend.'

'Good.'

'Good?'

'Unfinished business.'

And what's that?'

'Vikram Narayan.'

'Yours rather than mine, Frank.'

'I wasn't the one his sister asked for help.'

Stefan smiled. Frank Nugent wasn't such a bad policeman after all.

'I'll be heading back to India soon,' said the chief inspector.

'Run out of Indian nationalists to follow round London?'

'Nothing's happening here or at home.'

Stefan had heard Frank Nugent call India home before, but it registered now, in a pub in London's West End. He looked as if he belonged. He didn't.

'Nothing that matters. Games, no more than that. The Congress Party has no interest in cosying up to the Germans. The man who had didn't do himself any favours. You know enough about it. By going to Berlin, my friend Subhas Bose cut himself off from the rest of Congress, especially Gandhi and Nehru. Do they care? It's politics. He's a rival who sidelined himself. Unless Germany wins. But India's not thinking that way. Too far away to see a close-run thing.'

'And what about all these chats with the IRA?' asked Stefan.

'If a few fellers want to cheer on the Boys, why not? It means little enough in London, less in Dublin. And doesn't it keep them off the streets? Between Scotland Yard and Dublin Castle . . . everyone knows who they are.'

'And you've got enough double agents to chase them round in circles.'

'Am I alone in that? Isn't it one of Terry Gregory's specialities? But I'm done here. They want me home. Bigger fish may be coming our way in India.'

Stefan waited for Nugent to continue, but he didn't. He picked up his beer and looked round the Salisbury for a long moment.

'Have you noticed this is a queer pub?'

'Not really,' replied Stefan, looking round too.

'I've taken a leaf out of Sergeant Spiteri's book,' continued the chief inspector. 'Vikram Narayan. The unfinished business. We were pushed in the wrong direction. We took the bait. We didn't look at anything else. We didn't look at his friends . . . at what was going on around him. We looked one way.'

'Yes, someone made sure we looked the wrong way.'

'And that wasn't as hard to do as you might think.'

'No?'

'I'll be handing the Vikram case back to West End Central. Messrs Hardy and Dillon, inspector and sergeant of this parish. Do they fill me with confidence?'

Stefan Gillespie drank and waited. He knew Nugent well enough by now.

'I talked to a couple of people at the club, Billie's, where Vikram met your friend, Mac Liammóir. I didn't get far. But I was reminded of something Hindu Narayan said about one of her brother's friends being frightened. It was the photographer, the one he bought the camera stuff from. Of course, what Hindu was looking for was something to prove Vikram had the police, Special Branch, MI5 and me after him. She wanted to know what he said about that. Only there was nothing to say. But she pressed a trigger somewhere. Without knowing. Someone thought it was worth knocking her down. Don't forget that.'

'I haven't,' said Stefan quietly. 'You still don't buy the accident?'

'No, and I do know it certainly wasn't Lieutenant Yates.'

Chief Inspector Nugent beckoned the barman again.

'Sit down a minute, Kevin.'

The barman did so, wearing the same sour, sarcastic look.

'Tell my friend about how West End Central does business.'

'The Jack the Ripper job?'

Frank Nugent nodded.

'I hear that one's dead in the water now. You got the bastard.'

'Tell the story, Kevin.'

'Well, every so often, the superintendent at West End Central makes a show of clearing off his assorted poofs and pansies. Keep the good citizens onside. Mostly we're left alone, but a copper's got to do what a copper's got to do. So, they make some arrests, clear the cottages and the parks and make themselves unpopular in respectable public houses like this. But last time, Inspector Hardy thought he'd frighten us off with the bogeyman. He told us about the madman out there, waiting to cut us in pieces. He said how he did it. In some detail. Lots of blood. If he wasn't going to cut off your tail with his carving knife, he'd put a fucking frame round it . . . in a striking shade of red.'

'So, no shortage of people who knew about that,' said Stefan.

'Tell us about the blackmail, Kevin,' said Nugent.

'There's always blackmail, Mr Nugent. You know that.'

'This is a bit bigger, isn't it?'

'That's what people say. Been going on for years.'

'Have you been on the end of it?'

'I'm too big a faery, Mr Nugent.' Kevin laughed. 'No point!'

'What I heard,' continued the chief inspector, 'was that it

was well organised. Lots of inside information, photographs, letters, all sorts of evidence bought and sold. With threats of going to people's families, losing them their jobs. Even putting some anonymous tips in the way of the police.'

'They deliver,' said Kevin. 'No money, you're fucked. That's the word.'

Frank Nugent looked at Stefan. 'Something to be frightened of.'

'It would be.' Stefan nodded.

Kevin got up. 'Don't stay too long, gents. You're buggering business.'

The barman walked away. For a moment the two detectives were silent.

'Frightened enough to be worth killing for?' asked Nugent.

'Perhaps,' replied Stefan. 'But can you see Vikram Narayan . . .'

'As a blackmailer? He tried it on with Mac Liammóir, Stefan.'

'That's not the same thing. According to your man Kevin—'

'What about the camera, the telephoto lens? You said it, Stefan. What was it for? If this is a professional set-up . . . there's a lot of collecting and buying information. Vikram needn't have been running it. Maybe he was working for someone.'

Stefan frowned, then another thought struck him.

'No photos, Frank, remember?'

'What?'

'Expensive camera, expensive lenses . . . no photographs anywhere.'

'Except the roll in his pocket,' said the chief inspector.

'And what was on that?' asked Stefan. 'Not much, was there?'

'The funeral he went to, where he saw Mac Liammóir with Noël Coward. He took some pictures of them. The last ones he ever took. There were some pictures he'd taken before, somewhere else. He finished the reel at the funeral. The other pictures were of a woman, probably at a railway buffet, remember? One of the big London stations. A man with her, no clear shot of him. The side of his head, the back of his head. As if Vikram was trying to get a good angle.'

'But he wasn't going to risk getting closer,' said Stefan.

'I suppose so,' replied Nugent. 'There were a couple of photographs of the woman by herself at the station, presumably after the man had left. I'll need to dig them out. As I remember, she was posting letters. Then maybe going to get a train.'

'So, what does all that mean?' said Stefan. 'What's that got to do with blackmailing homosexual men? But if they were taken with the telephoto lens, the photos must mean something. Forget the ones of Micheál and Noël Coward. Vikram had pictures of them on his wall in Greek Street. They're what they seem, aren't they? I'd put money on it, Frank. He was a fan. Yes, he tried to threaten Micheál, maybe out of desperation, but those two were never good candidates for blackmail. Too important. So, it's the other photos we should be looking at. They're the ones that must be telling us something we don't know.'

'But what?' Frank Nugent shook his head.

'And what about the rest?' said Stefan. 'The ones that aren't there. Not a trace. How many photographs did he take? Where did he keep them? Why was he doing it? We know where he bought the camera, the lenses. We know the man he bought them from. His friend with a photography shop in Brixton. And when Hindu Narayan tried to speak to this friend about her brother, all she got was that he was frightened, very frightened. She thought he was scared of the police, even of you. That wasn't it. He was frightened of someone, though.'

'She saw that, and I didn't,' said the chief inspector. 'Jesus!'

'You weren't looking then, were you?' said Stefan. 'Now, we are.'

20

Coldharbour Lane

Driving over Westminster Bridge, through the Elephant and Castle, Kennington, Camberwell, Stefan noticed how the bomb damage drained away, street by street, as they came closer to Brixton. It was still there, in heaps of bricks and mortar and gaps in the Victorian and Edwardian terraces of high streets, but where whole sections of the city had been flattened close to the river – houses, shops, warehouses, factories – further south the damage was intermittent. Mostly high streets were still standing, ordinary, unexceptional, unremarkable.

Frank Nugent turned the black Austin off Brixton Road into Coldharbour Lane. He pulled up outside the shop: Coldharbour Cameras. It was a small, dark shop window; a glass door heavily taped in anticipation of blasts, sandwiched between a greengrocer's and an ironmonger's. There were a few cameras and lenses in the window, looking dusty and uncared-for, backed by bleached black-and-white photographs of the English countryside and a family at the seaside. The shop was open, but it looked as if it might as well be closed. It exuded a mood of failing and indifference. And the bleak interior felt just as weary.

A bell over the door tinkled as the two detectives entered.

The shelves displaying photographic equipment and stacks of film in boxes were half empty. It was difficult to find stock in wartime London, but here it seemed unlikely the proprietor bothered to look hard. He appeared several minutes after Stefan and Frank came into the shop. They heard him walk slowly from upstairs. He was a small, flabby man, grey-haired, in his fifties. He wore a well-pressed suit, a white shirt and a carefully knotted tie. His neatness was at odds with his shop.

'Can I help you, gentlemen?'

'Mr Hopkins, you may remember me. Chief Inspector Nugent.'

Edward Hopkins said nothing, but he did remember.

'This is Inspector Gillespie.'

Nugent had decided that for now Stefan's rank was explanation enough.

'I talked to you about Vikram Narayan, your friend . . . about a camera and some equipment he bought from you. In particular, an expensive telephoto lens.'

The man nodded.

'Friend or boyfriend?' said the English detective.

'There was nothing like that,' said Hopkins, almost indignant.

'Not important, I guess. We are still investigating Mr Narayan's murder.'

'I see. I thought you knew what happened. You said a man who killed—'

'I thought that at the time, Mr Hopkins. I was wrong.'

There was silence in the dark shop. The ticking of a grandfather clock.

'Do you develop photographs, Mr Hopkins?' asked Stefan.

'Yes. I don't do a lot of it now.'

'Did you develop any for Mr Narayan?'

The answer came with a hesitation and awkwardness that told both detectives something was being hidden. The shop-owner saw the need to be careful in what he said. There was also fear.

'I don't remember.' It didn't sound convincing. 'Some, perhaps.'

'Do you remember what sort of pictures he took?' asked Nugent. 'They would have been unusual, with that lens. Close-ups from a distance. A bit odd?'

'I said, some. It was a long time ago.'

'Not that long, surely?' said the chief inspector. 'This sort of thing . . .'

Frank Nugent took several photographs from his pocket and laid them on the counter. They were photographs of a woman at a railway buffet, sitting with a man whose face could only be partly seen; the same woman posting letters, on a station concourse. A picture of a tobacconist's shop and a street name.

'That's all we have. But odd, wouldn't you say?'

'They don't mean anything to me.'

'They were some of the last pictures Vikram Narayan took, before he was killed,' said Stefan. 'Undeveloped, a reel in his pocket. They were the only photographs we found in his flat. That's odd too, I'd say. For a man who was so interested in photography. It's hard to imagine that with a friend like you, he wouldn't have brought his films here to be developed. Especially as they wouldn't be the kind of pictures he'd want just anybody to see. That's what I think. That's what Mr Nugent thinks as well. What do you think, Mr Hopkins?'

'I don't know what you're talking about.'

Hopkins was not a good liar. The sweat on his face told the truth.

'I'll tell you then, shall I?' said Frank Nugent, harder. 'It's about blackmail. I don't know how. I don't know what. Photographs were a part of it. What else do you need a tele-photo lens for, except to spy? I don't know who this woman is or what she has to do with it. I don't know how it got your friend Mr Narayan killed, but maybe that's not difficult to guess. It might give you a good reason to be frightened, though, if you were working with him. What I do know – what is blindingly fucking obvious, Mr Hopkins – is that it involved extorting money out of homosexual men. And you know about it.'

The shop-owner was shaking his head.

'It's not like that. It's not that way, you don't understand . . .'

'Why don't you tell us what it is like, Mr Hopkins?' said Stefan.

It took Edward Hopkins several minutes to pull up a floorboard in the darkroom behind the shop. He levered it up with a claw hammer. He was calmer. He had stopped shaking. But he was still afraid. He took a package from between the joists. It was wrapped in oilcloth. He opened it up and took several paper wallets out. They contained black-and-white photographs. He spread some on the table. Several were versions of what Stefan and Frank had already seen from the reel of film found in Narayan's pocket: the woman, the man, the station, the tobacconist's. But they had been taken at other times. They were clearer.

'It's Waterloo Station,' said Nugent.

'Yes.' Stefan recognised it too.

'And the man,' continued the chief inspector. 'I know who he is. I thought from the profile there was something I recognised. A man called Pettit. He's the maître d' at Billie's, the club where Vikram had his run-in with Mac Liammóir. I talked to him. He knew Vikram, of course. It's his world, isn't it?'

Stefan nodded, looking down at the pictures.

'He'd know a lot of people, Frank. He'd see everything.'

'You know this man?' Nugent turned to Hopkins.

The shop-owner shook his head.

Stefan laid out more photographs. There were several of the woman, getting on a train. There were images of a street – a village street it looked like – and the woman getting into a grey car in the same street. There were photographs of a long, straight stretch of road, somewhere in the countryside. There was a house, old red brick, surrounded by a clump of trees. It was in the country too, somewhere near the long, straight road. It looked dark, isolated.

'Is that it?' Chief Inspector Nugent asked Hopkins.

'Yes.' The shop-owner nodded.

Stefan looked up and shrugged.

'Doesn't look like great shakes on the blackmail front.'

'So, if it isn't blackmail,' said Nugent, 'what the hell is it?'

Hopkins stepped back and sank down on to a chair.

'Those are the people doing it, doing the blackmail, they're the . . .'

Frank Nugent exchanged glances with Stefan. This was unexpected.

'It was when David died . . . Vikram said someone had to do something.'

'And who's David?'

'He was my, he was my very . . . special friend, we . . .'

'Take your time, Mr Hopkins,' said Stefan. 'Don't worry.'

'David was a policeman, you see.' Hopkins looked at them blankly. 'You'd think he could have done something, but he couldn't, not without people finding out. His family was so proud of him . . . only a constable, not like you, but he would have lost his job, you know that, don't you?' Hopkins gazed from Stefan to Frank Nugent, shaking his head. 'So, he paid the money. But he couldn't keep paying. I tried to help. They wanted more, all the time. They had letters he'd sent to a man, when he was hardly out of his teens. They sent them to Scotland Yard. He didn't wait for . . . he hanged himself.'

259

There was silence in the darkroom. The clock ticked outside.

'I told Vikram, and he said someone had to stop it. We all knew men who were being blackmailed, and no one did anything. Some people did tell the police. They tried. But nothing happened. I don't know if they even looked at it, most of the time they're more interested in putting us inside. Maybe it's easier to do. But Vikram said if there was evidence, if he found out who these people were, the police would have to do something. He said he knew a policeman. Someone important. If he gave him all the evidence he could put together, if he got photos and details . . . then this man would do something.'

There was a different kind of silence now. It came from Frank Nugent. Stefan could feel it. He knew the policeman Vikram Narayan intended to go to.

Stefan waited for Frank Nugent to continue the questioning, but the Englishman said nothing. He picked up one of the photographs. He seemed distant. The silence hung in the air. Even Hopkins was waiting for a question.

'Do you know who these people are,' asked Stefan, 'in the photos?'

'No, Vikram didn't say. He reckoned the less I knew the safer I'd be.'

'Did he tell you where these places are, the village, the house?'

'No. Once he mentioned Guildford, I think. Near Guildford.'

Stefan looked at Frank. The chief inspector nodded, still distracted.

'Could be. I think . . . the village doesn't mean anything . . . but I've maybe been on that main road.' He indicated a picture of a long, empty stretch of tarmac, with trees lining it. 'It looks like somewhere I've seen. I'm not sure.'

'What about the tobacconist's?' Stefan looked back at Hopkins. 'That's in London.'

'I don't know where. I think people sent letters there, money.'

'Well, there's the name of the street,' said Chief Inspector Nugent. He spoke sharply, pointing at another photograph, as if stating the obvious.

Stefan nodded. When Nugent unexpectedly said no more, he was the one who now turned to Hopkins again.

'Did Vikram know if they'd found out what he was doing?'

'I don't know; I think, perhaps. I think he realised . . . he'd been noticed. But he wasn't sure he could prove anything. Not without help. He was full of it at first, then he was . . . afraid suddenly. He said it didn't matter what he found out. No one would help him. That was when he started saying he wanted to get away. I shouldn't have let him do it. Looking into these things . . . it's better to leave it alone. I should have known. But he was determined to do something . . . at the start. Something right. That's what he said. But it changed, and the last time I saw him, he was simply desperate . . . He said he had to leave England.'

'Or what?' said Stefan. 'Did he say he was frightened . . . for his life?'

'No. He didn't . . . He was afraid – of all sorts of things, Mr Gillespie. I don't know what they were. I only know he couldn't see any way out of it.'

Frank Nugent still said nothing. It was as if he hadn't listened to what Hopkins had been saying. He was gazing down at the photographs. He pulled out a packet of cigarettes. He took one and lit it. Stefan looked at the bland photographs again. Pieces of paper. Could they be worth a man's life?

The chief inspector started to gather up the pictures. He seemed almost clumsy, flustered, as if he didn't want to look at anyone, either at Stefan or at the shopkeeper. Stefan couldn't decide whether he was angry or impatient. Finally, with all the photographs bundled together, Nugent turned towards Stefan.

His face was tight and intense. There was none of the calmness Stefan was used to.

'Let's find this fucking tobacconist's. I think I know the street.'

The tobacconist's shop that acted as a letter-drop was easy to find. Along with the photographs of the shop and of Charlie Pettit, the maître d' at Billie's, going in and out, there was a wider shot of the street and its name. It was close to Vauxhall Bridge, a road off Kennington Lane. Frank Nugent drove there from Brixton. It wasn't far. The Englishman was quiet. Stefan was too. They were closer to the Thames; the streets reflected that. The rubble was piled higher. There was more empty space where houses had been. When the car stopped outside the shop, at the corner of a row of terraced houses, half of the other side of the road had gone. It had happened months before, long enough to be unremarked, but only now were the bulldozers clearing the site.

Chief Inspector Nugent looked up at the tobacconist's doorway.

'A Mr Leonard Walshe, licensed to sell tobacco.'

Stefan waited. Frank Nugent gave a wry smile.

'I think this one's less of the softly-softly, more of the heavy hand.'

'You're the boss,' said Stefan. 'I'll follow your lead.'

'I'm sure you didn't get where you are, Stefan, without knowing how to put the screw on. This bastard's probably the sort who's got it coming anyway.'

'Not entirely my philosophy, but close to my superintendent's heart.'

They walked into the shop. The proprietor leant on the counter, a pipe in his mouth, reading a list of runners in the *Sporting Life*. He looked up, smiling.

'Couple of good nights. No bombs this side.'

'Could be worse,' said Nugent.

'It is getting better. Must be tiring the buggers out.'

It was the usual, idle bomb-speak.

'What can I do you for, gents?'

'Let's see, Mr Walshe. Hopefully, you can avoid a few years inside.'

The tobacconist frowned. 'What the fuck's that supposed to mean?'

The chief inspector held up his warrant card.

'It means you're operating a letter-drop. All very discreet, I imagine.'

'Nothing illegal about that.'

'That depends what's in the letters.'

'They're not my bloody letters. People just pay to use the address.'

Stefan smiled at the tobacconist. He let Nugent talk.

'And what if one of your customers was using this address, let's say, for the sake of argument, to collect money they were extorting by blackmail?'

'If I knew that, I'd be shocked. I'd go to the fucking police!' Walshe chuckled. He was pleased with that.

'I'm sure your ignorance goes deep, Mr Walshe. Why would you ask?'

'I assume people are honest,' said the tobacconist. 'Why shouldn't I?'

'Not always wise,' said the chief inspector. 'You'd be surprised what some people get up to.' He looked sideways at Stefan. 'You honest, Inspector?'

'I do my best, sir.'

'We all do,' said Nugent. 'Let's try, shall we?'

He put down photographs of the maître d', Pettit, at Waterloo Station.

'Do you know this man?'

'No, never seen him.'

'Does it ring any bells now?'

Nugent put down pictures of Pettit outside the tobacconist's shop.

'Where did you get these?'

The chief inspector grabbed Walshe by his jacket, pulling him forward across the counter, until his face and the tobacconist's were inches apart.

'Answer the fucking question, you bastard! Tell me about this man.'

'I don't know him. I don't know his name. He comes in now and again.'

'To collect letters?'

'I don't need to answer these bloody questions.'

'You do, you really do, I assure you.'

Nugent's words were softer, but he continued to glare hard into the tobacconist's eyes. Then abruptly he let him go. He turned to Stefan again.

'Why does he have to, Inspector Gillespie?'

Stefan picked up the copy of the *Sporting Life* and scanned it, as if it was of some interest to him. When he spoke, his tone was easy, mild, reasonable.

'Apart from being a law-abiding citizen, he has to do it because if he doesn't we'll plant enough evidence in his private post office, to tie it to so much extortion, robbery, pornography, and whatever else we can think of, it'll put him away for more years than he's had winners on the flat or over the sticks. Got it?'

'Don't you fucking threaten me!'

'It's not a threat, Mr Walshe. But it is a very sure promise,' said Stefan.

'You should trust him,' added Nugent. 'He is a policeman after all.'

The chief inspector picked up another photograph of the maître d'.

264

'So, I still don't know any more about this man, do I?'

'I told you. He collects letters here. He pays and he takes them.'

'And who are these letters for? For him?'

'How the hell do I know? He collects letters in the name of Mr Elliot.'

'That's more like it, Mr Walshe. Any letters for Mr Elliot here now?'

Walshe hesitated, but not for long. He nodded.

'Get them,' snapped Nugent.

The tobacconist went into the room behind the shop. Nugent lifted the counter flap and followed. Stefan Gillespie took the flap and did the same. In a small sitting room was a wooden cabinet full of cubby-holes and letters. Walshe took out a bundle of letters and handed them to Chief Inspector Nugent.

'How often does this man collect?' asked Stefan.

'Usually once a fortnight. On a Friday.'

'When is he due again?'

'This week.'

'The day after tomorrow?'

The tobacconist shrugged.

Frank Nugent flicked through the letters. There were seven. There was nothing to see; the name Elliot, c/o, and the address of the tobacconist's. He handed six of the envelopes back to Walshe and opened the seventh. He took out a ten-pound note and a piece of paper with a four-figure number on it. There was no letter. There was nothing to identify where the letter had come from.

'That's it, cash on delivery,' said Nugent. 'Simple. Neat.'

'The only weakness,' added Stefan, 'is you, Mr Walshe.'

'People can send money, can't they? Sending money means fuck all!'

Chief Inspector Nugent shook his head and tutted.

'I think in this case, Mr Walshe, it means fuck everything . . . So, put the other letters back. Business as usual. When our friend comes to collect on Friday, you hand them over, as always. You say what you always say, the less the better. If all that works, there's a chance we'll leave you to carry on your shitty trade, untroubled by the fact that it would be no bad thing to go through every letter here and see what's what. But if our friend gets even a whiff that anything is wrong, Inspector Gillespie will be back to plant the goods that will send you down for a substantial stretch. Who knows who you might bump into in Brixton or the Scrubs, maybe even the people you just squealed on?'

'That's bollocks! I haven't fucking squealed on no one!'

'The trouble is,' smiled Stefan, 'we'll tell them you fucking have.'

21

Waterloo Station

Charlie Pettit, maître d' of Billie's in Little Denmark Street, had no idea that he was being followed as he left Lennie Walshe's tobacconist's shop and made his way to the river and the Albert Embankment. The Irishman who was following him was unknown to Charlie. He was also good at what he was doing. He had every reason to believe he knew where the maître d' was going, and that meant he could hang back and follow in a leisurely, unobtrusive way. The journey he was making from Vauxhall to Waterloo Station was familiar. It hadn't always been Vauxhall. The letter-drops or post restantes changed from time to time. For safety. But nothing else did.

There was something of spring in the morning, and Charlie Pettit felt more content than he usually did at the prospect of an envelope from the woman. There would be good money this time. A fortnight ago he had provided a crop of names and addresses from the club, a list of clients from a male prostitute in Islington, some juicy letters from married men to unmarried men, and a reel of photographs of men at some of the West End's best-known cottages. He had paid through the nose for the photographs, but the photographer was good and that wasn't easy work. There were only two names to go with

267

the pictures, but the people he was giving them to would match more to names and faces they already had. That was their business. Collecting the money was their business. But he would be collecting his today. Tomorrow he would take the train to Stratford and spend the afternoon at the race meeting. A weekend off, out of London. There were shortages everywhere, but money solved most of them. Life was easier than it had been. It was an odd thing to feel in the middle of the war, but Charlie was a survivor; he was surviving well. He was too old for conscription and like everyone else he had learnt to live with bombs. People kept saying it was easing off. They said it when any fool could see it wasn't. They always said it. But he couldn't help feeling it was true now, or truer. He didn't follow the war. He took in what was half heard on the radio and chatted about in the club. He scanned the newspaper headlines, but not much more. He read the papers for the racing pages. But all in all, things weren't so bad. He was more comfortable than he'd been for ages. The money from the man and the woman came regularly. It made a difference. The information they wanted was easy to get. It was business. Business was good.

Stefan anticipated the route the maître d' would take as soon as he reached the Albert Embankment. Waterloo Station would be the destination. The Embankment to Westminster Bridge and then the station. It wasn't difficult to keep the thin, angular figure in view, in his dark suit and trilby. He moved closer only as Pettit moved away from the river into York Road. The station would be full of people and it would be a lot easier to lose him there. He couldn't know what would happen at Waterloo. The assumption was that the maître d' would meet the woman in Vikram Narayan's photographs, but Stefan and Frank Nugent could not be certain. There might be a train journey. Stefan Gillespie needed to be near his quarry. When

Pettit mounted the stone steps that led up to the Victory Arch and the concourse, he was close behind.

A woman's voice echoed around the great, high space beneath the glass roof. Between the announcements of arrivals and departures, music played. The woman's voice was distorted and hard to decipher. No one listened. Instead, people stared up at the high boards that listed trains and stations, waiting for the rattle and click that would bring up information for each platform. They stared and walked and came back to stare again. No one listened to the relentlessly cheerful band music either, as much the sound of the war as the drone of engines overhead at night and the sound of bombs, always, hopefully, somewhere else. The station was not as busy as Stefan expected. The morning trains that brought commuters in from the southern suburbs had long gone. Most of the passengers were soldiers, travelling to army camps and waiting for troop trains to Southampton to ship overseas. They stood in groups round stacked rifles and kitbags. They packed themselves round trolleys with tea urns, drinking tea and eating biscuits. They pushed in and out of station buffets and newspaper kiosks. Over every troop and group and company hung the clouds of smoke that marked what every soldier did when there was nothing else to do.

The line Charlie Pettit took, through the groups of soldiers, brought him to a station buffet at the far end of the concourse. Stefan knew Waterloo, a little. On the right, the platforms, stretching the length of the station; left, the station buildings and buffets and ticket offices and waiting rooms; in the middle the kiosks of W.H. Smith, wooden benches and space to stand and wait.

Outside the buffet were tables and chairs. At one of these sat a woman. Charlie Pettit went to the table and sat down. Stefan watched from beside a newspaper stand. He recognised the woman from the photographs taken by Vikram Narayan. She

269

was probably in her late forties. She was elegant and tall, dressed in a suit that had cost good money; a strong woman, he thought. Her hair was blonde and permed; the colour wasn't hers.

Stefan turned to the newspaper seller and bought an *Evening Standard*. He walked on across the concourse and sat on a bench, close to a row of telephone kiosks. He had clear sight of the woman and the maître d'. The woman poured tea from a pot into a cup in front of Pettit. He didn't drink it. He took a folded manila envelope from his jacket and pushed it across the table. She opened her handbag and put it in. She took out a smaller envelope and gave it to Pettit. He tipped his hat, which he had not taken off. He stood up and left. That was it. Stefan watched as the maître d' walked through the concourse, the way he had come. The transaction had taken no more than five minutes. Hardly any words had been spoken. Stefan assumed that the money from Walshe's had been passed over, perhaps more, perhaps information, names, the stuff of blackmail. In return, another payment had been made, to Charlie Pettit. But whatever it was, it was done. Now Stefan would do what he and Chief Inspector Nugent had decided. They knew where to find Pettit. He would be picked up in due course. It was the woman they needed to know about. She was the one to be followed. That was even clearer to Stefan now. The woman was in charge. The maître d' worked for her.

The woman sat at the table for another few minutes. She smoked a cigarette. She looked about her, but she was at ease. She was confident. Like Charlie Pettit, earlier, she could have no idea that she was being watched, or any sense of why she should be. Stefan felt her calmness. It was helpful for the job he had to do.

When the woman stubbed out her cigarette and stood up, Stefan saw that she picked up two carrier bags: Fortnum &

Mason, Simpsons of Piccadilly. It was a nice touch, he thought. She was an ordinary woman, but well-heeled, shopping in Town. He watched her walk across the station towards the departures board. She stood looking up at it, then turned to walk to one of the platforms. He got up from the bench and followed her. He waited, letting her walk through the barrier. She continued past two dark green carriages, then opened the door and got on the train. Stefan looked at the board over the barrier: Surbiton, Weybridge, Guildford. Frank Nugent hadn't identified the stretch of a rural main road in some of Vikram Narayan's photographs, but he felt the area was right. Somewhere near Guildford, Hopkins had said, and that felt right. It felt more right to Stefan now. The woman was heading that way. He passed through the barrier with several other people. He carried a railway warrant that identified him as a policeman; it gave him the ability to go where she went. He walked the platform and glanced into several carriages unnoticed.

The train was made up of compartment carriages, with no through access. The compartments took up the width of the train, with a door on each side and facing seats. He saw the woman, sitting by the window in a compartment. He couldn't sit with her. It would make him recognisable at some point, however little she noticed him. He got into the first compartment in the carriage behind hers. Sitting by the window, on the same side, he would see her get out. He would need to watch for the platform side. If she went to Guildford it would be easy. The train terminated there.

The journey was little more than an hour. The train had filled up before it left Waterloo, but by Surbiton and Weybridge the passengers were thinning out. The woman had not left the carriage. The train reached Guildford and with a dozen other passengers, the woman got off. Stefan watched her for a minute, still sitting by the window in his compartment.

271

Getting out of the carriage, Stefan was surprised to see that the woman was still on the platform. She was sitting on a bench by the waiting room. There were other people standing on the platform opposite the one the London train had come in on. She was waiting for another train. Stefan walked to the far end of the platform and leant against the wall, behind a trolley full of postbags. He lit a cigarette. Moments later he heard another train approaching. He walked forward as the train stopped. Doors opened and closed. The woman got into a carriage. Stefan got into a compartment further down the train and waited.

The train had travelled only one stop, to the next station down the line, Wanborough, when the woman got off. Only two other passengers disembarked with her and Stefan walked slowly to the exit of the small station. In a place like this, where everyone would know everyone, he would stand out. He knew that the ticket inspector, peering at his warrant, identified him as a policeman.

Walking out of the station, looking towards the village, Stefan knew where he was. It wasn't the same shot, or the same view. But it was the same village in the photographs he had seen in Coldharbour Cameras.

In the station forecourt, the woman was getting into a grey Riley. There was a man driving. Stefan saw only his outline and the sun on the windscreen, as the car turned and drove away. He read the number. He made a point of not watching the car for more than a few seconds. As he turned away, he saw the ticket inspector, standing in the station entrance, looking at him.

'Are you wanting the police station, then?'

Stefan smiled. It felt like he was back in an Irish village. The village police station wasn't the first place he meant to go. He wanted to find out who the man and the woman were, before he did anything else. But this wasn't an easy place to ask questions. It was like arriving in Baltinglass. Whether he wanted to speak to the local police or not, they would soon know he was there. If he said he didn't want the police station, they would know quicker.

'I suppose I am,' said Stefan reluctantly. 'You'd better point the way.'

Stefan Gillespie's arrival at the police station in Wanborough meant a number of things to Sergeant Ernest Porter; irritation and inconvenience were at the top of the list, but wariness and mistrust were not far behind. Stefan said nothing that dispelled the suspicion that the Guildford train had brought the kind of trouble Wanborough was not used to. The fact that the Irishman offered no indication of what he wanted made matters worse. He didn't elaborate on who he was, except to give his rank, and say that his senior officer was a Special Branch Chief Inspector at Scotland Yard. Irishmen in British police forces, especially the Metropolitan Police, were not so remarkable. It was Scotland Yard, especially Special Branch, that the sergeant didn't like. He left his young constable to make Stefan a cup of tea while he went into his office to phone Guildford. No Metropolitan Police officer should be in Surrey without the permission of the Chief Constable, but when it came to Special Branch, and with the bloody war that turned everything on its head, it was difficult to know what to do. And after several phone calls Sergeant Porter was none the wiser. His superintendent in Guildford came back to the sergeant, finally, to say he should offer Stefan any help he needed, as it was a matter that related to national security.

This took over an hour, by which time the sergeant was in need of a cup of tea too and the constable went off to fill the kettle again. Stefan had spent the hour discussing the war and the Surrey countryside with Constable Harris and learnt that the constable's sister-in-law's father came from Carlow and they still had family there, though he couldn't remember the surname. His sister-in-law's cousin was called Michael. He wondered if Stefan knew him. It was then that a call came from Scotland Yard: Frank Nugent.

Sergeant Porter spoke to Chief Inspector Nugent first. The conversation at the Wanborough end consisted mostly of him saying, 'Yes, sir.' He interspersed it with some asides to both Stefan and Constable Harris.

'Chief Inspector says can we put you up somewhere? . . . He'll be coming down from London tomorrow . . . Any questions you got, Inspector? . . . He'll be driving down, first thing . . . It's all hush-hush . . . you hear, Constable?'

Eventually, Sergeant Porter handed the phone to Stefan.

'You're having a good time, Stefan,' said Nugent, laughing.

'I'm not sure, Frank. Plenty of tea.'

'That's something.'

'We've brought in Charlie Pettit. Picked him up at Billie's.'

'Good, did you get anything?'

'Oh, Charlie's totting up what he might do in the way of stir and putting it in his account book against what he might get off if he sings. He's being extremely tuneful.'

'So, you know who the woman is?'

'No.'

'No?'

'They've been at this a few years. She got hold of Charlie when he was up to his eyes in racing debt. The kind that gets you a couple of broken legs if you don't pay. And that's just for starters. She paid off his debts . . . they went into business. The name he has for her isn't real. It's all done face to face, letter-drops, phone calls. He doesn't know where she lives, just that it's her and her husband. Charlie gives information, they do the rest. Very successfully.'

'And what about the murder?'

'He doesn't know anything about that.'

'Well, he would say that, Frank!'

'I believe him. He still thinks Vikram was killed like the others . . . part of the Yates business. He did know him . . . in Billie's, around Soho. But the rest . . . No, I don't think so. He knows nothing about Vikram's photos. No idea he'd been followed or watched. But that doesn't mean the woman didn't know.'

'So, what do I do now?'

'Find out all you can about these people. But ensure your country sergeant keeps his mouth shut. I'm coming down tomorrow. We want to take them by surprise. As far as anyone there is concerned, it's a security issue so you can't say a fucking thing! You might mention murder, at least to Sergeant Porter. I think he needs to know this is a serious matter. But it's nobody's business but Special Branch's. I'm sure the sergeant has the poster up.' Nugent laughed. 'Walls have ears . . . Point it out to him!'

Stefan Gillespie put the telephone down. He smiled amiably. Sergeant Porter and Constable Harris looked at him with continuing wariness. Stefan took a piece of paper from his pocket. He had written the number of the car on it, from the station.

'Do you recognise this number, Sergeant?'

He handed the piece of paper to Porter.

'Not straight off . . . It's a Surrey number, all right.'

'It's a grey Riley, I think a Kestrel.'

'That's Mr Hollingsworth's car,' said Constable Harris.

'Course it is . . . Mr and Mrs Hollingsworth.'

'Do they live in the village?'

'Up on the Hog's Back, Swithins Barn.'

The sergeant looked at Stefan, frowning.

'Mr and Mrs Hollingsworth?'

'You know them, obviously,' continued Stefan.

'Course I bloody know them, Inspector!' Sergeant Porter was laughing as he spoke the words.

'Course he bloody knows them. Mr H is our ARP Warden!'

The constable echoed his sergeant, starting to laugh now too.

Sergeant Porter stood up, reaching for a packet of Woodbines.

'I think you Special Branch boys have got the wrong end of the stick!'

Stefan shrugged. Not so much a 'maybe' as a 'probably not'.

'That'll make a fucking story and a half . . . Mr and Mrs Hollingsworth!'

The sergeant shook his head, still chuckling.

The constable joined in. 'That'll make a fucking . . .'

His echo faded away at a disapproving look from his sergeant.

'Language, Tim!'

'Not a story you'll be telling anyone tonight, Sergeant . . . Constable.'

Although Stefan was smiling, the seriousness in his voice cut through.

'No, sir,' said Sergeant Porter. 'Whatever you say, Inspector.'

There was still a kind of snigger on Constable Harris's lips.

'The joke's over, Constable,' snapped Stefan.

'Yes, sir.'

'You will be with us tomorrow, gentlemen. We'll be arresting them.'

The two policemen looked bewildered.

'Can I ask what for?' said the sergeant.

'I don't know where it starts,' said Stefan, 'but it ends with murder.'

22

The Hog's Back

Where Surrey meets Hampshire, to the south and west of Guildford, a high, narrow ridge rises out of the gently undulating landscape of neat, square fields, tidy coppices and well-ordered villages. The road that runs along the top of the ridge, long and straight, looks down on all that. It is called the Hog's Back. It was a road of sorts for thousands of years before anything was neat or well ordered, when it was safer and drier than the forests that lay beneath its steep slopes. It marked now the place where the London Road to Portsmouth branched, and the south-westerly route, to Winchester and Southampton, climbed up to follow the ridgeway. Various armies had marched this way in the course of time, and it was busy with military trucks and transports again. Villages clustered along its slopes and there was always traffic, though there was nothing for it to stop for except the view. There was one hotel, a plain, red-brick building, distinguished by a square, central turret that had a lot of windows and no clear purpose. It was here, at the Hog's Back Hotel, that Sergeant Porter found Stefan Gillespie a room for the night, and where, next morning, Chief Inspector Nugent arrived to start the day's work.

The aftermath of Frank Nugent's knife wound from Malta was still there. The drive from London had left him in pain and it was Stefan who drove along the Hog's Back to the house where the couple they now knew as Mr and Mrs Hollingsworth, Ivy and Edgar, lived. Stefan had walked the two miles along the road the evening before to look at the house. Like the road itself, Swithins Barn was solitary. It lay back in a clump of high elms, at the end of a gravel drive, hard to see from the road, behind hedges and rhododendrons. The farm that gave the house its name was long gone. It was a dark, shut-in sort of house, Edwardian, built from the same red brick as the hotel. There was nothing remarkable about it, except its location. It didn't quite fit the ridge. It could have sat more comfortably in a suburban street in the leafier outskirts of London.

They drove from the Hog's Back Hotel to a lay-by near the house, waiting for the two policemen who would be cycling from Wanborough to meet them.

'Edgar and Ivy Hollingsworth,' said Stefan. 'They moved into the house about five years ago. Semi-retired was all Sergeant Porter had to say. Hollingsworth was a civil servant, but that's the limit of what anyone knows. There was talk that he had a nervous breakdown before they came here. They lead a quiet life. Not very sociable. No real friends, but they're liked by the local traders. He grows vegetables and exhibits at the local shows. She plays golf at Farnham but doesn't take part in the club's social activities. They appear at the church in Wanborough on high days and holidays. They travel up to London quite a lot. Shopping and shows . . . that was the sergeant's take on it.'

'Quiet and ordinary, then,' added Nugent.

'Mr Hollingsworth does his bit,' continued Stefan. 'ARP Warden.'

'As I said,' continued the chief inspector, 'our friend Charlie Pettit has no idea where they live. He calls them Mr and Mrs

Elliot, as per the letters. He's met the man, but she's the contact. I spent an hour in records after you called again.'

'Did you get something?'

'Edgar Hollingsworth was arrested in nineteen thirty-seven, for soliciting a man for sex in a public convenience in Carnaby Street. Unfortunately, the man was a police officer. West End Central on one of their missions, I assume. Hollingsworth was tried and got off with a suspended sentence. I think some strings must have been pulled. But he had a senior position in the Treasury. That was the end of that, of course. He lost his job. They moved from a house in Wimbledon . . . and here they are.'

'You still think Pettit doesn't know about the murder?'

'Yes. And I think we should come to that last. Might be better if they don't know we're even aware of it. We don't know what they left behind, once we start looking at fingerprints. My instinct is they didn't set out to kill him. If that's true, they maybe weren't fussy about leaving traces . . . till it was too late.'

'They thought a false trail would do,' said Stefan.

'It nearly did,' nodded Frank Nugent. 'Ah, reinforcements!'

Two weary cyclists in police uniform were approaching the car.

Stefan pulled up in front of Swithins Barn. Sergeant Porter and Constable Harris leant their bicycles against a tree. Frank Nugent walked to the front door. It was opened by the woman Stefan Gillespie had followed from Waterloo.

'Good morning,' she said cheerfully. She saw the Wanborough policemen standing uneasily behind two men she didn't recognise; she had no reason to think anything was wrong. 'You'll want my husband. ARP business?'

'It's not ARP business, Mrs Hollingsworth,' replied Nugent. He took out his warrant card. 'I'm Detective Chief Inspector

Nugent. This is Inspector Gillespie, who is assisting me.' The vagueness covered Stefan's position, just. 'We would like to talk to you and your husband. Mr Hollingsworth is at home?'

The first hint that this related to the part of Ivy Hollingsworth's life that had nothing to do with the solitary house on the Hog's Back stirred in her head.

'I'm sure if you would like to tell me what this is about . . .'

'If we can come in, we'd like to ask you both some questions.'

'About what?' she said, quite sternly.

'Can we come in?'

The woman stared at them. She showed no signs of fear. The expression on her face didn't change. It was hard, but somehow disbelieving. She was struggling with the idea that this had anything to do with the way money came to Swithins Barn. She had been so careful, so very careful.

'Do you have a warrant?' She half laughed, as if this was some banter. But it was a show of nerves. 'Isn't that how these things work, Mr Nugent?'

'I'm a Special Branch officer, Mrs Hollingsworth. I don't need a warrant if I suspect you've been gathering information for reasons I find suspicious.' Frank Nugent smiled. 'The fact that there's a war on covers me for pretty much anything I want, including searching your house. And I will be doing that.'

'Don't be ridiculous!' She looked at Porter. 'Who are these people?'

Sergeant Porter shuffled his feet. 'Scotland Yard, Mrs Hollingsworth.'

'Whoever they are, they can't just walk in here—'

The chief inspector pushed the door hard, and walked in. Stefan followed.

'Edgar!' Ivy Hollingsworth called out.

'I'm here, dear.'

In an open doorway stood a man in his late fifties. He was

heavy-set, almost jowly. He wore thick, horn-rimmed glasses. He was in his shirtsleeves. There was a faint smile on his face. Stefan saw he had heard the conversation.

'These men, Edgar . . . they say they are police officers.'

'I'm sure they are, if they say they are.'

'I have no idea what they want . . . they seem to think we're spies!'

Again, Ivy Hollingsworth produced a nervous laugh.

'I'd be very doubtful they believe that at all, Ivy.'

She gazed at him uncertainly. He seemed calm.

'We were just having breakfast, gentlemen. Would you like some tea?'

Now all four policemen were in the hall.

'I don't think so, sir,' said Nugent. 'I am Detective Chief—'

Hollingsworth cut him off.

'Yes, I heard. You'll want to make a start. Do come in.'

Edgar Hollingsworth turned back through the doorway he was standing in. A table was laid for breakfast. The linen was crisp and white. There was silverware and there were fresh flowers in a vase. Hollingsworth sat down. He picked up a pipe that lay by a plate of bacon and mushrooms. He lit it slowly.

'Sit down, dear,' he said to his wife. 'You might as well.'

Mrs Hollingsworth glared at him.

Frank Nugent and Stefan Gillespie stood in the dining room.

'We'll take a look round first, Mr Hollingsworth,' said the chief inspector. He glanced at Stefan. Stefan nodded. They walked back to the hall.

'Just keep them where they are, will you, Sergeant Porter?'

The two detectives took their own directions through the house. Nugent went upstairs. Stefan walked through a door into the kitchen. This was not a search, but Stefan understood what the Englishman was doing. There could be obvious things to see, but he wanted a sense of these people before he started talking to them. He had come into this cold. He wanted time to think through his approach: hard or soft, blunt or subtle. If evidence of the blackmail might be easy to establish, the situation with Vikram could prove more difficult. Stefan also knew that keeping the couple waiting, not knowing what the police knew, was putting pressure on them. They would make mistakes.

Stefan walked back into the hall. He glanced into another room, a sitting room, elegant and bright. He saw nothing interesting. There was a baby grand piano in the window. There was a chest of drawers with a vase of flowers. There was a mantelpiece with another vase of flowers. The only thing he noted was that on all the surfaces where you might expect to see photographs, there were none. He moved across the hall and opened another door. It was a study. There were few books. On some of the bookshelves there were small trophies. He read one inscription: *Surrey Show, 1939, Best Mixed Vegetable Basket.* On the desk he saw something he recognised: opened envelopes. They were the envelopes Charlie Pettit had collected from Walshe's shop. Against one wall was a metal filing cabinet, the kind that would normally be in an office. Stefan pulled out the top drawer. Inside were closely packed manila folders, alphabetically ordered, with numbers on tabs. The numbers had four figures. He remembered the piece of paper that accompanied a ten-pound note in the envelope Nugent had opened at the tobacconist's. Four figures, nothing more. It was a simple records system.

He took out one of the folders. There was a sheet of paper with a name and address. There were other names too, with dates. There was a copy of a bill from a hotel in Brighton. There was a letter that started with a declaration of love and a plea from one man to another, asking him to do what he had promised when they were in bed together: to leave his wife and family and come away with him. There were photographs: somewhere dark, blurred, two men kissing; the same men were at a station, one crying, both very identifiable.

Nugent came downstairs as Stefan Gillespie opened the study door.

'You should come and look at this, Frank. It's quite something.'

In the dining room, Ivy and Edgar Hollingsworth sat at the breakfast table, saying nothing. Hollingsworth smoked his pipe. Constable Harris stood in the doorway. Sergeant Porter sat on a chair by the wall, looking uncomfortable, apologetic and confused, all at the same time. He still had no idea why they were there, or what these two ordinary, upright citizens were being accused of.

The two detectives returned.

'I think the best thing we can do is take you both into custody.'

'For what exactly?' said the woman.

'If we take you to Wanborough now,' continued the chief inspector, 'we can organise transport to bring you to London. You'll be questioned fully there.'

'This is ridiculous. What are we supposed to have done?'

'Once we're at the station, Sergeant, if you can keep Mr and Mrs Hollingsworth in separate rooms or cells, whichever is more convenient, and then arrange with your superintendent in Guildford for two cars to take them to Scotland Yard, in custody, again separately. I don't think questioning is necessary at this point. It can wait. However, there is a lot of evidence to look at here . . . right? Inspector Gillespie and I will travel up to London tomorrow.'

'Yes, sir,' said Porter, standing up slowly. 'Can I ask what sort of charges we're talking about? I will need to say something to Superintendent Osborne.'

'Extortion, blackmail . . . that's the bulk of it. The first thing.'
Ivy Hollingsworth stood up, angry, shaking.
'This is madness! What sort of nonsense is this?'
'We'll deal with the nonsense in due course, Mrs Hollingsworth.'
'You have no proof of anything . . . anything at all!'
'Do shut up, Ivy,' said her husband quietly. 'They've been in the study.'
'What does that mean?' she said. 'We don't have to say anything.'
'There is a filing cabinet that speaks louder than words, darling.'
'Thank you, Mr Hollingsworth. Cooperation would be sensible. The details of the people you've been extorting money from speak for themselves.'
'You know who these people are,' said Ivy Hollingsworth angrily.
'I'm afraid that's hardly the point,' said Nugent in a clipped voice.
'Do you think these people should be allowed to do what they do?' Mrs Hollingsworth was looking from Stefan to Frank. 'Do you? Do you think all the disgusting filth they bring with them, the people they corrupt and destroy, the lives they ruin . . . do you think normal people don't have a right to try to stop it? The police don't! They turn a blind eye. Everyone does. They should be locked away; if you won't do that, people have a right to make—'
She stopped, struggling to speak, fighting tears of fear and frustration.
'Make them "pay" is the word you're looking for, Mrs Hollingsworth,' continued Chief Inspector Nugent. 'Well, one way or another, I'd say the two of you have achieved that. And you've lived well off it, too. However, all that can wait. You will find it easier just to tell the truth. If that sounds like the sort of thing a policeman always says, we have already arrested

Mr Pettit. He is finding it easier to speak than to keep his mouth shut. We can hardly stop him. Reflect on that. Reflect on what you'll say about Vikram Narayan.'

Stefan saw the surprise in Mrs Hollingsworth's face. He looked at her husband. He was relighting his pipe. He still seemed unsurprised and unfazed.

'The false trail didn't work. We know someone added the knife wounds to make it look like something else. With all the information you had, you'd heard of the other homosexual murders. We'll find something that puts you in Greek Street.'

Ivy Hollingsworth had run out of words.

Edgar Hollingsworth sucked on his pipe and exhaled the smoke.

'All this was my doing, gentlemen.'

He looked from Frank Nugent to Stefan Gillespie.

'I took it upon myself to put together a little bit of information that might generate some income. I had reasons. Something to be bitter about. I had no job and no prospect of getting one. It worked surprisingly well.'

'Edgar, you don't have to say—'

'Oh, I think I do, Ivy.' Hollingsworth turned back to the two detectives. 'I found ways to get information, more and more. When you start blackmailing people, you can get more than money, you can get even more information. People talk when they're afraid. I'm sure you know that well. It kept growing. I paid people to talk, and to spy, and they just kept on doing it, you see.'

'I have to warn you, Mr Hollingsworth—'

'I know. Anything I might say, and all that, Mr Nugent. Too late. But Ivy was never . . . I dragged her into it. She was the perfect foil. Who would ever suspect my dear wife? She could collect letters and drop letters and do all the secretarial work, while I dug the dirt. That's how it was, but Mr Narayan—'

'Edgar, stop!' Hollingsworth's wife was pleading.

'He started asking questions. He traced us, somehow. We heard that he had an idea who we were. He knew too much, he'd even taken photographs. I had to stop him. Naturally, I did. I didn't mean to kill him. We went to the flat to find out what he had, especially the photographs. I thought we could stop him then, with threats . . . or just money. But we found nothing. We didn't know what he'd done with the evidence. That was worrying. Then he came in. I panicked and hit him from behind. I knocked him out. That was when it seemed there was a simpler way to stop it, a reliable way. I smothered him. Ivy tried to stop me and pull me off. I did it anyway.'

Edgar Hollingsworth put down the pipe.

'Isn't that right, dear?'

Mrs Hollingsworth stared at him.

'And then I had the bright idea of pointing you chaps another way.'

He walked to the far end of the room, and the French windows that looked out on to the garden. 'It is a damn shame about the vegetables.'

'Will you drive, Stefan?' asked Nugent, turning away.

Stefan nodded.

'We'll take them to Wanborough.'

Stefan walked to the door to the hall.

'If you set off to cycle back, Sergeant—'

Suddenly, with unexpected speed, Hollingsworth opened the French windows and was through them, taking the key, locking the windows from outside. Nugent ran to the doors. They were heavy doors. The lock was strong.

'Silly bugger,' said the chief inspector. 'Let's go and get him.'

While Constable Harris stayed with Ivy Hollingsworth, Stefan Gillespie, Frank Nugent and Sergeant Porter raced through the open front door, round to the side of the house. There was no sign of Edgar Hollingsworth.

'Hang on,' said Stefan, listening.

'Can't be far,' snapped Nugent, irritated with himself. 'What's the fucking point!' He turned to the sergeant. 'Phone from the house. If we can't find him, alert all the local stations. Get some cars up here. Damn the man!'

'Listen, Frank!' said Stefan. 'It's a car engine.'

'You're right . . . where . . .?'

They looked towards a wooden garage. The engine revved, roaring now. There was a loud, splintering crash. The grey Riley cut through the door of the garage, out into the drive, racing fast towards the road.

'For fuck's sake! Get on the phone, Sergeant!'

Porter ran back to the house.

Stefan was already in the driving seat of the police Austin.

Frank Nugent slumped in beside him, slamming the door.

'Who's the silly bugger now, Stefan?'

'Could be you, Chief Inspector.'

Stefan sped over the gravel drive, out on to the Hog's Back. He could see the Riley ahead, going flat out. On the long, straight road, speed was easy, and the Riley was a faster car than the Austin. But it wasn't hard to keep it in sight.

'Try and keep on him. Once he's at the end of the Hog's Back, he'll have to slow down. Either he comes off into lanes and villages or he'll hit traffic and bends on the main road. Either way he won't keep that speed up for very long.'

'Well, he's fucking keeping it up now. Jesus!'

The Riley was moving faster than ever.

Stefan had the pedal flat on the floor; the other car was moving away.

'What the hell is he doing now?' said Stefan.

Ahead was a wide verge of grass to one side of the road, and beyond it a clump of huge, ancient elm trees. The Riley swerved off the road, on to the grass. It kept going. The speed didn't slacken. They heard the sound of the crash as

Edgar Hollingsworth's car hit the great trunk of an elm and shattered.

The black Austin crossed the verge of grass, following the tracks left by the Riley. Stefan stopped where the crumpled front of Hollingsworth's car seemed almost embedded in the tree. The two detectives got out and went to the car. They knew what to expect, given the speed of the impact. Edgar Hollingsworth's body had smashed through the windscreen as the car met the immovable elm. He was dead. Frank Nugent shook his head. There could have been no other outcome.

'How did he lose control on a road this straight, even at that speed?'

'He didn't,' said Stefan. 'I imagine he did exactly what he set out to do.'

23

Hungerford Bridge

That evening, Stefan Gillespie sat on a bench outside the bar at the Hog's Back Hotel, gazing out over the fields of the Surrey countryside. It was hard to say what the difference was between this landscape and some of the gentler parts of Ireland he knew, even the view looking from Baltinglass Hill towards Carlow. The English were tidier about the way they gave order to the land they farmed. It wasn't much more than that. He was ready to go home now. In every other area of life he stumbled on, one place was no tidier than another.

He looked up to see Frank Nugent walking towards him.

'Will you have a drink, Frank?'

'I've one more job for you, Stefan.'

'Don't push your luck. My superintendent will be sending Scotland Yard a bill. Not to mention my reputation for collaborating with the bloody English!'

'It's just a bit of babysitting.'

'What?'

'The fucking evidence at Swithins Barn. They want a guard overnight.'

'Wouldn't it be enough to lock the door?' Stefan grinned.

'Orders from on high.' Nugent shrugged. 'Poor old Sergeant

Porter and Constable Harris are stuck on the Hog's Back. I thought we'd do them a favour.'

Stefan finished the beer he was drinking and got up.

'All right, why not? I've got nothing better to do.'

It was getting dark as the two detectives arrived at the house on the Hog's Back. They found the sergeant and his constable sitting in the study, in front of a blazing fire, with several empty bottles of beer in front of them. They had settled in for the night, but they were glad to leave the job to others. They left the remaining beer. Stefan and Frank Nugent replaced them by the fire.

'What's happening with Mrs Hollingsworth?' asked Stefan.

'She's on her way to London now. Full circle. They'll hold her at West End Central. She'll be charged in the morning. And I can exit too, I guess.'

'How's she taking it?'

'Not as troubled as you might expect.'

'No, she seemed . . . phlegmatic enough about her husband's death.'

'She's abandoned the idea that they were on a crusade to save Britain from the depredations of homosexuals. She's turned into a bit of a mouse. Not quite the woman Charlie Pettit knew. He says she was the boss, no question. But that's not Mrs Hollingsworth now. She didn't like what they were doing, she knew it was wrong, that's the story, but Edgar, Edgar had to have his way. I think she'll do well. He said it was all him, didn't he, five minutes before he went out and topped himself? His last words. Next best thing to a death-bed confession. Juries are always impressed by those, judges too. If she sells that story, it'll go down well. He pushed her into it . . . he made all the decisions. And with Vikram Narayan, she can keep coming back to Edgar's last words. She pleaded with him to stop. He wouldn't. She had to look on, helpless!'

'You think that'll stand up?'

'Oh, Mrs H has a lot to be grateful for. A good barrister will make her another victim. A woman who stuck by her husband, loyally, honourably, after he was caught doing unspeakable things in a public convenience. She stuck by him, only to be pulled into his disgusting world when he decided to make money from it. An ordinary, decent woman manipulated by a husband who was a pervert. She was afraid of him. With good reason. And after all, his other victims were perverts too. No jury's going to spend very much time on them.'

'You think she'll get off?' asked Stefan.

'If she doesn't, it won't be much of a sentence.'

'But it's not how it was. You don't think so?'

'I don't. Do you?'

Stefan shook his head.

'I think we saw the real Mrs Hollingsworth briefly in this house. That was the woman Charlie Pettit knew. I guess there'll be others who say the same. People who sold names, stole letters, took photos. That's all Charlie remembers the husband doing, taking pictures. He was a bit of a photographer. There's a darkroom, behind the garage. But how far is this investigation going to go now? Not much further, I think. A trial for her and for Charlie. He won't do so badly either. And that'll be that. Don't turn over any stones that you don't have to.'

'I remember something,' said Stefan, 'from the flat in Greek Street.'

Nugent looked up.

'The pillow that smothered him. There were a couple of hairs. Not that long but bleached and permed. You've looked back at the reports, haven't you?'

'Yes, and I've thought the same thing you're thinking now.'

'She killed him.'

The English detective nodded.

'It's entirely possible. Maybe Hollingsworth hit Vikram, when he came through the door, but did she make the decision to finish him . . . and get rid of him for good? Was Edgar really the one pleading? Who used the knife? We'll never know.'

Stefan Gillespie nodded.

'And a couple of hairs won't prove anything, will they?'

Frank Nugent got up and walked to the filing cabinet.

'I also think she drove the car that hit Hindu Narayan. It had to be one of them. It must have felt as if Hindu was following up on what her brother was doing. I looked at the date and the ARP roster. Hollingsworth was on duty that night. He was nowhere near London. We'll never get near proving anything.'

Nugent opened a filing-cabinet drawer and flicked through files.

'There is a sort of account of the other murders in here – the Yates murders. A note of something Charlie Pettit said about a couple of men being killed. He'd heard rumours. They put that together with something a bit more definite, from people who were selling them material about homosexual men. I'm pretty sure that information came from our chums at West End Central. CID spread it about to put the frighteners on the faeries. Not much more. But that's how some of the details got out, knife wounds and so on. The notes in the Hollingsworths' files are all in her handwriting. Most things are in her hand. In the margin, next to her notes on the murders, she wrote, "This any use to us?"'

'It very nearly was,' said Stefan. 'But not quite useful enough.'

On a table by the filing cabinet, there was a decanter of whiskey. Frank Nugent picked it up, along with two glasses, and walked back to the fire. He set down the glasses and poured two drinks. He sipped at the whiskey, slowly.

'I don't suppose Mr Hollingsworth will begrudge us.'

'So, when are you back to India?' asked Stefan.

'Ten days or so.'

'Then?'

'The usual. Informers and political meetings. Keeping an eye on the politicians who want to kick out the British and take power. An exercise in futility, of course: they will be taking power anyway. As everyone knows.'

'You think so?'

'It depends on the war. Once it's over . . . independence follows, as night follows day.' Nugent smiled. 'Or the other way round . . . as day follows night.'

'And what does that mean for you?'

'Well, if I was an ordinary policeman, I suppose I'd be happy enough in an Indian police force instead of a British one. It won't change overnight. But I've made a different bed . . . I told you, the Great Game isn't for amateurs, and that's what I was. Maybe I didn't look where I was going. When I did, I was already in the snake pit. It was too late. A new India won't have any room for the lads from Indian Political Intelligence. Eventually, I'll end up back here. A country that's not my country, with a pension and a bungalow in Worthing.'

As he finished speaking, Frank Nugent got up and walked to the filing cabinet again. One drawer was still open. Again, he started to flick through it.

'You know what's in here, Stefan?'

'I've seen enough.'

'It's a treasure trove,' said the chief inspector, 'for people like us.'

'How?'

'There are files on close to three hundred people here.'

Nugent moved back to the fire. He took wood from the basket and threw it into the grate, banking it up higher. He stood, looking down at the flames.

'You could divide these files into two sections. In India, my boss would, and I don't doubt your Superintendent Gregory would too. Important people, some very important, and the rest. Mr and Mrs Hollingsworth were clever. They divided them into three. I don't know that they thought that out, but for practical purposes, important people couldn't be blackmailed. You'd think they were the obvious targets, but it's too risky. You've got politicians, major businessmen, a couple of bishops, even a few senior police officers up and down the country. There's a few stars of stage and screen, of course, and assorted artistic types and academics of one kind or another. It's a whole network. But these are men with power, with real influence. They know people who can come after you.'

'So, you leave them alone?'

'You keep your powder dry, anyway,' continued Nugent. 'Who knows? And then there are the ordinary, everyday oiks. Men with no money, so not worth bothering with. Except for getting information. Ten bob could buy some interesting names, even some letters. But it's the middle that mattered to Edgar and Ivy. Bank clerks and managers and shopkeepers and teachers and doctors and civil servants, and maybe a few not-so-senior policemen. They were the people who had lives to ruin and nobody to help them . . . plus a bit of money. Not much, but enough to pay. Of course, I'm sure our friends delivered on their threats of exposure if the money dried up . . . or . . . pour encourager les autres.'

'And if you went to the police, you'd be ruined anyway,' said Stefan.

Chief Inspector Nugent stooped and put another log on the fire, which was now blazing fiercely. Stefan watched him, puzzled. It was hot in the room. Nugent walked back across the study to the filing cabinet. He pulled all the drawers out, slowly, one after another.

'There's a van coming to collect all this tomorrow.'

Stefan nodded. 'It's evidence. No shortage either.'

'They're not coming from Scotland Yard or West End Central.'

'What do you mean?' Stefan could see Frank Nugent's frown.

'It's not about evidence. That's not it at all.'

'Then what is it?'

'It'll be fellers from Intelligence. I'd imagine MI5. Special Branch might get a peep, but this is for the big boys. And what they want is the people at the top. They won't worry too much about the others. Edgar and Ivy have put together information about the predilections of a whole slice of the great and the good that MI5 would take years to collect, even if anyone would let them do it. No one knows what you might need all that for, but there's always going to be a time. It won't be about money, quite a different sort of blackmail, that's why they want it and that's why someone has to sit here all night and keep it safe.'

Stefan nodded. Now it was said, it was obvious enough.

'How's that fire doing, Stefan?'

'I'm starting to sweat like a fucking pig, Frank.'

'Good. Get a bit of fresh air.'

'What?'

'In the back of the car there's a jerry can of petrol. I've still got this bloody pain, courtesy of Mr Yates. I can hardly lift the thing. Will you get it?'

Stefan stood up, frowning, not sure what Nugent was getting at now.

'That's right. There's going to be an accident. What a couple of fools, banking up that fire so high it tumbled out on the carpet! Careless or what?'

'You're going to burn it?' Stefan was looking at the filing cabinet.

'Why not? That'll be the job finished. Finished properly, I mean.'

Stefan Gillespie smiled and nodded. It felt right somehow.

'They will know there was petrol. It won't be hard to work out.'

'Yes.' Frank Nugent was untroubled. 'But what are they going to do about it? It's a secret they're taking the fucking stuff at all. I don't see them making a song and dance out of that. They can't touch you. You're a bystander. You're heading home to Ireland anyway. My boss wants me in India. He's more than capable of telling some arsehole behind a desk in MI5 to fuck himself.'

The two men looked at each other for a long moment.

Stefan laughed. He picked up the bottle of whiskey and poured two more drinks, filling the glasses. He walked to the cabinet and handed one to Nugent.

'Sláinte!' said Chief Inspector Nugent.

'Sláinte mhaith!' said Inspector Gillespie.

It was little more than ten minutes later that Stefan Gillespie and Frank Nugent sat in the black Austin, in the driveway of Swithins Barn, watching the front of the house. The fire was underway in the study, blazing fiercely after the liberal application of petrol to the filing cabinet and the carpet in front of the fireplace. They would wait a little longer, until the fire had taken hold of that part of the house strongly enough to ensure nothing survived. Then they would drive to the Hog's Back Hotel, and the nearest telephone, to call the police and fire brigade. The phone at Swithins Barn being too dangerous to access now. For several minutes neither man spoke. They smoked cigarettes in the darkness.

'Is that a debt paid now?' asked Stefan.

'A debt?' said Frank Nugent.

'To Vikram Narayan. This has always been personal for you, hasn't it? From the start. You didn't have to push investigating his murder, did you?'

'I didn't know what would come up, as far as he was concerned, with the work he was doing for me and Indian Political Intelligence. I couldn't be sure there wasn't a connection. Or that things wouldn't come out . . .'

'That always felt more like an excuse than a reason,' said Stefan.

'You're right. And whatever he was, whatever happened to him, some of that was down to me. A lot of that. It wasn't always about work . . . that took over. There was a time I was close to his family, to Hindu as well. My father brought me up to spend more time with Indians than with the British. He had Indian friends, and not many English ones – another thing my mother never forgave him for. I went to a boarding school with Indians, boys whose fathers worked for the civil service or the railways. I knew Hindu before I knew her brother. She was a lot older. There was a group of us then, all a long time ago . . . what mattered then is gone, long gone . . .' The Englishman let the words fade away.

'That's why she won't speak to you, Frank?'

'Why she hates my guts, you mean?' Nugent laughed.

'All right,' said Stefan. 'You were friends once.'

'As I said, we were close. She thinks I betrayed that. She's right.'

'Why did you?'

'Because I'm weak. Because I do what I'm told. Because I'm the kind of arsehole who runs an empire and doesn't even believe in what I'm doing. But I do it. Hindu Narayan knows. She knows that. Why wouldn't she despise me?'

Stefan could feel there was real pain behind Frank Nugent's words.

'There must have been more,' said Stefan. 'Did you love her?'

The Englishman started the engine. Flames were visible through the house's front windows now. Still the chief inspector gazed at it, unmoving.

'No,' said Frank Nugent, 'it was Vikram. It was Vikram I loved, once.'

Stefan said nothing. He knew he wasn't meant to. The words were a kind of confession, a kind of explanation. They were only addressed to him in part. They had to be said aloud. Even if only one person heard, they had to be heard.

'He did come to me.' Nugent spoke again after a long pause. 'About some people who were blackmailing homosexual men. He told me he was trying to find out who they were. I told him to stop. I started out laughing. Then I lost my temper. He was putting a lot at risk. He was drawing attention to himself. As for the idea I'd help him with this arsing around, that I'd get involved . . . I gave him a real bollocking. What the fuck did he think he was up to? He had a job to do. For me. For my boss in India. And back in Delhi they were already unimpressed with what he was bringing in. He was coming up short. He wasn't getting enough. Or he wasn't giving enough. What were his Indian nationalist friends doing? What were they planning? Who were they talking to in London? What were the instructions from India? No one gave a monkey's about a few queers getting blackmailed. It went with the territory. Queers do get the screw put on them. The sun rises in the east. It's not news. So, I put the fear of God in him. I told him the last thing he needed was to make a spectacle of himself playing the fucking detective. What did he think his friends would do if they found out he was already playing the detective, for real, for me, providing information to Indian Political Intelligence? And that was that.'

The IPI man put the car into gear and turned it round.

'I told him I was protecting him. But I was just another blackmailer.'

Frank Nugent took out a cigarette and lit it. Everything he had said, he had said looking out through the windscreen. He looked round at Stefan.

'You're not much good on the absolution front, Stefan.'

'Do you want absolution?'

'I don't suppose I do.' The man who could have no place in England or India now smiled. 'Who would I be then?'

He drove out from Swithins Barn, into the darkness of the Hog's Back.

The night before Stefan Gillespie left London to return to Ireland, he waited for Hindu Narayan to finish work at the Veeraswamy in Regent Street. He knew she still refused to see Frank Nugent. The past, that Stefan had only some small window into, left no room for any kind of reconciliation between the Indian woman and the Englishman. But he liked Frank Nugent and he liked Hindu Narayan, though he had barely seen her. He assumed Vikram Narayan's sister would want to know what had really happened. He had been a policeman a long time. People wanted to know. It was a need. He recognised it as part of why a death had to be investigated. It wasn't only about justice or revenge; it was the desire to feel the thing had been completed, finished. If it was left unresolved, the gaps and doubts and questions were a continuing pain in people's lives. He felt that Hindu would want to close those gaps, now that they could be closed.

He still wasn't sure how much to say. The truth about how Vikram Narayan died was simple, however complicated the circumstances that led to it. Stefan knew, for instance, from Chief Inspector Nugent, that the Hollingsworths' Riley Kestrel had been fitted with a new wing earlier that year. According to the garage in Wanborough, Ivy Hollingsworth had hit a stone bollard in the blackout, coming out of Guildford. It seemed impossible she hadn't damaged it running into Hindu Narayan in Regent Street. Was it right to tell Hindu that, if she still believed that somehow the British Police or Indian Political Intelligence – or Frank Nugent himself – had something to do with it? Shouldn't she clear her head of that? The facts were what she ought to have. Facts usually helped. And Stefan wanted them to help Hindu. He could have ignored her. But he was trying to do what Frank Nugent would have done himself, if only Vikram's sister would let him. She might not. She must still see him as a proxy for a man she hated.

Stefan Gillespie and Hindu Narayan walked through Piccadilly Circus, down to Trafalgar Square. She lived across the river, not far from Waterloo Station. The route she took, to the Embankment and over Hungerford Bridge, was one Stefan knew from a visit to London years before. The night was overcast and dark. There was no moon. It was the kind of night German bombers avoided, and they had done. The city was quiet, and the night hid the ugly scars of war.

Hindu Narayan was cool and polite. She knew that Stefan's intentions were good. But somewhere in her head she had forced a distinction between the facts of her brother's death, that may or may not have involved a man and a woman he was trying to expose as criminals, and the facts of his life, which would have been utterly different if Nugent had not betrayed his trust in her and her family. If there was one thing Hindu Narayan shared with Frank Nugent it was that personal betrayal lay behind Vikram's death. Surely, without that betrayal, he would still be alive?

She listened as Stefan spoke. She nodded. She heard what he said. But he found himself trailing away as they stepped on to Hungerford Bridge, on to the footpath that ran beside the railway line into Charing Cross. The rattle of trains coming in and out drowned his words. As they did, he realised she preferred not to hear them. He could see that she already had a number of versions of her brother's death, and of his life. All he was doing was giving her another one. He couldn't know what had reached Vikram's mother and father in India, or whether anything he said would be added to it. In that version,

Stefan felt sure, Vikram Narayan was still an Indian nationalist, fighting the good fight until the end. And in that version, too, Vikram Narayan's homosexuality had likely been erased.

Halfway across the bridge, as the rolling thunder of another train passed across the Thames, Hindu Narayan stopped. She smiled, taking Stefan's hand.

'Why don't you walk back, Stefan? I'm fine now.'

'I've said enough, you mean. Or too much.'

'I appreciate what you've done. I know what I need to know.'

The words were both an acceptance and a rejection of what he had said.

'I'm sorry if some of it is . . . not what you want to hear.'

'There's nothing I want to hear . . . unless it could all be undone.'

Stefan nodded. He knew Hindu meant more than her brother's death. There were whole lives – hers, Vikram's, even Frank Nugent's – in that wish.

'I wish it was a different time. And we were here for different reasons.'

The words came unexpectedly, unintentionally into Stefan's mouth.

'There is only one time,' said Hindu.

'I'm sorry.' These seemed the only words Stefan had left.

'Yes, I'm sorry too.'

She leant up and kissed him on the cheek.

'Thank you.'

Stefan watched Hindu walk away until she reached the steps at the other end of the bridge and disappeared. He turned back towards the Embankment. As he reached it and walked down the steps, he looked out along the Thames, west towards Westminster Bridge. He had not thought about the places he had been in over the last few days. He knew some of them, but what he had been doing had pushed that away. Now he had time to look. And something made him look. Perhaps it was no more than the brush of a woman's lips on his cheek. There were some familiar places from years back. Waterloo Station and the train south, through Clapham Junction and Wimbledon; then Hungerford Bridge and the Thames below; the Embankment and the walk into London. They were things that appeared as images in his life. The past was not a great narrative that held together in one piece. Elements of it had seemed that way once, so much so that he had tried to cling on to it. But it had fragmented. There were images, moments, pictures that stayed strong, but they came into his head when they were needed or when it mattered. He had visited London, not long after he and Maeve were married. A honeymoon. They'd had enough money for three days in a hotel in the West End, but that was all. Then they stayed with an aunt of Maeve's near Kingston and travelled in by train. There were images of that now. Leaving a theatre, after a play he couldn't remember, and standing in a street, laughing; a café by the Serpentine and a child feeding ducks. There had been a day they walked from Kingston along the river to Hampton Court. In Hampton Court Park, ambling towards the Long Water that led to the palace, they saw a deer, unlike all the other deer they had seen in the park, startlingly white, only feet away. They saw it for seconds; then it was gone. Now, walking away from Hungerford Bridge, leaving the Thames, heading through the dark into the West End, the images the bridge and the river had brought into his head momentarily were left behind as well. They had come and then, very softly, they had gone.

24

Kilranelagh Graveyard

Dublin

Detective Inspector Stefan Gillespie returned to Ireland with a certain amount of what Sergeant Dessie MacMahon called 'housekeeping' to do. Housekeeping was the tidying up that came with the end of an investigation. There was always something more to provide in terms of a report and there was all the filing away of statements and the consignment of evidence to the bowels of a police station or Garda Headquarters or the cellars of Dublin Castle. In Ireland there had been no day in court where the murder of James Corcoran was concerned. There was, eventually, an account of the trial in London. It was brief, amounting to no more than two typed pages that stated only that a trial had taken place, that evidence had been presented, and that John Eddington Yates had been found guilty of the murder of a number of men, in a number of locations, on a number of dates. Those men included the ones he killed in Ireland and Malta. There was no record of what had been said at the trial, either by the prosecution or by the defence; at least, none of those details crossed the Irish Sea. The trial was held in camera. The reason was a vague resort to the exigencies of war: the defendant was a serving officer, and details of military camps and bases, as well as troop movements, were needed in evidence.

The reality was that the association of such shocking crimes with the British Army was not something anyone wanted to see in the press, in Britain or anywhere else. The image of an army standing alone to save democracy, even civilisation, could not be sullied by John Yates. If no one wanted to open up the secret world of the men Yates had preyed on in Britain and Malta, it was also true that even at the start, when James Corcoran died by a lake in Kildare, no one wanted to look too hard in Ireland either. The account that came from the Home Office in London, to be filed with the details of the seminarian's death, ended with a single paragraph, of one sentence, that gave the date on which John Eddington Yates was hanged at Brixton Prison and buried in an unmarked grave in the prison grounds. The trial had taken place ten days after his return to England from Malta. It lasted two days. Only four more days passed between his trial and his execution.

However, housekeeping, especially where murder was concerned, involved more than paperwork. It took Stefan Gillespie back to Thomastown and the house where James Corcoran had grown up. He gave Mrs Corcoran as much of an explanation as he could of what had happened to her son. It was what he thought she wanted. Mr Corcoran was in Dublin when Stefan went to Kilkenny. He was now a Cabinet minister. Stefan had offered to meet him in Dublin, but Rory Corcoran had been too busy. It didn't surprise Stefan. He arranged to speak to Mr and Mrs Corcoran at home, but Minister Corcoran was too tied up at his ministry to be there. Stefan told James's mother that the man who killed her son had been hanged in England. She wanted few details, but he hoped what he gave her helped bring a kind of end. He knew she would tell her husband almost nothing, except that there had been a hanging. It was enough. They were moving on, as they had to. Mrs Corcoran said that. She said it too many times. Stefan saw that in the garden, the building that was James Corcoran's refuge had been brightly painted. He knew that the debris of his young life would have gone; some few precious things kept, but most of it discarded. He also knew the life had been sucked out of the house in Thomastown. It would be a long time coming back. Probably it never would.

Stefan called at the Gate Theatre. Micheál Mac Liammóir wanted to know what had happened to Vikram Narayan. The shock of what he had found in the flat in Greek Street had not left him, nor had the feeling – he could not shake it off – that a different response to what he now knew to be a desperate cry for help might have meant the difference between life and death for the young Indian. Stefan told him it was unlikely that that was true. The circumstances of Vikram's death had a dynamic that was nothing to do with whether Mac Liammóir could have given him a job in Ireland or helped him in any way.

The actor wanted to hear the details of what had happened, both of Vikram Narayan's murder and of the other killings. These crimes were ultimately unrelated, except for an attempt to disguise one thing as another, but for Micheál Mac Liammóir there were connections. The complexities of Vikram's life had brought him to live on the edge of an ever-growing darkness he couldn't escape from; had made him an informer, a cheat, a liar. Why? Only because of who he was. The things that had put him in a place where his life could be destroyed would not be so different from those that might have marked and marred the secret lives of the men murdered by John Yates. Somewhere, perhaps, those things even touched the black despair that had tortured Yates himself, that had plunged him into a pit of self-loathing almost beyond comprehension. Almost, but not quite. His darkness was so complete that it consumed him, and others with him. Mac Liammóir recognised how lucky he was. He could stand outside the darkness. Only just. He would not forget that.

★

When Stefan Gillespie made time for his own life, the first thing he found, grabbing a brief night at home in Baltinglass, was a crisis that was almost refreshing in its parochial simplicity. For the moment, as he arrived at Kilranelagh, it was what occupied everyone in the neighbourhood. It had been abrupt and unlooked for, a shock, and a considerable irritant to many, including the Gillespies. Michael Cashman, the principal at Talbotstown National School, Tom's school, had resigned. One day he was there and the next day he had gone. His house in Kiltegan was shut up. Someone saw him get the train to Dublin. He said he was taking a holiday. He had been away a week when Stefan came home.

Explanations for what had happened were many and varied. There was talk he had inherited money or won the Hospitals' Sweepstake, or that he had been offered a job at an expensive private school in England. None of that made sense of the speed with which he went. There was talk of money going missing from the school, though no one took that seriously. People spoke of a row between Michael Cashman and the parish priest. There had been arguments between the two before. The priest didn't like Cashman and the feeling was mutual. The priest controlled St Joseph's School's Board of Management and everything the principal tried to do that challenged the hold of the Church over school life was knocked back. Increasingly, there had been a feeling that some things were being knocked back out of the priest's bloody-mindedness. But Michael Cashman could be bloody-minded himself. The two men had argued for years without it interfering with the way the school ran. And St Joseph's School was Cashman's life. He gave it everything he had. Even if he had a reason to leave, surely he loved St Joseph's too much not to give good notice.

If the level of crisis Michael Cashman's departure was causing in Baltinglass and Kiltegan made Stefan smile, it annoyed him too. He would not be drawn into the full heat of what was going on, but he was disappointed. It wasn't long ago he had talked to the principal about the extra work he was doing with Tom to help him get a scholarship to secondary school. He had decided, despite the reluctance of his mother and father, to do what Cashman had suggested and make the break with the Catholic Church's demand that Tom go to a Catholic school. It would not be easy. David and Helena, with the Protestant instinct to lie low in Dev's Ireland, were reluctant to face the trouble that would inevitably come. Michael Cashman was an ally. Stefan wondered if Tom was something to do with what had happened. Had Father Brennan got hold of the plan? It seemed unlikely Cashman wouldn't have said something. Tom was unsettled by it too. There was a new teacher and the quiet understanding that had allowed Tom to take his own path while appearing to travel the same one as everyone else was gone. If it all seemed trivial in the world Stefan had just left, he was still pissed off.

While Stefan Gillespie concluded the housekeeping that surrounded the murder of James Corcoran, the usual regime in Special Branch continued. He found himself spending more time collecting information on the Indian community in Dublin. Superintendent Gregory had decided someone needed to specialise in this area of surveillance, and Stefan had drawn that straw. Small as the community was, it could cause friction between Ireland and Britain. There were few Indians actively engaged in the politics of independence who looked to the IRA for support, but there were some. There were fewer who dealt with the German embassy, but it wasn't for lack of trying on the part of the Germans.

Finding out who was pushing the boundaries mattered more than it had when Stefan left for Malta. Three German spies had been picked up while he was away, after landing on the coast of Cork. They had so little idea where they were that their first act was to stop local children and ask. Two of the men were South African, with accents distinctly uncommon in Cork. The other was an Indian, Henry Obed, who wore a white Gandhi cap and offered the children bars of chocolate. The men were, unsurprisingly, arrested. Their suitcases contained incendiary bombs, explosives and large quantities of cash. It was so clumsy that G2 were inclined to think it was a British false-flag operation. But Henry Obed had come from Berlin. He believed he was there to help Ireland fight the British in an imminent war and that somewhere along the line this would free India from British rule. Obed had been interrogated by the time Stefan returned to Special Branch, but he interviewed him himself in Mountjoy Prison, in an attempt to relate names in the Indian community to German espionage. He came to the conclusion that either Obed was a very good liar or he knew hardly any Indians in Ireland. As a spy, he was another incident to file under 'F' for 'farce'.

Farce, however, did not stop there. Stefan Gillespie had watched *The Great Dictator* at the Manoel Theatre in Valletta; indeed, he was one of the few people in Ireland who had seen the banned film. But there was a print in Dublin. Two students from Trinity College had brought it from Belfast. It was due to be shown, secretly, in Trinity. But invitations had been scattered widely around Dublin's student community. On the morning before the showing, Inspector Stefan Gillespie and Sergeant Dessie MacMahon arrived at a staircase in the Courtyard at Trinity College, with two proctors, to seize the film. One student tried to get Stefan to arrest him. A chance to embarrass the censor and the police was too good to miss. Stefan didn't oblige. One farce at a time was enough.

At Dublin Castle, Stefan dumped the film canister on Superintendent Gregory's desk. He knew it had amused his boss to send him to seize it. It was deliberate.

'Right, sir. *The Great Dictator*. A comedy.'

'But a very insidious one, Inspector.'

'We look like fucking eejits,' said Stefan.

'That's the job. As they say, someone has to do it.'

'It's bollocks.'

'You take yourself too seriously, Stevie. You know, I look at this . . .' The superintendent gestured at the canister of film. 'I look at this, and I find myself thinking, I know what's in Inspector Gillespie's head. He's thinking, if this is what it takes to defend the fucking state, is it even worth defending? Now go on, tell me I'm wrong. Tell me this doesn't make you angrier than everything else put together, all the spying, all the arrests . . . even the occasional execution. If we can't even show a fucking Charlie Chaplin film . . . then Jesus Christ!'

'It's not worth arguing about, is it, sir?'

'Not at the moment, no, that's the point. When it is, I'll join you.'

Stefan shrugged.

'Meanwhile, Stevie, if we have to look like a bunch of clowns, we can.'

Stefan smiled.

'I wish we didn't have to do it quite so much.'

Superintendent Gregory's expression changed.

'There's something you should see.'

He pushed aside the film and picked up a newspaper.

'I know this means something to you. I didn't say anything before . . . I heard you talking to Dessie about the teacher at your lad's school. Well, read this now.'

Gregory pointed at a small paragraph, headed 'Tragic Accident'.

Stefan read the article.

The bodies of two men were recovered from the sea off Bray Head yesterday morning, after what appears to have been a tragic swimming accident. The men have been identified as Mr Michael

Cashman, a school principal, of Kiltegan, Co Wicklow, and Mr
Kenneth O'Malley, a taxi driver, of Rathmines, Co Dublin. The
men drowned after getting out of their depth in a heavy sea.
Relatives of the deceased have been informed.

'Jesus,' said Stefan quietly. 'What the hell was he doing?'

'You don't know anything?' asked Gregory.

'I know he resigned from the school . . . it was all very sudden.'

'It wasn't an accident. That's one thing you can be sure of.'

'What do you mean?'

'He was due in court next week.'

'What . . . what for?'

'He was arrested, two weeks ago. In the Phoenix Park. Along with the other feller. Indecency, sodomy, I don't know. There was a sweep on. There'd been complaints about men in the park. You've been in a Dublin station. Some inspector says it's time for a clean-up. Your man was unlucky. I think someone tried to stop the prosecution, but they wanted him. A teacher. As an example.'

'Does anyone know . . .? I mean, do they know in Baltinglass?'

'The Guards will know now. So, the people who matter will know soon enough.'

Stefan stared at the newspaper again. There was nothing to say.

It was two days later that Stefan stood in the bleak graveyard on the slopes of Kilranelagh Hill. It was a bright day, but the wind was stiff as the body of Michael Cashman was lowered into the ground. Stefan held his son's hand. Behind stood David and Helena. There were a lot of people there. A lot of children. And a lot of people who had been children, years ago and not so many years ago. There were those who knew why Michael Cashman was dead. The parish priest who sprinkled

Holy Water over the coffin. The men who were the Board of Management of Michael Cashman's school. The Guards who had turned out in their best uniforms. There would be others, too, who had all the details to hand, though many, perhaps most, would not know anything of the real truth at all.

Stefan had not gone to the funeral service at Talbotstown church. He had no wish to listen to the people who did know talk about what a good teacher the principal had been; people who would have done nothing to help the dead man, who would only have wanted him out of the way. After all, however sad, this was easier than what might have happened, the scandal if Cashman had not chosen to take the course he did. And all the words were true. He was a good man after all, in almost every way. The small community that sent its children to Scoil Naomh Iósaf had recognised that for many years. But Stefan found himself wondering how many there would have been in that community to defend him. Who would have stood beside the principal if the truth had come out? He had always been a solitary man. No one noticed it. They only saw what he gave them. They measured him only by what he did. But when it mattered, when something needed to be given to him, Michael Cashman had no one.

Stefan led Tom home, back through the graveyard. Tom was crying. Stefan, who was not a man to shed tears easily, felt them in his own eyes. Father and son stopped, for a moment, to say a prayer, or something like a prayer, at the grave of Maeve Gillespie. It was not far from where Michael Cashman was being covered by the earth of Kilranelagh Hill.

For part of that evening, Stefan Gillespie sat in the small, dark bar at the pub in Talbotstown. It was busier than it usually was, after the funeral, but he did no more than nod at the people he knew. He sat on his own. He drank more than he intended, but he expected that. He walked home, past the school. It wasn't long ago that he had been talking to Michael Cashman about Tom. He would still do what the principal had believed was the right thing to do. It would be harder. He had not realised how much Michael Cashman's help and conviction meant.

At the farm, David was still up, but Helena had gone to bed.

Stefan went to the kitchen cabinet and took out the whiskey. He found a glass and poured himself another drink. As so often, it was something to do.

'Do you want one, Pa?'

'No, I'm going up.'

Stefan looked at his father.

'When did you know?'

David Gillespie frowned, as if he wasn't sure what his son meant.

'You know what I'm talking about.'

'I heard from the station. I don't think all the Guards knew.'

'Bollocks. They knew well enough, all of them.'

'Yes, you're probably right, Stefan.'

'I've had enough of this, I tell you.'

'Of what?'

'Dead queers, Pa. Dead for no fucking reason anyone can tell you.'

David Gillespie nodded. He didn't understand, but he felt Stefan's anger.

'No one ever knew about him . . . If it could have just stayed that way . . .'

'That's not an answer is it, Pa?'

David could feel that his son was looking for an argument.

'I'm going to bed. I'll see you in the morning.'

'What the fuck does any of it matter, Pa? Does anyone even ask that? Who fucking cares?'

Stefan Gillespie stood in the kitchen as his father went out and climbed the stairs. He drank the whiskey. He picked up the bottle and walked through into the sitting room. The fire was still burning. He knew it had been lit because he was home. They didn't normally use the room. He didn't light the lamp. He sat in the armchair by the fire. The room had a low, warm glow. He looked at the bookshelves, the piano his mother almost never played now. His eyes found a book that was next to him, on the shelf by the mantelpiece. He must have been half looking for it, but even in the low light he recognised the battered brown spine and the faint remnants of some gold lettering: Palgrave's *Golden Treasury*. He had last seen a copy beside the bed where Vikram Narayan died. He took it out and held it. It had been given to him by his parents, as it had been given to Vikram Narayan at school in India. One a present, the other a prize, both recognising an interest in reading, perhaps, what others weren't reading. It was a bridge his own son was crossing now, suddenly, and he hadn't seen it happening until Michael Cashman pointed it out to him.

Stefan couldn't know what else Vikram Narayan had liked in the *Golden Treasury*, but he had been reading one thing Stefan liked too, 'Dover Beach'. It had been bookmarked. He saw it when he picked up the book at the flat in Greek Street. Stefan knew enough to understand that the young Indian was not only reading it because he liked it. Stefan didn't have to strain to guess what the last words of the poem must have meant to him; a statement of the hard, bitter truth of his life. They offered no consolation, no way out. They were honest, maybe, where almost nothing in Vikram Narayan's life had been.

He remembered reading the poem to Maeve once, when they first knew each other; she hadn't liked it. She believed life was better than that. He thought he'd probably told her that wasn't the point. The poem was part of what made life better than that. It was its own refutation. She had laughed at that, of course. It sounded clever, but it didn't mean anything, did it? What made life better than that was simple. It was what was in

313

front of you. It was what you touched. It was the air you breathed. 'Ah, love, let us be true to one another'; everything began with that. It ended with that, too. Those were the words that mattered; the rest was nothing. At the time, it had seemed Maeve was right, and even if the other words of 'Dover Beach' were still in the air Stefan breathed, he picked out the ones she held on to and held on to them as well. There had been times since her death when he had still felt she was right. But there were other times when he knew she was wrong. He did not hear the poem in his head because it was simply a beautiful thing; he heard it because too many times there was nothing else to hear. Because the world that was so various, so beautiful, so new, really did have neither joy, nor love, nor light, nor certitude, nor peace, nor help for pain.

He opened the book and found the poem.

He looked at the all-familiar words. And where was anybody in that world, now more than ever, but on that darkling plain, swept by confused alarms of trouble and flight, where ignorant armies still clashed by night? He sat back in the chair. He drained the glass of whiskey and stared at the dying fire. And he smiled. The image was still there, unbidden, despite everything. The woman and the man, young still, almost not Maeve, not him, and through the trees, with the sun on the Long Water at Hampton Court beyond, the white deer grazing, shining too in the sunlight. And the only movement it seemed, in that bright picture, the only movement in all the world, was his hand as it touched hers.

Notes & Acknowledgements

Island One: Eire

The main action of this story takes place in the early months of 1941. Ireland was still pursuing its course of fierce neutrality; still frustrating the British government, especially over the refusal to let Atlantic convoys use its ports; still letting Germany believe neutrality disguised a non-existent desire for German victory. The show was what mattered. Reality was different. The cooperation between British and Irish Intelligence services was intense. Many records of this were destroyed at the war's end, particularly by the Irish. Even the MI5 history, only declassified in 1999, is selective. It doesn't even mention sharing Garda Special Branch surveillance information about Indian nationalists in Ireland.

Éamon de Valera's government, in 1941, was still haunted by the prospect of war coming to Ireland, even if the threat of Germany invading Britain had receded, along with the chances of Ireland being attacked by the Germans, the British, or both at once. Less pressing, as a result, was the possibility of any IRA uprising. The action of war was shifting elsewhere.

The Emergency, as the war was referred to officially in Ireland, was preoccupied with keeping ordinary life going, hampered by a lack of basic commodities such as coal and oil. But Dublin was still somewhere Britons with the opportunity and the cash could briefly escape the rigours of war. The government continued to frown on its citizens joining the British Armed Forces but did nothing to stop the tens of thousands that did. Even more people left to work in British industries, where their presence made a huge contribution to the war effort.

Germany dispatched a series of laughably incompetent spies to Ireland, most of them believing the country was about to rise up against Britain. What prompted the Abwehr to land an Indian, for instance, dressed as a Jawaharlal Nehru lookalike, is anybody's guess. The idea that the secretly anti-Hitler Abwehr was only ever 'playing' at its espionage in Ireland may well be true.

Island Two: Britain

In Britain, as the chance of German invasion receded, the Blitz took its place as a threat to everyday life. But even this danger would fall away in 1941. German bombing of the United Kingdom, especially London, never reached anything like the scale of the Allied bombing of Germany later in the war. The level of destruction was relatively small in comparison. Though the Blitz did continue in 1941, Hitler's attention was already elsewhere: on the Mediterranean and North Africa, but above all on Russia. That disaster, along with the most brutal manifestation of what Nazi warfare was really about, was waiting in the wings.

Island Three: Malta

War in the Mediterranean and North Africa brought the tiny island of Malta, a British colony since the expulsion of a

Napoleonic army in 1800, into the thick of the conflict. Malta had been a staging post for British shipping since the Suez Canal opened to give faster access to India, the supposed 'jewel' in the Imperial Crown, and to colonies beyond. The island's economy depended on the British naval dockyards, and the presence of British soldiers and sailors, mostly on their way elsewhere, was a part of Maltese life. While Maltese remained the language of the home, English had become the language of everything else.

Maltese history always connected the island to Italy. Before English, Italian had been the language of business and politics. It was a connection Italy's fascist dictator, Mussolini, approved of. His desire to expand Italian territory encompassed Malta. So, when he joined Hitler and declared war on Britain, it was time to grab the island. Italian forces were already attacking the British in North Africa, with the aim of invading Egypt. But Mussolini's war collapsed. His army in North Africa was routed and Malta, weakly defended, with barely any fighter aircraft, at least contained the bombers of the Regia Aeronautica. Hitler had no choice but to prop Mussolini up and intervene.

The Germans changed everything. In North Africa, Rommel's Afrika Corps devastated the British. And though Rommel would eventually be defeated, he came close to taking Egypt and cutting Britain off from India and its colonies. In Malta the Luftwaffe was a different prospect to the Italians for the ill-equipped RAF. The island could be bombed at will. The British could do little to stop it. Italian and German airfields were only a short distance away, in Sicily. The island was now under siege. British convoys could not get through with oil and ammunition or the basic foodstuffs the people of Malta needed.

This was not Malta's first siege. In the sixteenth century a few hundred Knights of St John, along with the people of the island, fought off a massive invasion by the Turkish Ottoman Empire in one of history's most remarkable feats of resistance against overwhelming odds. It was a lot more too. The victory played a crucial role in ending long-running Ottoman plans to conquer Europe.

The new siege could not be resisted by fortresses and bastions. Malta was almost helpless against the Axis bombers. Destruction was everywhere, and civilian deaths ran high. At one point, the island would be the most bombed place on earth. It is a grim statement about the Second World War that it would not hold that distinction for long. But the resilience of the people of Malta is one of the most extraordinary stories of the war. Eventually, Winston Churchill did more to help the island he called an 'unsinkable battleship'. New RAF fighters, including Spitfires to take on the Messerschmitts, did arrive. Convoys got through, often at terrible cost. And Malta's existence as a naval base made all the difference in preventing supplies, especially tank fuel, reaching Rommel. Yet even if things improved, it is still the case that for much of the time the British forces on the island, and the Maltese people, just had to stick it out.

For this reason, the island was awarded the George Cross, the highest British civilian honour for bravery, the equivalent of the Victoria Cross. It is only normally given to individuals. The cross still features on the Maltese flag. Not everyone in Malta feels it sits easily with the symbols of an independent nation, but most Maltese see it as a memorial to their past and to the fact that some wars are fought for ends that matter more than the self-interest that may be there too. We may not always be sure what our civilisation is, but the tiny island of Malta has played a disproportionate part in defending it.

Much of what I have written about in Malta is still there to be seen. The city of Valletta, in particular, small as it is, is one of the most beautiful cities you will see. And at the edge of that city, between Battery Street and St Ursula Street, the British Hotel still looks out over the Grand Harbour, just as it did in 1941.

Island Tongues

There are lines of Irish and Maltese in the story. Both languages look odd if you don't know them, but their alphabets are more regular than English. If you read aloud, this may help. Irish looks like it has too many vowels. Some are there to show how to pronounce adjacent consonants. So, *scoil*, 'school', is like the first part of 'scholar'. If you see *i* following another vowel, for simplicity here, ignore it. Beyond that, pronounce *sh* and *th* as 'h'; *ch* as in Scottish 'loch'; *bh* as 'v'; *c* as 'k'; *ao* as 'ai' in 'wait'. Maltese is a form of Arabic that was transformed and reimagined by absorbing mostly Italian and later English words. The letter *h* is silent; the unique, barred *ħ* is pronounced 'h'. The *q* is a glottal stop, as when we say 'be'er' for 'better'. The airfield at *Luqa* is 'Lu'a', though the British said what they saw: 'Looka'! The word for 'street', *triq*, has no final consonant to English ears; it's 'tri'. For the rest, at its simplest, pronounce *j* is 'y'; *x* as 'sh'; *z* as the 'ts' in 'sports'; *ż* as English 'z'; *għ* is silent at the beginning of a word and also between vowels in the middle of a word. All oversimplified but close enough!

Acknowledgements

Many books, over many years, have contributed to these stories, most of them forgotten. But here I must mention three. Micheál Mac Liammóir's not entirely reliable memoir, *All for Hecuba*; Matt Houlbrook's *Queer London*; Kate O'Malley's *Ireland, India and Empire*. There are many histories of Malta during the Second World War, some focusing on military aspects, others on civilian life. I have only scraped the surface of that story. The best all-round account is James Holland's *Fortress Malta*. I am also grateful to the *Times of Malta*. Its archive pages contain a poignant mix of war's devastation and the ordinary life that went on despite that. Only in those pages could I find that the British Army was giving prizes to soldiers who took an examination in Colloquial Maltese!

Two films should be mentioned. Without *Victim* (1961), the tale of a homosexual blackmail scam in London, I would not have arrived at my story. Several scenes are set in the Salisbury in St Martin's Lane, where a character is played by Micheál Mac Liammóir's partner, Hilton Edwards. Astonishingly, *Victim* contains the first use of the word 'homosexual' in English-speaking cinema. The 1953 film *Malta Story* was close enough to real events to echo their atmosphere. The Lascaris War Rooms sequence is a brief nod to the film.